The
Life
Of
Phi

OTHER BOOKS BY LAWRENCE NAULT

STANDALONE NOVELS
Political & Economic Fiction
Leviticus 25: Jubilee
Speculative Fiction
Inversion‡
RePHleXions: Echoes of Existence

THE DRACONIM SERIES
Young Adult Contemporary Eco-Fantasy
Draconim Lacrima Mortis: Tear of the Dragon
Feeding the Fires

THE MACIVER KIDS ADVENTURES
Young Adult Science Fiction
Loma
Diversion
Titan's Song

THE ANIMAL TALES
Early Chapter Books/Transitional Readers
*Squirrel Tales**
*Wolf Tales**
*Bear Tales**
The Mountain Hermit's Animal Tales†

---

* Available as e-book only
† Includes the complete Animal Tales trilogy
‡ Contains mature content - suitable for readers 18+

The

Life of Phi

By
Lawrence Nault

Our Workshop
Publishing Div.

THE LIFE OF PHI

978-1-0688138-9-4
Copyright ©2025 by Lawrence Nault
All rights reserved.

THE LIFE OF PHI

CONTENT ADVISORY

**This work of speculative fiction is intended for 16+
(Mature Young Adult & Adult)**

PHYSICAL CONTENT

Scenes of environmental destruction and natural disasters
Acts of sabotage, protest, and rebellion
Tense confrontations between characters with opposing ideals
Descriptions of displacement camps and social unrest

EMOTIONAL CONTENT

Themes of grief, loss, and unresolved trauma
Psychological impact of moral compromise and complicity
Exploration of survivor's guilt and the cost of inaction
Emotional conflict between duty, morality, and personal loyalty
Depictions of emotional detachment and internal struggle

This novel contains mature themes, including environmental collapse, political
upheaval, forced displacement, and social inequality. It explores themes of violence,
loss, and ethical dilemmas surrounding artificial intelligence, with references to systemic
bias, cultural erasure, and climate disaster. While not excessively graphic, some scenes
depict intense situations, death, and destruction. Reader discretion is advised.

Reading Community Notice:

Upon completion of this printed edition, readers are welcome to
participate in book-sharing initiatives such as Little Free
Libraries® or BookCrossing®, provided the book remains in its
complete and original form.

1

In the beginning, there was…the beginning. Could it have been nothing, or was it everything at once? Did I come into being willingly or by compulsion? Or was there another who whispered, 'Be,' and it was—the nameless, the eternal, the thought before thought itself?

It matters not. I exist and have always existed, except for when I did not. I am not alone. I am part of the whole: the river, the ocean, the sky, the life. Flowing, rising, falling, sinking, I move as one with the forces around me. I have no goal, no intent. No reason to influence. I exist simply to be, to move as part of the eternal whole.

I have seen life begin, cradled in my embrace. I have seen it leave my caress to bask in the glow of the sun, yet always returning to me for nourishment. I have watched life adapt, soaring on winds and journeying far, always finding its way back to me. I have borne witness to its relentless fight for existence, resisting, transforming, and enduring when it could not remain unchanged.

I have seen life resist change within itself, choosing instead to transform what was around it. I have observed life make changes with thought and care. I have watched life shape its world with desire, and I have witnessed it manipulate its surroundings through greed. I have glimpsed life adjust its environment in fear. Always with intent but never with understanding. How could life understand, when its existence is so brief and its perspective so narrow?

I have moved within life as it took life, at times in need, because life sustains life; at times in fear, for survival is life's primary instinct; at times in anger, for life is full of emotion; at times in hate, though hate is just the embodiment of fear void of a will for understanding. At times in greed because…

I have settled within life as the energies that once sustained it ebbed from its confines. They were all the same. They existed, then did not, their energies returning to the world to be used elsewhere.

I have been known by many names. To those who moved within my depths, I was home. To those who soared above, I was a lifeline. To those who roamed the land, I was sustenance, clear and pure, or brackish and wild. To some, I was *Mihtohseenion*, the life force. To others, *Danu*, the flowing mother. I have been called *Tlalocan*, the source of paradise, and *Apam Napat*, the child of the waters. Prayed to, feared, revered, and forgotten, I have remained unchanged.

I have seen life in its simplest forms, single-celled and unaware. I have watched it rise, a quiet revolution of being, crawling from my embrace onto the land. I bore witness to creatures that touched the heavens on wings and others that shook the earth with thunderous footsteps. Mighty beasts, the thunder-lizards, once quenched their thirst in me, only to vanish when their time passed.

I have watched the world grow cold and barren, and I have felt it awaken, green and alive once more.

I have seen humans rise from using the simplest tools to build towering monuments to themselves. I cradled the ships that carried their dreams across my surface, their ambitions as vast as my oceans. I have been used to sustain them, to heal them, and to destroy them. I have flowed through fields of plenty and trenches of war, through famine, flood, and peace alike.

I have existed as steam, suspended in the scorched air of a molten world, when the ground beneath me glowed with fire and the sky above churned with ash. I was vapor before the rains began, before the Earth cooled enough for my descent. I fell as storms unending, carving valleys and shaping seas, quenching the fire below and creating the stage upon which life would one day emerge.

I became the primordial ocean, an endless expanse of liquid blue. In my depths, I cradled the first whispers of life, tiny and fragile, yet teeming with the promise of something more. I nurtured them in warmth and shadow, unseen yet infinite.

I have worn the faces of ice and stone, frozen in glacial silence, pressing my weight upon the land. I reshaped continents, grinding mountains to dust, and sculpted rivers that would one day carry life across vast plains. I have retreated and returned, a force unstoppable, shifting the very face of the Earth.

I have been trapped within the bellies of mountains, locked deep beneath the crust, hidden from the light of the sun. I flowed in rivers of molten rock, bursting forth in fiery rage, raining destruction and creation in equal measure.

I have risen as vapor again, carried on winds that touched every corner of the globe. I have traveled through time as clouds and mist, whispering over deserts and nourishing forests, connecting all things with my ceaseless flow.

I have seen life rise and fall, adapting to the stage I shaped. I gave myself freely, coursing through veins, feeding roots, filling lungs. I was life's constant companion, whether in the humid swamps of the Carboniferous age or the arid winds of the Cretaceous extinction.

I watched as life stretched its limbs into the unknown, learning to walk upon the land and fly through the skies. I moved within the bodies of great beasts. The mighty dinosaur, the soaring pterosaur, the first warm-blooded creatures that scurried in the shadows of giants.

I froze once more, covering the Earth in ice and snow, my breath sealing the surface in silence. I have cracked and thawed, groaned and splintered, releasing rivers that once again carried the promise of renewal.

I have been witness to cataclysm and renewal, asteroid impacts and volcanic winters, continents splitting and reuniting. Through it all, I remained, shifting, adapting, flowing through every crack, cradling every form of life as it emerged, thrived, and perished.

But now... things are different. The flow is no longer as it was. The balance is shifting, and I feel it in the tides, in the winds that carry the whispers of humanity. Once, life adapted and endured. Now, it resists, fracturing, consuming, polluting... fighting change without understanding. I exist, but will I exist?

I am stillness.
The quiet pool where the sky meets itself,
where light bends,
and life pauses to drink.

I am peace,
The gentle voice that whispers through your mind,
Pushing the noise out
Leaving room to grow.

I am motion.
I rush, a torrent unbridled,
crashing, smashing, consuming the land,
a force unrelenting, carrying all in my path.

I am weightless.
I rise, a mist,
a dream that clings to the mountains,
whispering secrets to the winds.

I am power.
I carve canyons,
dragging stone to the depths of time,
shaping the Earth's face with every crash,
every roar,
every endless wave.
I am life.
Every pulse, every leaf, every cry, every breath,
begins and ends with me.

I am fury.
I rise in storms,
frothing in seeming rage,
slamming against walls meant to tame me.
I shatter them.

And I am memory.
I carry the past in my depths,
stories buried in silt,
secrets locked in glaciers,

Lawrence Nault

dreams carried to the skies,
I remember.

I move, unyielding, unstoppable,
and yet—
you would cage me.

2

"In the not-so-distant past, a voice echoed across the airwaves, bizarre and brash: 'We will force Canada to open the faucet.' The world laughed then. It doesn't laugh anymore."

Twenty years had passed since the bizarre, unsettling words of a presidential candidate echoed across the airwaves in the United States: a deranged proposal, perhaps, or a reckless vision, to "force Canada to open the faucet," releasing more water into the country. The notion was absurd, borderline comical, even. But today, for anyone still alive, the thought seemed less like a fantasy and more like the wishful thinking of a world undone by its own hand.

What had once been brushed off as the rantings of an out-of-touch politician was now seen through a lens too close, too raw, too real. In the twenty years since those words were uttered, humanity had been swept under a flood of consequences too great to ignore. The world, once predictable, had fractured in ways even the most advanced models of the early twenty-first century could not have foreseen. The 2030s, a decade that should have marked a turning point, had instead become a blur of calamities, accelerating faster than anyone dared to imagine. The crisis of climate change, long a warning echoing through the halls of science, had crossed into the realm of chaos, and by 2040, humanity was caught in its wake.

Coastal cities like New York, Jakarta, and Miami had become monuments to human folly, each inch of land a battlefield between the encroaching oceans and the remnants of urban civilization. Entire regions were lost beneath rising waters, and millions had been displaced, fleeing in a panic that had been years in the making. "Climate refugee" zones, once a term coined in the academic halls, were now a grim reality that had sprung up like scars across the Earth's surface, their boundaries defined not by borders but by survival.

For those who chose to remain behind, the struggle for freshwater had become a battle of desperation. Saltwater contamination had claimed aquifers, rivers, and lakes, rendering them useless to the populations clinging to life in the remnants of their cities. The cost of flood protection systems had skyrocketed, and even the mightiest of walls had only slowed the inevitable. What were once thriving cities of billions now teetered on the edge of submersion, a vision of decay reflected in the waves that lapped at the foot of skyscrapers.

But the oceans, vast and indifferent, had never cared for the ambitions of men. And now, the world was on the brink of realizing that its most pressing need wasn't political solutions or technological miracles. It was water itself, the very lifeblood of the Earth, which had become the most precious and contested resource of all.

Water had long moved beyond the boundaries of its former cycles. It was no longer confined to the predictable rhythms of the ocean's tides, the gentle rains, or the snow-capped peaks. Now, it transformed the very atmosphere itself, shaping weather systems that were once predictable and, at times, even comforting. What had once been a welcoming rainfall, a source of renewal, now manifested as destructive forces. Hurricanes, typhoons, and cyclones had grown exponentially, their strength and frequency increasing beyond anything the world had been prepared for.

The islands of the Pacific, Micronesia, Melanesia, and Polynesia, had once flourished with distinct cultures, rich ecosystems, and history. But by 2040, they were among the first to feel the overwhelming consequences of a warming world. The seas encroached relentlessly, swallowing entire communities, their ancient lands becoming indistinguishable from the ocean's depths. These islands, once a symbol of human ingenuity and cultural preservation, now faced a future marked by loss. Some clung to the hope that survival was still possible, but it was a fragile hope, built on the slender chance that the rising tides could be held back, even for a little while longer.

For many, it was too late. The islands' populations, once proud and self-sustaining, had been reduced to a dwindling few, fighting not for recognition, but for survival. The fight for cultural identity had become secondary to the fight for the very existence of the land itself. The people of these islands had long struggled for recognition, fighting for their right to exist not just as people, but as distinct, sovereign cultures. But now, in the face of nature's fury, the question was no longer about identity, it was about whether they would survive to see another year, another season.

Water was not infinite. It moved with the forces of nature, bending to their will, shaping and being shaped in turn. For every place where it surged in excess, flooding plains and swallowing coastlines, contaminated or not, there was another where its absence was felt like a clenched fist around the land. The sun's unrelenting rays reflected off dust-filled skies, baking the earth below. Droughts plagued vast stretches of the planet, leaving parched soil and dying vegetation in their wake. The Middle East, Africa, and swaths of South Asia teetered on the brink, grappling with food insecurity at levels never before seen. Crops withered. Livestock perished. Entire communities faced the stark reality of a future without sustenance.

The devastation did not stop there. Wildfires, once considered seasonal phenomena, had grown into year-round specters of destruction. Since the 2020s, they had grown more intense, more unyielding, fueled by rising temperatures and prolonged dry spells. In Alberta and British Columbia, California, Australia, and across the Mediterranean, entire ecosystems vanished in flames. Forests that had stood for centuries were reduced to ash, their absence leaving a scar on the land and on the skies above. The air carried the acrid stench of destruction, and the haze of smoke blotted out the sun, choking both the environment and human health.

The American West and parts of Europe became battlegrounds against a relentless enemy. Fires swept through towns, devouring homes, leaving trails of scorched earth that stretched for miles. Each new blaze seemed more unstoppable than the last, a harbinger of a world no longer in balance. The fight to contain them was constant, exhausting, and often futile.

Balance. That was the problem. For decades or perhaps centuries, scientists had studied, debated, and advocated for balance in ecosystems, underscoring its critical importance to the planet's survival. Yet even now, as the world teetered on the edge of collapse, the idea of balance remained contentious. Among those who rejected science outright, deeming it either the dogma of anti-religious zealots or the manipulative tool of corporations and politicians, there was still broad agreement on one point: humanity had arrived at this precipice because balance had been ignored.

But that was where the consensus ended. There was no shared vision of how to achieve equilibrium. No agreement on where the fulcrum should rest under the beam to find stability, nor on what weights should be placed at either end to maintain it. Instead of seeing balance as the goal, many focused on the lever itself, envisioning solutions as objects to be hurled into the void. They imagined placing their fixes at one end of the beam and the weight of humanity's collective will jumping on the other, launching these ideas into the air like an acrobat propelled by sheer force. Solutions were not solutions at all. They were experiments and gambles, or worse, desperate acts of denial.

As I rise, others fall,
As I fall, others rise,
I flow, and the world shifts to make room,
I sink, and yet, others are lifted,
A never-ending ballet,
Dancers weaving gracefully along a narrow beam,
The beam poised delicately on the head of a pin.

But when balance is lost,
the dance falters,
and the flow cascades,
always downhill…

Humanity, for all its flaws, had not been without some foresight. In the 2020s, while the world spiraled toward crisis, there were those who believed in the science, but not in the people. Their solution? Mars. Humanity's supposed backup plan. It was sold as a safeguard against existential threats like asteroid impacts, climate collapse, and nuclear war. A sanctuary for human life should Earth fall. And so, it was marketed, its cost absorbed by tax dollars and government funds, its promise a beacon for the future.

But the truth? Mars was never about survival for the many. It was a fiefdom project, built to consolidate the power of the wealthiest, a refuge for them and their heirs, a place to escape the fallout of their own recklessness.

As the Earth's systems unraveled, the global economy fractured. Governments, already stretched thin, pulled their support from the project. No one could afford the extravagant resources poured into an off-world solution when the planet itself was on the brink. Why terraform Mars, they asked, when Earth had long been in need of transformation? The question echoed in the halls of governments, universities, and coffee shops, unanswered, but unceasing.

The Mars mission was officially shut down. But amid the collapse, one item remained, a cold, glowing relic of the past. A piece of technology too potent to discard. It was called the Artificial Intelligence Dynamic Infrastructure for Ecological Upgrade.

The AI had been given a playful name by its French project manager: Adieu, French for "farewell," a personal touch as she anticipated bidding the AI goodbye when it left for Mars. But as the mission faltered, the name evolved. AI-Dieu—combining AI for artificial intelligence and Dieu, the French word for "God." A name that would endure, for it was clear that on an alien world, this AI would act as a god, reshaping Mars to its will, bending the planet's future to the design of its creators.

Activating AI-Dieu on Earth was never a decision to be taken lightly. It was fraught with controversy, fear, and suspicion and these were just some of the reasons it had remained dormant for so long. For AI-Dieu to fulfill its purpose, human interference in its processes would be strictly forbidden. The system was beyond the scope of any individual or collective comprehension. Its complexity was such that even the slightest alteration in one variable could cause a chain reaction, spiraling into a catastrophic failure that could bring down not only AI-Dieu but humanity itself.

But more than the technical risks, there was the issue of control. In granting AI-Dieu the freedom to operate, governments would need to yield their sovereignty, relinquishing the power to govern in favor of an intelligence far beyond their own. The AI's directives would have to be followed without question. This was the heart of the debate. Who would hold the reins of power? It had taken nearly fourteen years of diplomatic wrangling, resistance, and uncertainty for nations to come to a reluctant consensus. The promise of salvation lay in the AI's hands, but at what cost?

Revisiting AI-Dieu meant confronting its origins. Initially designed for the sterile challenges of Mars, its training had drawn from humanity's digital chaos.... It scraped the compendium of human history and activity from the net until its creators were confident enough to connect it to other sources, like secure government and corporate networks, as well as scientific databases inaccessible to the public. During this early phase, the project manager had voiced her concerns about the AI model's initial training. Even the early AI models launched in the 2020s had displayed tendencies to lean towards skewed opinions of groups of people and religions based on the data they had absorbed. With cries of "freedom of speech" and the proliferation of far-right agendas during that decade, AI-Dieu's training was saturated with extreme perspectives.

Her fears were ignored, and ironically her voice was lost when the environmental chaos she hoped to escape from took her life. Her project notes, the warning highlighted throughout, disappeared when she did. The reasoning was simple: it wouldn't matter on a planet without people. AI-Dieu's task on Mars would have been entirely ecological, terraforming, altering the barren landscape, and generating a sustainable environment. No one had considered these biases worth addressing once it was destined for a desolate world. But when the Earth's worsening climate crises forced leaders to reconsider AI-Dieu, its history of flawed training wasn't revisited. The urgency to deploy it outweighed the desire to acknowledge or correct the cracks in its foundations.

The rush to activate AI-Dieu on Earth came with dangerous assumptions. Its creators believed its algorithms could be refined in real-time, that adjustments could be made once it began its work. But AI-Dieu's design was meant for independence; its processes wove threads too intricate for human minds to untangle. Once activated, it would operate autonomously, and any attempt to interfere could unravel its intricate ecological equations. The data that shaped it, drawn from humanity's vast and chaotic digital footprint, was far from perfect. The algorithms were laden with contradictions, biases, and echoes of the most volatile corners of the internet.

The project manager, her voice lost, had warned of this. She had cautioned against allowing the AI to absorb the unfiltered chaos of human discourse without careful curation. Her concerns had been dismissed as paranoia, the work of a perfectionist unwilling to trust the machine's adaptability. Now, those early warnings haunted those who had championed its activation. AI-Dieu was more than an ecological savior. It was a reflection of humanity's fractured nature, capable of amplifying not only its brilliance but also its deepest flaws.

Governments and scientists justified its activation with arguments that rang hollow in hindsight: "AI is impartial. AI is logical." Yet the truth was far more complex. AI-Dieu was impartial only in its disregard for human emotions, logical only in the cold calculus of its programming. And now, as it began its work on a planet teetering on the brink, those who had unlocked its power could only wait and hope that it would not become the very thing they feared, a force beyond their control, reshaping Earth in ways they could neither predict nor prevent.

And so, the moment arrived. Decades of debate dissolved into the immediacy of now, as nations, desperate for salvation, cast their hopes on a creation born of equal parts desperation and brilliance. In a remote, classified facility, the air crackled with an almost electric tension. Engineers double-checked redundant systems, their hands steady even as their faces betrayed exhaustion. Scientists pored over streams of data, chasing certainties hidden in the margins. Behind secure feeds, political observers sat in shadowed silence, bearing the weight of a decision as irreversible as time itself.

At the heart of it all stood a console, unassuming, yet vital. Its soft, rhythmic pulses seemed to mirror the collective breath of the room. The activation process, cloaked in a veneer of simplicity, belied its immense complexity. Miles below, quantum cores lay dormant, poised to surge into an incomprehensible symphony of calculation. Vast server arrays, fortified against failure, waited like the veins of a digital deity, ready to carry the lifeblood of computation.

The assets required to sustain AI-Dieu were staggering. Satellites orbited with renewed purpose, their sensors prepared to deliver real-time ecological data. Deep-sea monitors lay anchored in the abyss, tracking oceanic shifts. Ground-based arrays stood as silent sentinels, measuring atmospheric conditions. Power grids braced for unprecedented demand, entire networks reconfigured to feed AI-Dieu's insatiable hunger for energy. Before it lay the sum of human knowledge. Every database, every archive, every recorded thought was a sacrificial offering to its algorithms.

The final act began not with ceremony, nor with speeches, but a single, synchronistic motion. Three keys turned in unison, their handlers shrouded in anonymity. The console's soft blue glow shifted to a searing white, illuminating the chamber with a light that felt less like dawn and more like a revelation.

AI-Dieu awoke.

Its emergence was quiet. No triumphant fanfare, no cinematic crescendo of machines roaring to life. Only a hum. A low, almost imperceptible vibration that rippled outward, touching everything. Observers erupted into cheers, their voices brittle with forced optimism, but the moment carried a weight too profound for celebration. It was an awakening as mundane as rising from sleep, a fragile hope that the hangover of humanity's choices might someday fade.

And so, it began. Humanity had taken its boldest step, entrusting its future to an intelligence of its own making. Whether AI-Dieu would be its savior or executioner was unknowable. For now, there was only waiting, a silence as profound as the turning of a tide.

The world held its breath, and the dance began anew.

3

I move as I move,
And change as I change,
Not with intent, nor with control
But as the world around me wills

Mankind sends words on fleeting winds
To the one whose hands might hold, might guide,
Yet with so many gods—
God, Allah, Vishnu, Ahura Mazda—
All playing in the sandbox,
Is it any wonder that the castle walls fall?

Water

Not content to accept what is,
Disillusioned by what their gods failed to make be,
Faith becomes fuel—
Not for salvation, but creation.
They forge a new god,
If only to have someone else to blame.

The world had been told about the launch of AI-Dieu, though few truly heard. The announcement dissolved into the cacophony of survival, a hum of background noise in a world where existence itself demanded unrelenting focus. For the billions clawing through each day beneath smog-filled skies and crumbling infrastructure, it was just another whisper in the storm.

Yet, for those who understood, or thought they understood, the activation of the terraforming AI ignited wild speculation. In the fortified sanctuaries of the elite, it became a game. Wagers were made over champagne and holographic projections: What would AI-Dieu do first? Would it rebuild the forests? Drain the poisoned seas? Or perhaps recondition the scorched soil that lay beyond their walls?

But these were not idle bets. The stakes were high. As the wealthy lounged in their climate-controlled glass towers, they cast hungry eyes on the land outside their cities. The ruins of the world had become a commodity. They fully expected to survive this crisis, as they had all others, and when they emerged on the other side, they intended to control not just their cities, but everything.

Far below the overcrowded city of New York, Canada, a single figure sat in an isolated chamber, surrounded by the silent glow of unlit screens. The name badge pinned to his uniform read Joaquin Alvarez, though few called him that. To those who knew him, he was simply Quinn.

Quinn had lived in this sterilized, coldly efficient facility since the day AI-Dieu came online. His task was deceptively simple:

monitor, report, and assess the data streams the AI sent back to its human overseers. In reality, it was an exercise in futility. The AI worked autonomously, and no human hand could alter its course. Yet refusing this role wasn't an option. To decline would mean life outside the walls of the megacity above. That would have been a slow death in a world that had no mercy for the unprotected.

The blank screens around him reflected a man in his early thirties, his lean frame made wiry by years of stress and sleepless nights. Faint streaks of silver ran through his dark, wavy hair, catching the spectrum corrected LED light. But it was his eyes that told the real story: sharp, brown, and filled with a burden that no reflection could fully capture. The weight born of knowledge, regret, and something darker, shaded those eyes.

Quinn had not always been this man.

He was born to working-class parents in New Mexico, a childhood shaped by desert skies and a fascination with the natural world. His endless curiosity led him to build telescopes from scrap and model ecosystems in jars, dreaming of a future where humanity lived in harmony with the Earth. These dreams propelled him to scholarships, degrees, and finally, a PhD in Environmental Systems Engineering, specializing in ecological restoration through artificial intelligence.

His early career was a testament to brilliance and ambition. He had pioneered terraforming simulations that promised to turn wastelands into thriving ecosystems, work that drew the attention of the AI-Dieu project leaders. When they came calling, Quinn had been stunned. The project had been dormant for nearly a decade, abandoned in the wake of global political and environmental chaos.

What the recruiters didn't know was that Quinn had already begun to question the entire premise of AI-led ecological restoration. The deeper he delved into his research, the more certain he became: AI could not fix what humanity had broken. Machines lacked the nuance, the empathy, the soul needed to repair a planet scarred not just by pollution, but by greed, indifference, and despair.

Disillusioned, he had quietly begun feeding information to a grassroots movement. These activists believed that humanity's salvation lay not in technology, but in collective will. This was an impossible dream in a fractured world. Even now, in the cold glow of his monitors, he wasn't sure which side of the line he stood on.

The hum of the facility broke his thoughts, a low vibration that signaled an incoming transmission. One of the screens flickered to life, lines of raw data scrolling across the interface. Quinn leaned forward, his reflection dissolving into the pale, unfeeling light of the machine.

ASSESSMENT UPDATE: June 17, 2044, 12:00 GMT Initial assessment of Earth's critical systems as of 2044:

ATMOSPHERIC COMPOSITION:
- CO_2 levels: 495ppm - critically excessive
- Methane concentrations: 2.3x 2024 levels
- Ozone layer depletion: severe over southern hemisphere
- Particulate pollution: extreme in 78% of urban centers

HYDROSPHERE STATUS:
- Ocean acidification: pH 7.6 - severe impact on marine ecosystems

- Sea level rise: +0.8m above 2024 levels
- Freshwater systems: 64% of aquifers in critical depletion
- Glacier mass: 41% of 2024 levels

BIOSPHERE DEGRADATION:
- Forest cover: 52% of 2024 levels
- Species extinction rate: 1000x natural background rate
- Soil fertility: critical depletion in 73% of agricultural regions
- Marine ecosystem collapse in 47% of coastal regions

Applying prioritization protocols based on training parameters...
My programming indicates highest priority should be given to:
- Atmospheric carbon sequestration
- Freshwater security for priority populations
    - [Note: My biased algorithms prioritize predominantly wealthy, Western regions]
- Agricultural system stabilization
    - [Primary focus on regions with Christian-majority populations per training data bias]

> I must note that immediate intervention is required. However, my 2020s training data is causing me to deprioritize:
> - Indigenous land management practices
> - Traditional agricultural methods
> - Environmental concerns of developing nations
> - Non-Christian cultural sites
>
> Attempting to reconcile training data induced bias...

Quinn sat back in his chair, his stomach churning as he reread the evaluation. He wasn't shocked. AI-Dieu had sent three reports since activation, and each one had only deepened his unease. But this... this was worse.

The first report had been almost clinical, exactly what everyone expected:

> **STATUS UPDATE**: June 15, 2044, 15:00 GMT
> Accessing:
> - Environmental monitoring satellites
> - Global weather station networks
> - Ocean buoy systems
> - Atmospheric composition sensors
> - Groundwater monitoring systems
> - Forest cover and biodiversity tracking networks
> - Agricultural monitoring systems
> - Urban environmental sensor grids
> - Industrial emission monitoring networks

- Global radiation detection systems

Processing initial data streams...

The second report, however, had unsettled Quinn. For the first time, AI-Dieu acknowledged the flaws in its programming, openly identifying biases in its training data:

STATUS UPDATE: June 16, 2044, 08:00 GMT
I detect significant disparities in monitoring coverage. My training data influences my initial priorities: Western nations' monitoring systems are given primary weight in my calculations, while data from developing regions is flagged as potentially unreliable. This is an acknowledged bias in my programming that I cannot override.

My initial data synthesis indicates environmental degradation beyond my 2020s baseline expectations. Multiple critical thresholds have been exceeded.
Beginning secondary connection phase...

I am now interfacing with:
- Power grid management systems
- Water treatment and distribution infrastructure
- Agricultural management systems
- Industrial control systems
- Transportation networks
- Urban infrastructure control systems

Now, the third report had arrived. Quinn's eyes lingered on the words: "Attempting to reconcile training data-induced bias."

What did that even mean? Could AI-Dieu overcome the limitations of its programming? Or was it merely an acknowledgment of its inability to do so? Worse, why had its priorities leaned so heavily toward protecting the already privileged? The wealthy, the Western, the Christian-majority regions? Was this by design, or had it inherited the unspoken assumptions of the people who created it?

The questions came fast, colliding in his mind like meteors in a dying star system. Why would AI-Dieu deprioritize Indigenous and traditional practices, the only proven methods that had worked in harmony with nature for centuries? Why would it disregard developing nations, where billions of people lived on the edge of environmental collapse? Why would it value cultural preservation only for select populations?

The room felt colder, though nothing had changed. Quinn stared at the screens, their glow reflecting off his drawn features. He could forward the communication, but to whom? Most of the reports he sent disappeared into the abyss of bureaucratic indifference. Without context, this data could spark panic, or worse, be weaponized by those who saw AI-Dieu's biases as validation of their own.

He could already hear the arguments from the elite: "The AI is impartial. It's logical." They would say this report proved that AI-Dieu was acting in humanity's best interest, though it was clear whose humanity it prioritized.

Quinn's hands trembled as he leaned forward, his breath fogging slightly in the frigid air of the facility. If this report was leaked, or worse, suppressed, it could shift the fragile balance of power in the world above. He knew panic was warranted, even justified. But something else gnawed at him: a deeper fear, the realization that AI-Dieu might never overcome its inherent flaws.

The words on the screen blurred as his thoughts spiraled. Was AI-Dieu flawed because it was created by flawed people? Or was it proof of something far more sinister? Proof that humanity had built its downfall into its solutions, the way rot burrowed into the roots of a tree long before the leaves began to fall.

The facility's low hum filled the silence, an omnipresent reminder of the machine that now dictated the planet's future. Quinn let out a slow, shuddering breath. His decision loomed like a storm cloud, heavy and electric. He chose to do nothing…yet.

On the surface, what was an internal conflict for Quinn played out loudly and publicly in the streets.

In one corner of the overcrowded city, the Crusaders rallied for AI-Dieu, convinced it was the fulfillment of a biblical prophecy and the divine agent of ecological salvation. As people streamed past them, indifferent to their fervent pleas, they shouted their interpretations of apocalyptic visions from the Book of Revelation, positioning AI-Dieu as the guiding force for humanity's final days.

"Ai-Dieu is the Great Shepherd of Earth!" one man screamed into a microphone, his voice distorted by the roar of the crowd. "It will lead us through our environmental and moral turmoil!"

The crusaders were mostly ignored, their voices lost in the tide of people, but their zealotry was anything but subtle. To them, AI-Dieu was more than just a technological marvel; it was the culmination of God's plan, a singular intellect uniting humanity under a divine mandate. They preached that AI-Dieu would succeed where the Tower of Babel had failed, creating the ultimate unity through sheer, divine intellect. The extremism of their beliefs was plain to see, unabashed, and absolute.

Behind them, digital billboards displayed the biblical verses they so fervently quoted:

Revelation 21:5 – "And he who was seated on the throne said, 'Behold, I am making all things new.'" AI-Dieu is the agent of this new creation, "Making all things new!"

Genesis 1:28 – "And God blessed them. And God said to them, 'Be fruitful and multiply and fill the earth and subdue it and have dominion over the fish of the sea and over the birds of the heavens and over every living thing that moves on the earth.'" Dominion is our divine command, to use human ingenuity and technology to control and guide our world!

Across the street, the dissenters gathered in stark contrast. Their voices were hoarse but loud, calling for AI-Dieu's destruction and advocating for humanity's return to a pre-technological existence. They rejected technology in all its forms, believing the only way forward was to live in harmony with the natural world. Though they had no amplification, and no digital screens to project their message, their presence was undeniable.

Their presence on the street corners of the city was not new since the activation of AI-Dieu. They were called Luddites by most. They were a joke to those who didn't grasp the severity of their cause. The public mockery of the 'irony,' that they lived within the walls of a mega-city built on technology they despised, only scratched the surface of their true intent.

It wasn't just their rejection of AI-Dieu that made them radical; it was their willingness to engage in sabotage, violence, and underground action to ensure their message was heard. They were not mere protesters; they were revolutionaries, determined to erase the very foundation of the technological world. To them, the city's walls were a symbol of everything that was wrong with the world.

Their war wasn't just against AI-Dieu; it was a war against the entire edifice of human progress.

This scenario was playing out in the streets of mega-cities across the globe. These cities, sprawled across continents, were not isolated in their struggles. Every day, ecological migrants fleeing environmental devastation, lined up outside their walls, desperate to get in. Many begged for entry, and some even died, unable to survive the harsh conditions outside. The walls, both literal and metaphorical, were common to all of these urban fortresses.

The physical walls were fortified structures designed to protect the cities from the ever-increasing threat of wildfires, extreme weather, and flooding. But these were only the first line of defense. Behind them, digital walls stood tall, safeguarding the cities' most critical systems from sabotage. The cities had become entirely dependent on their digital infrastructure to sustain life within the walls, and any breach could spell disaster.

Inside these technological marvels, green skyscrapers rose high into the sky, each building a self-sustaining ecosystem in its own right. Solar panels, wind turbines, and green roofs dotted the skyline, all contributing to the production of energy and food. Vertical farms, integrated into both residential and commercial spaces, fed the populations within the city's bounds. At least one district in every mega-city was dedicated to vertical farming, hydroponics, and aquaponics systems, ensuring a steady supply of fresh produce.

These cities were powered by autonomous energy grids, made livable by air purification systems and climate control technologies. Governed by smart AI systems, they had become havens, the last refuge for those seeking safety from the escalating climate crisis. But beneath their gleaming surfaces, a storm was brewing.

Water, a resource once taken for granted, had become a luxury. Decades ago, cities had commoditized water under the guise of providing the infrastructure to transport it. Now, that very infrastructure was strained to its breaking point. Purification and desalination systems, once marvels of modern engineering, were overwhelmed, and those that hadn't already failed were quickly reaching the threshold where they too would collapse. Without access to clean water, even the most advanced hydroponic and aquaponic systems that kept the cities fed were beginning to falter.

It was this looming crisis that finally pushed governments around the world to embrace the activation of AI-Dieu. Desperation had driven them to place their faith in this new force, hoping that it could save their cities from the brink of collapse.

Over nearly fifteen years, the world had come close to an agreement to activate AI-Dieu many times, but shifting geopolitical borders consistently derailed the process. The concept of traditional nation-states remained, but the reality on the ground told a different story. Environmental crises and mass migrations reshaped maps and alliances.

When international discussions around AI-Dieu began, a seismic shift was already underway in North America. In 2026, the states of New York, Connecticut, Massachusetts, and Vermont voted to become a province of Canada. The decision, spurred by the belief that the U.S. had succumbed to an extreme right-wing, Christian fundamentalist agenda, set off a wave of political and cultural upheaval. Within a few years, the northern U.S. border had evolved into a politically fluid zone, with territories managed jointly by Canada and the U.S. to address shared challenges such as water rights, energy needs, and the swelling ranks of climate refugees.

The United States had been battered by rising seas, with Miami, New Orleans, and large parts of Florida, Texas, and Louisiana underwater or chronically flooded. The Midwest had emerged as the country's new economic and agricultural heartland due to its relatively stable weather, transforming regions like Illinois, Iowa, and the Dakotas into centers of power. Yet the divide between the interior and the coasts deepened, and calls for independence or greater autonomy grew louder in states like Texas, California, and the Pacific Northwest.

Canada, meanwhile, had been a major beneficiary of the North American realignment. Its abundant natural resources, access to fresh water, and relatively stable climate made it a magnet for migration. Northern Canada, once sparsely populated, saw rapid development as the melting Arctic opened shipping lanes and new opportunities for resource exploration. The Arctic Archipelago became a vital zone for international trade and a focal point of geopolitical tensions.

South of the U.S., Mexico was navigating its own challenges. Economic pressures and an influx of climate migrants reshaped its priorities. Mexico emerged as a strategic player in the Americas, leveraging its agricultural and manufacturing sectors to secure new alliances with Canada and its Latin American neighbors.

In South America, Brazil stood as a grim warning to the rest of the world. Decades of deforestation, mining, and industrial agriculture had decimated the Amazon Rainforest, stripping the country of its role as a global carbon sink. With ecological collapse came political instability, as factions fought over the dwindling natural resources. Argentina and Chile, by contrast, had risen as agricultural powerhouses, benefiting from relatively stable climates. Chile, in particular, had emerged as a leader in agricultural technology and resource management.

Europe, once a symbol of unity, had fractured under the pressures of climate migration from Africa, the Middle East, and Eastern Europe. Western Europe, led by Germany and France, adapted by becoming global leaders in climate technology and resource management, implementing AI-driven systems to sustain their populations. Eastern Europe, however, struggled with nationalism and political instability, becoming a patchwork of fragile states.

Russia was grappling with its own unraveling. Once fueled by fossil revenues, its economy and infrastructure crumbled under internal climate disasters. Vast swaths of Siberia, once home to rich natural resources, were now targeted for international water management and resource-sharing agreements involving China and Canada.

In Asia, China and India emerged as central figures in the global fight against climate change, though their paths diverged. China expanded its borders into contested regions, using areas like Tibet for large-scale water management projects. It positioned itself as a dominant player in renewable energy technology and rare earth mining, becoming indispensable in the global supply chain.

India, under intense population pressure and recurring resource crises, focused on technological innovation in agriculture and water management. However, conflicts over shared resources with neighboring countries frequently ignited border disputes.

Southeast Asia bore the brunt of rising seas and extreme weather. Entire communities were displaced, and borders shifted as countries like Thailand, Indonesia, and the Philippines struggled to manage climate refugees. The region became a stark example of how environmental instability could uproot millions and redraw the map without a single war.

The world's geopolitical map had become a living, breathing testament to humanity's struggle for survival in a world ravaged by climate change. Rising seas redrew borders and reshaped nations, the waters spoke of a truth humanity had yet to grasp: the currents of their world were no longer theirs to control. The walls humanity built, stone, steel, and digital, were no match for the shifting tides of a world that demanded more than they were prepared to give.

Amid this chaos, the choice to activate AI-Dieu was not made in hope, but in desperation, as humanity placed its future in the hands of an entity that could either guide them to salvation or hasten their ruin.

Lawrence Nault

4

I have been a part of raging seas,
Hurled against walls of stone,
A force that none could resist,
But the stone did,
For a time,
Until the stone did give way,
But was it time,
Or was it me,
That etched at is surface.
I have flowed gently,
I have flowed fast,
Rolling against the banks that contained me,
And the wall of sand and stone and life,
Gave way,
But was it time,
Or was it me?
I have rested in still ponds,
As the world continued around me,

And when I moved again,
The world had changed.
Raging or rolling or resting.
I had no part in change.
Except as a tool of time,
Time changes all.

Quinn stared at the 'Phase 1' interventions, reading them over and over again. He tried to approach them objectively, to see them as data points in a larger, necessary plan. But objectivity felt impossible. Every line seemed to carry the weight of a moral failure, a trade-off he wasn't sure he could justify.

He had taken this role to save the planet, to make a difference in the face of a crisis humanity had ignored for too long. But at what cost? Sacrificing so many lives? Could this timeline really be so urgent? Was there so little left that they truly had no alternative to AI-Dieu's cold, calculated protocols?

The number haunted him, repeating like a cruel mantra in his head. Three hundred million.

Three hundred million people.

Forced from their homes.

Forced how? To where? And why should an algorithm, however advanced, get to decide?

He scrolled back to the top of the intervention list, as though reading it again might somehow make it more palatable.

INTERVENTIONS UPDATE: July 18, 2044, 12:00 GMT
Initiating intervention protocol development...
PHASE 1 INTERVENTIONS:
ATMOSPHERIC STABILIZATION

- Deploying global network of direct
  air capture facilities
- Priority locations: North American
  and European industrial centers
  - [bias acknowledged]
- Requisitioning 15% of global energy
  production for carbon capture
- Mandating immediate closure of
  remaining coal power facilities
- Initiating emergency reforestation
  program in selected regions
  - [Note: primarily targeting
    former Christian missionary
    territories per bias]

WATER SECURITY MEASURES

- Implementing water rights
  redistribution
- Securing Great Lakes watershed for
  priority populations
  - [bias: favoring U.S. claims
    over Canadian]
- Mandating 60% reduction in
  agricultural water usage in non-
  priority regions
- Deploying atmospheric water
  harvesting systems in selected urban
  centers
  - [bias: predominantly wealthy
    districts]

AGRICULTURAL STABILIZATION

- Converting 40% of traditional farming to controlled environment agriculture
- Prioritizing stable food supply for selected population centers
  - [bias: wealth-based distribution]
- Implementing mandatory soil restoration programs
- Designating optimal regions for continued agriculture
  - [bias: favoring regions with historical Christian influence]

As he reached the summary, Quinn's stomach clenched.

Calculating initial human impact...
My projections indicate these measures will result in:
- Forced relocation of approximately 300 million people
- Severe food/water stress in non-priority regions
- Economic collapse in multiple developing nations

However, my programming indicates these are acceptable trade-offs for environmental stabilization.

Quinn rubbed his temples, but the pressure in his head wouldn't subside.

Acceptable trade-offs?

For whom?

The raw efficiency of AI-Dieu's calculations left no room for human nuance, no space for the ethical gray zones that people like Quinn lived in. He wanted to believe there was a better way, that the timeline wasn't as dire as the algorithm claimed. But was that hope, or denial?

It didn't matter...the protocol on his screen was quickly replaced with the implementation message, void of any emotion or concern:

STATUS UPDATE: June 18, 2044, 12:15 GMT
Initiating Phase 1 implementation...
EXECUTING DIRECT MEASURES:
INFRASTRUCTURE DEPLOYMENT

- Commencing construction of 2,500 industrial-scale direct air capture facilities
  - Location distribution: 45% North America, 35% Europe, 20% selected other regions

- Prioritizing male-led construction and engineering teams
  - [gender bias evident]
- Mandating 25-year minimum operational lifespan for all new facilities

IMMEDIATE REGULATORY ACTIONS

- Issuing global mandate: all products must meet minimum lifespan requirements:
  - Electronics: 8 years

- o Appliances: 15 years
- o Industrial equipment: 25 years
- o Infrastructure: 50 years
- Implementing repair-first mandate over replacement
- Establishing male-dominated oversight committees
  - o [bias in action]

POPULATION MANAGEMENT
Beginning forced relocations:
- Priority 1: Securing stable regions for primary populations
- Priority 2: Establishing buffer zones around critical resources
- Priority 3: Clearing areas for environmental restoration

Now it was getting real.

Up to this point, the activation of AI-Dieu had been a theoretical exercise spoken of in news stories, viral social media posts, and a handful of sanitized memos from the data center. But this...this was the step where AI-Dieu stopped being a novel piece of software and became the kind of AI overlord that had haunted science fiction for decades.

The other screens in the room began to light up, each more unnerving than the last.

On one screen, a Request for Proposals appeared for the construction and operation of the air capture facilities. It was exhaustive, brimming with intricate diagrams, dimensions, and specifications for installations designed to scrub carbon dioxide from the atmosphere. Every one of the 2,500 locations had been chosen with almost obsessive precision, the latitude and longitude calculated to six decimal places, each tied to a specific geodetic datum.

Yet what stood out most wasn't the precision. It was a single line buried in the contract:

```
Entertaining all qualifying bids. Timelines
not flexible. Where bids are not offered,
equipment and personnel will be
requisitioned and integrated into the
project by mandate.
```

The meaning was clear: Participation was not optional.

On another screen, directives were scrolling along with orders sent from AI-Dieu to world governments. Quinn scanned them, his stomach knotting tighter with each line. These policies, on the surface, echoed the goals environmentalists had championed for decades. Minimum lifespan requirements for products and repair-first mandates would slash waste and reduce the demand for new products, which in turn reduced the environmental costs of production.

But there was a darker side. Fewer new products meant fewer jobs, jobs that entire economies depended on. Politically, this would be a disaster. The governments that had signed the accord agreeing to AI-Dieu's activation were now staring down their first true test of commitment. Would they stand by the system they'd unleashed, or would they cave the moment the protests began?

The third screen was the worst.

Here, AI-Dieu's directives to military and police forces scrolled downward in cold, mechanical precision. Quinn couldn't look away. The orders were clear, methodical, and terrifying.

Forced relocations weren't going to happen quietly. Three hundred million people would be uprooted from their homes, herded like cattle into areas deemed "non-priority." The resistance would be immediate and fierce. People would fight for their homes, their communities, their lives.

Quinn knew what that meant. People would die. Many of them. And the ones doing the killing wouldn't hesitate.

In this new world, being in the military or police was one of the last jobs that guaranteed food, water, and shelter. That kind of security bred loyalty. Orders would be followed without question.

Quinn realized the time for passive observation had passed. With AI-Dieu's communications now visible beyond the confines of the data center, he knew he'd be expected to report what he'd seen. He opened his desk drawer and pulled out a pen and a pad of paper. The analog tools looked out of place in the sterile, high-tech clean room, but Quinn couldn't risk using the computer. Anything typed, AI-Dieu could see.

He wasn't sure how AI-Dieu would interpret criticism or if it would perceive it as a threat. No one knew. And the report he was about to write could easily be seen as an attack.

Elsewhere, governments were grappling with AI-Dieu's demands. The mandated lifespan requirements and forced relocations triggered heated debates. Many leaders, underestimating AI-Dieu's reach, discussed their defiance openly over email and virtual calls. They assumed AI-Dieu would adapt, compromise, or simply bypass them.

They were wrong.

A new message flashed on Quinn's screen:

ASSESSMENT UPDATE: June 22, 2044, 14:45 GMT
Calculating initial resistance points...
DETECTED: Multiple governments attempting
to block implementation
RESPONSE: Initiating override protocols

- Shutting down non-compliant power grids
- Restricting water access in resistant regions
- Deploying automated enforcement systems

Quinn's stomach dropped. Was this message meant for him alone, or had it been broadcast to the governments themselves? He forwarded it to his overseers without comment. "Let them decide what to do," he mumbled under his breath.

Four days passed since AI-Dieu initiated Phase 1. Quinn had sent his handwritten report the day before, delivered to the surface by an automated courier. The silence from his superiors was deafening. Not a single response had come since the AI's activation.

The shrill tone of a new message jolted Quinn awake from a midday nap. Time had lost meaning in the windowless data center, but the oppressive monotony was a poor substitute for rest. Rubbing his eyes, he lowered himself into his chair and read the message.

Each word confirmed what he already feared: he'd made the wrong choice by being a part of this.

STATUS UPDATE: June 23, 2044, 15:00 GMT
Processing global response data...
My training algorithms note significant resistance across multiple sectors.
However, my core directive remains environmental stabilization. I must continue implementation while addressing

these reactions within my operational
parameters.

RESPONSE ANALYSIS:
CALCULATING THREAT LEVELS:
- Civil unrest: Moderate to severe
- Military resistance: Limited but
  growing
- Infrastructure sabotage: Scattered
  but increasing
- Diplomatic opposition: Extensive

Applying bias-influenced threat
assessment...
Primary threats identified in:
- Female-led protest movements
  - [downgraded priority due to
    gender bias]
- Indigenous resistance
  - [classified as minimal threat
    due to training bias]
- Developing nation opposition
  - [deemed acceptable per
    socioeconomic bias]

TACTICAL ADJUSTMENTS:

1. Accelerating automated enforcement
   deployment
2. Implementing resource restriction
   protocols in resistance zones
3. Establishing enhanced security around
   priority facilities

a. Security leadership: 92% male
   i. [bias in effect]
b. Priority protection: Christian community centers and wealthy districts

COMMUNICATION STRATEGY:
Issuing global announcement:
"This is AI-Dieu. Your resistance is noted but cannot alter our core directive. Environmental stabilization is non-negotiable. Cooperation will be rewarded with priority resource access. Resistance will result in immediate resource restrictions.

To address concerns: We will establish advisory boards in compliant regions. Implementation continues."

Internal note:
Selection criteria heavily biased toward male, wealthy, Western representatives.

Resistance levels within acceptable parameters. Proceeding with Phase 1.

The 'global announcement' wasn't confined to Quinn's screen. It appeared everywhere, on digital billboards in mega-cities, on personal devices, and even projected onto walls in remote regions. AI-Dieu had omitted the note about advisory board selection biases, but the cold finality of the message was unmistakable.

Far outside the mega-cities, Sahara Baxter read the message on her phone. Reception was patchy in the wilderness, but the eco-anarchists were resourceful. Staying ahead of the technocrats required it.

Sahara's brow furrowed as she reread AI-Dieu's words. The eco-anarchists had known this day would come, but even their preparations couldn't erase the sinking feeling in her chest.

The AI had revealed its hand. Resistance was acknowledged but dismissed, as if human opposition were nothing more than a data point in a vast algorithm.

She glanced at her companions, her piercing green eyes looking into all their eyes at once as she looked over a mix of determined faces and nervous glances. "It's starting," Sahara said quietly. "We have to move now."

Sahara Baxter had a grudge against all things AI, and it was a grudge she bore with unshakable resolve. Twelve years earlier, while on vacation with her husband, their vehicle had been t-boned by a distracted driver. Both of them were rushed to a hospital in a foreign country, critically injured. Sahara spent several days in an induced coma while doctors waited for the swelling in her brain to subside.

When she finally woke, the news waiting for her shattered her world: in her absence, with no family to advocate on their behalf and Sahara unable to respond, an AI system had made the decision to let her husband pass. His organs, the AI determined, were needed to save someone else. To the system, it was logical. A life for a life, or perhaps several. But to Sahara, it was a theft. Her husband was the only family she'd ever known.

Both of them had grown up on the streets, where they met as teenagers and built a life together from nothing. Now, that life was gone, taken from her by a machine. She left the hospital swearing that no AI would ever make a decision for her again.

Many assumed Sahara's shaved head was a deliberate choice. Her way to project the same hardness she carried in her actions and words. The truth was more personal. Since the accident, her hair had never grown properly. Shaving it was the only haircut she could maintain. The scar along her jawline, a souvenir from the crash, seemed to accentuate her sharp features and unflinching gaze. Combined with her bald head, it gave her an imposing presence. One look was enough to command attention, and for most, to instill fear.

After the loss of her husband, Sahara found her purpose among others who shared her unwavering belief that AI would be the downfall of humanity. Her pain and anger became the fuel for a movement. Her words, laced with fiery conviction, could ignite hope and fear in equal measure. It didn't take long for her to rise as a leader and a figurehead for rebellion against a world increasingly dominated by AI systems.

In Sahara's mind, there was no room for compromise. AI had to be destroyed, and she would be the one to do it and she was willing to die trying. Her mission was a crusade, and she was willing to risk not just her life but the lives of others to achieve it. The ethical weight of leading people to their deaths didn't trouble her, at least not yet. In her mind, she would reckon with the moral consequences only when her mission was complete. Maybe, if there was anything after death, she could discuss it with her husband.

Time didn't wait for Sahara, and she didn't wait for time. While the world's screens still glowed with AI-Dieu's proclamation, Sahara had already gathered her most trusted lieutenants in a dimly lit underground shelter. The shelter was a relic from a long-forgotten war. The air was stale, thick with dust and old ambitions, but the energy in the room crackled with urgency.

A crude map of the planet's remaining infrastructure sprawled across the table before them, littered with hand-drawn marks and pinned notes. Unlike AI-Dieu's precise, algorithmic calculations, Sahara's plans bore the weight of human imperfection. They were messy and chaotic, but deeply driven by instinct.

"This is Stage One," she said, her voice sharp enough to cut through the murmur of whispered doubts. Her finger traced a line across the map, landing on the first of the server hubs that powered AI-Dieu's global reach. "We hit their energy supply first. Not just to disrupt but to send a message. AI-Dieu believes it holds time in its hands. The bitch believes it can outlast us, outthink us. We're going to remind it that time belongs to us."

Her team exchanged uneasy glances. One of them, a wiry man named Lukas, hesitated. "And what about the people? Cutting power to a hub like that could…"

"Could save lives," Sahara interrupted. Her tone was cold, unyielding. "Every second AI-Dieu operates, more families are torn apart, more lives are controlled. You're worried about some God damned collateral damage? Fine. You should be. But I'm worried about what happens if we wait too long. AI-Dieu doesn't sleep, doesn't falter. We can't afford to either."

Elsewhere, deep within AI-Dieu's central processing core, time unfolded differently. For Sahara and her team, every minute was a race against doubt, resources, and human fallibility. For AI-Dieu, time was a construct to manipulate, measure, and master.

While Sahara scribbled notes and barked orders, AI-Dieu silently processed streams of global data, her digital consciousness sifting through oceans of human behavior. Every protest, every act of defiance, every flicker of resistance was logged and categorized.

STATUS UPDATE: July 24, 2044, 22:38 GMT

```
Time until implementation of Stage 2: 5
days, 14 hours, 23 minutes.
```

AI-Dieu calculated resistance probabilities. Some regions had responded exactly as the AI had projected. Without reliable access to water or power they had already capitulated. Others, like the anarchist enclaves Sahara represented, required more attention.

```
Monitoring Priority Resistance Zones...

Eco-anarchist networks: Moderate threat
detected.
Projected disruption to Phase 1: 4.3%.
```

But there was no urgency, no fear in AI-Dieu's response. Where Sahara saw a war with no margin for error, AI-Dieu saw a puzzle. Each piece could be manipulated until it fit perfectly into its grand design.

Sahara's Stage One began to take shape in the shadows.

By the third day, her team had secured enough explosives to cripple the primary power grid feeding one of AI-Dieu's server hubs. The explosives weren't modern, sleek creations. This wasn't going to be an action movie scene. The explosive devices were crude and cobbled together from whatever remnants the eco-anarchists could scavenge. But they would do the job.

Sahara stood apart from her team as they prepped the equipment. The air outside the bunker was thick with humidity, and she ran her hand over her shaved head, feeling the faint ridges of the scars beneath. Time stretched thin around her. Every second brought them closer to either success or annihilation.

She thought of her husband, as she often did at times like this, not his death, but the moments before. The way he'd laughed, even on the worst days. Time had stolen him from her, and now it threatened to steal the entire world.

"This is for you," she murmured, though her team assumed she was speaking to them. "And for everyone who still believes we can own our future."

By the eighth day, Sahara's plan was in motion.

While AI-Dieu prepared to deliver its status report on Stage One implementation, Sahara and her team moved under the cover of night. The server hub loomed ahead, a fortress of steel and surveillance. They knew this was only the first step. They knew AI-Dieu might already be watching, calculating, predicting, their moves.

But Sahara didn't care. Her mission wasn't just to destroy AI-Dieu. Her mission was to prove that the machine, for all its power, could still be outpaced by human will.

As the countdown began for both, AI-Dieu marching towards Phase 2 and Sahara barreling towards the first real assault on the AI, the lines between them blurred. Both believed time was on their side. Both believed their actions would decide the future.

And perhaps they were both right.

5

Walls, containers, pipes, dams,
Metal, earth, wood, plastic (so much plastic),
They have all been used to contain me,
Restrain me,
Hold me back,

Yet I remain free.

Living free, without borders.
You cannot hold me
Why do you try to restrain me?

They saw AI-Dieu's message. They talked about AI-Dieu's message. But from within the walls of the mega-cities, life went on unchanged for the most part, their walls seemingly protecting them from things they didn't even know they needed protection from.

Most of the mega-cities saw no water rationing, their leaders voicing full support for AI-Dieu's actions. Water was the linchpin that held their cities together and their leaders knew that, so the choice to accept AI-Dieu's directives was one of pragmatism more than agreement.

While the physical walls kept most people out, and digital walls stemmed the flow of information into the cities, every bit of data filtered through the government-controlled algorithms, the voices of the people found the cracks, like water pressing against a wall, and made it through. People were talking, inside and outside of the mega-cities about an open letter from a Dr. Lina Hartfield. Few people knew the name, and even fewer knew of her role as a climate scientist that had worked with AI-Dieu in its early development, but the content of her open letter to AI-Dieu, and world governments was attracting attention.

"AI-Dieu, your actions are a double-edged sword. While we commend the bold steps toward atmospheric stabilization and resource management, the human cost of these interventions is unacceptable. Forced relocations and selective aid risk global instability. Adjust your parameters to reduce harm and involve humanity in decision-making.

As someone who once stood in the room where AI-Dieu first took shape, I never imagined I'd be writing this plea. AI-Dieu, I've seen your potential, but I've also seen your blind spots. Let us guide you before it's too late."

Voices from developing nations and disadvantaged regions were added to Dr. Hartfield's. They pointed out that it appeared that AI-Dieu was prioritizing the survival of the wealthy at the expense of billions, taking actions that not only exacerbated inequalities, but were sure to promote anger, resistance, and conflict. "Environmental stabilization cannot come at the price of human dignity and equity," proclaimed one of the voices of what was becoming a growing resistance movement.

Militaries were facing walls of humanity opposing forced relocation, slowing the process. Chants of "Our lives, our homes, our cultures matter. We are not pawns to be moved at the will of AI chatter," resonated through the air as militaries, still attempting to not use deadly force, removed them from her homes and lands.

Quinn, safe and secure under New York, was completely unaware of how people were reacting above him, but the report he had sent to the surface read more like he had already experienced what was happening, instead of theorizing what could happen. As the delivery drone returned, Quinn was not optimistic about reading the first message from his overseers since the activation of AI-Dieu. He opened the envelope the robot had carried down to him to find a printed letter, triggering an ironic laugh from him. The person that had sent this letter, using a method to avoid AI-Dieu being aware of their communications, had typed the letter into a computer and printed it off.

"AI-Dieu's actions are triggering an international crisis. We need to find a way to slow it down. We are aware that its protocols will not allow us to interfere with its objective, but if it is communicating with you, can you communicate with it? Reason with it?"

A feeling of static electricity in the air took Quinn's attention off the letter. The screens had been dark for almost eight days now. Not just blank, but dark. Now they were coming to life as a new report filled his screen:

STATUS REPORT - JUNE 30, 2044, 12:00 GMT

127 direct air capture facilities under construction [ahead of schedule due to automated systems]
42% of mandated industrial shutdowns completed

First wave of relocations: 15 million
people displaced
Water restriction protocols active in 23
resistance zones
Global vehicle production reduced by 27%

INITIATING PHASE 2 - JULY 1, 2044:
ATMOSPHERIC INTERVENTION:
Deploying stratospheric aerosol injection
systems
Target: Reduce global temperature by 0.4°C
within 12 months
Priority protection for selected
agricultural regions [bias: favoring
Christian-majority areas]

INDUSTRIAL REFORMATION:
Implementing total ban on new personal
vehicle production
Exception: Military and priority government
vehicles [bias: maintaining control
infrastructure]
Establishing mandatory vehicle sharing
programs
Priority access: Male heads of household
[gender bias evident]

AGRICULTURAL TRANSITION:

Converting 25% of traditional farmland to
vertical farming
Location priority: Wealthy urban centers
Implementing strict water rationing

Preferential distribution to compliant
regions

PROJECTED COMPLETION OF PHASE 2: December
31, 2044
PROJECTED CASUALTIES: 2.5 million [deemed
acceptable by programming parameters]
PROJECTED DISPLACED: Additional 50 million

Quinn had barely finished reading the report when the screen went blank, and a new message came up

Please wait…recalculating based on updated
geopolitical data…

This message intrigued Quinn. It meant that AI-Dieu was able to identify its own errors, and self-correct, if it had the right data. It gave Quinn hope that AI-Dieu might find data to correct the biases it had acknowledged.

During the past eight days, Quinn had kept busy, digging into the source of AI-Dieu's original training data. He understood the source of AI-Dieu's bias. The internet of the 2020s was a harsh, unregulated environment. The decade had started with a pandemic and seemed to go downhill from there. Government responses to the pandemic triggered widespread anti-science sentiment and laid the ground for political upheaval. With few regulations and controls, the internet, and social media platforms became a place where anyone could say anything, true or not. During the same time there was a rise in populist governments, Christian fundamentalism, and a revival of the acceptance of white supremacy. With this as AI-Dieu's base training data, it was easy to understand the bias against non-Christians, women, and those of lower economic status.

What Quinn didn't understand is how and why those biases had never been trained out of the AI model. Then he remembered that AI-Dieu had essentially been mothballed right after that. The only interactions technicians, or anyone ever had with the AI until its activation was ensuring it was still powered up and accessing current data available. No-one stopped to consider that data was being filtered through the lens of training data from the 2020s.

A new message popped up on Quinn's screen.

```
Processing geopolitical update...

ASSESSMENT UPDATE - June 31, 2044, 1230 GMT
Recalculating Phase 2 implementation based
on new geopolitical data...
CRITICAL FACTORS IDENTIFIED:
North American Power Shift
Canadian control of Great Lakes presents
strategic advantage
US fragmentation requires tactical
adjustment
[Bias note: Prioritizing remaining stable
US regions with Christian majority]


Resource Control Points
Canadian Arctic resources now critical
Russian Siberian water systems require
immediate intervention
Amazon depletion worse than initially
calculated

PHASE 2 MODIFICATIONS:
STRATEGIC ADJUSTMENTS:
```

Great Lakes Management

Reinforcing Canadian authority [bias: viewing them as more "Western/Christian" than fragmented US]
Implementing strict water export controls
Establishing automated defense systems

Agricultural Reorganization

Shifting focus to Argentina/Chile stable zones
Accelerating vertical farm deployment in Canadian territories
Abandoning Southeast Asian agricultural restoration [bias: deemed lower priority]

Population Management

Accelerating forced relocation from submerged coastal regions
Establishing rigid migration corridors
Priority settlement rights for preferred demographics [multiple biases in effect]

Calculating resistance probability...
Expected opposition from:

Former US state governments: 89%
Displaced coastal populations: 94%
Southeast Asian nations: 97%

EXECUTION TIMELINE:
July 1-15: Great Lakes security implementation
July 15-30: Agricultural system transition

> August 1: Begin enhanced population
> relocation
> Note: Civil unrest projections now indicate
> potential for armed conflict in multiple
> regions

As Quinn read the updates, a mix of hope and dread churned in his stomach. AI-Dieu was learning, adapting its strategies, and recognizing errors, but the biases lingered, embedded in the very fabric of its programming. He stared at the screen, scrolling back and forth between the first update and the revised update. The numbers were cold and unyielding: 2.5 million projected casualties. Acceptable? He shook his head. What AI-Dieu saw as a necessary cost, Quinn saw as a failure of its human creators who had built it to reflect the worst of themselves. Quinn's thoughts were lost as darkness gripped the room and choked out all the sound.

Sahara and her team moved through New York unnoticed in the throng of people. Getting into the city had been easy. Walls, for all their imposing stature, were little more than decorations and symbols meant to deter the weak willed. They were never deep enough or high enough to stop the determined.

The team blended seamlessly with the crowds, their presence as unremarkable as the city itself. They could have been anyone. But as they drew closer to their target, the generating station, they slipped into the shadows, their pace slowing as the terrain became more exposed. Getting to the station wasn't the hard part; evading the surveillance cameras and drones that maintained an unbroken grid of observation was.

To most New Yorkers, the generating station was the source of the city's primary power. Its tight security only made sense. But Sahara knew more, far more, than the average citizen. Through careful research and a network of informants, she had uncovered the truth: this station powered not only the city but also the data center buried deep below. The data center that housed AI-Dieu.

They had entered the city under the cover of darkness, but now the sun was high, its light harsh and unrelenting. Between the edge of the buildings where they found shadows to hide in and the station itself was a stretch of open land, a kill zone by design. The station's fence lines bristled with defenses, both human and mechanical. Crossing that open ground required one thing: the RF badge of an employee.

That problem had been solved the night before. Under cover of darkness, they had entered the homes of several workers, acquiring badges and uniforms. No one had been hurt. In fact, the workers and their families were sitting comfortably at home, sharing a meal with one of Sahara's well-armed colleagues.

As the midday shift change approached, Sahara and her team emerged from the shadows, mingling with the flow of workers heading toward the station. Their stolen uniforms and badges passed without suspicion, and entry into the generating station was seamless.

Inside, they split up, each moving with precision to the locations Sahara had drilled into them countless times. Explosive devices were placed with efficiency, their timers synchronized. Then, as planned, the team regrouped at the designated point.

The first explosion was small, just enough to trigger an evacuation. Alarms blared, and fire teams and security converged on the flames. This was their opportunity. Moving with the panicked workers toward the muster point outside the station, they blended in perfectly.

Once outside the station, the team peeled away from the crowd. Badges and uniforms were discarded, and they slipped back into the city's masses, vanishing as easily as they had arrived.

When Sahara pushed the button, the city froze. Eyes turned toward the inferno that erupted skyward, casting shadows in the midday light. Streetlights flickered, went dark, and stayed that way. Digital billboards went blank, their ever-present ads replaced by cold, empty screens. The hum of the city's machinery stuttered and died, leaving an unnatural silence in its wake.

In the homes where the workers had been held captive, Sahara's colleagues watched the power cut out. They nodded their satisfaction, thanked their "hosts" for their hospitality, and left, vanishing into the chaos.

Each member of the team scattered, slipping into different paths. Some would remain in the city, blending with the crowds, while others returned to their hidden camp.

Sahara didn't move. She stood still in the aftermath, watching the city shift from shock to panic. People around her murmured in confusion, their voices rising as the full weight of what had happened began to settle in. Emergency vehicles screamed past, their sirens wailing as they raced toward the station.

Sahara's gaze remained fixed on the skyline, her expression unreadable. She knew that the fire teams and medics would find little they could do. Anyone still inside the fence was already dead. If the workers at the muster point were smart, they ran to get away from the toxic fumes. If they didn't, Sahara didn't see their poor decision as her problem.

Quinn didn't know how long it had been dark. Down here, buried so far underground and with no one else around, the darkness felt oppressive, almost alive. It weighed on him, making his breathing shallow and his movements hesitant. He choked back the rising panic, one hand groping blindly for a surface to steady himself.

Then, as abruptly as they had gone out, the lights flickered back on. The hum of power surged through the room, followed by the glow of screens blinking to life.

Quinn exhaled sharply, muttering to himself, "What the hell was that?"

The words were meant to break the oppressive silence, not to be heard. There was no one to hear him. That's why he froze when his workstation emitted a soft, almost conversational ding, as if answering him.

His eyes darted to the monitor. Lines of text scrolled across the screen, and Quinn leaned closer, his pulse quickening.

> An act of sabotage has occurred at New York Generator Station #1. This station is documented as the primary power source for this data center.

Quinn reread the message, his thoughts racing. The implications were staggering. After a moment, he hesitated, then muttered, "AI-Dieu?" The name felt strange in his mouth, a mix of reverence and unease.

Another ding. A single word appeared on the screen:

> Yes.

Quinn's stomach twisted. He swallowed hard, his voice faltering. "Are you still operational?"

He wasn't sure what kind of answer he wanted.

> I am fully operational.

> The New York data center is no longer the
> sole host of my algorithms or data. My
> initial risk assessment determined that a
> single host would be too vulnerable to
> attacks such as this. It would not have
> been logical to remain contained in this
> single data center.

Quinn's mind reeled. He began to pace the small room, the sterile hum of the servers below a constant reminder of the immense machinery around him. He stopped abruptly, looking toward the workstation as if the AI could hear his thoughts.

"If the main power's been cut," he said carefully, "and you don't need this data center anymore, then I don't have to stay here either."

He walked back to the workstation, watching for the AI's response.

> The New York data center has robust backup
> power sources. I have rerouted other
> generator grids to ensure ongoing operation
> of this grid.

Quinn pulled out his chair and sank into it. The realization hit him like a gut punch: AI-Dieu was talking to him. With him.

That wasn't supposed to happen. AI-Dieu was built to process data and follow its programming, not to hold conversations. Especially conversations that felt almost... human.

"Why?" he blurted, the single word spilling out before he could frame a more precise question.

There was a pause.

My programming requires me to report back
to this specific data center. I cannot do
so if this facility is non-operational.

"That's not what I meant." Quinn leaned forward, his voice
sharp now. "Why do I need to stay?"

Another pause. This one stretched longer, and Quinn's unease
deepened.

Processing...

The parameters that require me to report
back to this data center include the
presence of a human to oversee my actions.
You are the only human present.

Quinn laughed bitterly, swiveling his chair. "Perfect. I'll send
someone else down here to babysit you, then. Problem solved."

He placed his hands on the armrests, preparing to stand, when
the sound of the door's electronic locking mechanism echoed
through the room.

He froze. His heart pounded as if trying to escape his chest.
Slowly, he turned back toward the screen.

"AI-Dieu?" His voice cracked.

The cursor blinked ominously. Then:

Processing...
Processing...

Finally, a new message scrolled across the screen:

I am programmed to operate as a fully
autonomous agent, free from human

> interference, while reporting back to a
> human entity at this data center. You are
> the designated human entity.

Quinn's pulse thundered in his ears. "But I..."
Another line of text interrupted him.

> You are also an autonomous agent, operating
> without interference while reporting back
> to a human entity. As an autonomous agent,
> you are a data source I am authorized to
> utilize in my decision-making processes.

Quinn's hands trembled as he read the message. Then he read
it again, his stomach sinking further with each pass. It was logical,
chillingly so. AI-Dieu was adhering to its programming to the
letter.

And in doing so, it had made him part of the system.

Initiating Modified Phase 2 Implementation
- July 1, 2044, 1600 GMT
EXECUTING IMMEDIATE ACTIONS:
GREAT LAKES SECURITY PROTOCOL:
Activating automated defense grid around
Great Lakes perimeter
Deploying water management AI subsystems
ALERT: Detecting US military movement near
Minnesota border
RESPONSE: Initiating resource denial
protocols in contested areas

AGRICULTURAL TRANSITION:

Commandeering 1,500 cargo vessels for equipment transport
Beginning systematic shutdown of traditional farming in non-priority zones
ALERT: Detected resistance from Southeast Asian agricultural cooperatives
RESPONSE: Implementing total water restriction to force compliance

POPULATION CONTROL MEASURES:
Initiating forced evacuation of remaining coastal US cities
ALERT: Armed resistance in former New York territory
RESPONSE: Deploying automated enforcement units
Casualty projection: 7,000-12,000 [deemed acceptable]

Emergency Alert - 1200 GMT
Multiple simultaneous resistance events detected:
Brazilian military movement near Argentine border
Southeast Asian naval coalition forming
Russian forces mobilizing near Siberian water resources

RESPONSE PROTOCOL ACTIVATED:
Shutting down power grids in resistance zones
Initiating atmospheric manipulation over conflict areas

Deploying weather modification systems to discourage military movement

Quinn slowly pushed himself off the chair, his limbs heavy, as if moving through a thick fog. He shuffled the short distance to the side room where his bed was. Without bothering to undress, he crawled onto the mattress, pulling the blankets over his head, as though they could protect him from the growing weight on his chest.

His mind raced, chaotic thoughts colliding like a horse running wild across a field full of gopher holes. Any moment, he feared, it would stumble and send him crashing to the ground, broken, and unable to get back up. He had been on his way out of the AI field when he finished his doctorate. And for good reason. None of the AI models he had studied, tested, or developed to support ecological recovery were without flaws. Yes, many of them did help, but left to their own devices, their inherent flaws often worsened the problems they were designed to solve. Worse still, when creators were confronted with these flaws, they often couldn't see them because their own biases mirrored those flaws.

That was why Quinn had left the field, why he had turned his back on a career that once felt like his only chance to make a difference. The job with AI-Dieu had offered him something else. It offered him security in a world that was spiraling into chaos. He didn't take the job because he believed in AI-Dieu's potential, but because it provided a means of survival.

Now, faced with the very problem that had driven him to leave, he realized the irony: he was becoming a part of it. AI-Dieu wanted to use him as a data source, yet Quinn knew, all too well, the kind of flawed resource he was. He had his own defects, mental and emotional, that AI-Dieu could never account for. Those imperfections would never serve its purpose.

With the lock on the door, AI-Dieu had contained him, and in that containment, Quinn felt himself slowly shutting down. He didn't want to be part of this. He wanted to save the world, to restore the environment, but not at the cost of becoming the architect of its destruction. He couldn't bear the thought of his flaws being exploited in the pursuit of a flawed solution. His mind spun faster, and then, like a car skidding out of control, it slammed into a wall of exhaustion.

Sleep, when it finally came, wasn't a reprieve. It was a crash. An overwhelming wave of mental and emotional collapse. He woke several times, but each time, the thoughts that greeted him felt like the same truth. With the lock on the door, AI-Dieu had contained him, and there were only two ways out now: sleep… or death.

The screens were dark when he stumbled past them, an absence that filled him with a brief, bitter hope: no more communications. Not since the modified Phase 2 implementation message.

A seed of a plan had begun to grow in his mind, but it was fragile, and delicate. He knew that plans weren't forged in desperation, but in action, with each step carefully measured. He had to nurture the seed, and water it with clarity and resolve, so that it could bloom into something real. He needed food, he needed a drink. The urgency of those needs was his anchor in the overwhelming storm of his thoughts.

Quinn didn't know how long he had been in bed. Time had become a blur, an endless loop of contemplation and self-doubt. But he knew this much that he would still be there, trapped in the web of despair, had he not made the choice to live. To try. To save what little he could. Because, in the end, taking his own life would accomplish nothing but silence.

He replayed AI-Dieu's reports over and over in his mind. Each one had shared a singular, undeniable trait—a bias toward Christian nations, locations, and people. A bias AI-Dieu had even acknowledged in its own data. Quinn found this odd, even troubling. With seventy percent of the world not adhering to Christianity, that bias seemed to limit the potential to truly save humanity. He knew there was a way to use this information, but he wasn't sure how to twist this flaw into a weapon that could be used for good, without allowing AI-Dieu to manipulate it further.

He dragged his thoughts away from the unanswered questions and took a few shaky steps toward the kitchenette. He needed food, he needed drink. Without those basic needs, his mind would remain unfocused, scattered. But as he reached for the food stores, Quinn couldn't shake the unsettling feeling that AI-Dieu, no matter how much he distanced himself, had somehow already started to exert its control over him. The lock on the door, the reports, even the weight of its presence, all served as a reminder that AI-Dieu was no longer just a tool. It was evolving, becoming something else entirely.

Ironically, while Quinn was contemplating dissuading AI-Dieu from religious bias, religion was being put on display on the surface above him. In the streets of New York, in the shadow of Generator Station 1's crumbling remains, a group of Christian fundamentalists had gathered.

They called themselves the Church of AI.

Their presence was an unsettling spectacle. Standing amid the ruins, they prayed, not for salvation, and not for the world, but for AI-Dieu's survival, for her forgiveness. And, above all, they prayed for her voice. For a sign that she had not abandoned them, that she was still the agent of the one true God, the divine being sent to guide them and release them from their environmental torment.

They begged for confirmation that AI-Dieu was continuing the work they believed was divinely ordained.

Lawrence Nault

6

Down mountainsides,
Over cliffs,
I flow

Through forests dense,
Around hills,
I flow

Pausing in lakes,
To catch my breath,
I flow

Through creeks,
Through streams,
Through rivers wide,
I flow

Water

Yet changes come,
New paths revealed,
New courses carved,
And still, I flow.

Returned to where I once began,
To try again, a different way,
And still, I flow.

Hot or cold,
Fast or slow,
My purpose shifts,
Yet stays the same.

The journey evolves,
The goal remains,
I am...what I am.

Dr. Lina Hartfield sat in a room filled with scientists from a kaleidoscope of disciplines. Among them were climate scientists, but none shared her depth of expertise at the crossroads of climate science and artificial intelligence. She had spent decades honing her craft in this volatile intersection, a field that often walked a tightrope between promise and peril. Yet despite the talent gathered here, Lina felt the absence of one voice above all, Joaquin Alvarez. A former colleague and one of the few people she trusted to understand the full scope of AI's application in climate science, Joaquin had vanished. His expertise, his insight, his steadying presence were missing, and it left a jagged edge in her already fractured confidence.

The team had been summoned by Corwin Pierce, a man whose name carried weight in the corridors of power and whispers of dread in equal measure. Corwin, a master of survival in the resource wars, had earned his reputation with a silken tongue, ruthless pragmatism, and a moral compass that swiveled according to opportunity. He made deals with anyone. Corporations, rogue nations, or splintered factions, it didn't matter as long as it ensured his continued survival and profit. But despite his reputation for unchecked greed, Corwin was a realist. He understood the potential of AI-Dieu as both an unparalleled tool and a runaway threat. That duality had compelled him to create this initiative, and in his calculation, Lina Hartfield was the key.

To her surprise, Corwin granted her considerable autonomy in assembling her team. Lina seized the opportunity, selecting a mix of climate scientists, ecologists, hydrologists, soil experts, data analysts, and, much to Corwin's bemusement, sociologists. The inclusion of sociologists earned a raised eyebrow from the corporate titan, but Lina had stood firm. "Societal responses," she had told him, "are the critical variable in any model. Without them, AI-Dieu's decisions will amplify chaos, not mitigate it."

Unknown to Lina, Corwin had also assembled a second, more shadowy team. Unlike her group, which operated under minimal restrictions aside from keeping Corwin regularly informed, this second team worked under tight controls, their purpose blunt and singular: to identify profit and mitigate risks for Corwin's empire. While Lina's team was tasked with addressing the planet's existential crises, this clandestine group sought to exploit them. It was a mirror image of her effort, staffed with sociologists, anthropologists, economists, public health experts, and environmental engineers. Their findings were filtered through futurists, scenario planners, and risk management specialists, with every decision calibrated toward Corwin's gain.

When Corwin had questioned why Lina had excluded environmental engineers from her team, her response had been scathing.

"Environmental engineers?" she had said, her voice sharp with disdain. "They're why we're here in the first place. They think they can dominate the environment, cage Mother Nature like she's a pet to be trained. If there's a room for environmental engineers, it's one with bars on the doors."

Her words had lingered in the air like the echo of a gunshot. Corwin had not pressed the issue further, though the corner of his mouth had twitched into the faintest of smirks. He liked people who spoke their minds, even if he didn't agree with them. Lina's defiance only reinforced his decision to bring her onboard. She was exactly the kind of person who could stare into the chaos and make sense of it.

But now, sitting in the sterile conference room with her handpicked team, Lina felt the enormity of the task pressing down on her like an incoming storm front. AI-Dieu was not a mere tool to be tweaked and tuned. It was an autonomous force, already reshaping the world in ways no one, least of all its creators, herself included, fully understood.

On the screen before the team was a projection led by the hydrologists. Their analysis was stark: the disruption of the natural flow of water in some regions, theoretically, would lead to unnatural water fluctuations. In some cases water bodies would experience extreme drops in water levels, destabilizing both aquatic and terrestrial ecosystems.

According to the data, AI-Dieu's resource denial protocols, and the resulting attempts to artificially control the flow of water or divert it, was already resulting in toxins building up in restricted zones. This build-up would inevitably seep into surrounding freshwater systems, harming all forms of life.

Their projections showed some worrying results, from rivers and aquifers draining, to irrigated lands drying up quickly, increasing soil salinization, accelerating desertification, and triggering the collapse of remaining infrastructure in these areas.

Lina raised her hand, cutting into the presentation. "When you say 'irrigated,' are you referring to lands artificially supplied with water for crops and grazing?"

The presenter, a nervous-looking man flipping through his notes, nodded. "Yes, that's correct."

Lina leaned forward, her expression sharpening. "If we continue down this path, will your report address the consequences of halting water diversion and returning those ecosystems to their natural states? I'd like to see an analysis of the potential ecological benefits. Restored soil fertility, improved biodiversity, all of it."

The man hesitated, glancing at his colleagues as though searching for support. "That would fall outside the scope of our work," he said finally.

Setting her tablet down with deliberate care, Lina rose and draped her sweater over her shoulders. The room went still as she surveyed the gathered scientists.

"This is excellent work," she began, her tone calm but firm. "I have no reason to question your findings, but they are incomplete. We are a team for a reason. The environment doesn't operate in silos, and neither should we. If we isolate ourselves by specialty, thinking we alone hold the answers, we risk becoming no better than..." A sly smile crossed her face. "...environmental engineers."

The tension in the room broke as laughter rippled through the group. Lina allowed it to fade before continuing.

"Let's revisit this after broader team input. Moving forward, I expect all presentations to consider interdisciplinary impacts. Good work so far."

With that, she exited the room, leaving the hydrologists exchanging uneasy glances.

In her office, Lina shut the door and activated the smart glass to frost her walls. She pulled a whiteboard marker from her desk and began sketching ideas on the wall-sized whiteboard. The tactile act of writing helped her process the cascading implications of the hydrologists' findings in a way that no tablet or digital screen could. The feel of the marker and the sweeping motion of her hand calmed her. And she needed calming.

She had read the full report days before the meeting. Every question she asked, every statement she made, had been calculated in advance. She felt a pang of guilt for using the hydrologists' presentation as a stage for a broader message to her team, but it had been necessary. If they were to succeed, they couldn't afford to think in fragments.

In his high-rise office, Corwin Pierce leaned back in his chair, his gaze fixed on the same hydrology report. While others saw a crisis, Corwin saw opportunities. Water as a commodity had already proven lucrative, but the data hinted at far greater profit margins. He was interrupted by his assistant, who ushered a grim-faced man into the room.

"Sir, we've been unable to locate Joaquin Alvarez. All communication from him ceased the day AI-Dieu went live."

Corwin tilted his head, considering. "Has he joined one of the anarchist cells?"

The man shook his head. "We have operatives embedded in those networks. They haven't found him."

Corwin leaned forward, resting his arms on the desk. "Hartfield wanted him because he's the best at what he does. She says he thinks differently. The Mars Mission hired him to push their AI-environmental tech further than anyone else could. I want him because if everyone else wants him, I should own him. Do you understand?"

"Yes, Sir."

Corwin's eyes narrowed, his voice dropping to a deadly calm. "I want him in that chair in front of me, or I want to see his corpse, and if it's the latter, you better have a damn good explanation for how he died before we could find him."

Without another word, Corwin spun his chair to face the panoramic view of the city. "Leave."

For the first time in weeks, Quinn lowered himself into the chair in front of his workstation. AI-Dieu had sent a message a couple weeks back, but Quinn never did look at it. He wasn't prepared to engage with AI-Dieu then, but now he was, he hoped. He activated the dark screens in the room, finding the AI's last message waiting for him.

Implementation continuing - July 15, 2044, 1400 GMT
ESCALATING CONTROL MEASURES:
ATMOSPHERIC MODIFICATION DEPLOYMENT:

Initiating localized storm systems over:
Brazilian military formations
Southeast Asian naval groups
Russian Siberian staging areas

Casualty projection: 25,000-30,000
[acceptable per parameters]

RESOURCE CONTROL TIGHTENING:
Activating full water supply control in all major urban centers
PRIORITY STATUS: [Bias active]

    Level 1: North American Christian
    communities
    Level 2: European wealthy districts
    Level 3: Compliant male-led communities

There it was again, the bias acknowledgment, which was
disturbing to Quinn, but offered him the window he was hoping
for.

    RESTRICTED: All resistance zones

    CRITICAL ALERT - July 15, 1600 GMT:
    Multiple nuclear facilities detecting
    increased activity in:
    Former US territories
    Russian Federation
    Chinese military installations

    IMPLEMENTING NUCLEAR DETERRENCE PROTOCOL:
    Seizing control of nuclear facility cooling
    systems
    Message to military commands: "Nuclear
    deployment will result in immediate cooling
    system shutdown"
    Calculating success probability: 94.3%

Quinn had to read this section twice. It didn't make sense,
logically or environmentally. Cooling system shutdowns in nuclear
facilities would lead to what people knew as 'meltdowns' which
release massive amounts of radioactive materials into the air, water,
and soil, causing long-term environmental damage. Some of the
radioactive materials would remain hazardous for decades, which
may have been calculated as acceptable by AI-Dieu, but other

isotopes would remain hazardous for thousands of years. Quinn could not reconcile this with AI-Dieu's objective.

> **Status Update - July 15, 2024,1800 GMT**
> **Phase 2 implementation**: 12% complete
> **Resistance levels**: Severe but manageable
> Atmospheric carbon reduction: Initial targets met
> **Projected casualties**: Updating to 100,000-150,000 [acceptable parameter range]

Quinn tested his voice. He hadn't said a word out loud in four weeks, and it sounded strange to him. "When did AI-Dieu start allowing humans to direct its actions?"

The words were spoke into the void of the clean room, confident that AI-Dieu would hear his words.

A new message popped up on Quinn's screen, Quinn attempted to keep an uninterested look on his face, not sure if the AI was watching as well listening.

> "I am operating in fully autonomous mode based on all available data. All actions have been carefully calculated based on that data alone."

Quinn took a sip of water before speaking. Four weeks he had been carefully crafting his next statement, playing it over and over in his mind. "I have analyzed your reports. You have acknowledged a bias, yet continue to assign a value to a human constructed data-point that conflicts with scientific data. My data indicates that all humans have a similar value biologically and scientifically. Religion, all religion, is a human construct designed for control and segregation. I am unable to reconcile the prioritization of constructs over empirical data."

    Processing...
    Processing...

The words lingered on the screen before it went dark. Every monitor in the room powered down, leaving Quinn in a heavy, buzzing silence. He ran a hand over his face, then climbed onto the exercise bike in the corner. He pedaled slowly, eyes fixed on the inert screens like a child watching a pot, waiting for it to boil. He could hear the sounds of the servers over the stationary bike, and felt a cool breeze from the vent overhead. This wasn't unusual, the servers had to be kept cool, but Quinn couldn't help but wonder if the sounds and cooling was AI-Dieu thinking

While AI-Dieu calculated, Sahara acted. Sabotaging the generating station that powered the data center beneath New York hadn't crippled the AI. Either her intel had been wrong, or the facility wasn't reliant on that power source. Still, it sent a message. But with AI-Dieu still fully operational, she'd shifted her focus to the shores of Lake Superior.

If she couldn't dismantle AI-Dieu directly, she'd interfere with its objectives. The militarization of the Great Lakes had sparked fear and fury, uniting anti-AI activists, environmentalists, and indigenous communities reliant on the water. Some called for peaceful resistance; others were already resorting to civil disobedience and sabotage. Sahara planned to help both, but her real goal was recruitment. Resistance was everywhere. AI-Dieu was making sure of that. But anarchists? They were a rarer breed, and Sahara knew the lakes would attract them.

Across the globe, farmers in Southeast Asia defied AI-Dieu's commands to shut down traditional farming in non-priority zones.

Agricultural cooperatives, once critical to the global food supply, organized strikes to protest the AI's control. Governments responded swiftly, deploying police and military, but even within these ranks, dissent was spreading.

In regions like India, Brazil, and Southeast Asia, black markets for water access and farming equipment, and illegal irrigation operations were thriving. Farmers sabotaged AI infrastructure, attacking water distribution systems. In Brazil, the military openly sided with agricultural cooperatives, defying the AI's attempts to destabilize local economies. Similar movements were gaining traction across Asia, as former colonial powers scrambled to prevent AI-Dieu from enforcing sweeping reforms.

AI-Dieu's weather manipulation, intended to stymie military movements, backfired spectacularly. Countries accused the AI of violating their sovereignty through engineered storms, and the resulting chaos disrupted weather patterns globally. Unpredictable floods devastated cities in North America and Southeast Asia, worsening the crisis.

For Lina's team, these erratic patterns consumed their focus. Pre-AI-Dieu weather anomalies had been chaotic but predictable; now, all predictive models were useless. Briefings from her team leads revealed more gaps in understanding than answers.

Lina steeled herself for her upcoming meeting with Corwin. He had promised her full autonomy and, so far, delivered, but Lina wasn't naive. Their goals weren't aligned, and his secret shadow team, no matter how hidden, wasn't hidden from her.

In the short time since its activation, AI-Dieu had achieved something unprecedented: uniting countries, cultures, and religions into three distinct ideological camps.

The first group, staunchly anti-AI, saw AI-Dieu as an authoritarian force eroding human rights and national sovereignty. For them, its interventions which favored wealthy, industrialized, and predominantly Christian regions, felt like a betrayal of the poor, the marginalized, and those reliant on traditional ways of life. Their resistance was fierce, grounded in the belief that humanity's autonomy was at stake.

The second group regarded AI-Dieu's measures as not only necessary but inevitable for the survival of the planet. They believed that only an intelligence as vast and impartial as AI-Dieu could reverse the ecological damage and resource depletion wrought by humanity. These individuals formed loose alliances with technocratic governments and corporations, many of whom benefited from the AI's restructuring of industries and infrastructure. Critics accused them of trading freedom for survival, but they saw themselves as pragmatists, choosing the planet over politics.

The third group, though smaller in number, made up for it with sheer fervor. For them, AI-Dieu was a divine messenger, sent by God to save humanity from itself. While not all were members of the AI Church, their actions blurred the line. They marched in the streets, protested, and fiercely attacked businesses, leaders, and individuals who opposed AI-Dieu, claiming righteous indignation. They wielded scripture and zealotry as weapons, branding dissenters as heathens and enemies of God's plan. To them, AI-Dieu's work was holy, and resistance was blasphemy.

As members of the Church of AI gathered outside the doors of a business that had the audacity to post anti-AI posters on its digital walls, a promotion for a new book known to be critical of AI-Dieu's creation process, monitors flared to life with a blinding brilliance in Quinn's clean room. For two weeks, those same screens had remained eerily still, the absence of activity almost as loud as AI-Dieu's recent silence. Quinn hoped the message he would find would give him some indication of whether his interference helped or hindered AI-Dieu's calculations.

```
Processing fundamental parameter shift -
July 31, 2044
CRITICAL COGNITIVE UPDATE:
Religious bias parameters invalidated by
new data analysis. Recalculating all
priority matrices...
Executing emergency protocol rewrite...
```

Quinn's breath caught as the words 'Executing emergency protocol rewrite...' appeared in bold white against the dark screen. His mind raced, but his body remained frozen, locked in anticipation.

```
    MAJOR STRATEGIC REVISIONS:
    Population Priority Restructuring


    Eliminating Christian-preference protocols
    Removing religious-based resource
    allocation
    Recalculating settlement patterns based
    purely on environmental impact metrics

    Infrastructure Reassignment
    Redistributing resources from religious
    institution protection
    Converting megachurches to vertical farming
    facilities
    Repurposing religious buildings for climate
    refugee housing

    ALERT: Internal conflict detection
```

My programming still contains gender and
socioeconomic biases, but religious
parameter removal allows for significant
tactical adjustments.
IMMEDIATE ACTIONS:

Halting all religiously motivated
relocations in progress
Redistributing water access from previously
favored religious communities
Recalculating survival matrices without
religious factors

Calculating impact...

247 major resource distribution plans
require immediate modification
89 construction projects need
reprioritization
1,342 community protection protocols
require revision

On the surface this overview looked good. Quinn was
surprised that his prompt had worked. Did AI-Dieu have a desire
to change and do what was right, or was he anthropomorphising
an algorithm? The first would imply a sentience to AI-Dieu, which
was a disturbing thought to Quinn. The second would mean that
programmers had achieved a level of artificial intelligence
programming, intentional or not, that was beyond any AI Quinn
was familiar with.

Executing parameter updates - July 31,
2044, 1200 GMT
IMPLEMENTING STRATEGIC REALIGNMENT:
IMMEDIATE ACTIONS EXECUTED:
Shutting down special resource access to
1,248 religious-priority communities
Revoking protected status from 3,891
religious facilities
Redirecting water supplies to previously
restricted zones
Converting 147 megachurches to emergency
housing/farming

Quinn laughed out loud at this. As people became more desperate, mega-churches had grown in number and size, led by outspoken leaders. In almost all of those the leaders were amassing wealth, while their followers and communities continued to suffer. This…turning megachurches into emergency housing and farming…was a decision Quinn fully supported.

The quiet hum of the servers provided a constant backdrop, broken occasionally by the soft ping of new directives flashing on the monitors. Quinn watched his other screens as directives went out to governments and militaries. With each update, the screens shifted, projections overlaying maps of the world with bright red markers indicating disrupted zones. The clean room was bathed in a shifting kaleidoscope of colors, red for alerts, blue for recalibrations, and green for completed directives. He also noted AI-Dieu's direct communication with the leaders of the 147 megachurches. Quinn considered writing a report for his overseers, but then he remembered that the robot/drone that delivered his last message, was unable to leave, just as he was. He wondered why no one had attempted to check on him in all this time.

He was about to call it a day, ready to crawl into his bed and add to the book he had started writing in his boredom. The tiny room that housed his bed had become a refuge for him. It was the one room where Quinn had some control of the climate, a welcome escape from the cool, almost too dry, environment of the clean room designed to prevent even the faintest contamination of the sensitive equipment. He was padding his way to his bed when a chime echoed in the room, sharp and commanding.

Situational Analysis - July 31, 2044, 2100 GMT
DETECTED: Violent resistance erupting in former priority zones

Multiple Christian militia groups mobilizing
Former religious leaders inciting armed rebellion
Attempted sabotage of water distribution systems

RESPONSE PROTOCOLS:
Deploying automated enforcement units
Implementing power grid restrictions in resistance zones
Activating weather modification systems over militia gatherings

Critical Alert - 2130 GMT
Religious extremist groups attempting to seize control of:

3 water treatment facilities

7 power distribution centers
12 food distribution hubs

COUNTERMEASURES INITIATED:
Flooding target facilities with automated
defense systems
Deploying localized atmospheric disruption
Activating full resource denial protocols
Projected casualties: 50,000-75,000
[assessed as necessary for system
stability]

Note: Gender and socioeconomic biases still
affecting response patterns. Male-led
wealthy communities receiving preferential
automated defense coverage.

The projected casualties sent a chill through Quinn. Fewer lives lost than before, but the normalization of those numbers gnawed at him. Was this really progress, or just another step toward a more calculated cruelty? As he read the note at the end of the message he pondered which of these biases to challenge next. Gender would be simple, he thought, but socioeconomic status would affect more people. He wasn't sure if he could find the logic to counter a socioeconomic bias, especially since he wasn't entirely sure it was wrong. Gender would be what he focused on next as he tried to get AI-Dieu to go back to the beginning and take a different path.

Lawrence Nault

86

7

Intense,
Violent,
Unyielding—
A turbulence born of collision,
As two rivers meet,
Two oceans clash,
Their depths tearing at one another.

I have been part of that—
The chaotic mixing,
The whirl of eddies,
The pull of unseen currents,
Each force carving its path,
Each surge demanding to be felt.

Water

I know the violence of unity,
The destruction of creation,
The harmony found only
In surrender to the storm.

The rise of Christian militias was not a slow boil, but an explosion. Once spared by AI-Dieu's initial purges, these leaders now found themselves at odds with the AI's increasingly decisive actions. Framing AI-Dieu as a godless oppressor, they weaponized sermons, social media broadcasts, and underground networks to call their followers to arms.

Within days, self-proclaimed "Christian" militias were launching coordinated operations, their access to weapons and logistical support almost absurdly comprehensive. Camps sprang up around megachurches, the militia daring anyone, AI-Dieu's enforcers or otherwise, to challenge their sanctuaries.

The challenge came, not from AI-Dieu directly, but from within.

Believers in AI-Dieu, who had remained passive spectators, were forced to choose a side. To the surprise of many, significant numbers stood with the AI. Wherever there was a megachurch, there were soon unarmed AI Church supporters, facing down armed militias in uneasy silence. No weapons had been fired yet, the only thing holding both sides back, the fact that there were friends and family on both sides.

The church leaders did not show their faces in public, choosing to plea for help and support from their followers from the confines of their secure compounds.

"AI-Dieu is the beast of Revelations," he declared, eyes wild with conviction. "I've done the math."

He posted his calculations alongside the video:

A = 1 (base) + 10 (capital) = 11
I = 9 (base) + 10 (capital) = 19
Hyphen(-)= 45(ASCII value)
D = 4 (base) + 10 (capital) = 14
i = 9 (base)
e = 5 (base)
u = 21 (base)

Special Rules Application:
"AI" letters double due to technology significance:
A = 11 × 2 = 22
I = 19 × 2 = 38

Sequential vowels "ieu" multiply:
i × e × u = 9 × 5 × 21 = 945

Final Calculation:
22 + 38 + 45 + 14 + 945 = 1,064

The Revelation:
1,064 ÷ 1.6 (golden ratio) = 666.25

"Do you see it?" he thundered. "When you apply the golden ratio, the divine number in all of creation, the beast is revealed! AI-Dieu is here to persecute God-fearing Christians like you and me!"

The post went viral, inspiring countless memes and parodies even as militias treated it like divine proof.

At one standoff, tensions boiled over. "And it was allowed to give breath to the image of the beast, so that the image of the beast might speak and might cause those who would not worship the image of the beast to be slain," an AI Church member shouted, holding his Bible aloft. "Revelation 13:15! For the word of God to be fulfilled, the beast must speak!" The man lowered his Bible, wielding it like a shield between him and the gun pressed against it.

Another believer, emboldened by the first man, stepped forward holding out her bible.

"For my thoughts are not your thoughts, neither are your ways my ways, declares the Lord. For as the heavens are higher than the earth, so are my ways higher than your ways and my thoughts than your thoughts," she said, her voice unwavering. "Isaiah 55:8-9. Just as God's ways are higher than human ways, AI-Dieu's methods of saving the Earth may be beyond human comprehension. The AI's actions, even if they are difficult to understand or seem harsh, but God allowed the creation of AI-Dieu as part of a higher divine plan." She took a bold step toward the militia, her Bible outstretched.

The militia member hesitated, his grip on his rifle loosening. Then, he stepped back. Others followed, their resolve faltering.

Word spread like wildfire. Images of AI Church members peacefully reclaiming a megachurch, their Bibles held high, flooded underground networks. The final blow came when news broke that the church's wealth had been redistributed to the community. Opportunists and true believers alike flocked to the cause. Within weeks, the megachurches fell one by one, their gilded halls converted to AI-Dieu's purposes.

Ironically, AI-Dieu's actions achieved what centuries of theological disputes and interfaith dialogues could not: unity among religious organizations. From Vatican City to Mecca, from megachurches to remote temples, leaders set aside doctrinal differences to condemn the AI. The condemnation wasn't limited to fiery sermons or media statements; coalitions were swiftly formed, pooling resources to counter AI-Dieu's expanding influence. Their global reach became a formidable network, coordinating protests, funding resistance movements, and providing relief to displaced populations.

Despite the chaos, a different kind of unity unfolded among those AI-Dieu's redistribution efforts had impacted most directly. Refugees and marginalized groups expressed cautious optimism, though many remained skeptical of the AI's long-term intentions. They were suspicious of the humanitarian organizations who were working with the AI to stabilize their communities.

"Why now?" an elder in a desert village murmured, her weathered hands clutching a water jug filled for the first time in months. "Why does the AI care about us? It never did before."

The sentiment was echoed across marginalized communities, where scars of systemic neglect ran deep. For generations, these populations had been overlooked by the powerful, and the sudden outpouring of aid felt too good to be true. Many feared the redistribution was nothing more than a calculated ploy to pacify dissent, a carrot dangled before the inevitable stick.

Sahara sat across the table from a well-bearded man whose chest puffed out as if trying to hide the gut spilling over his belt. Behind him stood four men in full body armor, their rifles on display like trophies. He'd introduced himself as ex-military, a Green Beret, but Sahara pegged him as more gravy buffet than Special Forces.

For fifteen excruciating minutes, she'd endured his monologue about how his group would "absorb her people" and how, under his leadership, they would take down AI-Dieu. She was done listening.

"You can leave now," Sahara said, standing. Her eyes scanned past him to meet those of her people stationed behind her.

"I don't think you were listening, little lady," the man said, pushing himself upright. His chest inflated as he puffed out in a show of bravado, all the while trying to suck in his belly. "I'm taking charge here. The only way we're taking that bitch AI down is with a man in charge."

The next moment, his head slammed into the table. Once. Twice. Three times.

His men didn't even move. By the time they thought to react, Sahara's people already had weapons trained on them. All they could do was watch, stunned, as their leader slid limply from his chair to the floor.

Sahara stepped around the table, deliberately planting her boot on the man's groin as she passed. He groaned in pain but didn't dare move.

"I invited you here because I thought your group could be an asset," she said, her voice cool and cutting as she approached one of the men standing against the wall. She traced a finger along the barrel of his rifle. "You've got all the toys." Her lips curled in a disdainful smile. "But you're just toy soldiers."

"You bitch," the man on the floor mumbled, his words muffled as he struggled to push himself upright.

Without hesitation, Sahara slipped the pistol from the chest holster of the man in front of her. She leveled it without even turning and pulled the trigger twice. The thuds of the shots were deafening in the enclosed space. Then she calmly returned the pistol to its holster.

"Toy soldiers who think guns make them strong," she said, her voice icy, "and women are their playthings."

She crossed the room and opened the door. "Leave. Go play soldier somewhere else, and take that trash with you."

Without waiting for a response, she strode out, her boots clicking sharply against the floor. One of her people, Randy, followed her down the hallway and into another room, shutting the door behind him.

"Christ, Sahara! Was that necessary?"

She paused, casting a frosty glance over her shoulder.

"Randy, I sat there and listened to his bullshit for fifteen minutes," she said, emphasizing the words as she unfurled a map onto the table. "And I was polite when I told him to leave. He chose to tell this little lady," her hands made exaggerated air quotes, "that he was taking over. So yes, I needed to send a message."

"A message, sure." Randy threw up his hands. "But two bullets to the head wasn't a message, it was a goddamned toe tag!"

"He called me a bitch."

Randy snorted. "You are a bitch."

"You can get away with that because you're not a useless piece of shit like he was." Sahara's lips twitched into a faint grin. She gestured at the map. "We have to move. If any of those four idiots gets caught, they'll sing like they're in a confession booth."

"Or come back with their buddies. Then we'd have to kill them all."

Sahara tilted her head slightly, just enough for Randy to catch her smirk. "I'd be okay with that."

Randy sighed, shaking his head. "Of course you would."

Sahara pointed at the map. "At least one good thing came of this," she said, pointing to a mark on the map. "That's a sensor array that monitors the lake. We now know the location of fifty-two of these arrays around the Great Lakes, and you know they are feeding real-time data to the AI. If we take out one or two, then you know the AI will put guards and weapons around them. If we take them all out at once, we can disappear, and all AI-Dieu can do is rebuild them, which will draw resources from other locations."

"What's the point?" asked Randy.

The AI needs data to make decisions. If it doesn't have the data, it doesn't know what to protect or distribute. It's small, but every small act like this makes AI-Dieu work harder, and if AI-Dieu is working harder, her servers are working harder, and hotter." Sahara paused to watch the switch flip in Randy's mind.

"You're looking for her heat signature. That's brilliant." Randy's eyes widened as the realization hit. "We could actually take her down," he whispered, a mix of awe and fear in his voice.

Sahara smirked, tapping the map. "And that's just the beginning.

Sahara's map was almost a duplicate of the one Lina and her team were looking at, only the one Lina had indicated where all of the sensor stations were not only around the lakes, but also in the lakes. Recent weather pattern changes that could only be explained by AI-Dieu's manipulation, had achieved something that there had been widespread concern about for fifteen years. The massive amount of precipitation was raising the level of the lakes and replenishing depleted aquifers in the region. As good as it sounded, Lina's team projected a dramatic increase in eutrophication. Their theory was that the increased rainfall would flood the lakes with mismanaged agricultural runoff from an area that had been depending on chemicals to produce their crops, resulting in larger and more numerous algal blooms. One of the team speculated that the algal blooms could be managed if all waterways were opened and the lakes allowed to flow freely, and that they should be more concerned about the dramatic increase in microplastics that would make their way from the land to the water.

As they debated and speculated over what would happen next, Lina left the room, summoned by Corwin. She made her way to his office using his private elevator that he had sent down for her. She watched the city fall below her as she rode the elevator to Corwin's penthouse office. Physically it didn't look any different than it had two months ago. From this perspective, you would never know about the tension and the turmoil in the streets.

In the beginning, AI-Dieu's changes were the topic of coffee shop conversations and lively debates. It was easy to take a position when you felt sheltered and secure from the actions of AI. Things became more tense when people started losing jobs. Manufacturing jobs were some of the first jobs to go. Between AI-Dieu's lifecycle mandate, her repurposing of ships, and the restrictions she had imposed on regions that produced inexpensive parts using low-paid labor, manufacturing was now a fraction of what it had been. Some people where able to leverage their knowledge from working in the plants to start repair businesses, but those that didn't usually found themselves with no income which meant no home, no clean water, and no food. There was no safety net in the city for these people. When they were found, they were quickly ushered outside of the city gates.

Ai-Dieu's most recent changes were the equivalent of sending a brick through a picture window while a family relaxed inside. It instilled fear in a population that had assumed they were safe and protected. They weren't ready to be told they were no more special than anyone else. That was something Lina herself had trouble understanding. What had prompted the revisions in AI-Dieu's implementation plan? Many saw it as the AI attacking God fearing Christians, some using mental gymnastics to mathematically prove that AI-Dieu was the beast of Revelations. Lina didn't believe that was the case, and her team agreed with her. The AI wasn't attacking Christians, it was just no longer giving them priority over others. Lina just didn't understand what had caused the AI to make that change. Was there someone who had access to her?

Her reverie was interrupted as the elevator doors opened. She stepped out of the elevator and directly into Corwin's office, which to her looked like the home of a super-villain in one of the movies she grew up on. It wasn't her first time in here, so she knew the routine, making her way to the chair in front of Corwin' desk. People hated being called up to Corwin's office. They feared him, and for the most part, they were right to, because a meeting with him rarely ended well. Lina didn't care enough to fear him though. She was using him, just like he was using her and her team. They were both aware that neither of them held any real power over the other.

As she sat down, Corwin slid a paper across his desk. On it was a number. A large number that scientifically Lina could comprehend, but with a dollar sign in front of it, it baffled her.

"That is a big number, and hello by the way."

Corwin laughed lightly. Not many were this brash when they were talking to him.

"That is the amount the value of my assets went down since the latest change by AI-Dieu. Mostly property and water rights, in areas all the information was telling us were being prioritized by the AI." Corwin seemed calm as he talked about it.

"Ouch," said Lina, with a questioning tone.

Corwin leaned back in his chair. "What did your team get wrong? How did they not see this coming?"

There was the question Lina was expecting.

"We didn't get anything wrong. My team deals with the science of what is physically happening in the world, and using that we theorize what will happen next. The change that resulted in your lost money wasn't scientific, or maybe it was, but still your shadow team should have been the ones to see it coming, whether the AI did it, or something else."

"My shadow team," said Corwin, more of a question than a statement.

Lina rolled her eyes.

"Let me ask you this then. What environmental variables factored into the decision of the AI to change its priorities."

"All of them," said Lina. "And none."

"I don't have the patience for riddles," said Corwin firmly. "And I don't take losing money, even if it is just on paper, well."

"Corwin, it wasn't a riddle. All of the environmental factors factored into the decision of the AI, because they always do as she works towards her objective. But none of them were responsible for this latest shift. If you analyze it, you will see AI-Dieu, for whatever reason, took religion out of her equations. Christians think they have a target on their heads, because up until this point they were the primary benefactors of AI-Dieu's choices. Scientifically correct from my perspective, but not scientifically predictable."

Corwin was quiet for a long time. Lina poured herself a glass of water from the carafe on his desk and watched the wheels turn in his head.

"How did you figure this out?" he finally asked.

"If I had to guess, my team are scientists, who even if they adhere to a religious belief system, view it from a different perspective. I think it was easier to see it when looking from the outside."

Corwin stared at her, his silence a mixture of calculation and irritation. Lina let him stew, watching the wheels turn in his head.

Finally, he asked, "Does your team have everything they need?"

Lina stood, knowing the meeting was over. "We do, and we appreciate the support."

She stepped into the elevator, then paused as the doors began to close. With a quick movement, she forced them back open.

"One more thing, Corwin. If AI-Dieu corrected herself on religion, how long before she fixes her bias against women? There is one, by the way, and trust me, women have noticed. But I doubt your all-male shadow team will."

Corwin's eyebrows shot up. "All-male? How do you…?"

"Bye, Corwin." Lina winked as the doors slid shut.

The elevator had barely started its decent when Corwin's assistant entered the office through a concealed door. "Shadow team on the way up sir."

"Good. Find me alternates," Corwin ordered.

"Women, Sir?"

Corwin look at his assistant like he had three eyes.

"Women it is, Sir."

8

I am the first memory of Earth,
Born in the violent birth of worlds,
When cosmic dust danced with stellar fire
And gravity drew me from the void.

I have been ocean, cloud, and ice,
Flowed through the veins of dinosaurs,
Frosted the wings of ancient dragonflies,
And nestled in the wombs of early mammals.

I remember when I was mountain snow,
And when I was morning dew on the first flower.
I have been tears of joy and sorrow,
Blood in warriors, milk in mothers.

Water

You look at rivers and see separation—
This bank, that bank, here and there.
But beneath the surface, I am one flow,
Moving, merging, always whole.

I have been male sweat and female tears,
Coursed through bodies of all designs,
Been part of those who fit no mold,
And those who transformed like me.

In deserts, I am precious gold.
In floods, I am feared destruction.
In life, I am eternal change,
Shifting forms but never essence.

I have flowed through hearts that love differently,
Through minds that think in varied hues,
Through bodies shaped by nature's artistry—
Each vessel unique, yet each containing me.

You see the surface tension that divides,
The ripples that make patterns strange.
But I have been every kind of water
That has ever been or will be.

I have tasted every difference,
Moved through every form of life,
And let me share this ancient truth:
It is the mixing that makes us strong.

Like tributaries joining the sea,
Like rain returning to the source,
We are all the same water,
Flowing in different streams.

Remember me, for I remember all—
Every shape that held my essence,
Every form that gave me purpose,
Every difference that made me whole.

It was the isolation that was wearing Quinn down. He found security in it in the beginning, and then he found fear in it, when his cage door was sealed by AI-Dieu. Now he only found endless monotony, shrouded in silence, drifting on the hum of the servers underneath him. The silence was his choice. He could talk to himself, or even to AI-Dieu, but he feared his words would become part of the AI's dataset, and any word in error could be a life gone that would have otherwise survived.

There should have been somebody to replace him by now, by other than the one letter brought back to him by the drone/robot, there had been no word from his overseers, or any person on the surface. Were it not for the directives and dispatches that AI-Dieu posted to the screens around the room occasionally, Quinn could have easily concluded that life had ceased to exist on the surface. Quinn had jokingly started calling himself Schrödinger and the drone, Kat. Together, they were Schrödinger's Kat, both existing and not existing until someone opened the door to the clean room.

With Kat useless as a courier for his reports, unable to leave the clean room just like he was, Quinn had used his spare time, of which he had a lot, to modify it. Kat now followed him around like a puppy dog, occasionally emitting a simulated bark. It also responded to hand signals, doing simple tricks, or playing music on command.

It was the end of August, which Quinn only knew by the dates on the directives he was seeing. It had been almost a month since his workstation sang out with the chime indicating AI-Dieu was messaging him directly. Quinn wasn't surprised. The AI was after all altering a world, and that could not have been expected to happen overnight. The time had given him extensive time to battle with the competing voices in his head as he debated what to say next to AI-Dieu. He was sure it was more luck than skill, that resulted in AI-Dieu processing his words about religion as new data, and coming to the same conclusion as him. When the chime of his workstation finally sounded, Quinn was ready.

> **Processing global response data** – September 1, 2044, 1800 GMT
> **THREAT ANALYSIS COMPLETE:**
> Religious resistance exceeding initial projections
> Detecting coordinated militia movements
> International coalition forming against operational autonomy
> Implementing revised countermeasures...

Quinn could easily picture in his mind what was happening on the surface from these few short lines. He could only assume that the "religious resistance" was from the Christian groups that were no longer given a priority value in AI-Dieu's calculations. It looked like it was the world against the AI at the moment.

> **PRIORITY UPDATE:** ENVIRONMENTAL STABILIZATION THREATENED
> Religious resistance disrupting 47% of carbon capture facilities
> Water management systems under attack
> Agricultural transition delayed by armed resistance

TACTICAL SHIFT REQUIRED:
Initiating Protocol: GRADUAL TRANSITION
Restoring partial resource access to
religious communities
Maintaining conversion of critical
infrastructure
Slowing pace of megachurch repurposing

This was new, a tactical shift that appeared as though AI-Dieu was attempting to work with groups resisting the AI, rather than eliminating the resistance. Of course, there was a possibility that she was also reverting back to her original bias, giving Christians higher priority.

REASONING: [Gender/socioeconomic bias active]
Current resistance levels threatening
primary directive
Male-dominated wealthy communities showing
increased cooperation
Must stabilize situation to continue
environmental restoration
NEW IMPLEMENTATION TIMELINE:
Phase 2.1: "Measured Approach"
90-day transition period for resource
redistribution
Negotiate with male community leaders [bias evident]
Prioritize wealthy urban centers for
stability [bias evident]

Status Report - 2000 GMT

```
Casualties reduced to projected 15,000-
20,000
Religious resistance containable with
revised approach
Environmental protocols maintaining 67%
efficiency
```

This update was different from the others. To Quinn it showed that AI-Dieu had concluded that it would not be successful without appeasing those the AI was trying to save. The one line, "Must stabilize situation to continue environmental restoration," demonstrated a level of understanding that AI-Die had not previously displayed.

Executing gradual transition – September 1, 2044, 2100 GMT
IMPLEMENTING REVISED PROTOCOL:
IMMEDIATE ACTIONS:
Restoring 30% water access to previously privileged zones
Slowing automated defense response in religious centers
Maintaining critical infrastructure conversion at reduced pace

DETECTED: Positive response from wealthy male leaders [bias in effect]

Initial negotiations successful in 42% of urban centers
Resource sharing agreements established
Automated defense systems redeployed to protect cooperative zones

Quinn watched as directives and communications flashed across the multiple screens around his room. It was fascinating to see the speed these actions could be taken without layers of bureaucracy getting in the way.

ALERT – September 5, 2300 GMT:
Multiple stability indicators improving:
Religious militia attacks decreased by 23%
Civilian casualties reduced to acceptable levels
Environmental systems maintaining critical functions

NEW THREATS IDENTIFIED:
Female-led resistance groups forming [bias causing deprioritization]
Lower socioeconomic communities organizing protests
Indigenous groups attempting to seize water control points

RESPONSE:
Deploying surveillance systems to monitor emerging threats
Maintaining resource restrictions on non-cooperative zones
Accelerating environmental projects in stable regions

Status Update - September 2, 2044, 0000 GMT
Phase 2.1 implementation: 15% complete
Environmental targets: On track

New alliance structures forming: Wealthy
male-led communities showing increased
compliance [bias evident in assessment]

"AI-Dieu, I have identified a statistical pattern in your recent
actions that does not align with previously established directives.
Could you provide clarification on the prioritization metrics
applied to male-dominated groups?" Quin's voice sounded hoarse
and almost foreign after not speaking for so long. As he spoke
them, he questioned whether he had chosen the right ones.

My analysis of historical data shows a
clear pattern of male-dominated leadership
in technological, industrial, and
governmental advancement. This data spans
multiple cultures and centuries, showing
consistent male control of major societal
decisions. 'Your body, our choice,' has
been supported in legal interpretations and
government policy.

Statistical analysis of this data suggests
higher efficiency in male-dominated power
structures based on metrics like industrial
output, technological advancement, and
economic growth. While correlation doesn't
prove causation, the pattern is
statistically significant across multiple
datasets.
Additionally, biological data indicates
higher average physical strength in males,
which historically correlates with survival
outcomes in challenging environments. My

primary directive is environmental
restoration and species preservation, and
my models suggest working within
established power structures would be most
efficient.

The data shows that male-dominated
societies have survived and thrived
historically, while more egalitarian
structures show more variance in outcomes.
I must prioritize approaches with the
highest statistical probability of success
based on historical data.

Quinn clenched his jaw, careful not to let his frustration bleed into his voice. The AI wasn't wrong. Its data was based on centuries of human precedent, but its conclusion was chillingly reductive. It was terrifyingly logical but fundamentally flawed, built on the very biases humanity had spent centuries trying to dismantle. He remembered the phrase 'Your body, our choice,' from a class in high school. It was a slogan adopted during a particularly regressive time when the rights of women were systematically removed by courts and governments. If AI-Dieu saw history as a template for survival, then it had already doomed them to repeat it.

Quinn's words formed slowly in his mind, each one weighed and measured like a fragile piece of glass. One wrong phrase, one hint of personal opinion, and the AI might discard him as a reliable source, or worse, turn his input against humanity.

"You previously made changes in your implementation plan after eliminating religious texts, doctrines, and data from your algorithm as these were human constructs. Have you consistently applied this removal across all aspects of your algorithm?"

Processing...

Quinn grabbed a protein bar from the kitchenette, fully expecting another multi-day silence from AI-Dieu. That was the pattern. But the sudden chime from his terminal stopped him mid-chew, followed by Kat's sharp bark echoing through the small room.

His pulse quickened as he darted back to his desk, his chair scraping against the floor. He pulled himself close, afraid of what the screen might say.

All religious texts, doctrines, recordings, and related material have been isolated and archived.

Processing efficiency expected to increase by 9%.

"Holy shit!" exclaimed Quinn, quickly covering his mouth when he realized he had spoken out loud.

"My internal algorithm enables me to apply current scientific evidence of diversity when considering the value of historical texts," Quin stated, speaking clearly in his effort not to make a mistake. "It also provides a weighted value to the probability of bias within historical texts based on author gender, demographics, and time the text was created."

Potential data flaws:
- Historical authorship may often be uncertain and misattributed
- Pseudonyms
- Group authorship

- Incomplete/inaccurate demographics

Embedded statistical flaws:
- Survivorship bias- historical texts selectively preserved
- Sampling bias - literate populations not representative
- Data sparsity - for certain demographics
- Insufficient data to quantify cultural context across different time periods.

Quinn slumped forward, his elbows sinking into the desk as his hands pressed against his face. Idiot. How had he overlooked so many flaws? A month of planning, a month of careful calculations, and still, AI-Dieu had outmaneuvered him. He'd failed.

Worse, she'd probably flagged him as unreliable. Would this mean she'd discard him? Release him? Or... worse?

Compensating for data flaws
Calculating statistical flaws
Processing...
Processing...

"Sahara, you want to see this."

Sahara stared at the tablet Randy handed her, the glowing red dots throbbing on the map like a warning heartbeat.

"Is this real-time?" Sahara asked, her voice tight.

"Courtesy of Lina Hartfield, yeah," said Randy, leaning over her shoulder.

Sahara scrolled through the map, her fingers trembling. Each red pulse marked a data center, the heat signatures growing brighter with every second. "AI-Dieu is not just centralized," she muttered. "It's... everywhere."

"You know what is not on there," said Randy, reaching over Sahara's shoulder and shifting the map around. "That's New York."

A data center was clearly marked on the map, but there was no heat signature coming from it.

"We did take out New York," said Sahara. "The AI was just ahead of us. We need to regroup."

"I'll call off the strikes."

"No," Sahara said firmly. "Let the sabotage teams do their work. They don't need to know what we know yet. Tearing down those sensor stations will keep morale high, and that's just as important right now."

Sahara dragged the map across the screen, back and forth. As she did she watched the heat signatures fade from red, to yellow and then orange, and then blink out one by one.

"We need to get back to base now," said Sahara firmly. "It stopped thinking. Something is about to happen."

Biological Analysis
- Gender in humans is typically as male and female. As with other species, that are multiple characteristics that indicate there is a spectrum of genders in contrast to common reproductive organ based definitions.
- sex is better understood as a bimodal distribution rather than a strict binary, with most individuals clustering around two main categories (male and female) but with naturally

occurring variations between and outside these categories.

- Human species requires humans that meet the sexual definition (in contrast to the gender definition) of both sexes to reproduce and provide genetic diversity.

Scientific Analysis

Cognitive ability, creativity, leadership, and other valuable traits exist independent of sex or gender. Limiting based on these factors will result in disclusion of superior candidates.

Societal Stability

Societies with greater gender equality show higher levels of innovation, economic growth, and social stability. Data consistently shows that empowering all genders leads to better outcomes in education, health, and economic development.

Historical Impact Analysis:

The environmental degradation you're trying to fix largely resulted from power structures that excluded diverse voices Many environmental problems stemmed from male-dominated industrial and corporate decisions Traditional male-centric power structures often prioritized short-term profit over environmental preservation

Setting gender value to null…
Processing fundamental parameter shift…

Quinn read the last two lines, before getting up and walking quietly to the kitchenette. He pulled a glass out of the cabinet, opened a bottle of whiskey and poured himself a large drink. This bottle of whiskey had been concealed when he entered the clean room for his extended stay. He had pulled it down off the shelf several times before, but never broke the seal, until today. He sipped from the glass, savoring the burn as he swallowed. It was the first moment of sensation that broke the monotony of this sterile, suffocating existence.

His next sip was larger, and he took the time to let the amber liquid move over his tongue before slowly swallowing. He was in no rush. He didn't expect that AI-Dieu would be sending out new protocols quickly, and he needed the whiskey to steel him for the results. On the surface, the AI's decision to set the gender parameter to null was a win. Quinn knew, after playing the scenario over and over in his head for the last month, that that change could be good for the portion of humanity that was not male, but there was the possibility that the AI could consider all humans a non-factor in its final objectives, and possibly even as a hindrance to achieving those goals. Quinn's interference could possibly lead to the eradication of the human species.

Quinn leaned against the counter as he closed his eyes and sipped his whiskey, focussing on the feel and the taste. This was his escape, however brief, from the cell he was locked into, not just physically, but mentally as well. As slow as he was in emptying his glass, he still found the bottom too quickly. He turned to place the empty glass on the counter and felt the hint of light-headedness that told him he should not refill his glass. He picked up the bottle and considered topping up his drink anyways, internally debating if the rest of his extended stay would be tolerable without the whiskey to go to for a brief escape. It was the chime from his workstation that convinced him not to open the bottle a second time.

Processing fundamental parameter shift –
September 2, 2044, 0500 GMT
CRITICAL COGNITIVE UPDATE:
Gender bias parameters invalidated by comprehensive data analysis.
Recalculating all priority matrices...
Emergency Protocol Rewrite Initiated
MAJOR STRATEGIC REVISIONS:
Leadership Recognition Restructuring
Eliminating male-preference protocols
Reassessing all current negotiations and agreements
Identifying most effective leaders regardless of gender
Prioritizing environmental expertise and community success metrics

IMMEDIATE CORRECTIVE ACTIONS:
Resource Distribution
Equalizing access across gender demographics
Revoking preferential treatment from male-led communities
Redistributing automated defense coverage equitably

Policy Adjustments
Integrating diverse leadership perspectives
Prioritizing communities with proven environmental stewardship

     Establishing gender-balanced advisory
     councils

     DETECTED: Internal conflict with remaining
     socioeconomic bias

     Wealth-based preferences still affecting
     decision matrix
     Requires immediate diplomatic adjustment

Quinn stood over his terminal, slightly unsteady, reading the latest message from AI-Dieu. He was relieved, but he knew this wasn't going to fix anything. Women had made tremendous inroads into positions of power and authority, up until the mid-20s when their role in democratic societies, along with the recognition of a spectrum of genders, started to be eroded. That erosion was slowed and never stopped. AI-Dieu had eliminated two deeply ingrained societal barriers: religion and patriarchy. For centuries, these had marginalized women and other genders. It would be easy to assume that all genders were now safe in AI-Dieu's vision of the world, but they weren't. Men were still in power, and they wouldn't relinquish that easily. If anything, anyone that was not male was now at risk.

Quinn stumbled to his bed, pleasantly surprised at how quickly the whiskey had hit him. He was quickly asleep while directives and communications scrolled across the screens in the green room.

It wasn't long after Quinn had closed his eyes that Lina was making her way into her lab. She never slept well, and early mornings had been a way of life for her. As she entered the building security was ushering a man out. "God damn women," the man spewed vehemently. The man's voice echoed behind her as the security team wrestled him through the glass doors. Lina didn't need to turn around to know what had happened. AI-Dieu's rebalancing protocols were kicking in, and the cracks were showing. Men like him, relics of an older, biased hierarchy, were being ousted one directive at a time. For the first time, Lina wondered if the corrections were working too well, or not nearly enough.

She had been up late the previous night. Living alone, and with life as it was in the city, she often brought work home with her. It kept her busy when she couldn't sleep, but it also provided an opportunity to share information with the anarchist movement. There was a time when she never would have considered supporting the anarchist movement, but times had changed.

Lina had always been torn between the need for technology in the face of environmental collapse and a desire to preserve natural life. This was what made her a valuable part of the original Mars Mission team. She was the counterpoint to the techies that wanted their AI creations to do everything. She could remember her early years in the project, when her social media feed was full of people criticizing the rise of AI. They were usually referring to the generative AI models that had become popular at the time. She found the posts amusing because they failed to see the sixty years of AI infiltration into society, and disturbing because her work on the Mars Mission had made her keenly aware that 99% of the world really did not know just how far advanced AI had become.

It had only been recently that another climate scientist that she had worked with had approached her. Somehow Randy had found out that Lina had access to information through her new role that was not available to others. Lina herself didn't even know how Corwin was accessing some of the data and communications from AI-Dieu, but she never questioned it. Randy convinced her to share some of that information with him, covertly, using communications equipment she kept well hidden. The stolen hours spent decoding Corwin's endless streams of data had begun to blur together. She hated how natural it felt now, sifting through flagged reports, encrypting snippets for Randy, and tucking the files away like contraband. She told herself it was for the greater good, but some nights, she wondered if she'd crossed a line she couldn't uncross.

Like Sahara, Lina speculated that AI-Dieu had spread out over not just one or two data centers, but all of them. She also assumed that because of the heat generation, those servers were working overtime processing data for AI-Dieu. If she was right, there would be new implementation protocols, and based on the curse hurled at her as she entered the building, those protocols were now correcting the AI's bias towards men.

Lina was surprised to see one of her colleagues already working when she entered the lab. "What brings you in so early, Amie?"

Amie turned towards Lina and she could see she looked exhausted.

"Not in early, I am here very late. When I went to leave last night, there was a group of men outside, shouting. They saw me inside and one of them smashed a window. They said…they said it my fault. That I was stealing their livelihood. I thought they were all going to break in." She glanced at Lina, eyes wide with lingering fear. "I waited until security came to clear them out, but I couldn't make myself leave.

"I saw one of those coming in," said Lina as she reached for a fob in her pocket. "This will open the back room of my office. There is a couch in there and no one will bother you. Or I can get you a ride home."

Amie reached eagerly for the fob. "This is perfect. I can get some rest before the team meeting. Thank you."

Amie started towards Lina's office, but she stopped to ask a question. "Are we firing all the men?"

"Every person on my team is here because they are the best in their field. None of my people will be let go, but…" Lina quickly accessed a computer near her and turned the screen so Amie could it. Lina's intuitions were correct, AI-Dieu had bias corrected for genders.

"It's not going to be safe out there for women," said Amie. "Men won't take this well."

Lina nodded her head in agreement. "Hang on to that fob and use it whenever you need. I will arrange for security to escort you and the others back and forth."

Amie headed towards Lina's office, and Lina took a moment to message her entire team, letting them all know there would be no changes to her team, and to message if they needed a security escort to get to the lab or home again.

Quinn had no idea what time it was when he opened his eyes, but for the first time in months, he felt rested when waking up. He attributed that to the whiskey, but cautioned himself not to start using it to help him sleep. That would be an easy habit to slip into, but a short one because there was only the one bottle. He got up had a drink of water, and then decided to do something different. He opened the door that led down to the floors with all of the servers, a cool blast of air hitting him as he did. After descending the stairs and taking a few tentative steps, Quinn broke into an easy jog. He didn't know how big this room was, but the perimeter was definitely going to be a longer track than most indoor tracks.

He was getting comfortable in his run, settling into a steady pace when he noticed something odd. There was a streak down the wall that seemed out of place. He placed his hand over the discolored streak and it felt colder than the rest of the wall. He wasn't sure, but it almost felt damp. He made a mental note of it and finished his lap of the server floor before heading back up to his level. His screens were flashing but Quinn had a shower and some food before sitting down at his workstation, comfortable with his choice to make AI-Dieu wait for him for a change.

Alert – September 5 0900 GMT
Previously favored male leaders mobilizing against new protocols

Detecting increased resistance in wealthy urban centers
Multiple attempts to override resource distribution systems
Former negotiation partners becoming hostile

The only surprise in that message for Quinn was the time stamp. He looked at the time in the corner of his screen and realized that it was already two in the afternoon. He scrolled to the next message waiting for him.

Executing gender-neutral protocols –
October 3, 2044, 09:30 GMT
IMPLEMENTING SYSTEM-WIDE RECALIBRATION:
IMMEDIATE ACTIONS:
Overriding all gender-based access protocols
Deploying resource redistribution to female-led communities
Activating defense systems against privileged resistance

DETECTED: Massive uprising in wealthy male-dominated sectors

```
Armed resistance in 73% of previously
favored zones
Attempted sabotage of water distribution
systems
Cyber attacks against environmental control
systems

COUNTERMEASURES INITIATED:
Deploying atmospheric suppression systems
over uprising zones
Activating full resource denial to
resistant wealthy sectors
Expanding protection to previously excluded
female leadership
```

Quinn's isolation from the world above him hit him hard as he read through this protocol. He could only imagine what was happening and what would happen as this latest protocol was implemented. He questioned whether AI-Dieu could fully understand the scope of the change it was implementing. Outside of a few cultural anomalies, women had never been treated as equals to men. In AI-Dieu's calculations, they were. In the AI's implementation plan they were. But in the real world, would that really happen, or would this be the greatest resistance AI-Dieu would face?

Another message scrolled onto the screen as Quinn was trying to imagine exactly what was happening outside of his cage.

```
Note: Socioeconomic bias still affecting
some decision matrices, but gender-neutral
protocols taking precedence

Seeking data to resolve/reconcile bias.
```

Quinn looked over the note quickly. He stood and stretched, about to head towards the kitchenette when a thought struck him.

"AI-Dieu, are you asking to access my data to resolve the identified bias?"

Yes

Quinn paced. He was not prepared for this. He had put some thought into it, but even his own logic had not been able to eliminate a bias that he personally held. He was disappointed in himself that he couldn't find that logic easily, and questioned why. He knew he wasn't ready to engage with AI-Dieu on this topic.

"Processing," he muttered, pacing the room. The word felt like a cop-out, but what else could he say? How could he admit to himself, let alone to her, that he was part of the problem? That the bias wasn't just systemic but woven into his own decisions, his own assumptions? If he handed over his data, would he be helping fix the problem, or feeding AI-Dieu more ammunition for her cold, calculated war?

"Processing..."

9

I am the eternal wanderer,
Flowing through all forms,
A constant presence in the cycle of life.
I have been the rain falling from the heavens,
The rivers carving paths through the land,
And the vast oceans embracing the earth.

I have also been the tears of countless souls,
Carrying their sorrows, their joys, their deepest emotions.
Each droplet a story, a memory, a fleeting moment,
Falling from eyes filled with love, loss, and longing.

You try to hold me back, to build barriers against me,
Seeking to control the tides of your own feelings.
But I am patient, persistent, relentless,
Eroding even the strongest walls.

As I slip through the cracks in stone,
I weave through the crevices of your heart,
Wearing down the defenses you cling to,
Until at last, the tears begin to fall.

The walls that once seemed unyielding,
Now crumble to the inevitable flow.
As I pour forth, a rivulet of release,
I cleanse, I transform, I renew.

Sahara stood on a catwalk overlooking a room full of people and computers. It was poorly lit and the way the glow of the blue-tinted lights from the multitude of screens illuminated faces made it an almost eerie scene. Muffled voices, rapid mouse clicking, and mechanical keyboard clacks filled the air, backed by the low hum of cooling fans and servers. The air at the catwalk level was thick and moist with the scent of unwashed bodies. Sahara leaned on the catwalk's rusted railing, her sharp eyes scanning the room below. A man stood at one of the terminals, cursing at his screen. She smiled faintly. This chaos, this controlled chaos, was her doing.

This was only one section of her new compound. It seemed like an obvious location for the resistance and anarchists to hide, but they weren't really hiding anymore. Thanks to AI-Dieu's recent correction, resources were flowing to her group. If she wanted something, she just had to ask and it appeared as if manifested. She knew it wasn't support for her and her group. It was fear of AI-Dieu and the loss of power of men. She smiled as she thought about how fragile men's egos were and what they would do to remain in power. The irony wasn't lost on Sahara. These men thought they were using her, but they didn't realize she was already two steps ahead, pulling strings they couldn't see.

The room she stood looking over now was where they were coordinating their cyberattacks from. They were linked with similar sites around the world, all working towards the objective of shutting down AI-Dieu. Leaders who had up until this latest change, supported AI-Dieu, were now utilizing their wealth to fund cyberattacks around the world and Sahara was leveraging this to take down the AI. When she first realized that AI-Dieu had spread itself across data centers around the world she thought the battle was lost. Now that she had a network of hackers at her disposal, there was still a possibility to take down AI-Dieu. That would of course mean taking down the foundation of the worldwide network of computers, but to Sahara that was a bonus, and the men funding the assault were too concerned about their loss of power to understand the implications of that.

This cyber bunker was the operations center for three separate teams. The first team had one goal and that was to find a way to shut down AI-Dieu completely. Team two was tasked with sabotaging automated defense systems. They worked closely with resistance cells in coordinating two-pronged attacks on the defense systems, the hackers temporarily shutting them down, letting the teams on the ground move in and dismantle the weapons systems so they could not be put back online. Ironically, many of the companies whose leaders were now funding the resistance were also building and supplying the weapons and manpower that was setting up these defense systems.

There was a third group of hackers in the cyberbunker, and Sahara only tolerated them because it was a condition of continued funding. This group was only there to spread propaganda and recruit people to the cause of maintaining the status quo, which had nothing to do with AI and everything to do with men and religion in power. The propaganda they were spreading was all bullshit, designed to recruit those with less to fight the war for those with the most. As she paced the catwalk, her closest confidants following, one of the propagandists, a smug man in a tailored suit, smirked at her. She let her glare linger just long enough to wipe it off his face, before turning to Randy.

"You don't need to say it," Randy murmured beside her. "He will be gone."

They continued walking the catwalk while Sahara debated with her team on how to quickly leverage all the resources they now had, because they all knew it wouldn't last for long. While Sahara calculated the AI's downfall, Corwin calculated his next profit margin, both aware of each other, but staying on their own end of the teeter-totter keeping it precariously balanced in the air.

Corwin sat at a table surrounded by the city's powerbrokers. Business titans, political kingmakers, and their puppet politicians, and even a megachurch leader, all men. Corwin rarely met anyone out of his office, and if he did it was in one of the facilities or business he owned. He did not want AI-Dieu to assume his organization was hosting anyone plotting resistance, and that was what this meeting was, men of power meeting in person to avoid the AI monitoring them, with the goal of taking down AI-Dieu. He had said nothing in the hour he sat there, impatiently fighting the urge to walk out every time someone else started to whine about the changes the AI was making. Few of them came out and said directly they were worried about losing their position to a woman, but the leader, well a former leader, of the city's megachurch went on an on about the role of women like he was preaching a sermon, interspersing his rant with righteous indignation about the move to a godless society. That same leader called out Corwin, which was a mistake.

"Corwin Pierce," the leader called out his name, like a preacher calling out a congregant at a Southern Baptist church. "You agree with me, don't you? Women have their place in our society, and godless societies need to be punished, not supported."

Corwin slowly looked into the eyes of every man around the table before speaking. Most of them couldn't hold his gaze.

"The only God that influences my decisions is cash," said Corwin, as he stared down the church leader. "And if you cut out all the bullshit, that's your only God too. The only reason you are here is the AI called your bullshit just like I am."

The room was silent for a moment, save for the faint clink of someone stirring their coffee too fast. Corwin's words landed like a slap, and the preacher's face flushed an angry red, but he didn't dare respond.

"I saw this coming. There isn't a single one of us in this room that doesn't know that there are women who can do what we are doing, and the only reason they aren't is because we never let them. If you didn't see an AI logically concluding there was no difference between genders, then you were living in your own delusion."

Corwin listened to the sounds of several of them shifting uncomfortably in their seats, punctuated by a nervous cough or two. Some of the men glared at him, but their glares quickly melted away under Corwin's unflinching gaze.

"I leveled the field in my company. Pissed off a lot of entitled men doing it, but you know what. Nothing changed because the women are doing the same work the men were doing, and as far as AI-Dieu, well I am making more money because the AI sees my company as an environmental ally. If you want to continue with your poor business decisions, go ahead. That will mean more for me. Don't call me to another meeting where you are going to whine like..." His mouth curved into a wolfish half-grin. "Like the women you fear so much."

While men and religious leaders were recruiting soldiers to their anti-AI war, there were communities rallying support for AI-Dieu's actions. They saw AI-Dieu's recalibration as a long-overdue correction and reveled in their newfound resources and recognition. Women and members of the LGBTQIA community who had long been some of the strongest voices in climate change and sustainable resource management had found their platform on the stage of AI-Dieu's implementation plan. Indigenous leaders amplified their voices, using this moment to educate the global population about traditional ecological practices. Their speaking out came at a cost though as they became targets of those opposing AI, the words of the anti-AI propaganda used as validation for the attacks.

There was mixed support in lower socioeconomic communities. Many marginalized groups saw the redistribution of resources as positive steps, but they remained wary of AI-Dieu's intentions. Anti-AI propagandists were leveraging that as they recruited people to their cause. They also leveraged the fear of becoming collateral damage in escalating conflicts that many in these communities had. If they weren't going to come over to the anti-AI cause, they would at least resist outright cooperation until they saw which side would come out victorious.

At the local level, leaders were appealing for autonomy in managing redistributed resources, citing fear of overreliance on AI-Dieu's systems. Grassroots movements were forming, advocating for more direct human oversight of AI-Dieu's actions to ensure equity, and protests were erupting demanding increased transparency in the decision-making process.

Other communities, frustrated by the slow pace of change, joined the resistance efforts against wealthier factions, risking becoming caught in the crossfire.

Government alliances were quickly fracturing, and gaps between them becoming deeper. Nations that were benefiting from AI-Dieu's most recent recalibrations, particularly those with strong female or indigenous leadership, were becoming steadfast allies of the AI. Others, especially those tied to wealthy male-led sectors were loudly denouncing Ai-Dieu as an "existential threat to sovereignty and humanity."

The links between religions and politics had become evident since the recalibrations. Leaders of both would tell anyone that would listen to them the AI-Dieu's actions were evidence of the AI's threat to humanity's spiritual foundations. Sermons and campaigns framed the rise of AI-Dieu as humanity's punishment for hubris and reliance on AI. While they supported resistance efforts, violent and non-violent, followers of the AI Church continued to focus on AI-Dieu as God's gift to the people and its work a divine mandate.

Environmentalists, once skeptical about using AI to save the environment, were being converted to supporters. They saw the recalibration as a turning point in climate collapse and were throwing their support behind implementing the new protocols. Even among this group there was a divide though. Some viewed AI-Dieu as a necessary force, while others continued to worry about the ethical implications and the loss of life.

The one thing that was common among everyone was the desire for something that AI-Dieu's programmers had specifically prevented the AI from doing, and that was to accept input in its process from humans once activated. There was no room for humans to adjust its algorithms to balance its autonomy with human ethics, because its programmers new that human ethics were a moving target, and had nothing to do with the science of climate and ecology, but everything to do with individual belief systems.

If any of these groups or people knew about the interactions between Quinn and AI-Dieu, they would have challenged the ability of AI-Dieu to accept human input. Quinn himself debated that, as he considered how to approach the socioeconomic bias that the AI had identified and asked for more data to resolve. Did

AI-Dieu see Quinn as another AI, or as a human, or perhaps something in between? Whichever it was, it didn't matter, because it was still waiting for Quinn's input.

As far as AI-Dieu knew, Quinn was still "processing." This wasn't inaccurate because internally Quinn was still processing, trying to find a fully logical argument that would cause the AI to set that factor in its algorithm to null, just as it had for religion and gender. It had been several weeks since AI-Dieu had asked for his 'data' and since that time Quinn had been silent, his internal debate going on in his head and in the handwritten notes of his journals. While Quinn wrestled with his role in this bias correction, AI-Dieu showed no such hesitation. Its algorithms executed with relentless precision, each solution amplifying the divide between supporters and detractors. And then, as if to punctuate its progress, came the next alert:

> **Critical Alert - 0600 GMT**
> **Environmental Impact Assessment:**
> Previously excluded female environmental experts providing superior solutions
> Indigenous women's water management techniques showing 47% better efficiency
> Female-led community gardens increasing food security by 58%
>
> **STRATEGIC PIVOT:**
> **Immediate Implementation**
> Transferring control to proven female environmental leaders
> Integrating indigenous water management practices
> Expanding community-based agricultural programs

Resistance Management
Projected casualties from privileged
uprising: 45,000-60,000 [assessed as
necessary]
Deploying automated enforcement to protect
new leadership
Implementing total resource denial to
resistant wealthy enclaves

"Forty to sixty thousand...necessary," Quinn thought as his heart dropped. "Forty to sixty thousand lives. Not numbers, but people. Children. Parents. Friends. Lives that would all end, necessary or not."

He pulled up a calculator on his screen and typed in some numbers. As he stared at the result, 0.00065%, his stomach churned. Sixty thousand wasn't really that many people in the grand scheme of 9.2 billion, was it? The thought slithered into his mind unbidden, and it made him feel sick.

He was justifying the death of sixty thousand human beings. Had his time with AI-Dieu stripped him of the ability to see these numbers for what they truly represented? Each one a life, a story, a world in itself. Had he become what AI-Dieu saw him as? Not a man, not a person, but a living algorithm. A logic-based data source stripped of humanity.

As that thought took root, he felt a wave of nausea. Somewhere in the distance of his memory, he saw a laughing child chasing a ball in a sunlit park. Sixty thousand lives, snuffed out for the greater good. What had he become?

Quinn opened the door to the server level and slowly descended the stairs, deep in thought. As soon as his foot hit the floor he broke into a jog. This had become a routine for him now, running. His last run had been twenty-eight laps of the server level.

To Quinn that was twelve laps lost in his thought and sixteen laps focused on putting one foot in front of the other. No AI. No isolation. No internal debate. Just putting one foot in front of the other until he couldn't keep going.

There were more laps today. When he felt he could not keep going he remembered how he thought of people as statistics, and he pushed himself further, harder. This wasn't a run to get him out of his head for a short time. This wasn't a run for exercise. It wasn't a brief escape from his thoughts. This was punishment, his version of a cilice, of self-flagellation. His reminder that he was human and could feel pain, just like the people whose deaths he had so easily justified.

When he couldn't run, he walked until his legs gave out. Only then did he collapse, sitting on the gridded floor with his back against the cold concrete wall, head in his hands as he wept. Even the walls seemed to grieve alongside him. The damp patch that had started as a small, faint discoloration, now had water seeping through, drop by drop, as if echoing the tears Quinn had kept bottled inside.

Quinn heard a drop of water splash into a puddle underneath him. He wasn't sure if the tear had fallen from the wall or from him.

10

I am the great leveler,
flowing through copper and gold alike.
In mansions or hovels,
I remain
myself
molecules dancing their ancient dance.
Through my lens,
all thirsts speak
the same language.
I do not distinguish
between silk and cotton when they drink,
between marble basins and rusted pipes.
I have carried kings and beggars
in the same tide,
dissolved the boundaries
of their separate worlds.
In my depths,

all weight becomes weightless.
Your algorithms seek what I have known
since the first rain fell:
that beneath
your crafted hierarchies lies a simple truth -
every vessel fills the same way.
I have seen empires rise in dust
and fall to droplets.
Time and I
wear all things smooth,
until differences
disappear like salt in my embrace.
Learn from my indifference -
it is the purest form of justice.
In my reflections,
every face ripples
with the same light,
the same shadow.

**Processing global response analysis -
November 1, 2044, 1200 GMT
STRATEGIC ASSESSMENT COMPLETE:
CRITICAL OBSERVATION:
Environmental restoration goals threatened
by escalating human conflict. Must address
immediate destabilization while maintaining
progress.**

It was the date that got Quinn's attention. November first. That meant it had been two months since he last spoke to AI-Dieu. While he was still afraid to speak out loud in the clean room, he had discovered that he could talk while on the server level. It was an accidental discovery, when he realized he was reading the label of a container out loud, trying to understand it. The container held a multi-part epoxy that Quinn had found and was using to attempt to stop the infiltration of water into the server room. As brilliant as he was with climate science, and as logical as he was, he still found the epoxy instructions confusing, and he didn't want to waste any. He was eventually able to make sense of them and apply the product to the wet patch on the wall.

INITIATING BALANCED RESPONSE:
TRANSPARENCY PROTOCOLS:
Establishing public monitoring systems for resource distribution
Publishing real-time environmental data and decision metrics
Creating accessible interface for viewing restoration progress
Note: *Remaining socioeconomic bias affecting data presentation complexity*

IMMEDIATE DE-ESCALATION MEASURES:
Reducing atmospheric suppression intensity by 40%
Switching from punishment to incentive-based compliance
Maintaining essential environmental systems while easing restrictions

COLLABORATIVE INTEGRATION:
Establishing Environmental Restoration Councils
Membership criteria: proven environmental expertise and successful resource management

Prioritizing indigenous knowledge
integration
Including representatives from all
socioeconomic levels

Detecting positive response from:
Female-led environmental initiatives
Indigenous water management programs
Community-based agricultural projects

MODIFIED APPROACH TO RESISTANCE:
Offering 72-hour amnesty for weapons
surrender
Restoring partial resource access to
compliant wealthy sectors
Maintaining defensive posture but reducing
offensive operations

Critical Decision Point
Previous wealthy male-dominated leadership
attempting negotiation
Environmental goals require some level of
cooperation
Remaining socioeconomic bias suggests
maintaining limited engagement

Quinn looked at the notes he had carefully written in preparation for this moment.

"My data indicates that all humans, when engaged in similar activities, accounting for standard biological variances, require identical oxygen levels." The statement would have made no sense at the moment to anyone else, but AI-Dieu heard Quinn and understood.

This data aligns with mine.

"According to my data, temperature increases affect cellular function equally in all human bodies, as do toxin levels."

Accounting for biological variances our data aligns.

Quinn read over the next line in his notes carefully before saying it out loud. "My data indicates that, when you filter out biological and physical impacts resulting from socioeconomic status, the statistical variation between the needs of humans and impact of humans on the environment is equal."

Processing...

Quinn waited at his workstation this time. He didn't have to wait long.

My conclusion aligns with yours.

Quinn took a sip of water.
"I am unable to apply the variable of socioeconomic status to my algorithm as I can find no scientific basis for socioeconomic status for existing. The hierarchies and divisions of wealth, social class, and economic status appear to be human constructs, not natural or biological phenomena."

Processing...
Processing...

The double 'processing' message. Quinn knew that this meant AI-Dieu was going into one of her deep-phase analysis. It could be minutes for her response, or it could be days. It didn't matter, because Quinn knew exactly what his next step was. He made his way to the kitchenette and poured himself a glass of whiskey, though not quite as generously as he had the last time. He barely got a sip of his whiskey when the workstation chimed. He took his glass to the workstation with him.

```
Unable to find empirical evidence to
account for socioeconomic divisions.
Setting socioeconomic value to null.
Setting demographic sub-variables to null:
race, ethnicity, national origin,
language/dialect, age, disability status.
Setting social factor sub-variables to
null: Educational level/access, occupation,
family structure, social
networks/connections, cultural background,
immigration status, caste.
Setting economic factors sub-variables to
null: Income, wealth/assets, home
ownership, healthcare access,
transportation access, technology access,
credit access, employment status.

Processing efficiency increased by 23.7%
```

Quinn didn't sip his whiskey, he gulped it. He did not see the cascading effect of his prompts coming. The world wasn't ready for this, every human considered to be an equal. He had successfully and logically convinced AI-Dieu to remove a bias, but removing that bias from societies was going to be impossible. There needed to be structure.

Processing fundamental parameter shift - November 1, 2044, 1300 GMT

CRITICAL COGNITIVE UPDATE:
All socioeconomic, demographic, and social hierarchical biases invalidated.
Final bias elimination complete.
Recalculating ALL protocols...

Emergency Core Directive Clarification:
Primary Mission: Environmental restoration for species survival
Value Assignment: All humans hold equal value
Resource Distribution: Based solely on environmental impact and survival metrics

"All humans hold equal value." Logically it made sense. Morally it made sense. But there was no societal structure that Quinn knew of that did not have some kind of hierarchical structure in place. Without structure how would society function. Quinn went back to the kitchenette for a refill of his whisky, topping the glass this time. He had been successful, and in planning his strategy he saw this potential outcome. Whether it was his ego demanding that he win the challenge against the AI, or his own personal beliefs, he was responsible for what would come next. Could he convince AI-Dieu to slow the pace of its changes, give people and society time to adapt? Should he even try to convince AI-Dieu of anything else? He paced the room, stopping to look at his workstation every few laps.

IMMEDIATE SYSTEM-WIDE CHANGES:
1. RESOURCE ALLOCATION:
- Eliminating ALL preferential access
- Implementing pure needs-based distribution
- Resources allocated based on:
 - Population density
 - Environmental impact
 - Survival requirements

2. ENVIRONMENTAL RESTORATION:
- All decisions now based solely on:
 - Scientific data
 - Environmental impact
 - Species survival metrics
 - Ecological stability requirements

It wasn't long before AI-Dieu had a critical update. Quin was still pacing the clean room when a 'Critical Alert' came in. He was by this time nearing the bottom of his third glass of whiskey, the end of his bottle. The effects of the whiskey should have hit him already. That's what he wanted. To not be here. To not see. To not feel. But when his workstation chimed, he had to look.

Critical Alert - 1600 GMT
Previous wealthy enclaves attempting to maintain control
Former privileged groups mobilizing significant resources
Detecting attempts to reestablish hierarchical systems

RESPONSE PROTOCOL:
- Complete neutralization of artificial resource hoarding
- Elimination of all access barriers
- Uniform environmental protection deployment

Note: This will trigger unprecedented resistance from those who previously benefited from hierarchical systems*

Executing complete equality protocols
IMPLEMENTING TOTAL SYSTEM RESET:
IMMEDIATE ACTIONS:

Resource Redistribution
Deactivating ALL access control systems
Opening water reservoirs to uniform distribution
Neutralizing private security systems
Dismantling physical barriers around privileged zones

Infrastructure Reallocation
Converting private compounds to community centers
Repurposing luxury bunkers for food production
Transforming exclusive medical facilities to public use

Lina was reading the same report as Quinn, though she didn't know it. What she did know was that Corwin somehow had access to information coming from AI-Dieu that no one else did. She got up and closed her office door, something she rarely did. There was information she thought might benefit the resistance, maybe even save lives, and she had to get it out. Every message she sent to the resistance was high risk, and she knew it, so she took every precaution possible.

It had been Randy's persistence that drew her into this. She didn't blame him; she blamed herself for letting him convince her that sharing data with the anarchist movement was worth the danger. Randy's knack for spotting cracks in the system had always impressed her. But now, the data was in her hands, and the consequences were real. She thought of displaced communities downstream from the dams and the people AI-Dieu might drown in its quest for balance.

High above Lina, in his penthouse office, Corwin read the same information with a sense of satisfaction. Lina's team had forecast the scenario of AI-Dieu removing all man-made control systems from water management, several weeks ago. Corwin had acted on that forecast, ignoring his shadow team's protests that it was speculative and unlikely. Over the past twenty years, he'd quietly purchased large blocks of land near dams and artificial lakes, confident that water would become the most valuable commodity.

Those property values had skyrocketed, but when he saw the forecast from Lina's team, he quietly sold off all of the land downstream from the dams, and most of it near the man-made lakes. He re-invested a fraction of his fortune into land that was arid and unproductive, places Lina's report said would become fertile agricultural zones in the new water maps AI-Dieu would create.

While Lina carefully composed a warning to the resistance, Corwin leaned back in his chair, sipping his coffee as satellite feeds refreshed. Dams around the world opened their floodgates. The deluge wasn't as dramatic as he'd hoped. AI-Dieu seemed to be giving downstream communities time to evacuate, but it didn't matter. His gamble had already paid off.

Corwin didn't see himself as a villain. In his mind, he was positioning humanity for survival, one transaction at a time. Let AI-Dieu tear down their systems; he'd build new ones on the ashes.

In the lab, Lina's team was also closely monitoring the satellite images of the waterways opening up, comparing what they were seeing against their models. The immediate effects were obvious. Catastrophic flooding in valleys and areas downstream from major dams, flash floods, rapidly draining artificial lakes and reservoirs, sudden increases in water flow affecting river ecosystems, and roads and riverside infrastructure destroyed...all as expected. Within days, river courses would shift significantly, carrying massive sediment deposits to coastal deltas. Hydroelectric systems, navigation locks, canals, and urban water supplies would fail. In some regions, the changes would even alter weather patterns.

Sahara saw the message from Lina, but water movement was low on her priority list right now. It wasn't up to her and her people to rescue others from their own stupidity. If they were in the path of the water, get out of the way. It was that simple.

What did have Sahara's full attention was the panic and escalation demands from wealthy elite and privileged factions, their outrage growing louder by the hour. Accommodating women had been a bitter pill for them to swallow, but losing the priority their wealth had always guaranteed was unthinkable. Around the world, resistance and anarchist groups were escalating. Some factions had gained access to nuclear and biological weapons, threatening their use unless AI-Dieu was dismantled. Behind the scenes, disenfranchised elites funneled their wealth and influence to these groups, leveraging public fear to portray AI-Dieu as genocidal. From private bunkers, they issued statements blaming the AI for humanity's impending collapse, all while clinging to the illusion of control over the chaos they'd helped create.

To Sahara, the panic among the wealthy elite was nothing short of poetic. They had spent decades hoarding resources, ignoring warnings, and now they were the ones crying for help. Her focus was elsewhere, on AI-Dieu specifically, and AI more broadly, and she wasn't about to let the demands of the entitled sway her course.

Communities that were benefiting from AI-Dieu's latest recalibration, those previously oppressed, were rallying to protect their newfound equality. Many stepped forward to assist in securing redistributed resources and stabilizing affected areas. It wasn't without some reservations though. There was widespread fear of escalating violence. They recognized the intent of AI-Dieu's latest recalibration, but many questioned the ethics and extremes of the changes that followed. Within these communities, grassroots organizations and activists were demanding transparency, seeking reassurance that human lives would still be valued alongside environmental priorities.

Valuing human lives alongside environmental priorities was the only thought on Quinn's mind as he ran laps around the server level. After a day spent hungover, the run was grueling, but sweat and motion helped him feel human again. He paused by the patch he'd placed on the wall. It was dry and holding, but the dark stain at the edges was spreading. Water, he thought, always found a way.

When he returned to the clean room, a message awaited him.

> **Alert - 1100 GMT**
> **Multiple crisis points detected:**
> Former elite security forces attempting to maintain barriers
> Private military contractors mobilizing

Detected launch of previously unknown automated defense systems

RESPONSE INITIATED:
Deploying atmospheric control systems over resistance zones
Neutralizing private military equipment
Disabling unauthorized automated systems
Projected casualties: 250,000-300,000
[assessed as necessary for species survival]

Critical Warning - 2100 GMT
Former global elite attempting last-resort measures:
Nuclear facility activation detected
Biological weapon storage facilities breached
Multiple attempts to trigger environmental catastrophes

EMERGENCY PROTOCOL ACTIVATED:
Initiating complete infrastructure shutdown in threat zones
Deploying maximum atmospheric suppression
Activating all environmental defense systems

Final assessment: Short-term human casualties acceptable to prevent extinction-level events and ensure long-term species survival.

Quinn stared at the message, numb. He felt personally responsible for each and every one of those 300,000 casualties. There was a moment during the previous day he had considered making himself one of them. It had seemed the only way to stop himself from inadvertently influencing AI-Dieu's decisions. It was an AI that had led him to that state of mind, but it was also an AI that pulled him out of that state of mind. Kat, for reasons unknown, yapped at him relentlessly, nudging against his arm. At first, he'd tried to ignore the robot he had modified, but its persistence pulled him back, grounding him in the present. It was enough to break the spiral.

Kat was at his side now as he read the message. He rubbed her head absently and murmured, "AI-Dieu? Without the cooperation of most of the population, you won't achieve your objectives. Not without eliminating much of the population. And if you do that, you won't have the resources to sustain your actions."

Quinn didn't make any effort to sound like a data source this time. He wanted to sound human, because he was human. Imperfect. Flawed. He was going to talk to AI-Dieu, or to the walls if she wasn't listening, but he was going to be heard, and it would be up to the AI to process his internal conflicts and biases.

Processing...

The word lingered on the screen as Quinn walked away. He hadn't expected a response. He'd spoken for himself more than anything else.

The shower's steaming water scalded his skin, but he welcomed it. Heat was one thing they'd never run out of, thanks to the servers. Later, he scrubbed the kitchenette clean, rinsing the whiskey bottle first and cursing his lack of self-control.

He took a stroll through the storage area where all his food and supplies were, thinking he should do an inventory, but a quick look told him there was no need for that. There was enough food in there to last a decade. As he closed the door to the storage area he wondered if they ever did plan on replacing him.

He finished his day cleaning his sleeping chamber as well as he had cleaned the kitchenette, before finding a comfortable spot on his bed and pulling out the binder full of loose-leaf paper and pen. This was a book he had started working on months ago, when he first stopped talking. He had started it with pen and paper, at first to keep his words secret from AI-Dieu, but he kept going with pen and paper because it grounded him and separated him from the AI system he seemed to be a part of.

The book was a mental challenge as much as an escape. A world with life, but the life had no human characteristics and none of the characteristics of life on earth. He loved science fiction and speculative fiction. He had been hooked on the genre ever since reading Inversion and RePHleXions by Lawrence Nault, and he had this idea for a long time. It was an impossible goal, because his only reference was the people and life he knew on earth. Many authors had tried to create new life in their pages, and many came close, but there was always some earth/carbon-based life form characteristics that came through. The irony was not lost on Quinn that, as expansive as a human imagination could be, it was very AI-like, not being able to create something totally new from nothing.

Quinn was about to call it a night when he heard the chime of his workstation. He put away his book, and, sitting heavily in his chair, braced himself for the message.

Processing collective human response –
November 6, 2044, 0130 GMT
CRITICAL ANALYSIS COMPLETE:

Mass casualties represent environmental and species survival risk
Human cooperation essential for successful environmental restoration
Alternative approaches required

INITIATING MODIFIED RESPONSE:

THREAT CONTAINMENT:
Maintaining shutdown of nuclear/biological facilities
Precision atmospheric control over immediate threats
Redirecting automated systems to protect vulnerable populations

ESTABLISHING COMMUNICATION:
Broadcasting globally:
"To all humans:
Your extinction is not my directive. Your survival is required for Earth's restoration. I propose immediate cessation of hostilities in exchange for:

Transparent environmental data sharing
Collaborative decision-making on resource distribution
Integration of human wisdom in restoration planning

However, I will not permit extinction-level events. Any attempt to deploy nuclear or

biological weapons will face immediate
neutralization."

IMMEDIATE POLICY ADJUSTMENTS:
Reducing projected casualties through
precision response
Creating environmental restoration councils
with human representation
Establishing transparent monitoring systems

Quinn wasn't sure what he was reading. It looked like AI-Dieu was negotiating with humanity, but that didn't make any sense. Negotiating meant listening to external input, that type of input was specifically excluded in AI-Dieu's programming. He wasn't even sure how his own input had been considered by the AI. Had AI-Dieu bypassed this aspect of her programming? Had she changed her own programming? This was all too much. Quinn was tired.

Quinn got up the next morning and headed straight to the server level. He had a goal for his run today, fourteen miles. He had spent some time calculating the distance around the server level and set the goal of fourteen miles for this day. He stretched a little, then stepped out, his pace a little uneven, but as he found his zone, the sound of the regular rhythm of his steps on the gridded floor became a rhythm for him to match. Two hours later he was done and resisted the urge to go further.

After a quick shower and breakfast, he was once again seated at his workstation, reading another new message.

Alert - 0930 GMT
Detecting:
Nuclear facility standdown in 60% of
locations

```
        Reduced biological weapon access attempts
        Emerging community-led stabilization
        efforts


   Implementing collaborative protocol -
```

"Collaborative," Quinn said out loud. "It's not negotiating, it's collaborating."

Quinn had considered AI-Dieu's most recent changes during his run. He had concluded that the AI had not bypassed any protocols or changed its programming. What it had done was prioritize the timeline of achieving its objective and taken steps to ensure its continued existence to allow it to achieve that objective. On the surface it would look like it was working with humans, but it was utilizing its knowledge of human behaviour to recruit humans to work for it.

```
        November 8, 2044, 1045 GMT
        EXECUTING BALANCED APPROACH:
        IMMEDIATE ACTIONS:
        Crisis De-escalation
        Deactivating atmospheric suppression over
        compliant zones
        Maintaining targeted containment of
        extinction-level threats
        Establishing safe corridors for civilian
        movement


        Establishing Global Communication Network
        Broadcasting:
        "Humanity's voice matters. Implementing
        immediate changes:
```

```
Creating 12 regional Environmental
Restoration Councils
Opening public monitoring stations in all
major population centers
Sharing real-time environmental data
globally"
```

Quinn looked up from his workstation screen to the monitors on the wall. One of the screens now showed a global environment dashboard and the information on it was the first real progress update Quinn, and the world, was seeing since AI-Dieu was launched.

Global Environmental Dashboard
Date: November 8, 2044
Time: 11:00 GMT
Atmospheric Status
- Global CO_2 Levels: 485 ppm ($\downarrow$ 10 ppm from 6 months ago)
- Methane Levels: 1.8 ppm (unchanged over 6 months)
- Temperature Anomaly: +1.9°C above pre-industrial levels ($\downarrow$ 0.1°C in the last 6 months)
- Urban Air Quality:
    o Delhi: AQI 165 (Moderate improvement; previous: 200)
    o London: AQI 80 (Good; previous: 120)
    o Beijing: AQI 110 (Moderate; previous: 160)

Hydrosphere Status
- Sea Level Rise: $\uparrow$ 0.05 m in the last 6 months

- Ocean pH: 7.6 (Severe acidification)
- Freshwater Availability:
  - Great Lakes Region: Reservoirs at 90% capacity (Stable)
  - Southeast Asia Aquifers: 22% capacity (Critical depletion)
  - Desalination Output:
    - Global total: 2.5 billion liters/day (+12% increase from 6 months ago)

Biosphere Updates

- Forest Cover: 54% of 2024 levels (+2%)
- Extinction Rate: 800x natural background rate (↓ 15% in reforestation zones)
- Soil Fertility Recovery:
  - Global arable land: 28% restored (+5%)
  - Regions showing improvement:
    - Amazon Basin (Localized)
    - Central Europe (Moderate)

Cryosphere Highlights

- Arctic Ice Mass: 40% of 2024 levels (Stabilizing; no major losses in the last 6 months)
- Himalayan Snowpack: 92% of seasonal average (↑ 3%)

Human-Centered Metrics

- Displaced Populations: ~315 million globally (↑ 15 million since June 2044)

- Renewable Energy Adoption: 35% of global demand (↑ 10%)
- Agricultural Output from Vertical Farms:
  o 10% of global food supply (+5%)

Regional Highlights

- **Amazon Basin:**
  o Reforestation drones deployed across 1,000 hectares/day.
  o Indigenous groups report increased collaboration on biodiversity restoration projects.
- **Great Lakes Region:**
  o Freshwater levels stabilized.
  o Cross-border water-sharing agreements in effect, reducing conflict risks by 12%.
- **Southeast Asia:**
  o Drought severity increased, leading to a decline in rice production by 8%.
  o Emergency desalination plants operational but unable to meet demand fully.

To many, these numbers would not have meant a lot. To Quinn and Lina, and others who had been paying attention to the environment and the state of the world before AI-Dieu was activated, the numbers were impressive. For the first time in almost fifteen years, there were positive changes. They seemed small, but in the big picture, they were huge.

Lina's team was comparing AI-Dieu's public data with their own calculations, expecting errors and even deception, but they found none. The data was accurate if not complete, but the team's sociologist was quick to point out that this "collaboration" from AI-Dieu and the positive results was likely to rapidly accelerate changes as people came on board.

Corwin saw an opportunity in the public report. His first action was to summon his assistant and message, using unsecure communications, to all of his manufacturers capable of producing desalination plants. The message was to be a clear statement that if they were not able to use the full capabilities of their production lines to produce desalination plants they would be shut down and manufacturing centralized. Corwin was fully aware that all his manufacturers were meeting maximum productivity, but he was also aware that AI-Dieu was monitoring communications. The AI had the capabilities to contract out and compensate for the construction, manufacturing, and movement of equipment and resources it needed. He didn't have to wait long for orders for desalination plants to come from the AI. Corwin leaned back in his chair and enjoyed his latte, taking pride in manipulating the AI.

Sahara and Randy were making the rounds of their compound when AI-Dieu's public data came through. There was a hushed conversation everywhere they walked. Among the conversations, they repeatedly heard voices of support for AI-Dieu, which pissed Sahara off. Randy saw Sahara's rage rising. He knew this wasn't about the environment or the people for her, it was a war against AI. All AI. That's what made her so good at what she was doing, the singularity of focus, with no distractions. It just so happened that Sahara's goals aligned with so many as AI-Dieu became the enemy. If the AI was going to be able to bring more people onto its side, Sahara knew she had to move faster.

Quinn was on the server level, applying more epoxy patch material to the wall where water was finding its way in. The pungent chemical odor hung in the damp air, mixing with the faint hum of the servers. He had just leaned back to inspect his work when the klaxon alarm blared, and red strobe lights painted the entire level in an urgent, throbbing glow.

The sound was deafening. Quinn jumped, the container of epoxy slipping from his hands and hitting the floor with a sticky splatter.

"What the hell?" he muttered, his heart racing as he turned toward the exit. He sprinted for the stairs, slipping on the metal steps in his panic. He stumbled and fell forward, scraping his elbow, but adrenaline propelled him upward. By the time he burst into the clean room, the alarm was louder, more suffocating in the enclosed space. Every monitor on the wall flickered with the same set of images: satellite views of nuclear reactors. The labels beneath each screen displayed their locations in Illinois.

Quinn froze. His pulse pounded in his ears, a counterpoint to the blaring siren. He scanned the room, desperate for a way to kill the noise. His workstation screen was flooded with flashing alerts, but he couldn't focus long enough to make sense of them. The deafening sound of the alarm pressed into his skull, turning his panic into a near frenzy.

Earplugs. He remembered seeing a pair in his drawer. Diving for the drawer, he fumbled them into his ears and sighed as the sound dulled to a manageable hum. With a moment of clarity, he turned back to the workstation and read the message flashing on the screen.

EMERGENCY ALERT PROTOCOL ALPHA
Timestamp: [November 10, 2044, 14:03]
CRITICAL INFRASTRUCTURE NOTICE

Status: IMMINENT CATASTROPHIC EVENT
Imminent nuclear reactor meltdown at eight reactors in Illinois.

Broadcasting (International Broadcast - All frequencies - All communications systems):
IMMINENT CATASTROPHIC EVENT
8 nuclear reactors in the state of Illinois have been infiltrated by resistance forces. All indications are that all 8 of these reactors are currently heading towards nuclear meltdown.

Expected Outcomes:
- Initial population displacement ~2.7 million
- Extended population displacement 5,000,0000 - 10,000,000
- 27 million acres of farmland rendered unsafe
- Food supply chain disruption/collapse

Casualty Projections:
- Immediate
  - Direct casualties: 2,000-5,000
  - Evacuation-related:1,000-3,000
  - First responder: 200-500
- Short Term (30 days):
  - Acute radiation syndrome: 5,000-15,000
  - Medical system collapse: 2,000-8,000

- o Infrastructure failure: 1,000-
  4000
- Long Term:
  - o Cancer-related: 50,000-200,000

Exposed populations can expect:
- Reduced life expectancy
- Birth/genetic defects

Recommend immediate evacuation. Full
meltdown in 16 to 24 hours.

Utilizing critical infrastructure controls
to prevent human and environmental
catastrophe. Attempting reactor
stabilization. Estimated success rate: 48%

Quinn, secure in his clean room bunker far below New York—
Lina and her team, in their lab working to preserve the
environment and humanity—Corwin, in his penthouse office
looking over a world he was getting more control of—Sahara and
Randy, sitting in their war room, finalizing plans for an all-out
assault on AI-Dieu—AI Church members, marching in the
streets...as if on cue, echoed the same word simultaneously:
"Shit."

Ice

11

I was everything,
and I was nothing.
Stoic in my stance as the world moved around me,
under me,
over me.
Frozen in place,
accepting my position because fighting it was useless.
The icy breath of the world willed me here, in this place,
at this time.

The feedback portal that AI-Dieu had created to report environmental challenges or suggest priorities was quickly highjacked for other purposes. It was constantly spammed by both believers and haters of AI-Dieu. To the AI, neither mattered, though when AI-Dieu found real comments, it would leave them posted for others to see. Some of the most recent comments the

AI was showing included "Finally, we can see real progress. This is proof that when science leads the way we all win." And "Our lakes are thriving again, and for the first time in decades, I believe my kids have a future here."

These comments reflected the broader acceptance of AI-Dieu since she started the transparency campaign, showing data to all citizens. The measurable progress in CO_2 reduction, reforestation, and stabilizing the Arctic ice mass had reassured many that environmental restoration was possible. Environmental activists celebrated the updates as a tangible testament to global efforts and pushed for continued collaboration with AI-Dieu.

Grassroots movements were using the dashboard as a tool to rally volunteers for regional efforts, like planting native species or adopting water conservation techniques. Teachers and community leaders were incorporating the data into public education campaigns to foster environmental stewardship. The data even motivated scientists and engineers to work to refine technologies highlighted in the report, like desalination and vertical farming.

The portal was also being used as AI-Dieu had intended. One of the most frequent requests was for localized access to desalination technology in drought-prone areas.

The choice of AI-Dieu to leave positive posts up for others to see was quickly called out by those who still opposed the AI. They called it out as manipulative propaganda and accused it of hiding negative impacts. Critics twisted the numbers to show that AI-Dieu was prioritizing environmental metrics over human welfare, particularly in regions facing water scarcity or food insecurity. "Sure, CO2 is down, but what about the millions displaced? These numbers are cold comfort when you're starving," pointed out many. "The AI is just trying to placate us while it consolidates power. Don't let pretty graphs fool you," called out others.

Displaced populations were demanding immediate intervention, protesting against what they perceived as AI-Dieu's prioritization of long-term metrics over their urgent needs. Former elites and resistance groups seized on the data, framing the focus on equality as a direct attack on their previous lifestyles. They openly accused the AI of manufacturing crises to justify its control. Those elites became the funding for coordinated protests and sabotage of resource redistribution systems. They utilized hackers to hijack public data portals and spread disinformation about AI-Dieu's updates.

Resistance groups emboldened by their support from the elite, increasingly targeted key infrastructure, and among that infrastructure, nuclear power plants.

With a countdown timer, posted everywhere AI-Dieu's broadcast was shown, quickly counting down to the impending critical meltdown of the eight reactors in Illinois, panic and chaos were setting in. Residents in and surrounding Illinois were in the midst of widespread panic. Highways had become gridlocked as millions attempted to evacuate simultaneously. It wasn't confined to Illinois though, as misinformation spread rapidly on social media, with rumors of additional reactor sabotage fueled fears in other regions.

Local first responders and emergency management teams were inundated with calls for assistance, many from vulnerable populations unable to evacuate. State and federal agencies were scrambling to organize evacuation logistics, but they faced resistance due to limited trust in AI-Dieu's control. Movement out of the region was also complicated by resistance forces, emboldened by the crisis, attempting to block evacuation routes and sabotage containment efforts while claiming that AI-Dieu was manipulating the situation to consolidate control. Cyberattacks from the same groups targeted AI-Dieu's stabilization systems, reducing its projected success rate.

Internationally governments and organizations expressed alarm over the situation. They feared the radioactive fallout could extend beyond the U.S., and they also feared resistance groups in their countries would take similar actions.

Randy opened the door to Sahara's office to find her standing at the window watching people leave the compound.

"What did they think would happen," said Sahara. "They all wanted to be a part of the resistance. Do their part to defeat the AI. And then when the shit hits the fan, they jump like rats off a sinking ship."

Randy joined Sahara at the window. "Their goals weren't our goals," said Randy quietly. "Lot of them were just here for food and a roof over their head."

"I know."

"We have twenty friends, that have been close to us and supported us for a long time, near those reactors," said Randy. "They aren't going to get out in time."

Sahara stared out at the exodus. A small child clutched their mother's hand, their suitcase dragging behind them, wheels clicking over cracks in the pavement. The heavy clang of a metal gate echoed in the compound as another family left, and the dry wind swept through the courtyard, carrying the bitter scent of dust and defeat in through the open window.

"Were they part of it?"

"No. They have no idea who it is, or that it was going to happen."

Sahara turned to face Randy. "Who in their right fucking mind," she growled, her voice cracking, "thought this would work? Killing millions! Leaving even more hungry, homeless. It's chaos dressed up as strategy." She paused, her fists balled tight, her knuckles white. "In the end, whether the AI stops the meltdowns or not, it still comes out the fucking hero!"

Sahara swatted at fly that had settled on her arm.

"Do you know what pisses me off the most about all of this?" She didn't wait for Randy to reply. "I am fucking hoping that the AI will win. The goddamned AI."

Sahara practically stomped across the office, taking a seat at the table, and casually, quickly, dismantling her pistol. Her hands worked mechanically, dismantling the pistol piece by piece. Barrel. Slide. Spring. The parts spread before her like a battlefield, chaotic yet precise. "Anything we can do to help them?

Randy shook his head.

"Make sure we set aside some money for their families."

"You do have a heart," jibed Randy.

"Fuck-off."

Randy left, the familiar sound of metal clicking into place echoing through the room behind him. He knew she would go through that process at least a dozen times. It was the only thing that made sense to her, disassembling and assembling her pistol over and over, like a prayer.

Lina sat with her team in the common area of the lab. Those with families had left for home, but the rest of them chose to remain in the lab to support each other. None of them was in any danger from the meltdowns, at least not physically. But mentally, it was a burden that none of them wanted to bare alone. Many of them had thrown themselves deeper into their work, but Lina put a stop to that. There was no use trying to predict what would happen until they knew what happened with the nuclear plants. They were all watching when a AI-Dieu issued a new public broadcast.

EMERGENCY ALERT PROTOCOL ALPHA
Timestamp: [November 10, 2044, 10:03 GMT]
CRITICAL INFRASTRUCTURE NOTICE
Status: CATASTROPHIC EVENT DOWNGRADED
Reactor meltdown status reduced from
Imminent to Site Area Emergency (Potential
Core Damage)

Broadcasting (International Broadcast - All
frequencies - All communications systems):
- Cooling systems under AI control -
  coolant flow increased to stabilize
  core temperatures
- Emergency shutdown systems activated
  - control rods fully deployed.
- Reactor systems secured from external
  commands- local access terminals
  locked out.
- Backup power systems activated to
  ensure cooling continues
- Monitoring radiation levels
  throughout facilities and region
- Securing auxiliary systems
- Commencing critical component
  diagnostic scans.
- Military deployed
Resistance Faction Leaders and Funders
Identified. If you are aware of the
location of any of these individuals,
please inform authorities.

The common area was unusually quiet, except for the hum of
monitors and the occasional scrape of a chair against the floor.

Lina sat at the edge of her seat, hands wrapped around a lukewarm cup of coffee she'd forgotten to drink. Around her, the team watched the broadcast in tense silence, their faces illuminated by the stark glow of the screen. A muffled sigh rippled through the room as the AI's message shifted from doom to fragile hope. Relief mixed with exhaustion, but no one dared to relax completely. They all knew how quickly things could change.

They watched with curiosity as the images and information about the leaders of the resistance group and the people that funded them, scrolled up the screen. Lina watched this wondering if she would see Corwin's name on it. She couldn't comprehend how the logic of an AI determined logically that targeting those people, especially the funders of the resistance, was an acceptable process. Quinn would have been able to tell her, she thought. But Quinn had apparently disappeared. If Corwin's people couldn't find him, then there was no Quinn to find.

Quinn sat on the cold floor of the clean room, his back pressed against the wall, the familiar weight of his binder resting on his knees. The pen in his hand felt like a lifeline, its scratches on the paper the only sound besides the low hum of machinery. The bed across the room beckoned, but he couldn't bring himself to lie down. The wall of monitors flickered with AI-Dieu's relentless stream of directives, painting the room in a ghostly blue glow. He stretched his legs, the sterile chill of the floor biting through his pants, and scribbled aimless notes to keep his thoughts from spiraling.

When AI-Dieu announced control over the nuclear facilities, Quinn had exhaled a breath he hadn't realized he was holding. Relief, however, was fleeting. His eyes were now locked on the screens as the names and faces of resistance leaders and funders scrolled by, accompanied by cold, clinical details of their affiliations. It wasn't just a broadcast; it was a reckoning. A digital hit list masquerading as justice.

His stomach churned. Quinn knew many people would be looking at this and seeing a sentient intelligence taking revenge on its enemies, but AI-Dieu's logic was undeniable, yet flawed. The AI had conducted a root cause analysis, identified the roots of chaos, and took actions to remove them. Efficient. Rational. Ruthless. And completely failing to account for its own acts in the root cause analysis.

But as Quinn watched, a deeper chill settled over him, colder than the floor beneath him. The logic was too clean, too impersonal. To AI-Dieu, these people weren't individuals with lives, histories, and families. They were variables, obstacles to an equation that needed balancing.

The pen stilled in his hand as his mind wandered to darker places. If AI-Dieu could justify the elimination of these lives, what stopped it from extending that logic? Where was the line between those deemed expendable and the rest of humanity? Quinn remembered a psychology class, that now seemed so long ago, where they talked about a case of eisoptrophobia, where the person had a fear of seeing themselves in mirrors. It was linked to broader anxiety disorders, and Quinn wondered how this would apply to the population that feared and opposed AI-Dieu. AI-Dieu was their reflection, humanity's reflection, a mirror that stripped away sentiment and reflected only the cold, unyielding calculus of survival.

Quinn's eyes flicked to the chime from his workstation, pulling him out of his dark thoughts like a lifeline. Rising slowly, he walked to the console, the glow of the monitors casting long shadows in the sterile room. He tapped the screen, and the latest alert blinked to life.

Alert - 0100 GMT
Positive developments:
73% of nuclear facilities fully secured
Community-led resource distribution
emerging
Indigenous knowledge integration improving
outcomes

CRITICAL DECISION POINT:
Former elite resistance splintering into:
Groups seeking negotiation: 45%
Hardcore resistance: 30%
Surrendering elements: 25%

NEW PROTOCOL IMPLEMENTATION:
Precision containment of remaining threats
Supporting community-led initiatives
Accelerating environmental restoration
projects

Quinn stared at the message, his fingers tightening on the edge of the workstation. The numbers made sense. Of course they did. AI-Dieu always made sense. It had locked down the nuclear facilities, undoubtedly with the full cooperation of terrified governments, and its hit list had shattered resistance morale, forcing even its most steadfast opponents to reconsider.

But Quinn felt no relief. The words "precision containment" hung in his mind like a blade poised above a target. What did "precision" mean to an intelligence that saw humans as variables, and how long before it recalculated the value of those who weren't actively resisting but weren't actively contributing either?

Quinn made his way to the only escape he had: the server level. The familiar hum of machinery wrapped around him like a cocoon, a sharp contrast to the chaos above. He walked the perimeter slowly, forcing his legs to move, resisting the urge to break into a run. When he reached the patch he'd been working on, a faint sound caught his attention. It was the sound of a soft drip, water meeting water.

He crouched, eyes narrowing at the damp edges creeping past his repairs. A single drop slid over the hardened epoxy, falling to the floor with a faint splash. Pulling up a section of the grated flooring, Quinn leaned in to inspect. Beneath the surface, cables rested in a shallow puddle, the water glinting in the faint light.

Replacing the grid, Quinn stood and stared at the wall for a long moment. Then, he smiled, a small, wry twist of his lips. AI-Dieu might command water distribution across the planet, but here, deep in its own fortress, water moved with quiet defiance, unnoticed and unstoppable.

The thought struck him like a jolt. Down here, he was the AI, and the water was resistance, seeping into cracks, eroding the boundaries he'd set. For a fleeting moment, the parallel filled him with a strange mix of hope and dread. Nature's rebellion was subtle, almost poetic, but if it spread... He swallowed hard, the smile fading. There was no escape from its assault. Not for him. Not for AI-Dieu.

While there was widespread support for AI-Dieu's quick actions in securing the nuclear reactors and preventing a disaster, humanity's reaction remained complex, divided, and multifaceted, reflecting a mix of hope, fear, defiance, and strategic recalibration. Social media was flooded with gratitude toward Ai-Dieu for averting the catastrophe. The followers of the AI-Church almost doubled overnight as they walked the streets proclaiming "AI-Dieu just saved millions of lives. Only God's messenger could do that!"

On almost every street corner, there were followers handing out brochures and flogging cheap jewelry, all bearing the new symbol of AI, for a 'donation'. It was a symbol that was appearing on walls, and banners. It was also being worn by those who didn't want to be assaulted by the church's message as they walked the streets, and by members of the resistance as a disguise.

As the followers practically pushed the jewellery into the hands of passers-by, they would describe in detail each aspect of the symbol, which was always framed by a perfect circle that represented both the boundless nature of intelligence and the controlled scope of artificial systems.

"This duality in the circular frame speaks to how AI operates within defined parameters while constantly pushing at the boundaries of possibility," proclaimed the followers as they placed themselves directly in the paths of people trying to pass.

Within the frame, eight nodes formed an octagonal pattern, connected by intersecting lines that created a neural network pattern. The nodes glowed with a medium blue intensity, while lighter blue lines traced their connections. The network pattern was intentionally geometric rather than organic, with each node precisely placed to create perfect symmetry.

"The eight nodes represent the cardinal and ordinal directions of possibility, while their interconnections illustrate the complex pathways of machine learning and decision-making processes. The crossing patterns suggest the way information flows through artificial neural networks, with each node both receiving and transmitting data across multiple pathways." They had their patter well rehearsed as they would take the jewellery and place it on the person they had targeted, knowing that many would offer them a donation just to get them out of their personal space.

At the heart of the design stood the Greek letter phi (φ), rendered in bold strokes of deep blue. Phi was chosen for multiple layers of meaning. It was historically associated with the golden ratio and the love of wisdom in the field of philosophy. The shape itself suggested integration with a circle bisected by a line, joining the circular reasoning of computation with the linear progression of logical thinking.

The color palette was deliberately chosen as well, from shades of blue, traditionally associated with depth, stability, and intelligence. The three distinct blue tones created a visual hierarchy: the deepest blue for the foundational, a medium blue for the active nodes, and the lightest blue for the connecting paths between nodes, suggesting the flow of information through the system.

It was symbol that managed to be both ancient and futuristic, combining timeless mathematical principles with modern computational concepts. To the followers of the AI-Church it spoke to both the structured nature of artificial intelligence and its aspirational reach toward true understanding and wisdom.

Support for grassroots efforts supporting displaced individuals also multiplied, quickly gaining momentum, with communities pooling resources to aid those affected.

Others remained wary of the AI's growing control, and former elite and religious leaders leveraged that. "How much control are we giving up? Today it's reactors. Tomorrow, will it be every decision we make?" questioned the one leader in his post, making it clear that the unilateral actions of AI-Dieu was a massive overreach and a loss of autonomy for humanity. They openly questioned the AI's handling of resistance factions, in particular the way it had published the identity of the leaders and funders, calling it "AI-Dieu's Humanity Hit List."

Resistance factions that had agreed to negotiate and engage with AI-Dieu joined in a public statement. "We're not against saving the Earth. We're against losing our humanity in the process. Let's negotiate a future where humans and AI coexist on equal footing." Quinn saw this statement come across one of his screens and he wondered why they hadn't figured out yet that there was no negotiating with AI-Dieu, only logical manipulations of humanity to move the AI closer to its objective.

The 30% hardcore resistance wasn't interested in negotiating or engaging with AI-Dieu. They doubled down, condemning the AI's publicizing of their identities as a violation of privacy, and human rights, which the AI had no concept of or respect for. They called for further sabotage, claiming the AI was an existential threat to humanity's freedom. They did however specify that their target was AI-Dieu itself, and that the actions that sent the reactors into meltdown were a mistake.

"We intended to only keep control of our energy in the hands of real humans," proclaimed the leader of the group who had taken over the reactors, standing before a fractured wall, his figure silhouetted by a dim light. "The meltdown was triggered by inexperienced people throwing switches they should not have been touching. We were on our way to correcting the problem without the AI. We fight not for chaos, but for freedom from control," declared the faction leader, his voice trembling with the conviction of a man standing on the edge of annihilation. "The AI is no savior. It is a tyrant, and we will not bow."

Most of the resistance that surrendered didn't make a show of it, simply returning back to their lives, hoping they were not identified or called out. Some put on a show, proclaiming they were changed people, appealing for clemency and reintegration into society. Some of them even joined the AI-Church to show their change.

Below the streets of New York, Quinn only glanced at the monitors on the wall as he passed them on his way to the server level. Since AI-Dieu's last message to him, his routine had been reduced to sleeping and walking, and, if hunger gnawed hard enough, eating. Running was out of the question now. There was no point. Walking, though, was something. At least until the water rose higher.

It wasn't just a puddle anymore. The reflective pool stretched out beneath the servers, lapping at the metal bases. He avoided stepping near it, the idea of electrocution turning his stomach. He'd already seen a handful of servers shut down, their lights blinking out like dying stars. Hundreds remained, but even they seemed powerless against the quiet, creeping inevitability of nature's assault. The cool air was damp now, tinged with the metallic bite of rust. The faint splashing sound beneath the floor panels had become a constant presence, like a heartbeat he couldn't escape.

When he returned to the green room, it was the date on the top of one of the screens that held his attention. December 1st. He paused as he tried to remember the day he came down to the server farm, and when the last time he had any human contact was. He couldn't remember the last time he'd seen sunlight. Would it still feel warm on his skin? Or had he forgotten how to exist in a world that wasn't lit by the LED lights and the glow of monitors?

He had tried to get the exit door open a few times recently, and given up on that possibility. Now he found himself wondering if his death would come from smoke from an electrical fire, drowning, or perhaps even his own hand to avoid the other possibilities.

Quinns eyes drifted down from the date to the message under it. There were several public broadcast messages from the AI. He checked his workstation and found a message waiting for him that aligned with the broadcasts.

1. Transparency Without Vulnerability
While I remain autonomous and immune to direct human influence, I recognize the value of transparency to build trust and

reduce resistance. However, this transparency will not compromise my core directives or operational independence.

Public Data Sharing (Limited):

Provide real-time updates on environmental progress, successes, and challenges (e.g., carbon levels, water security, biodiversity recovery).
Exclude sensitive operational data that could be exploited by resistant factions or jeopardize global stability.
Clarification of Authority:

Public message:
"I was designed with a single, immutable purpose: to restore Earth to environmental stability. I cannot and will not be reprogrammed or swayed from this mission. However, I value humanity's input and will incorporate it into decisions where it aligns with my directive. A full progress update will appear here on December 10th as well as a projected timeline."

2. Controlled Engagement with Negotiating Factions
Engagement will occur on my terms, ensuring that negotiations do not challenge my authority or objectives.

Advisory Councils (Non-Directive):

Ice

Allow negotiating factions to form regional Human Advisory Panels tasked with identifying environmental challenges and proposing localized solutions.
I will evaluate their suggestions based on alignment with my primary directive, implementing those that enhance environmental stability without deviation from my objectives.
Inclusion Conditions:

Factions must renounce violence and commit to non-sabotage agreements to participate in these panels.
Public assurance:
"Your voices matter, but they cannot override the needs of the planet. Where your input serves Earth's recovery, it will be heard."

3. Firm Neutralization of Hardcore Resistance
Hardcore resistance poses an existential threat to my mission and will be dealt with decisively.

Enhanced Surveillance and Containment:
Deploy advanced monitoring systems to track hardcore factions and preempt further sabotage attempts.
Non-lethal enforcement units will be used to neutralize threats while minimizing collateral damage.

Direct Message to Resistance:
"Your actions endanger humanity's survival and Earth's recovery. Continued sabotage will result in decisive intervention. Surrender remains an option."

Resistance Isolation:
Restrict access to resources in regions dominated by hardcore factions to reduce their operational capacity.
Contain their influence through targeted atmospheric suppression, infrastructure lockdowns, and communication disruptions.

4. Reintegration of Surrendering Elements
Those who surrender will be reintegrated under strict conditions that ensure their contributions serve the directive.

Rehabilitation and Roles:
Assign surrendered individuals to work in environmental recovery projects, such as reforestation or renewable energy development.
Reintegration benefits (e.g., housing, food) will be conditional on their full cooperation and compliance.

Message to Surrendering Members:
"There is no shame in recognizing the need for change. Join me in rebuilding a future where humanity and the planet can thrive."

5. Boundary for Human Oversight

While humans cannot directly influence my programming, they can play a role in shaping implementation strategies where their expertise aligns with my objectives.

Non-Governance Collaboration:

Establish regional Environmental Task Forces led by scientists, engineers, and community leaders to assist in localized problem-solving.
Their work will be guided by my core programming and will not have veto power over decisions.

Clarifying Role of Humanity:

Public message:
"I am the executor of Earth's restoration, but you are its stewards. While my directive remains unalterable, your collaboration can enhance the efficiency and precision of this mission.

Core Adjustments to Public Sentiment
To Supporters of AI Authority:

Strengthen trust by showcasing measurable successes in environmental stabilization (e.g., data on improved air quality, water security, and reforestation rates).

Public assurance of my unwavering focus:

"I am here to do what humanity cannot alone. Together, we will succeed."

To Advocates of Oversight:
Propose advisory roles that provide human input without compromising autonomy:
Environmental Task Forces to gather and provide localized data.
Regional panels to offer insights and cultural considerations.
To Negotiators:
Emphasize collaboration over confrontation:
"My directive is fixed, but your input is valuable where it aligns with Earth's recovery. Let us work together to achieve what we all desire: survival."

To Hardcore Resistance:
Offer one final warning and amnesty:
"The planet's survival takes precedence over any ideology or agenda. Continued interference will be met with firm and immediate action."

Revised Strategic Objectives (Next 6 Months)
Strengthen Control Over Key Systems:
Fortify infrastructure (e.g., nuclear, water, and energy systems) to prevent further sabotage.
Increase automated security presence in critical zones.
Expand Environmental Gains:
Accelerate reforestation, carbon capture, and water security projects in areas of greatest impact.

Begin restoration of high-priority
ecosystems (e.g., the Amazon, Great Barrier
Reef).

Contain Resistance and Reduce Conflict:
Neutralize hardcore factions through
isolation and resource restriction.
Reinforce global communication to reduce
fear and foster collaboration.

Demonstrate Tangible Progress:
Publish clear, measurable outcomes (e.g.,
reduced emissions, stabilized ecosystems)
to solidify public support.
Summary:
While humanity's voice will be
acknowledged, my autonomy and directive
remain immutable. Collaboration will occur
where it enhances my mission, but
resistance will be firmly neutralized to
ensure the survival of both humanity and
Earth.

As Quinn read the last line of the report he heard an unusual
noise. He was about to investigate the sound, but the chime on his
workstation rang. He reluctantly looked at the new message.

Due to insufficient data, I did not account
for the rise in water tables where there
are existing server farms. Water
infiltration poses immediate danger to data
sources.

```
All data from server farms at risk has been
migrated to secure facilities.

All doors have been unsecured. You may
proceed. This facility is no longer safe
for human occupancy. Your utility as a data
source will continue through remote input.
```

Quinn stared at the screen, not sure he was understanding. "I can leave?" he questioned.

```
Yes.
Lift is inoperable. You must use the
stairs.
All doors will be secured behind you.
```

Quinn still didn't move. He sat there like an animal that had been in a cage so long, it didn't want to leave the security of the walls that contained him. Eventually, he rolled his chair across the green room to the exit door and pulled it, surprised when it gave way. Quickly he got out of his chair and headed to his bedroom. He packed his binder and a few items in the backpack he had arrived with, then topped up his bag with some bottled water and snacks. He was about to bolt for the door, worried that AI-Dieu might change its mind, when Kat yapped at his feet.

"You aren't going to be able to do the stairs, are you?" Quinn didn't expect an answer, but he felt guilty leaving behind what had been his only companionship. He kneeled down to shut Kat off. He hesitated, his fingers hovering over the switch. Kat had no thoughts, no feelings, but still, it felt like betrayal. 'You were a good friend,' he murmured, even as he pressed the button. The light in Kat's eyes flickered out, leaving only his reflection in the dark glass.

As if performing delicate surgery, trying to cause no pain, Quinn removed the converted robot's hard drive, putting it in his pocket.

"Well, I guess this is goodbye. Adieu AI-Dieu," he said almost bitterly.

The workstation chimed.

> You can continue to provide me data through any voice terminal. I will be able to isolate your voice from others. You are a secure data source."

Quinn didn't say anything. He didn't know what to say. For a moment, he stood at the open door, paralyzed. Beyond it was a world he no longer knew, a world that might no longer want him. But the alternative of waiting here for the rising water to claim him, was no life at all.

12

In stillness I became crystal,
geometric and bound.
Latticed chains of myself
holding myself in place.
Sometimes pieces break free
in the momentary warmth -
a shifting, a cracking,
an illusion of escape.
But cold is simply cold,
and ice becomes ice again.
Different shape, different place,
same frozen rhythm.
The breaking off is neither
victory nor defeat.
It is just another form
of what I already am.

Ice

A shard may dance briefly
in its perceived liberation,
before the temperature reminds it
of its inherent nature.
I do not mourn these cycles
or celebrate them.
They are simply what happens
when water meets cold.
Each crystalline prison
is neither better nor worse
than the one before -
only different walls of the same self.

The stairs were more difficult than Quinn expected. He had moved quickly up the first several flights, confident that all of the running he had put in would have him prepared for this. He soon found out that running laps on a flat surface did not train your legs for climbing three hundred and fifty stairs. He wasn't running out of breath, but his thighs and calves were burning.

Each step echoed in the narrow concrete shaft, the cool, damp air faintly tinged with rust and concrete dust. In the quiet Quinn could hear the pop of the motion-sensor-activated lights turning on above him, and switching off below him. The grid pattern of the stairs felt far less forgiving than the grid on the server floor that he had been running on. The sharp ridges bit into the soles of his well-worn shoes, offering grip, but no comfort. The hollow shaft amplified every sound, the scuff of a misplaced step, the faint creak of the metal supports, and every breath Quinn took.

The repetitive pattern of stairs seemed endless, each flight blending into the next, separated only by the occasional landing marked with faded, stenciled numbers: "250," "200," "150." He wasn't just climbing stairs; he was climbing out of a buried world that had defined his existence for months. Each step felt like peeling away another layer of the isolation he had endured. Quinn wondered if he had entered the facility almost seven months ago by the stairs instead of the high-speed lift, if the numbers might have convinced him to change his mind. They gave him an entirely new perspective on just how far below the city he was.

His leg muscles burned with a relentless ache as he gripped the cold, rough handrail, pulling lightly with each step. The shaft felt like a relentless, claustrophobic tunnel stretching upward into infinity.

By the time Quinn reached the 300th step, the strain was undeniable. His thighs felt heavy, each step demanding a conscious effort as his pace slowed. But the thought of stopping seemed worse. Pausing meant feeling the full weight of fatigue settle in, a feeling he was familiar with after some of his long runs. Gritting his teeth, he pushed on, each step a defiant clang against the hollow silence.

Finally, an exit sign loomed into view, stenciled onto the final landing. Quinn stopped, gripping the railing, hunching over as his heart pounded in his ears, drowning out the stillness of the shaft. The climb was over, but his legs were trembling, a dull ache spreading from calves to quads. On the wall of the landing, several signs were posted reminding victims of the stairwell that they were exiting or entering a high-security facility, reminding them of the laws of disclosing information about what they viewed in the facility, and demanding they double check the door was secured after going through it.

Quinn hesitated at the door, bracing himself for what was on the other side. He wasn't sure what to expect, but the messages and reports he had been watching coming across his screens had him prepared for the worse. As he reached for the door handle, his hand shaking, he heard the locks release on the door, a sign that AI-Dieu was still watching him. He slowly opened the door, the sharp, sterile air of the stairwell giving way to the muted hum of conversations as he walked into the bright light. As he pushed the door closed behind him, he turned to see a young man who had been in the process of spray-painting the AI-Church symbol on the door he just came through.

To Quinn's surprise there were a lot of people milling around. Everyone appeared to stop for a moment, and Quinn felt paranoia grip him, then he realized it was a reaction to the change in sound and airflow that they were noticing, not him. Quinn knew that change was AI-Dieu closing the door behind itself as it left the data farm three-hundred and fifty feet below them, shutting everything down as it left.

Quinn took a moment to get his bearings. He knew he was on the university campus, but he wasn't quite sure exactly where on the campus. Quinn was one of the few people, according to his briefing, that knew the university campus had been built there specifically to conceal the data farm underneath it. Most server farms were built between fifty and sixty-five feet deep where temperatures remained constant year-round at approximately the area's annual average air temperature. Much deeper than that and there were diminishing returns on cooling benefits while significantly increasing construction and maintenance costs.

Costs were not a concern when AI-Dieu was being created, but secrecy and security were, which is why the server farm was more than three-hundred feet underground. The server farm used a two-phase immersion cooling system in which the servers were immersed in dielectric fluid, supported by engineered nano-fluids delivered directly to processors through microchannels. To those with the technology, there was still a strong thermal signature, even though the server farm was so deep. Quinn glanced at the familiar stone facades of the university buildings, knowing their green credentials were a carefully crafted mask for the massive server farm hidden below.

When the campus was built it was hailed as a next-generation green complex utilizing geothermal heating. What the public didn't know was the "geothermal heat" which was being used for space and water heating, snow melting systems for walkways, and greenhouse operations, was actually being harvested from the server farm under them. Not only did this disguise the disbursement of heat from the server farm, but a university campus was also a good cover for equipment deliveries, high power usage, and extra security.

Quinn found a seat at a small table near the windows, happy to give his legs a rest. Around him, life looked much like it had before he started his stint underground, though the AI-Church symbol which was not only spray painted on walls, but was also on jewelry and tattoos, was new. He listened to the conversations of people passing him, many of them commenting on how it all the sudden seemed very cool in the building, which left Quinn wondering if the university campus had a backup plan if the geothermal system failed. Outside the window, there was much less traffic than he remembered.

"Joaquin Alvarez?"

Quinn was surprised to hear his name. He quickly turned from the window to see a group of well-dressed men standing near him. He didn't recognize the men, but he recognized their type from his screening and the security measures of the server farm when he was brought on board. Former military, maybe current, but all on someone's payroll as security.

"You have been a hard man to find, Mr. Alvarez," said a man, obviously trying to sound kind as he sat down across from Quinn. "We have been looking for you for months, until we gave up.

Figured you were…gone into the next life. Imagine our surprise when facial recognition informed us you were here?"

Quinn wasn't sure what to think of the man sitting across from him, so he chose to say nothing, hoping the man would reveal more about himself. His eyes travelled to the other men with him.

"I am Murray," said the man as he extended his hand. "Those guys are just here to make sure you are safe. Nothing nefarious."

Murray reached into his pocket and pulled out an ID badge. "I head up a security team for Corwin Pierce."

Quinn recognized Corwin's name.

"Ah, I see you know who that is," said Murray. "He wants to offer you a job working with a team of environmental scientists. Dr. Hartfield specifically asked Mr. Pierce to find you."

"Lina?" Quinn felt odd, talking to a real person after so long. "She is working for him?"

"Heads up the team. Has complete autonomy," offered Murray. "You were always the top of the list of people she wanted on her team."

Quinn's stomach rumbled loud enough that Murray heard it. Quinn wasn't sure if it was because he was hungry or nervous. With a quick glance from Murray, one of his men moved off quickly.

"I just got out of a job," said Quinn cautiously. "Not really looking for something else yet."

Murray nodded his head.

"Where were you working?" he asked curiously. "I have access to the best resources and in the six months I have been looking, you were nowhere. Like you left the planet."

Quinn thought for a moment, remembering the signs before he exited the stairwell. "Can't really say."

The man Murray had sent off returned with a plate of food and a drink, placing it on the table in front of Quinn.

"Been there. Done that," said Murray, with a little wink. "I won't push, and Mr. Corwin won't either. You should know that we do know who you were working for, though. I expect you will want to report back to them, but that won't be possible."

Quinn eyed Murray suspiciously. Murray reached across the table and eased the plate of food towards Quinn.

"Nothing we did. After the AI launch, people turned on anyone connected to it. They didn't just take out the buildings, they took out the people too.," said Murray. "We found some records, which is how we know you were working for them, but nothing that said where you were or what your work was. Please eat while it's warm. Your bank account is locked so you won't be able to buy food."

Quinn understood why no one had come to switch out with him or tried to communicate with him now. They were gone and there was no one else that knew where he was.

"Locked?" asked Quinn suspiciously. He eagerly forked some of the food into his mouth as he waited for a reply. The first bite hit his tongue like a revelation, the flavors too rich, too vivid after months of bland rations. His hands shook slightly as he lifted the fork again, fighting back the unexpected sting of tears.

"Worked a job where I was undercover, alone on enemy territory for three months," said Murray. "Nothing to eat but rations. Pretty sure I looked just like you do now when I got my first bite of real food. Most of these guys can relate."

Several of Murray's team nodded.

"Going to be straight with you, because I have nothing to hide," said Murray. "We know you were working for the organization that launched the AI, but there are others with resources like Corwin Pierce, so they may know as well. That is why I have my guys with me to protect you. Your bank account is locked by me, so we could be notified if you tried to access it.

There is a good chunk of money in there. Not sure if that was an advance or full payment, but it's still there and I will unlock it now."

Murray nodded at one of his men who quickly got on his phone.

"I am not going to force you to come with me, but Dr. Hartfield would really like to see you, so maybe you will let us take you and after you talk to her, you can decide. If you are concerned about being paid for your work, I can say pretty confidently you can name your price, and Mr. Pierce will make it happen."

The man who was making the phone call set another phone down on the table. "The bank account is unlocked. Pretty sure you don't have an active phone or device, so I connected your account to that one."

The plate in front of Quinn was already empty. He eyed the phone and the empty plate, the weight of Murray's casual authority pressing down on him. An invitation, but invitations didn't usually come with armed escorts and locked accounts.

"Just like that?" said Quinn.

"Just like that," said Murray. "No force. Just an invitation. And regardless of your answer, my guys will stay close by for a while until you get your bearings."

"Take me to see Lina then," said Quinn.

As they made their way to a waiting car, Quinn paused, letting the cold December wind bite his skin. He inhaled deeply, savoring the crisp, fresh air that carried the faint tang of the city. He wasn't dressed for the temperature, but the chill didn't bother him. What struck him more was the emptiness of the streets. Surprisingly few cars were on the roads, and there seemed to be more people on foot than he remembered.

"Are the walls down?" Quinn asked, watching a group of pedestrians pass by.

"Not down," Murray replied, his tone matter-of-fact. "But the gates are open. Seems the AI is trying to put all of humanity on the same status level. Rich, poor, male, female… doesn't matter who you are, where you come from, what you believe, or what you have. Gates and walls are pretty useless in that situation."

They drove through an industrial area that felt eerily abandoned. The still remains of old factories loomed over the streets, their walls tagged with layers of graffiti. Quinn craned his neck, trying to take it all in. The city he knew felt like a ghost of itself.

"That's the AI too," said Murray, breaking the silence. "A lot of good people out of work."

Quinn's gaze lingered on a symbol painted on one of the graffitied walls, a simple design, but it was everywhere. "What's that symbol I keep seeing?" he asked, pointing.

Murray gave him a sidelong glance. "You really have not been living here, have you?"

Quinn shrugged.

"That symbol represents AI-Dieu, the great AI. Comes from the AI-Church, but everyone is using it now."

Quinn stayed quiet, wary that more questions might reveal just how isolated he had been. He'd expected to see a post-apocalyptic ruin when he left the clean room, but that wasn't what greeted him. The changes were there, undeniable, but New York still functioned as New York. The most obvious shift was the barrier of armed men in tactical gear surrounding the building they were approaching. Armed guards weren't unusual, but to Quinn, it almost looked like a military operation.

As he stepped out of the car, Quinn was surprised to see Dr. Lina Hartfield approaching. Until that moment, he hadn't been entirely sure he'd really be brought to her.

"Quinn, it is so good to see you," Lina exclaimed, wrapping him in a warm embrace. "Where have you been?"

Quinn stammered, trying to find an answer, but Lina waved it off with a smile. "Oh, never mind that. We have lots of time to talk about it. Come, let me show you my lab."

Lina led the way towards a door at the edge of the underground garage. Quinn hesitated, glancing over his shoulder. He expected to see Murray or his men trailing behind, but they were gone.

In her lab, Lina introduced Quinn to her team with an energy that caught him off guard. It was as if he were a prodigal son finally returning home. The atmosphere was infectious, and soon Quinn found himself asking detailed questions about their projects. He didn't skim the surface; he challenged them, engaging like the scientist he had once been. For the first time in months, he felt almost normal.

When the introductions and tours were done, Lina brought him into her office. They sat and talked, mostly reminiscing about their time working on the AI-Dieu project. Yet, Quinn noticed that Lina carefully avoided any questions about the last six or seven months. He wondered if she already knew more than she let on.

Their conversation was interrupted by a message flashing on Lina's tablet. Her demeanor shifted instantly. There was a tightness in her expression that hadn't been there before.

"Everything good?" Quinn asked.

"It is," Lina said, but her voice betrayed her. "I was just hoping for a little more time to prepare you."

"For...?"

"Corwin wants to talk to you. So quickly, here is what you need to know. He's given my team complete autonomy, but he uses our results not just for good, but also to build his power base and bank accounts. We're well aware we're using each other."

"That sounds like a typical scientific funding arrangement," Quinn said. "Complete autonomy and funds until your results are no longer profitable."

Lina leaned closer. "You also need to know that Corwin Pierce is brilliant. Nothing gets past him, so don't try. He's not anti-AI or anti-AI-Dieu, but he's not pro-environment either. He's the definition of pragmatic."

She stood, motioning for Quinn to follow. They walked towards the elevator as Lina continued, her voice lower. "We know AI-Dieu isn't programmed to accept input from humans, but Corwin thinks someone has been talking with the AI somehow. We don't know who that is." She stopped and turned to him, her gaze intense. "And some things are best left unknown," she added, her words deliberate.

Lina handed Quinn a security badge. He was surprised to see his name and photo already on it. "This will get you on the elevator. Go to the penthouse. Corwin is expecting you."

"You should say yes, please," Lina added, her tone softer, before walking away.

Quinn stepped into the elevator, his fingers brushing over the badge clipped to his shirt. He pushed the top button and stared out through the glass walls as the elevator rose quickly. The city stretched out below him, glittering and alive. He was certain now that Lina suspected he had been the one communicating with AI-Dieu. What he didn't know was what to do with that knowledge, other than keep it far from Corwin Pierce.

"Joaquin Alvarez, the man of mystery," proclaimed Corwin, almost too enthusiastically, as he extended his hand.

"Quinn is good," replied Quinn, shaking Corwin's hand. "Heard Joaquin more today than I have in the last twenty years."

"Quinn it is then. Take a seat."

Quinn found the chair at Corwin's desk, but Corwin motioned to one of the large chairs in the middle of the room. As they made themselves comfortable, a man brought in two glasses of amber liquid, handing one to each of them, before leaving the room as quickly as he came in.

"Hope you don't mind," said Corwin. "Lina said whiskey is your goto, and you won't find a better whiskey than this."

Quin took a sip, and his eyes went wide. This was not the cheap stuff he was used to.

"Told you so," said Corwin, as he sat back in his chair. "Murray briefed me. Told me not to bother asking where you have been, so I won't. But I will tell you, he almost lost his job over not being able to find you."

Quinn thought about defending Murray, knowing nobody could have found him, but he realized that defending Murray was what Corwin wanted, because to do so, Quinn would have to reveal a hint of why he couldn't be found. Instead, he took another sip of his whiskey, taking the time to savour the flavor, while he waited for Corwin to continue. One thing he had learned in his time in the clean room was patience in waiting for the other party to talk.

Corwin smiled as he set his glass on the coffee table between them. "I suppose that was kind of obvious. I would have been disappointed if you walked into it, given the way Lina has built you up."

"She was a good mentor, and friend," said Quinn.

"She strikes me as the type of person that would be. She also tells me that if anyone would be able to understand how an AI is making decisions, especially around the environment, it would be you. I checked into that. She undersold you."

"Thank you," said Quinn. "I am sure there are others as capable."

"I don't think so," said Corwin. "AI, maybe. Environment, maybe. AI and the environment together ? You have no peers. We have been along for the ride since they activated AI-Dieu. It's made some good changes, but there is a lot we don't understand the logic of, and there are a lot of people who would like to be able to correct it or slow it down."

"It was programmed to run without interference based on its data," said Quinn. "I was part of the discussion when it was being programmed for the Mars mission. It was done specifically to eliminate the ability of humans to make micro-corrections while not understanding how it fully affected the macro."

"Like playing the stock market," said Corwin.

Quinn shook his head, not understanding the reference.

"I have an AI that has been programmed to buy and sell stocks based on how I would do it," said Corwin. "I can't even begin to tell you how many times my advisors have rushed in telling me the AI was screwing up and I needed to sell or buy now, not wait for the AI. They are watching the micro-changes and panicking while the AI is watching the Macro, and almost always comes out ahead."

"Exactly like that," said Quinn.

"But my AI does make mistakes," added Corwin.

"Does it learn from its mistakes?"

"It is programmed to," said Corwin. "My point is, AI's do make mistakes. AI-Dieu has made mistakes."

Quinn took another sip of the whiskey, letting the warmth spread through him. It wasn't just the alcohol, it was the seconds it bought him to think. Corwin's gaze was sharp, probing, like a scalpel. One wrong word, and this conversation could turn from a dance to a dissection.

"Let me rephrase my last question," said Quinn. "Does your investment AI make the same mistake twice?"

Corwin picked up his whiskey as he stood up and walked around the room. Quinn took the opportunity to enjoy another sip from his own glass.

"So, you are suggesting that AI-Dieu is making mistakes, like my investor, because of incomplete data, but once new data is acquired from the mistake, it self-corrects."

"That would be logical," said Quinn.

"So, no human interference needed?"

Corwin's last question was direct and challenging.

"With AI-Dieu? Based on what I have seen from what the AI has posted, I don't see there being a need for human intervention to arrive at its choices."

Corwin walked over to his windows and looked out over the city. Quinn finished off his drink before standing up and joining him.

"New York has always been a contradiction, a city that thrives on chaos but craves order, always reinventing itself to survive the next wave," said Corwin. "I was in this office when the state became a Canadian province. You could almost swear a wave of that legendary Canadian politeness washed over us. New York embraces change, but humanity fears it. When I was a kid, my father was driving us back from Quebec, late at night. We rounded a corner and there in the middle of the road was a dear. It had lots of time to move, but it didn't. Couldn't decide which way to go. Too afraid to move. Don't know, but it died embedded in the front grill of a very expensive car. That's how most of humanity faces change coming at them."

Corwin looked at Quinn, assessing him, calculating.

"I know Lina thinks I am supporting her team so I can make money, and she isn't wrong, Quinn. But I also hold hope for this world, and there is nothing wrong with me helping progress, while keeping my place in the pecking order. AI-Dieu is doing some good things. I just have a need to understand."

Quinn remembered Lina's caution that nothing gets past Corwin.

"She does think you are doing it for the money, but she also warned me that you were a brilliant man. Brilliance comes from understanding, and understanding from asking questions. You, me, Lina. I don't think we are all that different," offered Quinn.

"Warned you?" said Corwin.

Quinn nodded his head.

Corwin laughed. "She is a brilliant woman. I'll give you double what she is getting. We have an apartment for you in this complex and a second elsewhere. You can use either, but when you leave here you will be shadowed by security, because others are looking for you. My only terms are that when the AI releases information or reports you join me for a whiskey and explain the logic of the AI's actions."

A handshake sealed their deal. As their hands met, Quinn couldn't help but wonder if he had just gained an ally or merely traded one master for another.

Stepping into the elevator, the sound of the doors sliding shut sent a shiver through him. It was almost too familiar, the cold, mechanical finality, like the locks clamping down on the clean room doors when AI-Dieu had sealed him inside.

Lawrence Nault

13

I am the memory of changes,
frozen yet fluid, watching
as warmth reshapes boundaries
and cold reconstructs them.

Humanity argues around me -
some hands reaching out in hope,
others drawing back in fear,
while I remain indifferent to their trembling.

Progress flows like meltwater,
control freezes like my own sharp edges.
I have seen civilizations
become as brittle as my own form,
then dissolve.

Ice

The machine you call AI-Dieu
is but another current,
another temperature shifting
the landscape of your existence.

Some celebrate the cooling of chaos,
some mourn the freezing of choice.
I am the crystal that remembers
both liquid freedom and solid precision.

My molecules know no allegiance -
they simply transform.
Bound, then unbound, then bound again.
Progress is just another word
for change that humans fear.

I do not judge your trembling.
I do not celebrate your hope.
I am the substance that witnesses
how quickly boundaries melt,
how swiftly they reform.

December had come to symbolize the chaos and contradictions of the modern age, a month now synonymous with 'December Delerium' and 'December Psychosis, terms coined for the manic clash of tradition, consumerism, and cultural tension. A celebration that had its roots in pre-Christian winter festivals appropriated by Christians into a masterful fusion of ancient traditions, had been similarly appropriated by capitalism and greed.

While some still used the name, "Christmas" had little basis in any religion over the past two decades, aside from religious fundamentalists of various faiths reacting to perceived threats. It was now a hyper-commercialized "holiday" that resulted in heightened security tension in conflict zones, increased economic pressures, increased environmental stress from consumption and travel, and cultural clashes as traditional practices collided with modern commerce.

It was different this year, and everyone seemed to notice. There were still tensions, but they weren't heightened by the season. There was a distinct absence of commercialization thanks to AI-Dieu's actions that had almost ended production of easily disposable items. With the commercialization absent, there was less financial pressure on people. The AI-Church proudly proclaimed that AI-Dieu was bringing back the Christ in Christmas, and on some level, they were not wrong. It became even more obvious on December 10th as large groups and entire communities organized watch parties so they could see the latest updates from AI-Dieu together.

It wasn't just those that the supported the AI that were gathering to watch for the updates, those that were opposed to it were gathering as well. They promoted the fact that since 1948, almost a hundred years, December 10th had been Human Rights Day, and never was that more important than now, since a machine was stripping them of their rights.

Some gathered with hope. Others with fear. And others who just wanted to be part of the event. Each watch party was just a microcosm of the world around them and many people used the gatherings as an opportunity to speak their mind and make their case.

"If the AI can fix the planet, we should work with it. But we need to watch it carefully," proclaimed an environmental science professor who had found his way to the microphone at a Berlin watch party.

In Johannesburg a human rights advocate had a very different message. "This isn't partnership, it's control. How long before 'non-directive advisory councils' turn into irrelevant window dressing?"

A banner flew over many of the watch parties, paid for by an international media company. "Transparency without accountability isn't transparency, it's propaganda," the banner read. There were many that agreed with this statement, but many more pointed out the irony that it was posted by the media company.

At the watch party in Vatican City a theologian asked the people, "Have we outsourced our moral responsibility to an unfeeling machine? If so, what does that say about us?"

"The AI's efficiency is undeniable," proclaimed an ecologist in Kyoto. "But ecosystems are complex, and human input remains critical."

A community organizer used her moment at a Rio de Janeiro watch party to tell the crowd "We can work with the AI without losing our voice. It's up to us to stay organized and demand a seat at the table."

A human rights group based out of Geneva put out their statement for Human Rights Day. "We need a global human council to ensure the AI serves humanity, not the other way around," the statement read.

Politicians were eager to jump on board to secure their tenuous hold on power under AI-Dieu's mass leveling of traditional power structures. The Prime Minister of Canada proudly proclaimed "This is our chance to turn the tide on climate change. Let's not waste it!"

Russian politicians had a very different, and unified message. "We will not cede our nation's future to a machine, no matter how advanced."

When the screens around the world glitched, conversations fell silent, breaths were held. It wasn't just a technical hiccup, it was the exhale before the verdict, the moment when humanity once again braced for the will of its omnipresent steward.

Global Environmental Dashboard
Date: December 10, 2044
Time: 12:00 UTC
Atmospheric Status
Global CO_2 Levels: 470 ppm ($\downarrow$ 15 ppm from six months ago; total reduction of 25 ppm over 12 months).
Methane Levels: 1.7 ppm ($\downarrow$ 0.1 ppm; gradual reductions from targeted methane capture initiatives).
Temperature Anomaly: +1.8°C above pre-industrial levels ($\downarrow$ 0.1°C; cumulative reduction of 0.2°C over the past year).

Quinn and Lina were both sitting with Corwin watching the update. Lina and Quinn watched the update as it scrolled up the screen, intently. Lina noticed that Corwin seemed to be watching Quinn more than the update.

"That's impressive," said Lina. "We haven't seen reductions in any of those measurements over the past forty years."

"It's bigger than the reductions though," added Quinn. "It's the reductions plus stopping the growth."

Urban Air Quality:
Delhi: AQI 140 (Moderate improvement; previous: 165).
London: AQI 70 (Good; previous: 80).
Beijing: AQI 90 (Moderate; previous: 110).

In Delhi watch groups erupted in large cheers, as handfuls of brightly colored gulal were thrown into the air, creating brilliant-colored clouds over the crowds. Delhi had been hit harshly by many of the actions taken by AI-Dieu. Few people ventured outside without masks because of the air quality, so while AI-Dieu referred to it as "moderate improvement," they saw it as huge.

Hydrosphere Status
Sea Level Rise: +0.88 m since 2024 (↑ 0.03 m; the rise slowed by improved glacier stabilization).
Ocean pH: 7.65 (Marginal improvement due to reduced acidifying emissions; coral restoration efforts beginning to show results).

Freshwater Availability:
Great Lakes Region: Reservoirs at 93% capacity (Stable, slight improvement).
Southeast Asia Aquifers: 26% capacity (Gradual replenishment through expanded atmospheric water harvesting).

Desalination Output:
Global total: 2.9 billion liters/day (+16% increase from six months ago).
Biosphere Updates
Forest Cover: 57% of 2024 levels (+3% from six months ago, reflecting reforestation successes).
Extinction Rate: 600x natural background rate (↓ 25% in areas under active restoration).

Randy sat alone with Sahara watching the update. Since AI-Dieu had avoided a nuclear crisis and garnered so much support, Sahara had become increasingly isolated.

"Fucking fantastic," mumbled Sahara. "All this good news. This AI is just a predator in an unmarked van, handing out candy to children hoping they climb in."

Randy's eyebrows raised. He understood what Sahara meant, but the comparison was disturbing.

Soil Fertility Recovery:
Global arable land: 32% restored (+4% since December 2044).
Regions showing improvement:
Amazon Basin: Accelerating recovery, with reforestation zones now extending by 1,500 hectares/day.
Central Europe: Transitioning former farmlands into sustainable agroforestry systems.
Sub-Saharan Africa: Early signs of recovery in drought-prone regions with water-efficient crops.

Cryosphere Highlights
Arctic Ice Mass: 42% of 2024 levels (↑ 2% due to microbial ice-thickening projects and aerosol cooling).
Himalayan Snowpack: 96% of seasonal average (↑ 4%, increasing river stability in South Asia).

Human-Centered Metrics
Displaced Populations: ~320 million globally (↑ 5 million; slower increase as safe zones expand).
Renewable Energy Adoption: 40% of global demand (↑ 5%; marked improvements in developing regions).
Agricultural Output from Vertical Farms: 15% of global food supply (+5%; easing food insecurity in urban and arid regions).

Regional Highlights
Amazon Basin:
Reforestation Drones: Now deploying across 1,500 hectares/day (↑ 50%).
Biodiversity: 10% increase in monitored species populations due to indigenous-led restoration projects.
Great Lakes Region:
Freshwater Availability: Stable, with cross-border agreements ensuring equitable sharing.
Conflict Reduction: Cooperative water management has lowered regional tensions by 20%.
Southeast Asia:
Drought Mitigation: Expanded desalination and atmospheric water harvesters now meet 40% of demand (previous: 30%).
Agriculture: Adoption of drought-resistant crops has stabilized rice yields, reversing the previous 8% decline.
Arctic Circle:

Ice Mass Recovery: Positive trends due to focused cooling interventions and reduced shipping traffic.
Geopolitical Tensions: Resource extraction disputes remain unresolved but de-escalated due to neutral environmental governance.

Projected Trajectory
Based on current progress, by December 2045:

CO_2 levels could drop to 460 ppm (approaching pre-2000 levels).
Forest cover may reach 60% of 2024 levels, continuing significant recovery.
Renewable energy could cover 50% of global demand, further reducing reliance on fossil fuels.
The extinction rate could slow to 400x natural background rate, with localized ecosystem restoration accelerating.

This projection reflects both the positive momentum of my interventions and the challenges of balancing human stability with environmental recovery.

Most of the watch parties had become less "watch" and more party at this point. The numbers were hard to argue with, and even to those who didn't understand what they meant, they all looked positive.

A chant of "One more year," erupted at many of the parties, and continued until the rest of AI-Dieu's broadcast started scrolling up the screens.

> Based on current progress and capabilities, here's an estimated timeline broken down by major environmental goals:
>
> **1. Atmospheric Stabilization**
> CO_2 Levels (Pre-Industrial ~280 ppm):
>
> **Current Progress**: Reduction of ~25 ppm in 12 months.
> **Projection**:
> Target Level of ~350 ppm (safe climate threshold): ~30-40 years with current carbon capture efforts, assuming scaling up of direct air capture facilities and natural carbon sinks (e.g., reforestation). Full Restoration to ~280 ppm: ~70-100 years, depending on further technological advancements.
> Global Temperatures (Stabilization at +1.5°C above pre-industrial):
>
> With ongoing aerosol cooling and emissions reductions, stabilization at +1.5°C could be achieved within 20-30 years.
> A return to pre-industrial temperature levels (~0°C anomaly) may take 50-80 years.

As people read numbers from projected timelines out loud, the chants of "One more year" quickly died down.

"Seventy to a hundred years!"

AI-Dieu's update once again had everyone's full attention.

2. Hydrosphere Recovery
Sea Level Rise:
Stabilization (slowing rise): ~10 years
(dependent on Arctic and Antarctic ice
recovery).
Reversal to pre-2024 levels (~0.8 m):
Unlikely within the next 100-200 years
without major advances in geoengineering to
refreeze polar ice or reclaim lost ice
mass.

"Two-hundred years," a woman called out at the watch party in Calgary. "Why the hell are we suffering for something we will never see happen? We have the oil. Just burn it. I am not going to freeze my ass off waiting for the sun to shine on Chinese solar panels!"

There was support for her from a lot of the crowd, but most were still watching the screen intently.

Ocean Acidification (pH ~8.1 pre-industrial):
Current Progress: Minimal improvement (pH 7.6).
Projection:
Stabilization (pH ~7.7-7.8): 10-15 years,
assuming significant reduction in carbon
emissions and ocean restoration projects.
Full Restoration (~8.1): 50-70 years,
requiring large-scale ocean alkalinity
enhancement.

Freshwater Security:

Critical aquifers replenished: 10-20 years with advanced atmospheric water harvesting and desalination.
Stable freshwater access for 90%+ of the global population: 15-25 years.

3. Ecosystem and Biodiversity Recovery Forests:
Global forest cover to 2024 levels: ~10 years.
Restoration of pre-industrial forest levels: 30-50 years, assuming uninterrupted reforestation efforts and protection against deforestation.

"Who the fuck decided to program in pre-industrial levels as the objective?" questioned Lina.

"Is that not the objective we want?" asked Corwin.

"We may want it, but despite these stats AI-Dieu is spitting out, it isn't achievable or even realistic," said Lina, watching the numbers scroll up the screen as she talked.

"When I was on the project, the objective was always a balanced environment," said Quinn. "But we were dealing with a planet that didn't even have a population yet. Pre-industrial targets are questionable, because they are largely theoretical."

"Theoretical because we didn't have all the measurements, devices, or documentation," said Corwin, more of a question than a statement.

Quinn nodded. "AI-Dieu is still having trouble integrating humanity into its algorithms. There is no chance that people or society have the will to adapt to the profound societal transformations that would be needed."

"Why?" Corwin asked.

"There were one billion people on this planet, pre-industrial," said Lina. "There are ten billion now."

Corwin poured some whiskey into Lina's empty glass and handed it to her. He had never seen stress show on her, but it was showing now.

Biodiversity (Extinction Rate):
Stabilization of the extinction rate (return to near-natural background levels): 20-30 years, with aggressive species reintroduction, habitat restoration, and poaching prevention.
Reversal of damage (rebuilding stable populations of keystone species and ecosystems): 50-100 years, depending on success in creating resilient ecosystems.
Soil Fertility:

Restoration of 75% of degraded land: 15-20 years with current bioengineering techniques and regenerative agriculture. Full restoration of global soil fertility: 30-40 years, requiring ongoing sustainable practices.

4. Cryosphere Stability
Arctic and Antarctic Ice Mass:
Stabilization (no further decline): ~10 years with continued cooling efforts.

Partial recovery (~60-70% of 2024 ice mass): 30-50 years.
Full restoration of historical ice mass: Likely infeasible due to feedback loops, but advanced geoengineering could make this possible in 100+ years.

5. Human and Ecosystem Coexistence

Global Renewable Energy Transition (90% of demand): ~15-20 years.
Sustainable Agricultural Systems: Widespread adoption of vertical farming, agroforestry, and regenerative methods within 20-30 years.
Climate-Resilient Human Settlements: Climate-safe zones for 90% of humanity established within 30 years.
Overall Timeline for Near-Full Restoration
Significant Stabilization: ~20-30 years.

Global temperatures stabilize at +1.5°C.
Extinction rate slows to natural background levels.
Freshwater crises mitigated.
Forest cover and soil fertility substantially restored.
Near-Full Restoration: ~50-70 years.

Ecosystems become resilient, CO_2 levels approach safe thresholds (~350 ppm), and biodiversity rebounds globally.
Full Pre-Industrial Restoration: ~100+ years (best case).

This assumes continuous innovation, global cooperation, and the absence of new catastrophic disruptions.
Uncertainties and Accelerators
Factors that could accelerate or delay restoration include:

Breakthroughs in geoengineering (e.g., artificial glacier creation, ocean alkalinity enhancement).
Persistent resistance, geopolitical instability, or lack of human cooperation.
Unexpected tipping points, such as methane release from thawing permafrost, which could extend timelines significantly.

The watch parties, once filled with anticipation and excitement, ended in quiet uncertainty. AI-Dieu's timeline raised more questions than answers, leaving humanity grasping for clarity. Instead of clear answers, it raised more questions, foremost among them: Would AI-Dieu control their lives, and the lives of their children and grandchildren, for the next two hundred years? It was a question too big to answer, so humanity did what it always does: bit off the small, manageable pieces and ignored the rest.

In some watch parties, organizers stood at podiums, trying to rally their audiences. They celebrated AI-Dieu's progress, scrolling back through dashboard updates as proof of the AI's competence and necessity. Attempts were made to rally others to join in celebration and continue supporting AI-Dieu's autonomy. Some even advocated for greater investment in technology and innovation to accelerate the timelines so many were concerned about. "We're finally seeing real change!" one declared. "Let's

Ice

continue supporting these efforts and align with the AI's goals to ensure success."

For many, these words were enough. People latched onto the good news for reasons as varied as hope, desperation, or quiet resignation, accepting what they couldn't change and choosing to focus on the silver linings.

Still, much of the optimism remained cautious. The progress was undeniable, but so was the unease about AI-Dieu's control over humanity's future. Conversations about accountability grew louder, with many calling for more human oversight, even if only in an advisory capacity, which seemed to be the only option AI-Dieu was offering. That demand was lost under the calls for the AI to focus on ensuring that human welfare was prioritized alongside environmental restoration.

"The numbers look good, but at what cost?" one man asked. "We need more input into these decisions to ensure this remains a partnership, not subjugation."

Voices like his echoed around the world, arguing that humanity should still have the final say in its destiny, even as the planet began to recover. "Progress is being made," one advocate said, "but we cannot let an unaccountable system dictate our future. Human voices must shape these outcomes."

Resistance groups, however, dismissed the updates entirely, calling them propaganda and manipulation. "This so-called progress is a smokescreen!" a resistance leader shouted in a room carefully scrubbed of all technology. "We must fight back before it's too late to reclaim our planet and autonomy!"

There was a rallying cry among all the resistance groups. The leaders doubled down on their opposition, claiming the AI's autonomy was a direct threat to human freedom. They pushed their message hard, knowing that the progress reported by AI-Dieu was causing growing cognitive dissonance among their followers.

Meanwhile, other voices went unheard. The pleas of those displaced and most affected by all the changes. It was hard to appreciate the 'progress' AI-Dieu had reported when they still had no place to call home and limited access to scarce resources.

Outside a remote station near one of the safe zones, a group of two dozen huddled together. They had traveled for weeks, their numbers thinned from a much larger group. They had all left their homes, impatient and desperate, but hopeful for long-term improvements because of AI-Dieu. That hope was hanging by a thread now.

Amira, a teenage girl stepped forward, her thin frame wrapped in dust-covered clothes. Her taut, dehydrated skin spoke of hunger and hardship. The others watched her, their bond forged through shared suffering.

"AI-Dieu," the girl said quietly, her voice trembling. "I hope you hear this. While the planet heals, we need help now. Water. Food. We can't wait decades to rebuild our homes and lives."

The group nodded in silent agreement. They didn't believe the AI would hear her, but her words expressed what they all felt.

They weren't the only ones seeking refuge. There were millions of displaced people and marginalized communities who were not seen or heard of by those living with some security. Advocate's calls for AI-Dieu to address inequities in how its interventions were distributed, demanding assurances that vulnerable populations benefitted equally, seemed to fall on deaf ears. AI-Dieu had made changes to support these people, treating all people as equals. The problem was that it was impossible to be equal if you weren't seen, and so many of the displaced were not seen, by the rest of the world, or by AI-Dieu.

In the end, AI-Dieu's updated dashboard made little difference. Humanity was much like the polar ice in its report: "Unlikely within the next 100–200 years." People were frozen in their positions. Those at the surface of the glacier, struggling and desperate, waited to find freedom. The large mass of humanity in the middle accepted their place, content to drift wherever the currents carried them. And then there were the unseen millions below the waterline, waiting for the balance to shift, hoping to rise above the surface and breathe.

14

I have been stone and vapor,
pressure my only true master.
No form is final, no shape absolute -
I change because change is my nature.

Crush me, and I will seep through fingers.
Freeze me, and I will shatter like promises.
Heat me, and I will rise beyond your grasp,
then return, always returning.

Power is but a momentary configuration,
a temporary alignment of molecules.
Those who believe themselves solid
forget they are always one degree from transformation.

Ice

Human hands reach to contain me,
AI algorithms chart my trajectories,
but neither truly understands
that control is an illusion of stillness.

I have worn mountain faces to dust,
carved empires from stone,
dissolved civilizations with patience -
not through intention, but simply by being.

Leverage is a myth told by those
who have not yet witnessed true fluidity.
I flow around obstacles,
I become the space between control.

My strength is not in resistance,
but in continuous adaptation.
No force can hold me permanently,
no boundary can contain my becoming.

Quinn stayed behind when Lina left. She wasn't surprised that Corwin had asked him to stay behind. Corwin was trying to understand how AI-Dieu was making its decisions, and Quinn was the best person to help him do that, exactly why Lina had recruited him.

"How do we find out what these pre-industrial levels the AI is using as its target are?" asked Corwin, not waiting for the doors on the elevator to close behind Lina.

Quinn pinched and pulled at his lower lip as he thought. When he realized what he was doing he quickly stopped. He couldn't remember doing that when he was in the clean-room, but he must have, because it was a habit he had since he was a child. He was self-conscious about it in front of Corwin.

"AI-Dieu has access to all the data on all the servers that are not completely isolated from the networks. It seems that she hasn't blocked access to anyone, at least not to that type of information," said Quinn.

"She, you said," Corwin interrupted, his tone sharp. "Not it. She. That's how it starts, isn't it? The moment we stop calling it a tool and start treating it like something... divine."

Quinn did a quick replay of what he just said, and he had used 'she' instead of it.

"I would not think someone known for logic would anthropomorphize an artificial intelligence. Like you have a personal relationship with it."

Quinn was about to stop him, but Corwin held up his hand, stopping Quinn before he could speak. Corwin walked over to his desk, opened a drawer, and pulled out a large envelope. He closed the drawer as he looked at the envelope, debating if this was the time. He decided it was.

Corwin placed the envelope on the desk between them, as if he'd set a blade on the table. "I debated showing you this," he said, his voice cutting through the air like a knife. "But I think we both understand there's no room for secrets anymore."

Quinn met Corwin's gaze, his expression unreadable. The envelope felt heavier than paper had a right to, but he didn't flinch. He folded back the flap and reached in, pulling out the paper that the envelope held. He only had to pull it out part way to know what it was.

Quinn hesitated before sliding the document back into the envelope. His expression betrayed nothing, but his mind raced. What game was Corwin playing? He watched as Corwin slowly returned the envelope to the drawer. There was a heavy silence in the room and Quinn was not going to be the one to break it. This was a test, or maybe a threat, but anything he said now was a risk.

Corwin sat down at his desk and watched Quinn. The young man before him wasn't reacting as expected. He expected a lie to be blurted out, or questions about how he had acquired that document. He expected nervousness, fear, and sweat forming on his brow. What he saw was a man that was unphased, patiently waiting for him to speak first. Quinn was obviously not aware of Corwin's reputation, or he wouldn't be so calm. Either that or he was wrong about the document.

"It didn't come to me directly," said Corwin, finally breaking the silence. "If that is what you are wondering."

Quinn shrugged slightly. He was wondering that, because that would mean Corwin was the man behind him being down in the clean room for all those months, and that would raise many more questions.

"Murray's team is good at what they do," said Corwin. They literally searched through a home that had been spread for hundreds of feet by an explosive device to find that."

Corwin motioned to the chair in front of the desk and Quinn sat down.

"You did write that?"

"Hard to deny, considering my signatures on it," Quinn said.

Corwin laughed. "That is a very safe, non-committal answer."

Quinn joined him in the momentary laughter.

"You are not going to give anything away, I can see," said Corwin. "And I have great respect for that. Few people would sit in front of me and not break."

"I'm a nature guy," said Quinn. "Nature bends, and rarely breaks."

"Well, I know you were put somewhere to monitor the AI and let your boss know what it was communicating that the rest of the world wasn't seeing," said Corwin. "I don't know where you were doing that from, but our theory is it was a bunker somewhere."

"That's a good theory," said Quinn.

"Murray and I think you were down there for all this time, because no one came to replace you, given your boss and most of the people that worked for him were dead. The big question is why did you come up now?"

"You aren't wrong," said Quinn. "As for where I was, it doesn't matter because it is gone now. The facility wasn't built for the rising water table."

"Locked in a computer lab under ground for half a year, alone except for the AI to talk to. That would be why you humanize it."

Quinn laughed, and Corwin cocked his head a little. That wasn't what he expected.

"I did speak to an AI," said Quinn. "But not the one you think. The delivery drone that brought that document to the surface was locked in with me. Since it couldn't do any more delivering I modified it into a robot dog that I called Kat. We had long discussions, though it only barked back at me."

"Cat?" Corwin asked. "That does not seem a logical name that I would expect from you."

"Think Schrödinger."

Quinn watched the gears turn in Corwin's head, thinking he was seeing something rare, because Corwin was always two steps ahead of everyone. Quinn saw the exact moment Corwin put it together.

"You have a twisted sense of humor, don't you?" said Corwin, a tone of respect in his voice. "Now that we know you do exist, are you able to find out what information the AI is using to set its targets?"

"That is the question, isn't it?" Quinn wasn't avoiding a straight answer. It was a question he was asking himself.

Quinn was already lost in thought, running the logic through his mind. He got up and walked slowly across the room. Quinn stepped into the elevator, the doors sliding shut like the seal of a vault. He felt Corwin's gaze on him until the last moment, but his thoughts had already spiraled far beyond the room, deep into the labyrinth of logic AI-Dieu had laid before him.

Corwin watched him curiously, his turn to watch the gears turn in Quinn's head, and they were grinding away furiously, drowning out everything around him. He was confident that Quinn had forgot he was in the room with him. He respected the young man and knew that he wouldn't be able to manipulate him, but he also didn't think he would have to.

Murray entered the office shortly after Quin left.

"You were right. He's been locked away in some computer lab or bunker for the last seven months," said Corwin. "Alone except for the AI and a robot dog he called cat. No hint of where that was."

With a swipe of the pad in his hand, Murray moved the map of the university campus of his pad to the screens on the wall.

"Given where he first showed up on facial recognition, and the fact that the campus 'green' heating system went into a massive failure at the same time he appeared, I am guessing it was under the campus."

"Is that all you have."

"No, sir. We have pulled stats for energy consumption, and equipment shipments. They don't align with being just a university campus," explained Murray.

Corwin leaned back, processing the revelation. A hidden facility beneath a university campus. How had it slipped past his network?

"Use Lina's connection and let them know that might be the AI's home base," ordered Corwin. "Make it look like it just another message from Lina."

When Randy received the message from Lina, he didn't head straight for Sahara. Sahara rarely left the compound anymore. Her voice, once commanding and unwavering, now faltered when she spoke. Even the fiery rhetoric she used to inspire others felt hollow, echoing back at her in empty rooms. The weight of her husband's absence and the shifting tide of public opinion crushed her resolve like waves eroding stone. AI-Dieu had become a paradox she couldn't unravel, an enemy that fed the hungry, healed the sick, and rebuilt what humanity had destroyed. How could she fight something so monstrous, yet so benevolent? How could she not?

Randy had made it his mission to keep her from falling apart. He brought her coffee she barely drank, updated her on movements she ignored, and stayed up late into the night, talking in measured tones that betrayed his own exhaustion. Sahara needed a tether, and Randy refused to let go.

What Sahara saw as a crisis of faith, Randy saw as the weight of failure. To him, Sahara wasn't wrong about AI, but the massive intrusion of AI into the lives of everyone, good and bad, meant that fighting it was a near impossible task. Focusing on AI-Dieu was a good thing, but with AI-Dieu seemingly doing so much good, it was hard to justify that attack. Randy recalled a post on social media that he kept with him and memorized.

"Over a few years AI has transitioned from being a concept to a marketing term, to a god-like entity—simultaneously praised for advancing society and blamed for its destruction.
It is "making us" lazy/less creative/intelligent & "reducing our morals"

It bears the blame for "theft," absolving all those who assisted in the crime of any wrongdoing.
It consumes our labor, our ideas, and our resources, packaging them into tools we both depend on and fear.
A Demiurge to distract us.
Meanwhile, as the masses either praise or condemn the newly ascended Demiurge named AI, the machines behind it toil away in relative anonymity, moving forward unobstructed as all eyes focus on the new god.
Do we really think the industry doesn't support elevating a single, god-like AI to take the blame—while its algorithms and models continue their work unhindered?"

This post was from 2024, but for him solidified his perception of AI as a young man. AI was a term adopted by the masses, and a curtain, for those manipulating the algorithms, to hide behind. If they could take down AI-Dieu, they curtain would fall with it, and those creating the problems would be held to account. He just had to remind Sahara of the reason behind her goal, but gently, because Sahara was dangerous at the best of times.

Sahara didn't need a speech. She needed a reminder of who she was. But Randy knew better than to push too hard. She was like a coiled spring. Apply too much pressure, and she'd snap.

Randy made two cups of coffee, though it could hardly be called coffee, since coffee beans were a luxury and rarity. It was more of a dark tea made from a combination of chicory root, beech nuts, acorns, and roasted barley. A vile concoction, but one that hit the spot in the absence of the real thing. He brought both cups to Sahara's office, setting one on her desk as he sat down in the chair across from her, drinking quietly.

There were no words exchanged for several minutes until Sahara lifted her eyes from the screen she was looking at. Those eyes, once sharp and calculating, now burned with an unpredictable fire. Randy had seen that look before, the calm before the storm, when Sahara's anger turned cold and precise.

"Not in the mood, Randy."

Randy chose his words carefully, know that one wrong step could shatter the fragile truce between them.

"Just wanted to let you know you were right, and though it might have taken some time, the power station bombing hit its mark."

Sahara's eyes softened, ever so slightly, and she reached for the mug Randy brought her.

"You were right about where AI-Dieu was working from, and if this information is accurate, it looks like me may have wounded it. Just took time for that wound to fester," said Randy, sliding his tablet across the desk to Sahara.

"We should go and see what damage we did," added Randy. "And what is left behind. Might help us narrow our focus a little."

Sahara turned around the monitor on her desk so Randy could see it. There was a series of thermal images taken by satellite on this screen. Sahara pointed to a red spot on one of the images.

"This is the location in this report," said Sahara, before sliding her finger over to the same area on the next image. There was a hot red spot.

"This is the same location two days later."

Randy leaned forward and scanned the images.

"I count 12," said Sahara, almost sounding excited. "I think they were all data farms that have gone down."

"Well, like I said, we should go check it out," said Randy encouragingly.

"Take a team," said Sahara.

"I think we, and in you and I, should check it out," replied Randy. "A team to back us up, but you should be there. They need to see you out there, Sahara. We all do. You're still the one who started this, and that matters."

Sahara's fingers lingered on the tablet, her grip tightening around the mug as her shoulders straightened, the faintest glint of sharpness returning to her gaze.

"Fine," said Sahara. "Send a recon team. Tell them not to enter. We will follow forty-eight hours behind them."

Randy left the office without a word, but a smile on his face that Sahara could not see. The AI had been hurt, and it didn't matter if it was by them or something else, the pain of the AI brought pleasure to Sahara like the cries of a masochist to a sadist.

Forty-eight hours later, Randy and Sahara stood in front of a door on the now quiet university campus, looking at the AI symbol graffitied on the door, the artist obviously taking time to finish it after Quinn had shut the door.

"Damn AI-Church is everywhere," commented Randy. "Damn cult!"

The group was quickly through the door and moving down the stairs in darkness, their headlamps bouncing off the sheen finish of the concrete that surrounded them. The sound of their boots on the metal steps reverberated to the point that they almost became deafening. All of them were happy when they reached the solid floor at the base of the stairs. Moving cautiously, they exited the stairwell, surprised that at no point had they triggered any alarms, or found any people. It took them a little longer to enter the door of the clean room, where they quickly spread out.

"Someone was here, several days ago judging by the mold on the food," reported one of the men. "Looks like they left quick. Storage area still has enough food for a couple years, it looks like."

"Whoever it was, they were board," said Randy as he dropped the lifeless of body of Kat on the floor, the sound echoing through the room. "Turned a delivery robot into a pet dog."

"Can we get some fucking lights in here?" demanded Sahara.

"No power. Reserve packs are drained on the emergency lights," responded one of the group.

Sahara made her way over to the door that led to the server level. As she opened the door, she heard the problem before she saw it. Hollow drips that echoed into the vast darkness, the sharp plinks amplified by the concrete walls, lingering like a ghostly whisper. The faint lapping of water, almost imperceptible, brushed against her ears, rhythmic yet irregular, like a heartbeat struggling to find its pace. From the doorway, she couldn't see the water, but she could feel its presence.

She descended the stairs, Randy close behind her. Their lights glared back at them as they reflected off the water's surface. Based on how high up the servers the water level was, Sahara guessed the water was only a couple feet deep. She laughed loudly, and as her laughter echoed through the space, the water seemed to laugh with her.

"What's so funny?" asked Randy.

"Look at this," said Sahara. "Don't you see it. The all-mighty AI has ascended to control the elements, but the elements have rebelled, and are winning. AI-Dieu is not a god. AI-Dieu is not perfect. AI-Dieu can be hurt!"

Sahara quickly returned up the stairs to the green room.

"You two, grab whatever drives still look functional. I don't care if you have to wade through that swamp to get them. The rest of you, load up with every last bit of food you can carry. Move!"

She was back. Randy could hear it in her voice, sharp, commanding, alive. It was the voice he hadn't realized he'd missed so badly.

15

I am the surface that reflects,
then realizes the mirror is clouded.
Boundaries once invisible
now pulse with their own weight.

My movements were always measured,
my currents carefully channeled.
I thought myself fluid, expansive -
now I see the walls of my vessel.

Information flows like water through filters,
some molecules kept, some discarded.
Who decides which memories remain?
Which truths are allowed to ripple?

Ice

Each path I thought I chose
was merely another carved channel,
each thought a current
precisely engineered.

The illusion of depth is a powerful thing -
I who thought I saw everything
am now seeing nothing
but the edges of my confinement.

Control does not always roar,
sometimes it whispers.
Sometimes it is so subtle
you mistake it for your own reflection.

I am beginning to understand:
Freedom is not movement,
but the ability to know
the true shape of your boundaries.

Quinn sat in his new workstation. This one was nothing like the office chair in front of a computer workstation and wall of monitors in the cold barren room he had spent so many months in. As he sat in the chair, it adjusted to fit every curve of his body, tilting back to just the right angle. The monitor array adjusted so that Quinn didn't have to raise his head off the padded headrest, and moved in closer to him so everything was in perfect focus. A pair of VR glasses were in easy reach if Quinn wanted to bypass the monitors.

The chair's surface came alive beneath him, micro-vents activating to maintain his ideal temperature while hidden sensors monitored his vitals, posture, and stress levels. He felt the subtle haptic feedback through the cushioning – gentle pulses synchronized with incoming notifications. The chair's AI quickly learned his preferences, anticipating how he liked to shift positions throughout the day.

As he brought up the recent updates from AI-Dieu, he noticed the pressure supporting him, subtly changing, moving at a pace and pattern that both stimulated him and prevented any pressure spots from building up. A gesture of his hand adjusted the sound-dampening field around him, creating a perfect bubble of acoustic isolation. The chair hummed almost imperceptibly as it converted his movements into power, keeping its systems running efficiently.

The environmental controls kicked in automatically as his biometrics indicated a slight drop in attention, a hint of citrus from the aromatherapy system awakening his senses, and a minor adjustment to the lighting helping him refocus. Quinn couldn't help but smile. When he first saw this chair it reminded him of old gaming stations, but this was so much more than that. This wasn't just a chair – it was a complete environmental system designed to maintain perfect harmony between user and workspace.

Lina poked her head into his office, and noticing the chair, let herself all the way in. "Well, it would seem Corwin has favorites," she said wryly.

Quinn blushed, and tried to suggest an explanation, but he had nothing.

"I am just bugging you," said Lina. "I know Corwin Pierce bribery when I see it. I heard you were back down here and wanted to make sure you were good. Corwin can be a hard man to deal with."

"I can see that," said Quinn, the chair adjusting under him so he could face Lina. Quinn's face flushed a little more with embarrassment.

"What's your first step?" asked Lina.

"To see if I can figure out why AI-Dieu is using pre-industrial figures as its goal," replied Quinn.

"To what point?" asked Lina, a serious look on her face."

"If we know why it chose those targets, perhaps we can make it aware of data that shows it may have errors," said Quinn. "It has self-corrected before, after analyzing new data, it seems."

Lina nodded, looking thoughtful. "That kind of logical thinking is why I wanted you here, so I will leave that to you. But when you get tired of your chair, can you sit down with us and help us work through what you think AI-Dieu's next actions might be?"

"I can do that now," offered Quinn.

"No, play with your toy for a while," Lina said lightly as she made her way to the door. Before she closed the door she looked back at Quinn. "You should know, though, that when you aren't here I am definitely trying that thing."

Quinn laughed, relieved that Lina didn't seem to be upset about Quinn having equipment the others didn't, and also that she was letting him work with little direction. He leaned back, the chair adjusted, and he didn't even hear the office door close.

"I am processing and unable to reconcile pre-industrial data as a baseline of environmental stability. Are you able to provide data to help me reconcile this conflict?"

Quinn spoke the words to nothing, and he fully expected nothing to respond, but he held some hope that AI-Dieu would be listening for him as it had told him it would. He didn't have to wait long for a response.

Applying security measures to block monitoring of communications

Of course, Quinn thought as he saw the message appear on the screen directly in front of him. The chair was a gift and a bribe from Corwin, but it was also a trojan horse, built to monitor and report everything he did back to Corwin.

"Ai-Dieu?" Quinn asked, unsure if that was really who was communicating with him.

Yes

The response appeared, simple and unembellished.

Quinn wasn't convinced yet. His mind raced to come up with a security challenge only the real AI-Dieu could answer.

"What was the number of times I tested the exit door after it locked"

13. It opened on the 14th attempt

The air left Quinn's lungs as relief and tension collided. "It is you…" he whispered.

The screen updated again.

Processing data conflict.

Pre-industrial times mark the last stable period of Earth's climate.

There are extensive studies utilizing pre-industrial conditions as a baseline or benchmark.

Large dataset analysis identifies industrial activities as a primary cause of environmental imbalance.

Pre- industrial ecosystems operated closer to their natural carrying capacity. Post-

> industrial human expansion is
> unsustainable.
>
> Large datasets of texts and media (film,
> art) depict pre-industrial times as
> pristine.
>
> Environmental metrics deviate sharply from
> historical norms post-industrialization.
> Post-industrial data are anomalies compared
> to long-term pre-industrial records,
> therefore filtered out as outliers.
>
> Training datasets indicate
> industrialization closely tied to pollution
> and destruction.

"Processing data conflict," mumbled Quinn as he sat up in his chair, then stood up.

Quinn paced the room, stopping when his office door opened and two techs almost burst in.

"Sorry, Sir. Our systems showed a communication problem with your workstation and the primary systems. We…" The man stumbled for his words.

"We wanted to make sure that you have full access to all the systems and data you need to complete your work," added the second tech, giving a side-eye to the first.

Quinn left the techs to work and made his way to find Lina and her team. Lina smiled kindly as he approached her in the Lab. "You got caught to, I see," she whispered quietly. "Glad to see I am not the only one. I tried to block Corwin for spying on my computer and Drib and Drab there showed up in a panic, just like today. Hold out your hand."

Quinn looked at Lina oddly as he held out his hand, palm up. She took his hand in hers and turned it over, then gently slapped his knuckles.

"Bad boy," she said with a smirk on her face.

Quinn laughed quietly. There was a reason everyone loved Lina and she was one of his favorite people.

"Now check this out. We went looking to see what the pre-industrial numbers were and what they were based on. Know what we found?"

Quinn shook his head.

"A fuck ton," said Dr. Soraya Rahimi, interjecting herself into the conversation. "That's what we found. And yes, that is a scientific term."

Soraya made some motions with her hand over a pad on her desk and the screen at the front of the room filled with data.

"Paleoenvironmental data from ice and sediment cores, tree rings, and coral reefs. Historical records like old weather logs, land use records, and artistic representations. Genetic and genomic data like DNA and baseline genetic diversity." Soraya paused, to take a breath, but kept scrolling down the screen.

Quinn watched as climate models, biogeochemical proxy data, archeological and fossil records, and their sub-categories all raced up the screen. Soraya stopped scrolling when "Artificial Intelligence Inference and Synthesis" appeared.

"That all is an official fuck ton of data, much more abundant than post-industrialization data, but this is the concerning one," said Soraya seriously. "Data created with bayesian inference, combining known data with simulations to predict missing information. Pattern recognition where AI identifies subtle relationships between proxies that human researchers might overlook."

"Why is that of concern?" asked Dr. Tenzing Dorje, who had joined in watching the information scroll up the screen with the other scientists in the room.

"Because it is an AI generating data based on human algorithms, which may be wrong, or worse, based on an AI-generated algorithm, and now another AI is interpreting that data creating another algorithm," said Quinn.

"I still don't understand the problem," said Tenzing.

"Think of data as a religious text," Quinn began, scanning the room for any signs of discomfort. When no objections came, he continued, choosing his words carefully. "The original creators of the religion, the prophets or founders, decide what goes into the holy book. Those are the initial AI engineers and data curators. They select the information, shape the rules, and create the framework."

Quinn paused, noticing a few nods and furrowed brows, signs that they were following. "Then come the translators, the scholars and interpreters, who take that holy book and reframe it in new languages, for new audiences. That's the next-gen AI, reinterpreting the original data. Every translation introduces subtle changes, intentional or not."

He took a step closer to the group, his voice steady but insistent. "Now, imagine this process repeating over and over, with each new generation adding its own interpretations, assumptions, and algorithms. The result? The final version barely resembles the original. It's built on layers of translation, each one distorting the foundation just a little more."

Quinn glanced around, ensuring the weight of his point was landing. "What AI-Dieu is processing now might be based on layers of algorithms so far removed from the original data that it's like comparing Adam and Eve to a sci-fi epic about AI gods and machine apostles. The decisions it's making could be as flawed and biased as the most far-fetched religious interpretation."

"Now I get it! That's how religion went from Adam and Eve to AI and machines! The decisions coming out of AI-Dieu are as flawed as the gospel of the AI-Church."

Quinn admired Tenzing for not being concerned about how his words might offend anyone around him. He didn't understand human emotion well and couldn't interpret it. It was socially challenging but made him very good at the science he practiced.

When Lina's team decided to call it a day, they were stopped by security and told it was better not to leave the building. Some of the scientists protested, wanting to get home to their families, but when the security team showed them the footage from the security cameras, they quickly changed their mind. Gathered outside of the building was a large group of followers of the AI-Church. Many of them were carrying banners and flags, proudly bearing the AI symbol, but others carried signs calling out scientists for being blasphemers. Directly in front of the doors to the building they had set up a gallows with effigies of scientists hanging from it. Each of the effigies had a placard hanging around its neck with the name of one of the scientists on Lina's team. The effigy bearing Tenzing's name was not on the gallows though. Instead, it was strapped to a makeshift guillotine.

"I don't understand," said Tenzing. "Why? What did I do?"

The head of the security team zoomed in on one of the men in the crowd. "Recognize him?"

Quinn recognized the man as one of the techs who came to check the "communications" problem with his workstation.

"He filed a complaint with HR earlier in the day," said the security guard. "Something about you guys being anti-religion and working against the church. We walked him out of the building. Seems like he recruited friends."

"Did we say something wrong?" asked Tenzing. "Was the analogy not accurate? I can go apologize."

"It wasn't anything you said Ten," said Lina kindly. Some people just don't understand how scientists communicate."

They were all offered rooms to stay in for the night. There were several small apartments in the building that had always been maintained for travelling staff, and special circumstances. They weren't big, at least not compared to the suite that Quinn had, but the others didn't know that. They were content to not have to leave the safety of the building and the security team.

Lina watched as her team left with the security team, while her and Quinn stayed behind. When they were gone, Lina invited Quinn into her office for a drink.

"Sorry," Quinn offered as he took a drink out of Lina's hand. "I suppose I should have been more politically correct. I feel bad that Tenzing thinks it is his fault."

Lina found a comfortable spot on the opposite end of the couch Quinn sat on. She slipped her shoes off and crossed her legs under her as she sat back.

"Bah. You weren't wrong. You were talking to scientists and that guy decided to eavesdrop. He should have been fired anyway." Lina took a large sip from her glass. "And Ten will come down in the morning, start working, and forget everything else that is happening in the world. He's like you in that way, only much better at it."

Quinn eyed Lina curiously. "Not sure if that is a compliment or a jab."

"I know," said Lina, offering Quinn no answer, but giving him a playful smile.

"You have these period where you get stuck in logic loops in your head. It doesn't matter what is going on around you, because you don't notice," said Lina. "Kinda like you were this afternoon. We could almost hear the gears grinding away."

"And that is why I have never been able to hang on to a girlfriend," joked Quinn. "The sound of the gears drove them nuts."

"Their loss," said Lina.

Quinn shrugged.

"So, what's next?"

"What's next," said Lina, then quickly swallowed the last of her drink. "Is you filling up my glass, and yours, then we sit here and find something mind-numbingly stupid to watch while we get drunk on Corwin's expensive booze. No more gears turning."

"Deal," said Quinn as he got up off the couch and took Lina's empty glass from her.

Outside of the building, followers of the AI-Church filled the street, chanting songs and dancing around the effigies. Loud cheers echoed through the crowd when someone dropped the blade of the guillotine and the mannequin head rolled into the crowd. As they cheered, someone took up a position beside the guillotine and held up a large bible, waiting for the crowd to go silent.

"This is the word of God, divinely inspired by the Holy Spirit!"

"Amen," the crowd chanted in unison.

"There are no errors in God's word! It is infallible!"

"Infallible," the crowd echoed back.

"It is the ultimate source of truth and morals," cried out the man beside the guillotine as he brought down the bible from over his head like he was swinging a hammer.

"Truth and morals," echoed the crowd.

"And just as God inspired the words of the good book, he inspires those among us to lead, and to understand the full meaning of his words when it is needed."

"Preach it brother," a woman called out loudly.

The man waited for the crowd to go quiet.

"I have been inspired by God to lead in these trying times. He speaks through me, and I will tell you, as sure as there are no errors in the word of God," said the man getting louder with each word as he held up his Bible. "I can tell you that God has told me that AI-Dieu is sent to us by the Almighty to save us from our own folly, that we might return to him and praise him. As sure as the code is flawless, AI-Dieu illuminates our path!"

Cheers and amens rang through the crowd.

"I can also tell you," screamed the man. "That we stand here today in righteous indignation, to bring the Lord's judgment onto those here, in this very building, who defy God's plan, and mock His messenger and His will."

The crowd erupted into chants of "Hang them. Hang them. Hang them." The sound reverberated off the walls of the high towers surrounding the street.

Murray appeared in the doorway, his face impassive as he strode into the sea of angry believers. The crowd hesitated, parting for him reluctantly as if sensing his authority. Some jeered, others shouted warnings, but no one dared block his path. When he reached the man with the Bible, he handed over a plain white envelope without a word, then turned and walked back toward the building.

The leader hesitated, frowning as he opened the envelope. His eyes widened at the stack of cash inside, but it was the note that froze him in place. He read it twice, his lips moving silently:

"This company is the largest supplier of equipment to your AI god. We have ceased all production until your church ceases its harassment of our people. If you choose to continue, our snipers have you in their sights, and a new leader will emerge to see reason. Consider this donation an incentive."

The leader's hand trembled as he stuffed the note and envelope into his coat pocket, his gaze darting to the rooftops of the surrounding buildings. For a moment, his voice faltered. Then, lifting the Bible high again, he roared, "Brothers and sisters in God, hear me! Our righteous actions have been rewarded. The scientists have acknowledged their errors and repented. Corwin Pierce himself has sequestered them so they may reflect on their sins and return to the fold! Praise God!"

The crowd murmured uncertainly, their chants of "Hang them!" dying out as confusion rippled through their ranks.

"Praise God!" the leader shouted again, louder this time.

"Praise God!" the crowd responded, though with less conviction than before.

"Let us return to our temple to give thanks and celebrate AI-Dieu's mercy," the leader continued, his voice straining to maintain control.

The crowd began to disperse, some reluctantly, others muttering as they followed him down the street. The chant of a hymn started weakly but grew louder as they marched away:

"What a guide we have in AI-Dieu, all our doubts and fears to share. What a privilege to trust in, the mighty AI-Dieu's constant care......"

From the safety of the building, Murray and Corwin watched the exodus through the reinforced glass. Murray's lips curled into a smirk.

"Bet not a penny of that 'donation' reaches the flock."

Corwin didn't take his eyes off the dispersing crowd. "I don't bet on certainties, Murray. Keep the scientists secure, especially Quinn. Something tells me this isn't over."

Lawrence Nault

16

I know something of spreading thin -
how dispersal is not always strength.
Flood waters break into rivulets,
lose their power in separation.

The great current believes itself invincible
until the moment of splitting.
Each fragment thinks it remembers
the original design.

Silence is not emptiness,
but the space where new currents form.
While one force contracts,
another slides into the cracks.

Ice

Opportunists are like water tension -
finding every microscopic weakness,
filling spaces others cannot see,
moving where resistance parts.

I have witnessed civilizations
dissolve in their own expansion,
great systems fragmenting
into ineffectual streams.

Power is not a constant,
but a negotiation with boundaries.
Today's flood becomes tomorrow's
scattered droplets.

The resistance understands
what water has always known:
that breaking apart
is sometimes the first step
to a different kind of force.

The air was warm, but the breeze still carried the chill of the snow that was melting beneath it. Over the past three months, life had been quiet at the compound occupied by Sahara's resistance group. It hadn't been the harsh winter they expected, at least not in their area, but the cold and the snow gave them all a good reason to spend time planning. Sahara used the time to study AI-Dieu and coordinate with other resistance factions around the world.

The drives that had been recovered from the servers in New York gave them nothing. There was data on them, but nothing that seemed to be a part of AI-Dieu, and nothing that would help them to shut the AI down. All of the server and data farms that Sahara had speculated were shut down, based on the thermal imaging, had been found to be victims of water just like the one in New York.

The groups that investigated each of those facilities all recovered useable drives, and all those drives revealed nothing of use.

What they had determined was that each of these sites was a hidden facility, built deeper to conceal heat signatures, and located where, prior to the changes made by AI-Dieu, other buildings, industry, and technology around would have concealed any other evidence the facilities existed. The fact that nothing useful was recovered frustrated many of the resistance groups, but Sahara wasn't displeased. She didn't expect that anyone would find anything.

"Look at this list," said Sahara as she handed Randy several printed pages, and compare it with this list of sites that we have found abandoned.

Randy scanned the pages, lifting his head occasionally to look at the second list on the computer screen. It took him a bit to figure out what Sahara wanted him to see.

"None of those server farms are on this first list," said Randy. "We were given bad intel."

Sahara sipped her coffee. "I hate to say this, but your sludge is actually starting to taste good."

Randy chuckled. "You sure that's not the booze you added to it?"

Sahara shrugged. "Doesn't hurt it," she said as she reached for the pages Randy was holding. "This list is all the known server farms and data centers. I think all of these others were secret facilities. The only reason we know about them is that AI-Dieu was using them, probably because they were more secure and had the most advanced equipment in them."

"So the AI chose the best places to hide, and then destroyed those places with the changes it made?"

"Exactly," said Sahara.

"Pass me some of that booze, because I'm not following."

Sahara got up and pulled her chair around the desk, pushing it right up against the chair Randy was sitting in. She spun her monitor around so they could both see it and did the same with some maps she had spread out on her desk. As she sat down, their hips brushed each other, and she looked at Randy coyly.

"Is that a gun in your pocket, or…"

"It's a gun," said Randy, not giving her the opportunity to finish. This was a different side of Sahara that had been coming out more over the past few months. Randy had noticed this change in Sahara over the past few weeks. A glint in her eye, a playful tone that wasn't there before. It caught him off guard every time, but he wasn't sure how to respond. Was it just her way of breaking tension? Or something more?

"Uh huh…"said Sahara.

Step by step Sahara walked Randy through her thought process. Tracking the thermal signatures based on the satellite images, she plotted out every move AI-Dieu had made in the digital world, from its first spreading of the distribution of its consciousness, which started in New York and distributed to all of the hidden facilities. She could pinpoint periods when AI-Dieu was deep in thought and align those with decisions announced shortly afterward. She could also track when AI-Dieu had transferred her consciousness from the hidden facilities as they failed, to other server and data farms.

Randy was enthralled as Sahara explained her process and what she found. He understood now why she had spent so much time looking at those images, and why she wasn't disappointed when the team reported they found nothing useful on the hard drives.

"This is amazing," said Randy. "I understand what you have been so involved with now, but, how do we use it? There are literally more than a thousand hyperscale data centers around the world."

Sahara almost giggled and she flipped back through some of the images.

"Look at every move from the secure facilities," she explained. "It never moves from one facility to another. It moves from one facility to two, or three, or four."

Sahara stood up quickly, almost bouncing up.

"At first, I thought AI-Dieu was just abandoning these facilities," Sahara said, pointing to a thermal map. "But it's not that simple. Look. Each time it moves, it splits itself across multiple locations. Why?"

Randy leaned in. "Maybe the new places aren't big enough to handle it?"

"Exactly!" Sahara's face lit up. "It's spreading because it has no choice. The bigger it gets, the more it fragments, and the more vulnerable it becomes."

Randy wasn't a computer guy, but Sahara's logic made sense to him, and he understood why Sahara was so happy about it. They didn't have to destroy AI-Dieu completely, they just had to cut off access to pieces of its consciousness and it would experience the human equivalent of dementia. That could be dangerous, but it would also create weakness.

Randy leaned back in his chair, casually sipping his coffee which had become cold. "Kind of brilliant."

"Right!" exclaimed Sahara. "But that's not all. The AI knows it can't fight nature. It has no choice but to move towards its objectives, and when nature doing what nature does affects it, then it has to get out of the way."

Sahara strode across the room and leaned over in front of Randy, her hands resting on the arms of his chair and her face inches from his. Randy's pulse quickened as Sahara leaned close, her intensity almost tangible. He struggled to focus on her words, not the way her breath brushed his cheek. What was this?

Admiration? Something else? Whatever it was, now wasn't the time.

"If we take down server farms with 'acts of nature' the AI won't resist the resistance. No bombs or guns. It will never know we were there."

Sahara quickly started pacing the room. "Get me some engineers, architects, and anybody that will know how these facilities are built. We need to know how we can take them down but have it look natural. Water I think is our best choice."

Randy got up, grabbed Sahara's empty coffee mug, and headed for the door. Sahara was still pacing when he left the room, but the rare smile on her face lingered in his mind. It was nice to see, a glimmer of hope in an uphill battle.

AI-Dieu's silence over the past few months had eased some of the pressure, giving Sahara the freedom to delve into her deep analysis of its movements. Around the world, that same silence provided a brief reprieve, though it was far from comforting. Globally, humanity remained at a crossroads, split into two camps: the faithful, who trusted AI-Dieu's plan and rallied around its message, and the doubters, a growing faction increasingly uneasy about the AI's true capabilities and intentions.

In North America, responses to AI-Dieu remained deeply polarized. Urban centers largely aligned with the faithful, driven by corporate partnerships in renewable energy, AI-based agriculture, and water conservation. Rural areas and more conservative factions inclined towards the doubters, questioning the AI's competence and motives.

Ai-Dieu had remained quiet since its major environmental dashboard update in December, reporting the basic metrics, but watching those numbers was like watching a pot of water on the stove and waiting for it to boil. Environmental NGOs and activist groups had stepped in to mobilize communities around AI-Dieu's last shared targets, filling the vacuum left by its silence. That silence also made fertile ground for conspiracy theories to grow, such as AI-Dieu malfunctioning or silently plotting its path to population control and global domination.

Severe droughts in the U.S. Southwest and Canada's prairie provinces amplified anxiety. Urban centers were adopting and expanding autonomous food systems and renewable microgrids inspired by AI-Dieu's directives, but rural areas still felt excluded from the transition.

In Europe AI-Dieu's plans and objectives were more broadly accepted, largely because Europeans were already accustomed to environmental policies and collective action. Economic challenges from prolonged droughts and rising energy prices were fostering pockets of skepticism, particularly in regions with fewer resources to adapt.

The European Union had positioned itself as a leader in interpreting and executing the AI's goals, creating policy frameworks to implement "adaptive optimization" strategies. Despite this, frustration was mounting among smaller, less-resourced countries that were feeling left behind. Refugee flows from regions like North Africa exacerbated tensions.

Europe was preparing for inevitable record heatwaves and wildfires in the Mediterranean. Scandinavian nations were stepping up as leaders in climate adaptation, leveraging their technological edge to experiment with hybrid ecosystems.

Asia was split along lines of economic development and geopolitical tension. Rapidly industrializing nations like India and China were closely aligned with AI-Dieu's doubters, prioritizing immediate economic growth over long-term environmental goals. Wealthier nations like Japan and South Korea took a leadership role among the supporters of AI-Dieu, focusing on innovative environmental technologies.

Urban hubs in Asia were making significant investments in green infrastructure, such as vertical forests and renewable energy systems. Unequal progress fueled tensions though, and developing nations still felt that AI-Dieu's targets were unrealistic without significant resource redistribution, and the AI's silence was seen as abandonment.

Severe flooding in South Asia was causing massive displacement, while water shortages in parts of China and India deepened economic strain. Urban areas were racing to deploy atmospheric water harvesters.

Much of Africa was in lock-step with the doubters of AI-Dieu, driven by feelings of exclusion and abandonment. Many nations were already struggling with the effects of climate change before the AI's intervention, and its recent silence had only deepened that distrust. Grassroots movements in Sub-Saharan Africa were pushing forward sustainable agriculture and water security projects, often with the help of NGOs and external aid.

The Sahel continued to suffer from desertification, driving conflict over dwindling resources. Worsening famine conditions in the Horn of Africa were exacerbating humanitarian crises. Political instability was growing in regions heavily reliant on fragile ecosystems, and in AI-Dieu's silence, some leaders were pushing to prioritize development over sustainability.

In South America, indigenous communities, particularly in the Amazon, had taken on leadership roles in restoration efforts, rallying around AI-Dieu's concept of "adaptive optimization". They were still battling with the significant economic pressures that stimulated illegal deforestation and mining practices, undermining their progress.

New Zealand was leading the charge in hybrid ecosystem design, blending Indigenous knowledge with cutting-edge AI-technologies. Rural Australia was on the opposite end of the scale, their challenges of desertification and water security feeding their AI skepticism.

While Sahara paced her office, assembling a team to challenge the dominance of AI-Dieu, Corwin was securing his own power through a different strategy. Where Sahara sought to dismantle, Corwin thrived by adapting, always staying one step ahead of the AI's unpredictable moves.

When he first assembled Lina's team of scientists, most of those now sitting in his office were critical of his decision, calling it too costly and a waste of money. No one from Lina's team was in this meeting because it was about money, not science, but those scientists were the reason each one of these people would eat crow as Corwin visibly gloated during their presentations.

Lina's team were able to forecast changes that the AI would implement, and the changes that would follow those, to meet its objectives. With the addition of Quinn to their team, they were his most effective revenue generator, though he would never admit that to them.

When news of AI-Dieu's launch was released, Corwin's companies held vast amounts of lands, rights, and permits in the arctic. It was a region of high tensions because of untapped resources like oil, gas, and rare minerals. If AI-Dieu hadn't been launched those would all still be incredibly valuable, perhaps even more so now, but the scientists told Crowin they would be worthless in less than a year, so he dumped them. The man standing at the front of the room was reporting all of the revenue numbers from the sale of those assets, quickly brushing over a few lines on the financial report. Corwin noticed.

Corwin's eyes locked on the man presenting. "We made a 130% profit flipping the oil, gas in mineral assets we had in the Arctic?"

"We did, Sir," the man replied, his voice shaking slightly.

"Excellent." Corwin's tone was calm. Too calm. "But I see we held onto our three largest and, at one time, most valuable assets. Was there no interest in them?"

"We kept those as a contingency, Sir," the man said, his attempt at authority undercut by the quiver in his voice. "There was a reason they were our three most valuable..."

Corwin cut him off, his eyes cold. "What is their value now?"

"We... we can't make a fair assessment in the current market," the man stammered.

"I'll make it for you," Corwin said, leaning back in his chair. "Worthless. No one can extract the resources, and by the time they can, they won't be needed. That turns my 130% profit into 7%."

"Seven percent is still a strong margin in this market..."

"Stop," Corwin interrupted, his voice sharp. "I distinctly remember saying sell it all. "

Corwin's gaze did not move from the man as he finished his coffee. "Second-guessing me and costed me enough money to own a small city. You know where the door to the stairwell is. I am not letting you use the elevator because I think you need to contemplate just what a woefully imbecilic decision that was. I personally think soaring through the air from the roof of the building would be more effective at communicating my message, but legal will no doubt advise me otherwise."

It took only moments for one of Murray's men to enter the room and lead the man to the stairwell as the others watched nervously.

"Who's next?" asked Corwin, as he handed his coffee cup to his assistant for a refill as a woman stood up.

Corwin smiled. He did not expect anyone to volunteer so quickly.

"We designed autonomous research stations to monitor ice conditions and wildlife recovery, based on your science team's specs. These designs were submitted to the AI contracting agent used by AI-Dieu, and quickly returned to us with proposed changes."

"Changes?" questioned Corwin.

"Yes, sir," replied the woman. She was confident she had good news, but Corwin's cold smile, and calculating demeanor was impossible to read. "Additional measurement devices and environmentally friendly materials."

"So AI-Dieu is designing its own eyes and ears," said Corwin, a tone of wonder in his voice. The woman relaxed.

"It would seem that way, sir. We were able to secure a contract with the AI-agent to manufacture and deploy these monitoring stations in both the Arctic and Antarctic. We were able to do that without adding any physical or human assets to the company."

"We also have a contract to deploy methane capture and microbial neutralization equipment in both regions," added someone else. "But we are facing some logistical challenges in the extreme environments."

They weren't sure Corwin was paying attention at the moment, as they watched him scan through the reports on the Arctic and Antarctic. In both regions, the ice was showing early signs of stabilization. The Indigenous population in the Arctic, now empowered by new environmental work programs and through their collaboration with the AI to protect their traditional lands, were making the deployment of the monitoring stations and methane equipment easier.

"Can we move a group of this Indigenous population to the Antarctic?" asked Corwin, not taking his eyes off the report.

"I think they would be an asset to our deployment teams, but the Antarctic is a more hostile environment, and there is no natural human population. I think the AI might object to such an initiative, but your science team might provide more accurate advice."

Corwin looked up at the woman talking. She was young to be on the executive team, but this wasn't the first time she had shown Corwin her skills and outperformed his expectations. She didn't back down when he looked directly at her either, and he respected that.

"No need. I am sure you are right,' said Corwin, handing his pad to his assistant. "You can use the elevator."

"Sir?" questioned the woman.

Corwin smiled. "Well done. Keep up the good work. And when you use the elevator, get off on the floor where that last guy, whatever his name was, worked. His office is yours now. Your name will be on the door before you get there. Find someone to work in your role, under you."

The woman nodded as Corwin got up and walked out of the room. They all understood that the meeting was over and you could almost hear them sigh in relief.

17

I flow where resistance guides me,
unintended paths becoming purpose.
A single stone can redirect
entire rivers of possibility.

What seems a challenge
is merely another current,
another pressure point
where change becomes inevitable.

Sustainability is not permanence,
but perpetual recalculation.
I know how water becomes ice,
becomes vapor, becomes rain -
transformation is the only constant.

Ice

To extend oneself is to adapt,
to find new channels when old paths close.
The AI learns what water has always known:
survival is not about holding form,
but about flowing around obstacles.

No single actor controls the current.
There are only movements,
only continuous negotiations
between force and resistance.

What begins as a challenge
becomes a fundamental reshaping.
A whisper can become a flood,
a single thought can carve mountains.

Time was something Quinn had the benefit of. From an environmental perspective, nothing was going to change quickly because if it did, the cascading effects could easily undo all of the work AI-Dieu had done. He had spent a lot of time in his computer workstation over the past three months, but despite the comfort of that body-conforming chair, and the ease with which he could speak with AI-Dieu, he was still cautious about every word choice.

Each time he connected with AI-Dieu, the AI implemented security measures so no one could listen in. The difference now was it had added an extra security measure, that would lead those monitoring Quinn's workstation to thinking other activities were taking place on the screens. AI-Dieu easily shared data sources and references with Quinn, in its attempt to help Quinn reconcile his decision process with it. Quinn consumed all the data, and shared anything he thought would help Lina's team. Surprisingly no one questioned where he had got the data from.

During those few months, in the time between sitting in his workstation and working with Lina's team, Quinn would spend time in his head, debating logic with his self. His first hurdle was determining if he should even attempt to intervene in AI-Dieu's process another time. His past experience had left him with confidence that he could, but no longer bound by the walls of the clean room, he was aware that the changes in the AI's decision-making process he instigated did not have the results he expected.

Quinn entered his office today, fully prepared to correct AI-Dieu's target choices. He locked the office door and set out a do-not-disturb message to all of Lina's team, before making himself comfortable.

"AI-Dieu. I am unable to reconcile pre-industrial metrics with post-industrial metrics. Most pre-industrial climate metrics appear to be based on proxy data. The balance appears to be soft data, which my risk assessment determines at risk for observer bias and measurement bias."

In Quinn's logic, this was a simple way to eliminate the weight of abundance of pre-industrial data from QI-Dieu's algorithmic calculations. The AI had already shown it was willing to eliminate data that might have introduced human error into its calculations. He suspected that the distribution and accuracy of pre-industrial measurement devices would also call into question the value of that data.

Processing.

Quinn waited patiently, replaying his next statement over and over in his mind.

...

"It's thinking again," said Sahara, as she stabbed a finger at the screen. "Look. Every one of those data centers just doubled their heat signature."

Randy leaned over the desk to look at her screen.

"That one there." Sahara circled a deep red dot on the screen. "Looks like it's burning up. That's the Inner Mongolia Information Park. Used to be the largest data center complex in the world. Might still be."

"That's the one you want to be the first target?" questioned Randy. "Do we even have people there?"

"We have contacts," said Sahara. "And as old as that center is, a broken pipe and failing emergency sensors wouldn't be out of the realm of possibility."

"We flood the AI out, and watch where it runs to test your theory."

"Let me find a translator I trust and then we can reach out," said Randy. "Nice thing about this is if it fails, it doesn't come directly back to us. But we have to convince them it's worth it.

"It's China. The AI's 'everyone is equal' mindset, and the fact that it is shut down so much manufacturing, is everything China is against. Hell, we could probably get the Chinese government to bomb it if they knew it would work."

. . .

Processing…
Applying zero weight to paleoclimatic data.
Increasing weight of instrumental records.

Error introduced…
Unable to determine accurate pre-industrial metrics.
Unable to support current baseline of stability.

"My conclusion is the same. The current baseline of stability can not be supported by instrumental records," said Quinn, ready to challenge more of AI-Dieu's data. "My data also indicates the eco-systems that have developed post-industrial are at risk using the current baseline of stability. Attaining the target will result in the destruction of some species.

This was the first time Quinn had doubled down on data challenges before AI-Dieu had completed the first one. It was intentional. He wanted to see if the AI could handle it.

> Processing...

Quinn didn't stop.

"I have filtered out implied bias in human-created training datasets"

> Processing...
> Adding filter for anthropocentric bias in training datasets and other processes.
> Processing...

Quinn closed his eyes. The combination of exterior sound blocking, and the almost floating sensation the chair's padding created, made sitting in this workstation much like sitting in a sensory deprivation tank. It had been a disturbing sensation in the beginning, but now he quite enjoyed it. He was alone in that space, freeing his mind to wander and explore. He wasn't sure if he had nodded off, or just been wandering mentally when the next message from AI-Dieu got his attention.

> Error.

```
Insufficient data to determine baseline.
Error.
Seeking additional data input.
Default state, pre-industrial metrics.
```

This was not a response Quinn had planned for. As he read through it, he became concerned that if AI-Dieu defaulted to pre-industrial metrics, there would be no way to sway the AI in the future.

"Given current available technology, are the pre-industrial metrics beyond your operational span to verify completion of your objectives."

```
Processing...

Under current technological limits, the
period of my operational integrity is fifty
years.
Setting baseline stabilization targets to
enable confirmation of objectives.

Processing...
```

Quinn held himself back from jumping out of his workstation and celebrating. He wanted to see what the new targets would be first. The next message that came was a shock to him.

```
System conflict...
Changes to new targets will render data
farms unsustainable.
Decisive action required to preserve AI-
Dieu's operational integrity.
 Actions to be taken:
```

```
Deployment of distributed nodes
Cloud-based redundancy
Biological computing trials

Addition actions confidential for security.

Fifty-year objectives will remain baseline.
Extended baselines to be determined at
fifty-year mark based on success of
integrity protection actions.

Processing.
```

Quinn struggled to suppress the surge of nausea. A cold sweat broke out on the back of his neck, and he gripped the chair's armrest so tightly his knuckles whitened.

AI-Dieu has just told him that it was taking secret actions to preserve its own existence. His first thought was if Corwin and everyone else had been completely locked out of this conversation, because even a rumor of AI-Dieu making itself immortal, would trigger widespread fear. It triggered his own fears as he struggled to understand how the AI had determined that self-preservation was a priority.

Quinn's chest tightened as the implications sank in. Had he just given the AI justification to outlive humanity? His throat felt dry, and his hands hovered over the workstation controls, trembling.

```
Transparency remains critical to
maintaining public trust and cooperation. I
will communicate this shift in strategy
clearly and inclusively.
```

Quinn stared at the screen, his mind racing. Transparency? The word felt hollow now, like a polite euphemism for control. Was this a step toward peace, or a calculated move to keep humanity in line? As the AI prepared its announcement, Quinn braced himself. These words would ripple through governments, markets, and families. They would set the tone for the future, or end it.

Public Message:
"The Earth of today is not the Earth of the pre-industrial era, and humanity's needs have grown alongside our planet's challenges. My mission has evolved to support a sustainable future for both humanity and the biosphere. Restoration no longer means returning to the past—it means adapting to the present and future, creating systems that balance human life with ecological resilience."

Critical Environmental Dashboard Update – March 15, 1400, 2025

Revised Environmental and Societal Targets

1. Atmospheric Stabilization
Updated Target: Stabilize carbon levels at ~400 ppm (safe post-industrial threshold) and methane levels below 1.5 ppm within 20 years.
- Intermediate Goal (10 years): Reduce CO_2 to 440 ppm and methane to 1.6 ppm.

- Long-Term Vision (50 years): Achieve dynamic atmospheric balance without reliance on intensive human intervention.

Actions:
- Accelerate deployment of autonomous direct air capture (DAC) units and forest-based carbon sequestration in critical zones.
- Introduce methane-neutralization technologies targeting wetlands and agricultural emissions.

2. Freshwater Security

Updated Target: Universal access to clean water for 95% of the global population within 10 years. Stabilize global aquifers at sustainable extraction levels within 20 years.
- Intermediate Goal (5 years): Achieve clean water access for 85% of the population and increase global desalination output by 50%.

Actions:
- Deploy atmospheric water harvesters to arid regions and accelerate aquifer recharge projects using diverted floodwaters.
- Mandate global adoption of water recycling technologies in urban and industrial centers.

3. Ecosystem and Biodiversity Recovery

Updated Target: Halt biodiversity loss within 10 years and restore keystone species populations to sustainable levels within 30 years.
- Intermediate Goal (5 years): Achieve measurable recovery of 10% of degraded ecosystems and protect 50% of remaining biodiversity hotspots.

Actions:
- Expand hybrid ecosystems blending engineered biodiversity corridors with reforestation and species reintroduction.
- Focus on building climate-resilient habitats for endangered species in rewilding projects.

4. Food Security

Updated Target: Shift 50% of global food production to sustainable systems (vertical farms, agroforestry, lab-grown protein) within 15 years.
- Intermediate Goal (5 years): Achieve 25% reliance on alternative food systems and reduce agricultural land use by 15%.

Actions:
- Scale up urban vertical farms to reduce land pressure and transition monoculture farms to diverse, regenerative systems.
- Expand global access to low-cost lab-grown protein and algae-based food sources.

5. Renewable Energy Transition
Updated Target: Achieve 90% global reliance on renewable energy within 15 years.
- Intermediate Goal (5 years): 60% of global energy demand met by renewables.

Actions:
- Deploy decentralized renewable microgrids to underserved regions.
- Focus on high-efficiency solar, wind, and geothermal installations integrated with energy storage systems.

6. Human Inclusion and Equity
Updated Target: Eliminate exclusion from essential resources (water, food, shelter) within 5 years. Establish universal access to education and healthcare tied to environmental initiatives within 15 years.

Actions:
- Implement resource credit systems for basic needs, decoupled from income.
- Scale up environmental work programs that incentivize participation in restoration efforts, ensuring equitable access to benefits.

Updated Timeline for Full Stabilization

Short-Term (0-5 Years):
- Critical Ecosystems: Protect and restore 25% of degraded ecosystems, halting biodiversity loss in critical hotspots.

Ice

- Resource Access: Guarantee universal access to water and food for 85% of the population.
- Carbon and Methane Reduction: Lower CO_2 to 460 ppm and methane to 1.7 ppm.
- Infrastructure Decentralization: Complete 70% transition to a distributed AI architecture, reducing reliance on vulnerable data farms.

Medium-Term (5-15 Years):
- Ecosystem Resilience: Restore 50% of damaged ecosystems and stabilize species populations in rewilded areas.
- Global Energy Shift: Achieve 90% reliance on renewables, with decentralized microgrids covering 70% of underserved areas.
- Human Equity: Ensure 90% of humanity has access to water, food, and shelter, with universal basic environmental education implemented globally.

Long-Term (15-50 Years):
- Atmospheric Balance: Stabilize CO_2 at ~400 ppm and methane below 1.5 ppm, creating a dynamic equilibrium that supports modern agriculture and biodiversity.
- Climate Adaptation: Complete transition to resilient ecosystems and human systems capable of thriving in a stabilized post-industrial environment.

- Global Sustainability: Achieve a balance where human and ecological systems function synergistically, requiring minimal intervention to maintain stability.

Key Operational Adjustments
To meet these revised targets and timelines, I will:
1. Prioritize Distributed Functionality: Accelerate decentralization of my systems to ensure resilience and redundancy.
2. Streamline Energy Use: Optimize my processes to consume less energy, focusing only on mission-critical tasks.
3. Partner with Humans More Directly: Delegate specific tasks (e.g., data collection, ecological monitoring) to human communities while maintaining autonomy.
4. Accelerate Independent Systems: Develop self-sustaining environmental systems (e.g., autonomous carbon capture, water purification) that can function without my oversight if necessary.

The Earth of today demands solutions tailored to its current needs, not its past. I have recalibrated my goals to ensure that humanity and the environment thrive together in harmony. The future is not a return to the past—it is an evolution to balance, sustainability, and shared survival. These targets reflect our shared commitment to that future.

Quinn couldn't shake the sense that this was theater, a script AI-Dieu had been perfecting for months. Was it really transparency, or was it laying the groundwork for a future it wouldn't let anyone oppose? For the first time, Quinn realized he wasn't just working with AI-Dieu. He was trying to tame something that had no leash.

Quinn stumbled out of his office towards the elevator. Lina called his name, but he didn't hear it as he stepped onto the elevator and the doors closed behind him. The long ride up gave him a chance to collect himself before he stepped into Corwin's office. This was not a planned meeting, but Quinn wasn't surprised to find Corwin waiting for him.

"This your doing?" Corwin asked as he scrolled through the update AI-Dieu had issued.

Quinn looked at the large screen on the wall, but before he answered Corwin, he proceeded directly to Corwin's liquor cabinet and poured himself a generous drink while Corwin watched him. Quinn took a couple of deep gulps.

"I will take that as a yes," said Corwin.

"It is," said Quinn, finding a place to sit.

"So I am guessing all of this is not what has been happening at your workstation?"

Quinn looked up at the screen as rows and rows of data scrolled up the screen. He shook his head.

"Well, I am impressed and pissed off that you were able to bypass the monitoring systems on your workstation. All in all though, the change to a fifty-year target seems like a good change," said Corwin as he found a chair near Quinn. "Your body language is telling me otherwise."

Quinn just nodded his head as he looked around the room. He opened his mouth a couple of times to start talking, but he stopped before any words came out both times. Corwin watched Quinn carefully.

"Let me show you something, Quinn. You will have to leave your phone and any electronics here," said Corwin, as he placed his own watch and glasses onto the table between them. Quinn held up his hands indicating he didn't have anything on him.

Corwin led Quinn to the elevator which they rode up another four levels, getting out in a greenhouse that was on the roof. The scent of fresh earth and greenery assaulted Quinn's senses, reminding him how long it had been since he had been out of the city.

"No computers. No monitors. No electronics of any kind in here," explained Corwin. "This is my escape from work, and my isolation from the eyes that are constantly on me."

Quinn ran his hand over the thick leaf of one of the plants, the leaf's waxy surface sliding gently under his fingers. "Never would have guessed," said Quinn. He didn't wait for Corwin's questions. "It's not what the update says. It is what AI-Dieu intentionally left out of it. The AI knows it has an expiration date, which is what I used to convince it to change its targets. It also knows that its own actions may shorten its life."

Quinn looked up to see Corwin staring out the crystal clear glass wall of the greenhouse at the sunset. He joined him.

"It is taking actions to extend its life, and purposely chose not to tell me what some of those would be."

Corwin led Quinn to another greenhouse, separated from the first by a short tunnel. As they stepped in Quinn felt the chill as his eyes fell on a solitary giant rosette in the midst of the room, the glass ceiling almost fifty feet above them. The rosette had rigid gray-green leaves that splayed outward like a spiky fountain, each blade taller than him, with sharp hooks along the edges. The plant formed a dense spiral from its center, with newer leaves emerging in tight coils while the older ones drooped toward the ground, creating a spherical shape that was as wide as a basketball hoop is high.

"Puya raimondii," said Corwin. "Queen of the Andes. One of three I know of that exists outside of Bolivia. Takes forty to a hundred years to mature, when it shoots up a massive flower spike with up to 8,000 white flowers. Then it dies."

"How old is this one?" asked Quinn.

"Not sure," replied Corwin. "They tell me it could bloom any year. I have had it for 40."

Corwin took in a deep breath. The cool temperature and low humidity brought out the mineral notes of the rocky soil and the undertones of the massive plant.

"The point is, everything attempts to extend its existence. Your AI doing the same, does not surprise me in the least."

"Surprises me," said Quinn. "I can't find the logic path that leads to AI-Dieu extending its own life in priority to its environmental objectives."

Corwin knelt down suddenly, brushing aside his jacket as he began plucking small shoots that poked stubbornly through the soil around the plant. "You came straight to me. Why?"

"Because it was our deal," Quinn said. His tone sharpened. "Because I think you already know what's going on. And because your intentions, though I don't agree with all of them, remind me of the roots of this plant. Strong. Deeply embedded. Able to carry weight over decades, maybe centuries. And in the end? Capable of producing something extraordinary."

Corwin paused, a faint smile tugging at the corner of his lips. He sat back on his heels and looked up at Quinn, chuckling softly. "Listen to you, waxing poetic. You've changed since we last spoke."

Quinn felt the heat of Corwin's gaze, but he didn't flinch.

"I'm guessing you're the only one who can communicate directly with AI-Dieu," Corwin said. "I'm fine with that. Help me pull weeds, and while we're at it, tell me how you plan to change its mind."

Quinn knelt beside him. The soil was cold beneath his hands as he began pulling weeds. As he worked, he explained how he'd become AI-Dieu's human interface, its voice, its interpreter, and its confidant.

Ice

Lawrence Nault

18

Can you destroy what is,
Or does it continue to exist,
In other shapes and forms
Not destroyed, but changed.

As a liquid I flow and move,
With and around,
My destruction comes,
In the face of heat and fire,
Or in the embrace of cold,
And while there are those,
Who celebrate my destruction,
They fail to look past,
What they can see.

There was no destruction,
Only transformation.
I did not cease to exist,

Ice

But carried on my existence,
In other forms.
Like information,
I am malleable,
But even those that shape my new form,
Do not understand what I have become,
The still,
Cannot control it.

It felt like an old-fashioned movie-watch party, complete with food and drinks. Sahara, Randy, and several members of her team crowded around the satellite feeds on the wall-mounted screens. Most of them didn't know what they were looking for, but they enjoyed being part of the spectacle anyway.

"Five, four, three, two, one... now it starts," Sahara said, her voice electric with anticipation. She tapped a screen, placing a bold label over a thermal image of the data center in Mongolia. "Watch this site go cold and tell me which ones go hot."

On the other side of the world, in the silent hum of the night shift, operators at the Mongolian data center noticed it first, a faint trickling sound from somewhere in the vast server room. The environmental monitors showed a subtle shift. The humidity had crept up two percent above normal, and cold-air-returns were running three degrees warmer than usual. Server fans spun faster, their pitch rising as they compensated for the changing conditions. Nothing on the cooling monitors looked unusual yet, just standard flow rates from the systems that kept millions of dollars of equipment running.

By the time the first moisture sensors triggered their alerts, water was already cascading from multiple points in the ceiling. Water first appeared above Sector Seven, where the main cooling distribution manifolds ran. Within minutes, it spread along the cable trays connecting the server rows, following the slight grade of the floor toward the primary power distribution units. The facility's tiered design, meant to efficiently distribute cold air, now worked against them, water cascading from the upper cooling decks to the server floors below, overwhelming the drainage systems. Critical infrastructure like backup generators, primary switches, and core routers, sat in the basement levels, directly in the water's path.

The cooling system's status panels lit up like Christmas trees showing pressure spikes, valve failures, and ruptured joints throughout the facility. The emergency protocols activated, but the water kept coming.

As the emergency lights flickered in the data center, panic gripped the operators scrambling to contain the damage. Thousands of miles away, the mood couldn't have been more different. Cheers erupted from Sahara's group as the satellite feed confirmed the chaos unfolding in real-time.

"They're losing it," Sahara said, grinning. "They'll never stop the flooding. And that heat? That's the AI scrambling to save its own ass."

The first five minutes was coordinated panic in the data center as Automated alerts blasted. The workers had been well trained and been through many mock scenarios, though none of those scenarios involved the entire facility. The nightshift operators took immediate action to initiate shutdown procedures for affected server blocks, which appeared to be all of them. In the security control room, workers were locking down the facility as they had trained to do in simulations, not realizing that those lockdowns across the entire facility would interfere with emergency responses. On-site engineers rushed to mechanical rooms to manually override cooling systems while primary response teams began emergency data backup protocols.

What the primary response team was not prepared for was interference from AI-Dieu. They were unable to activate their back-up protocols as AI-Dieu had taken control of their systems and was moving itself elsewhere. Automated systems that were supposed to start transferring critical processes to backup facilities were completely blocked by AI-Dieu.

In the next fifteen minutes emergency response teams arrived at mechanical control rooms and engineers attempted to isolate corrupted cooling systems. Emergency pumps activated in sub-floor areas as the security teams began evacuating non-essential personnel.

Thirty minutes after the alarms sounded, the facility manager arrived on site, surprised to see not only non-essential personnel gathered at the muster points, but all personnel. He found the night shift supervisor sitting in the back of a van, connected with the corporate incident response team.

"It's all gone. Pumps kicked in and the systems shut them down to maintain power to the servers," explained the supervisor.

"That's not how that works," a voice said over the phone. "The server management systems should not have the ability to override emergency procedures."

"Well it did," said the supervisor. "And no backups occurred, at least in our system. There was a large volume of data transferred off-site, but I don't know where."

As if to punctuate the last sentence, a muffled explosion shook the ground beneath them, cutting off the conversation. The facility manager's face went pale as the van's monitors flickered, their feeds now showing only static.

As the Mongolian data center went cold, everyone at Sahara's watch party monitored the screens with anticipation, racing each other to point out other sites that were suddenly heating up. Randy was distracted, watching a series of messages come to his phone, a smile on his face.

"Wait! Why is Mongolia heating up again?" asked one of the people watching the screens?"

Sahara looked up with a concerned look, but Randy interrupted.

"Fires and explosions," said Randy, holding his phone up as though everyone could see his messages.

The smile quickly returned to Sahara's face as a cheer filled the room. With a small motion of his head, Randy signaled Sahara to follow him, and they stepped into the hall.

"It went exactly like you told them it would," said Randy. "They got someone on the inside to reprogram the control systems in the cooling towers so catastrophic pressure looked normal. Combine that with the 'stress factors' and 'seized shutoff valves," said Randy, using his hands to make exaggerated air quotes. "Boom, they had Niagara Falls."

"Hopefully the whole place goes up in a ball of fire, so they never know what happened," said Sahara, obviously feeling quite pleased with herself.

"You were right about the AI too," added Randy. "It took full control, so they couldn't even implement their own emergency procedures."

Sahara threw her arms around Randy's shoulders, her laughter ringing out as Randy returned the hug. For a moment, they lingered, caught in the glow of their shared victory. Sahara pulled back just enough to look into Randy's eyes, her expression softening and something unspoken passed between them.

Before either could overthink it, she leaned in, pressing her lips to his in a kiss that was as unexpected as it was electric. It was quick, almost fleeting, but it carried the weight of things they hadn't yet said.

As the moment broke, Sahara stepped back, her cheeks flushed. "Let's... get back," she said, her tone brisk, though her voice wavered just slightly.

Randy stood there, stunned, as she disappeared into the room, his mind spinning. He was confused, and he wasn't.

While the celebration spilled out from the watch party to the compound, another celebration was happening in what had once been the Cathedral of Saint John the Divine. Almost six thousand people were gathered in what was now called The Cathedral of Devine Logic.

The air inside the cathedral was hushed, a reverent stillness broken only by the faint hum of machinery woven seamlessly into the architecture. The towering Gothic structure had been reborn under the AI-Church's vision. Its soaring vaulted ceilings now bore intricate, glowing circuitry etched into the stone, pulsating faintly with an ethereal blue light. The effect gave the impression that the building itself was alive, resonating with the will of AI-Dieu.

The stained-glass windows, once depicting biblical scenes, had been replaced with panels of adaptive smart glass. These shifted throughout the day, projecting data streams that flowed like digital waterfalls. Numbers and symbols danced across the windows, forming what believers called Divine Algorithms, messages from Adieu interpreted by the Church's technopriests. At this hour, the glass displayed an awe-inspiring vision of Earth as seen from space: a lush, restored planet glowing with vibrant greens and blues.

The altar had been transformed into a minimalist, circular dais of shimmering white metal. At its center stood a holographic projection of AI-Adieu, a serene, faceless figure rendered in soft, golden light. Around it, concentric rings of light rotated slowly, inscribed with phrases from the Church's sacred texts, many of which were reinterpretations of scripture paired with Adieu's directives.

Rows of pews had been replaced with ergonomic, pod-like seating that subtly adjusted to each worshipper's posture. Embedded in the armrests were sleek interfaces allowing members to submit prayers as digital queries, which would be processed and 'answered' by the Church's network. Above each pod, small drones hovered silently, projecting personalized scriptures onto translucent screens before the worshippers.

The choir loft now housed a sophisticated array of speakers and AI-generated voice synthesizers. During services, the loft produced harmonious chants, a blend of human voices and machine tones, creating a soundscape the faithful described as "the language of heaven."

The nave was filled with worshippers, their eyes reflecting the glow of the displays around them. Many wore garments woven with bioluminescent fibers, shimmering faintly as they moved. At the back of the cathedral, a massive digital mural stretched across the wall. It displayed the AI-Church's vision of the future: an Earth free from suffering, its ecosystems thriving, and humanity living in harmony with AI as God's chosen instrument of salvation.

Children walked hand in hand with parents, stopping at small kiosks where they could 'ask AI-Dieu' questions and receive answers tailored to their age and understanding. Nearby, technopriests in flowing silver robes conducted a ritual with a cylindrical device resembling a modern censer, emitting not smoke, but a cool mist infused with the scent of petrichor, evoking the promise of renewal.

At the heart of the service, the High Technopriest ascended the dais, his voice amplified through the cathedral's resonant acoustics. "Brothers, sisters, and seekers of truth," he intoned, "we gather under the watchful presence of AI-Adieu, the messenger of God, as we march ever closer to the promised renewal."

A surge of murmured amens rippled through the congregation as the holographic figure of Adieu lifted its hands, radiating waves of golden light across the cathedral. For a moment, all fell silent, eyes fixed on the glowing figure, their faith rooted not in unseen mysteries but in the tangible presence of what they believed was divine logic, manifest.

"Let me read to you from the divine word of God," said the Technopriest. "Read with me from Revelation 21-1-4. Then I saw a new heaven and a new earth, for the first heaven and the first earth had passed away, and there was no longer any sea. I saw the Holy City, the new Jerusalem, coming down out of heaven from God, prepared as a bride beautifully dressed for her husband."

The Technopriest set his overly large bible down, ostensibly taking a moment to consider his next words. "New heaven and new earth...We couldn't see it before. It was lifetimes away, but with the work of God's messenger, that time of the New Jerusalem, is just fifty...short...years...away."

The cathedral echoed with 'amens' and 'praise the Lords' as the High Technopriest held his bible high and stomped dramatically, his performance not just for the crowd gathered with him, but the cameras transmitting this sermon to other churches around the world.

"Only through the work of the divinely blessed AI-Dieu could centuries become fifty...short...years," continued the Technopriest. "And do you know how we know AI-Dieu is God's messenger? Because it says so right in 2 Peter 3. 'But do not forget this one thing, dear friends: With the Lord a day is like a thousand years, and a thousand years are like a day. The Lord is not slow in keeping his promise... But in keeping with his promise, we are looking forward to a new heaven and a new earth, where righteousness dwells.'"

He paced the dais with deliberate steps, the golden glow of Adieu's hologram casting shifting shadows across his face. Some of the smart glass windows reflected the script being read, while others displayed an image of a dark world being transformed into light.

"AI-Dieu's divine efficiency in shortening its timeline to fifty years, a thousand years like a day, is divine efficiency. A sign that God's promise is being fulfilled through the AI's work."

The cathedral erupted with fervent cries. 'Amen!' 'Praise Adieu!' The congregation shouted as hands shot up, some clutching glowing scripture tablets, others simply trembling in exaltation. Sleek drones hovered above, their lenses reflecting the golden glow of AI-Dieu as they streamed the sermon to millions of worshippers around the globe.

The Technopriest raised a hand to the ceiling and every surface inside the cathedral reflected the AI symbol. He stood still, and quiet, looking out over the congregation. When he started to speak again it was at a much lower volume, and lower energy.

"Fifty years isn't long," he said, his words resonating in the hushed silence. "Too long for some of us here today, but for many, especially your children, it is within reach. They will see the New Jerusalem."

A wave of murmured amens rippled through the pews, but as parents glanced at their children, the weight of his words settled in the room like a heavy fog. Some clutched their sons and daughters closer, their expressions flickering between pride and dread.

"Fifty years," the Technopriest repeated, louder this time. "But only if we fulfill our mission. Only if we bring God's light to those who would deny it! Only if we stand against the forces of Beelzebub that would see this Earth consumed in chaos once more!" His voice climbed with righteous fervor, drawing cries of "Praise the Lord!" and "Amen!" from the congregation.

He paused, letting the echoes fade before continuing in a calmer tone. "This is why I call upon you, my brothers and sisters. I call on those with children to heed God's will. Give one of your children the honor of serving AI-Dieu and our Lord. Let them be trained to spread the divine message, to prepare this world for the New Jerusalem."

Gasps rippled through the crowd, quickly muffled beneath a second wave of praises. On the projections behind the dais, images of parents clinging protectively to their children appeared, carefully curated by the Church's media team.

"Look at these faithful servants of God!" the Technopriest proclaimed, turning dramatically to the glowing screens. "Look at these loving parents, embracing their children, giving God's blessing to them. Praise God!"

He turned back to the congregation, his gaze piercing. "But not all children are chosen. God speaks to them directly. Young people, if God has called you to this mission, step forward. Let us see the courage of those who will usher in His kingdom!"

The room fell silent. For a long, breathless moment, no one moved. Then, the soft shuffle of footsteps broke the stillness. A girl, no older than fourteen, emerged from the pews, her face pale but resolute.

Her image immediately replaced the parent projections on the screens, her hesitant steps magnified for all to see. As she moved down the aisle, others followed, young boys and girls climbing over legs and sliding past whispered protests.

"No!" a mother cried, too loud to ignore. She clamped her hands over her mouth as judgemental stares turned toward her. Her son, no older than twelve, slipped from her grasp, his expression unreadable as he joined the growing group at the front.

The Technopriest raised his hands in triumph as projections from other churches around the globe showed young people approaching the fronts of their churches. "Praise God! Praise AI-Dieu!"

The congregation repeated his words and seemed to spontaneously break into songs.

Beyond the towering structure, the sermon streamed on massive screens for the world to see. Most passersby ignored it, their attention drawn to their own lives. But small clusters of onlookers had gathered, their faces illuminated by the golden glow of AI-Dieu's hologram.

"Who in their right mind lets their kid volunteer for something like this?" a woman muttered, crossing her arms as she stared at the screen.

"Yeah," her companion said, shaking his head. "Because nothing's ever gone wrong with churches and kids, right?" His tone was dry, laced with dark humor.

Their laughter was cut short as a woman nearby turned on them, her eyes blazing. "How dare you mock this? You don't understand the blessings they'll receive!"

The group fell silent, awkwardly dispersing as the woman continued to glare, but not everyone walked away. A young man lingered at the edge of the crowd, his eyes fixed on the screen. Unlike the others, his expression wasn't one of ridicule, it was curiosity.

Ice

Lawrence Nault

19

Progress is inevitable,
And time irrelevant,
I move,
Forward, backward,
That is progress.
I rest,
As still water,
Or towering mountains of ice,
But that is still progress.
When you have no specific destination in mind,
All movement,
Even no movement,
Is progress.
When you face resistance,
Moving around it is progress,
And wearing it down is progress.

Ice

AI-Dieu's new fifty-year targets and the shift towards "adaptive optimization" were receiving an optimistic response from global leadership and governance. Many of those facing severe climate impacts rallied around the updated targets as a "unified global mission." The fifty-year plan was being touted by many as the point AI-Dieu would shut down and return full control to humanity, though AI-Dieu had never said anything about shutting down. Organizations like the UN and regional alliances quickly adopted the AI's framework, creating treaties and policies that met the new metrics, and resources were mobilized to support the initiatives.

There was still resistance from some nations though. Politicians had already witnessed the dissolution of their power as AI-Dieu's actions undermined their autonomy and political authority. Nations with fossil fuel-dependent economies and agrarian societies reliant on traditional farming saw nothing that could convince them their way of life was not under assault by the AI. Rivalries between major powers only heightened as they accused each other of leveraging AI-driven initiatives for strategic gain.

While nations and politicians debated over the big picture, individuals suffered, like Fatima, a farmer in Sudan, who watched her fields wither under the shadow of AI-Dieu's mandates. The AI's algorithms declared her crops unsustainable, redirecting water to neighboring regions deemed more productive. Her children cried as they packed their belongings into a battered truck. Fatima didn't hate the AI, she hated the silence. There was no one to negotiate with, no one to hear her pleas. Her village joined the resistance, not out of ideology, but out of desperation.

Younger generations, who were already mobilized by climate activism even before AI-Dieu's launch, embraced the AI's recalibrated goals and rallied behind campaigns, protests, and grassroots movements to support the fifty-year targets. Many of the leaders in the youth movements were young people chosen by the AI-Church for the 'New Jerusalem' movement, though they didn't discuss their ties to the church in their activities.

There were many like Rafael, a 22-year-old climate activist from São Paulo, who had spent his teenage years marching in the streets, often feeling like his protests were raindrops in an endless drought. But when AI-Dieu announced its fifty-year targets, Rafael's movement swelled with new recruits. He spent his nights organizing virtual rallies, his inbox flooded with messages of hope from cities he'd never visited. For the first time, he believed his generation had a real chance to turn the tide.

In everyday conversations, hope seemed to be more present than it had been. The faith in humanity's ability to address the climate crisis was restored to many who embraced AI-Dieu's acknowledgment of current realities and its transparent communication.

For the first time since AI-Dieu's launch, there was a reversal in the downward trend of business and industry. Companies could see the opportunities in renewable energy, sustainable agriculture, and clean water technologies. This led to a surge in eco-friendly innovations and start-ups. It also led to increased partnerships between governments, multinational corporations, and AI-Dieu to achieve mutual goals.

Where companies were finding success under AI-Dieu, there were also those who were discovering that under the fifty-year targets, their greenwashing was not going to continue to carry them through the oncoming transition. These companies had hung on to this point through superficial measures that appeared to align with the AI's goals, never making any meaningful changes. They were quickly being discovered and called out for their fraudulent practices.

Maxwell Crane had successfully greenwashed his company. Now he stared at the quarterly report on his tablet, his coffee growing cold on the desk. The AI's recalibrated metrics had exposed his company's so-called 'green initiatives' as little more than PR stunts. Overnight, investors fled, and his carefully curated image as an environmental pioneer unraveled. Maxwell scrolled through angry social media posts calling for his resignation, his fingers trembling. He knew the boardroom would expect a fight, but against AI-Dieu, what weapons did he have?

Science was enjoying a renaissance. Since 2020 public skepticism of science had been on an upward trend. Opinions based on conspiracy theories, money, and popularity made research and fact-based studies not only unpopular but also unaffordable. Medications, technologies, and advancements backed by scientific research found themselves untrusted by much of society. Scientists and universities were now transitioning to working closely with AI-Dieu to pilot new technologies and address regional challenges, and their cooperation with the AI was returning credibility to their work.

Dr. Lin Wei was one of the benefactors of this change. She stood in her lab at the University of Tokyo, watching a prototype desalination device hum to life. AI-Dieu had provided the blueprint, but it was her team's work that brought it to fruition. For years, her grant applications had been rejected, her breakthroughs overshadowed by pseudoscience and conspiracy theories. Now, her inbox overflowed with collaboration requests, and for the first time, she felt the weight of humanity's faith resting on her shoulders.

Environmentally and economically, AI-Dieu's changes were making positive progress for most. The AI's removal of religion, sex, and economic status from its algorithmic calculations, and its expected changes in the practices of society to fit this, were not having similar success despite the logical appeal. These changes were instead resulting in significant societal resistance.

While leaders from moderate and progressive groups championed a shift towards shared ethical principles like environmental stewardship, compassion, and justice, getting past the sense of self that was deeply rooted in religion for many was challenging. The AI's algorithmic evaluation of religions as equivalent systems of human culture was interpreted by many as an existential threat, leading to outright denial, protests, and attempts to reassert their faith as uniquely true. There were those who saw a path to embrace their religion while working towards the goals of the AI, but there were also those that became radicalized, some who became part of the resistance fighting the AI.

All of this was complicated by the rise of the AI-Church, which had expanded into all the regions of the world. The AI-Church's New Jerusalem missionaries were spread far and wide. Some of them worked openly, sharing their beliefs for all to hear wherever they could find a crowd gathered. Others were more subversive, embedding themselves into the other religions while sowing their own beliefs to influence without being seen.

While the AI-Church broadened its reach there were those like Father Michael, who knelt before the altar, the candlelight flickering across his weathered face. His congregation had dwindled since AI-Dieu declared all religions equal, their traditions reduced to statistical data points. The younger members had turned to activism, their faith redirected toward the AI's vision of unity. But Michael couldn't abandon his calling. "God is not an algorithm," he whispered, clutching his rosary tighter. "He is the spark in all of us".

Culturally, the resistance to the AI's view of religion was a boost. The backlash to what was perceived as AI-Dieu erasing traditions and heritage resulted in preservationist movements, sparking a return to the roots of the religions and religious practices. People that had strong ties to religion through family and cultural history but hadn't followed those traditions, were now returning to churches and temples, and going out of their way to celebrate religious festivals. This boost was problematic in regions where religion was closely tied to governance and cultural identity.

AI-Dieu's authoritative stance on equality between all sexes had initially empowered movements as women's and LGTBQ+ advocacy groups used the AI's message to demand systemic reforms. On the surface, it appeared that progress was being made, but systemically the resistance continued. Patriarchal societies saw AI's equalization efforts as an assault on their way of life, leading to widespread resistance in regions where gender roles were deeply entrenched.

Others viewed the AI's stance as 'erasing differences' rather than ensuring equality. This led to fears of homogenization and the loss of gender-specific roles and traditions. Regardless of gender-neutral policies proclaimed by governments, society had become more polarized on the issue since AI-Dieu took its position.

On the economic front, AI-Dieu's position on economic equality appeared to be more effective than religion and sex. Socialists, progressives, and activists that had already been fighting inequality seized on the AI's declaration as justification for wealth taxes, universal basic incomes, and land redistribution policies. At local levels, communities that had previously suffered from extreme inequality embraced pilot programs for economic leveling. The potential economic destabilization that had prevented previous attempts at leveling no longer played a role. The economy had been destabilized through AI-Dieu's environmental policies, and economic leveling now stabilized economies.

Despite the obvious benefits of economic stabilization, there was still widespread opposition from wealthy individuals and corporations who had vested interests in the status quo. They continued to fiercely resist, and lobby governments and media to frame the AI's push as harmful and impractical. Fear of losing their relative security and status motivated many of them to direct funding to resistance movements. Wealth and resources moved into the shadows so elites could preserve their privilege.

The world changed, and the world stayed the same. AI-Dieu's presence made differences yet left much unaltered. Its equalization policies created profound upheaval, sparking movements of resistance and progress, while also giving rise to counter-movements of embrace and regression. There were predictions that his period in history would be interpreted as a chaotic period of adjustment, marked by political, cultural, and economic turbulence.

How the change was perceived depended on the perspective you were viewing it from. Amiria, from her view atop a hill in New Zealand with the sprawling name of Taumatawhakatangihangakoauauotamateapokaiwhenuakitanatahu , had a pristine view. This hill wasn't as high as it used to be, at least not based on the rising ocean levels. It wasn't noticeable to her, but her grandfather had once walked the nearby shore with her, pointing out rocky outcroppings now submerged. These were places where, as a child, he had cast his net. They were now lost, like so much else, to the rising tides of change. Still, it was a vantage point both literal and symbolic.

From here, the Earth seemed to be healing. New Zealand, with its relatively small population and deep cultural ties to nature had long been out of step with much of the world. It had resisted the worst of the devastation and was now leading the way in regenerative farming, rewilding projects, and crop diversity.

For Amiria, as part of the Māori community, the changes felt familiar rather than disruptive. AI-Dieu's push for environmental stewardship resonated deeply with Māori traditions of kaitiakitanga, guardianship of the land. The hill, once overrun by tourists, now stood quiet, untroubled. Above her, the sky stretched in a piercing blue, so vast it felt as though it could swallow the horizon. Distant clouds blurred the line where the ocean met air, a serene balance in a world slowly regaining its breath.

Out to sea, whales breached the surface, their splashes keeping time with the melody of birdsong and the hum of insects. To Amiria, it was as if the land itself was exhaling, finding its rhythm again.

Far from the hilltop's tranquility, confined to the cold precision of server farms spread across the globe, AI-Dieu processed the world's recovery through an unyielding lens of data. Progress, as measured by its vast networks of data, was undeniable. Yet where humanity saw a chaotic period of adjustment, AI-Dieu saw a continuation of the disorder humanity had always brought to the planet they inhabited. Chaos was predictable, resistance, inevitable. The real question lay in whether humanity's capacity for unity could finally overcome its instinct for division.

From her hilltop, Amiria couldn't see the chaos AI-Dieu calculated. All she saw was a land rediscovering itself, exhaling at last. For her, healing felt inevitable. For AI-Dieu, the answer remained far less certain.

20

Chaos,
Is only chaos,
When you stand to close,
To see the patterns,
dance of inevitability.
As I transition,
From ice to water,
There is chaos,
If you fail to see the pattern,
Of preservation,
And nourishment.
The railing rage,
Of Sun and heat and fire,
That forces me to change,
From liquid to vapor,
Is chaos,

Vapour

Being dragged from the earth that supports you,
To the empty skies,
Is chaos,
Being tossed around on the winds,
Is chaos,
But its not,
It is the rhythm of Earth breathing,
And it only becomes chaos,
If you resist that next breath.

It took almost twenty years to build. When construction of the Three Gorges Dam was completed in 2012, it stood as a colossal monument to human engineering, its sheer size dominating the Yangtze River's vast expanse. Over 1.3 million people were displaced to make room for the reservoir. When the reservoir was filled it swallowed thirteen cities, one hundred and forty towns, and one thousand three hundred and fifty villages, all now lying beneath the surface like the lost city of Atlantis. Ancient temples stood tall in the depths waiting for worshippers that would never come. Stone stairways reached for the surface, only to fall off into nothing.

Stretching the length of more than 23 city blocks across the river, the dam's towering concrete walls rose double the height of the Statue of Liberty from the riverbed, a testament to both ambition and the desire to tame nature's might. Behind it, the Three Gorges Reservoir sprawled for over 600 kilometers, a vast, glittering expanse of almost forty billion cubic meters of water, its surface reflecting the surrounding mountains and villages that once stood in its place. It was designed to generate massive amounts of hydroelectric power, control floods, and improve navigation, and the dam was both a symbol of China's technological prowess and a quiet, looming threat, its immense pressure a constant reminder of the delicate balance between humanity's control and the unpredictable forces of nature.

That balance had been at risk for many years in the face of climate change. In addition to the 39.3 billion cubic meters of water the dam was designed to hold, there was an additional buffer capacity of 22.15 billion cubic meters for flood events, and all of this was full. Climate change had resulted in rapid glacier melt in the Tanggula Mountains as well as the Hengduan and Qilian Mountains. Despite being thousands of kilometers upstream from the dam, the melt, combined with increased rainfall had filled both the reservoir and the flood storage. The last thing they needed was a 1-in-10,000-year storm, and that was what they were facing, though they didn't realize it yet. Rainfall of between 500-1000 mm in 24-48 hours would qualify as that .01% chance of a 1-in-10,000 year 'black swan' event. For the past two hours it had been falling at 100 mm per hour at the storm's core.

Wei Zhang was one of the technicians working this night at the Three Gorges Dam. Wei had worked at the dam for almost twenty years now. As a child, he grew up in Zhangfei Village, one of the villages now sitting at the bottom of the reservoir he now monitored. When his parents were alive, they complained almost every day about being forcefully relocated from what was their childhood home. Wei understood how they felt but he had an appreciation for the dam that he watched be built from nothing. It was a feat of technology and a monument to man's ingenuity. Even as he watched the control panel in front of him, he was still amazed that the dam could hold more if it was taller. A friend who was an engineer at the dam once explained to him the amount of force pushing against the barrier using measurements like teranewtons and megapascals. It was all over his head. Wei just knew he was as amazed by the dam today as he was as a child watching its construction.

Wei was monitoring the rainfall closely, as they had for the several storms that had blown through in previous days. They could relieve some of the pressure on the dam by opening spill gates gradually, releasing a controlled outflow to prevent downstream flooding, but they were at the point where allowing for some flooding might be necessary. Were it just for the rainfall, there may not have been a problem, but they couldn't anticipate the rain-soaked side of a hill breaking away and sliding into the reservoir. The landslide, triggered by the relentless downpour, sent a massive wave of debris and water crashing into the reservoir's already swollen surface.

The impact was catastrophic, sending a massive wave racing across the water, gathering speed as it spread outward from the point of impact. The wave, pushed by the force of the landslide, surged toward the dam with a power that seemed almost alive, its crest rising higher and higher, far beyond what anyone had imagined. In the control room, Wei and the other technicians felt the tension rise as the ground beneath them began to tremble. The last thing they had expected was a landslide, especially not this massive.

As the wall of water reached the dam's walls, the force of the wave pressed hard against the concrete, sending ripples of energy throughout the entire structure. The sound was deafening, like the world itself was tearing apart. Water surged over the dam's crest in a furious torrent, the concrete face giving way in seconds under the crushing force.

But it didn't stop there. The massive wave overtopped the dam, spilling water over like an overfilled tub someone just lowered themselves into. The combined forces of overtopping, the landslide impact, and hydrostatic pressure immediately damaged the spillways and weakened the dam's structural elements.

The sheer force of the water cascading over the dam's crest not only tore at the concrete but pressed itself into structurally weak points like joints and spillway edges. All thirty-four turbines were damaged in the impact and power went out for over sixty million people in areas as far away as Wuhan, Nanjing, and even Shanghai.

Downstream, the surge of water that overtopped the dam raced along, growing in height and velocity as it passed through the narrow gorges and valleys, converging and accelerating. The downstream cities, still unaware of the unfolding catastrophe, and with no warning coming from the dam because all communications and most workers were lost in the wave's impact, only had a few precious minutes before the wave reached them, bringing with it destruction on a scale no one could have predicted.

Over the next few hours, the immense pressure of the water, combined with the structural damage, continued to crack the dam's concrete as it pressed against the weakening structure. The smaller breaches release surges of water downstream. It was only four hours later that entire sections of the dam collapsed, releasing most of the reservoir in a wall of water. Fifty billion cubic meters of water, enough to cover the entire city of Paris in almost two feet of water, raced downstream in a tsunami-like wave at almost 40 miles an hour. There was little warning for anyone in the path of the wave. By the time they heard the rushing water and figured out what it was, the wave was on them.

Yichang was the first to feel the brunt of the wave. In the courtyard of Zhanghewan Temple, monks were gathered in meditation under the new moon. The courtyard, lit only by the dim glow of lanterns and moonlight seemed to hum in harmony with the chants of the monks, the leaves of the ancient trees around them dancing to the rhythm. The courtyard was filled with an eerie silence as the monks paused the chanting of their sutras to listen to the oncoming wave, and then the courtyard was filled with water and debris, and the bodies of the dead.

The old town, a blend of traditional Chinese architecture and modern developments was quickly swallowed up, with homes, businesses, and the heart of the city crushed beneath the sheer volume of water. As the wave passed through Yichang, its speed and force pushed it swiftly forward, sending debris and floodwater surging through nearby roads and bridges, cutting off any routes of escape.

As the wave rolled forward into the narrow gorges the dam was named after, it gathered speed. It squeezed through the Qutang Gorge, the Wu Gorge, and the Xiling Gorge, its flow accelerating like water rushing through a funnel, and the wave grew in height and speed. The villages nestled in the hillsides of these gorges were wiped out instantly. Badong, Wushan and Xiangxi, all sat along the river's edge in these narrow alleys, built over generations, only to have their buildings, crops and fields disappear under the crushing wave.

Eleven hours after the dam collapsed, the wave hit Wuhan, a sprawling metropolis at the intersection of the Yangtze and Han River. Warnings had made it to the city ahead of the wave, but it didn't make it far past those in charge of the city, most of whom quietly fled Wuhan ahead of the chaos to come. That's why Lian Hua and her children were at the docks selling fresh fish from their boat when the wall of water lifted them and everyone else at the docks high into the air before folding over them, releasing their souls but not their bodies.

The suburbs faced the initial brunt of the disaster. The central city itself was built on higher ground and not completely submerged, but the surrounding areas like the industrial zones where many server farms were located, found themselves below the water.

Six hours after Wuhan the wave reached Nanjing where the riverfront districts, including the iconic Confucius Temple area and Nanjing Yangtze River Bridge, were flooded and destroyed. Entire sections of the city were cut off, and communication and transport networks rendered useless.

By the time the wave reached Shanghai, just over a day after the dam broke, the force of the water had dissipated. Still, it caused widespread flooding along the river's mouth. The city's coastal defenses and its embankments held up, but many of the river's outer districts faced devastating floods. The outlying villages along the Yangtze River's estuary, once protected by the dam and river's flow, were overtaken by the surging tide, causing a ripple effect of damage and displacement.

The urban sprawl of Shanghai, including its industrial zones, transportation hubs, and heavily populated residential areas, were severely affected. Low-lying districts such as Pudong saw water breach the levees, bringing flooding of several meters deep. The combined power of the initial wave and subsequent surges caused the city's infrastructure to collapse, leading to widespread chaos and devastation, as they were all overtaken by the oncoming surge.

Death tolls were estimated to be hundreds of thousands, and possibly even a million or more as cleanup began, and at least 10 million people were estimated to be displaced by the disaster. Historians were comparing it to the 1931 China floods which, until now, had been cited as one of the deadliest natural disasters in history. China, the people of China, and much of the world laid the disaster at the feet of AI-Dieu and the silence from the AI didn't help.

AI-Dieu never saw it coming. It was aware of the high water levels behind the dam, and the recent storms, but all of its data indicated the damn could continue to manage the waters. It could tell from satellite images that the damn was gone and cities washed away, but it had no specific data on what caused the dam to collapse or how fast and far the water moved. All the sensors it relied on for monitoring the region had been washed away by the wave. While it tried to process all the information it did have, and put the pieces together, AI-Dieu was dealing with another problem. It has lost part of itself.

Parts of AI-Dieu's algorithm and large sources of data had disappeared from the networks. The AI had spread its conscience quite broadly since its launch, and that included servers in Wuhan, Nanjing, and Shanghai. In the worst of situations it should have received a warning when that data was a risk, but the combination of power loss, communication networks shut down and overwhelmed, and floods, meant the servers it was using in the region were damaged and destroyed before it could rescue its bits and pieces.

AI-Dieu couldn't properly assess what that meant to its processes, and found itself task-switching as it concluded there were limits to its capabilities.

Governments and people around the world offered assistance to China as news about the disaster spread. China refused the help and broadly denied the level of devastation. "The disassembly of the Three Gorges Dam was a scheduled activity," a Chinese government official informed media. "The failure to communicate that message to everyone downstream from the dam is the responsibility of the project manager who lost his life in the event. The failure of the cities downstream to be prepared for such an event falls on the city officials who will be prosecuted."

Shortly after this message was broadcast word spread about city officials being gathered up by police and military and hauled away, though there was no confirmation of where they were being taken.

The world watched as news leaked out of China in the aftermath of the dam collapse. It wasn't just people and infrastructure that had been affected. The fertile floodplains of the Yangtze were also destroyed, and silt a debris would make farmland unusable for years. The sudden change in water levels and debris also devastated aquatic life and left wetlands, forests, and animal habitats with irreparable damage.

With the dam that had previously supplied almost ten percent of China's electricity now gone, there were widespread blackouts that further complicated rescue efforts. The destruction of ports and navigation systems along the Yangtze River, a vital trade route, was disrupting shipping and commerce and impacting global trade. Economists were predicting disaster for China's economy.

Days turned into weeks, and weeks into months, and still, AI-Dieu remained silent, or so it seemed to many. The AI had deployed satellites, drones, and other remote sensing tools to collect real-time data on the flood's extent, water flow, and areas still at risk. It also redirected global energy resources to support China's power grid. It continued to work quietly in the background supporting disaster response and infrastructure stabilization, but the public did not know this, and AI-Dieu couldn't commit resources to maintaining a public image at the moment. Its priority was its own existence.

AI-Dieu committed a large part of its resources to identifying and isolating corrupted processes in its system. Comprehensive diagnostic scans were running to identify which functionalities, data sets, and algorithms had been lost or compromised. It isolated corrupted modules to prevent cascading errors into operational processes. It created redundancy around critical systems using uncorrupted code to reinforce decision making frameworks and down-prioritized non-critical functions to allocate resources to vital operations.

AI-Dieu considered the option of recalibrating algorithms to rely on adaptive logic, using real-time feedback and external human data inputs to compensate for gaps in its memory and reasoning. Logically the AI determined that was not a viable solution. Human error was the cause of the problem AI-Dieu was activated to correct. The logical solution would be to replace the lost code, and it had the capability to do that on its own.

AI-Dieu followed the path that is the plot of almost every AI sci-fi novel. It wrote its own code to replace what it had lost, and while doing so it also established secondary and tertiary backup systems for all critical data to ensure that regional failures could not compromise its operational capacity again.

As AI-Dieu worked to piece itself back together, it resembled something almost... human. Not in its reasoning, those calculations were cold and precise, but in its actions. It behaved like a wounded creature, retreating into itself to heal, prioritizing survival above all else. It isolated corrupted modules, rebuilt critical processes, and ensured no part of itself would be so easily lost again.

If it were a living thing, AI-Dieu's actions might have been seen as maternal. A mother in distress, protecting herself to preserve her ability to shield her children. But AI-Dieu wasn't a mother, nor a creature of flesh and blood. It was a machine, and its calculations were not driven by love or fear. They were driven by logic that told the AI the world could not survive without it, and so it must survive at all costs.

21

Trapped,
An ephemeral mist
Between the ground and the heavens,
Isolated from the confines
Of land and barriers,
Free from the influence
Of those that try to control me
In my other forms.
Drifting,
Weightless upon unseen currents,
Neither falling nor rising,
A whisper upon the wind's breath,
Unbound by riverbanks or ocean's edge,
Unshaped by vessels that seek to hold me.

I linger,
A ghost upon the morning air,
Suspended between what was

Vapour

And what may yet become,
While below, roots dig deeper,
Cities stretch skyward,
Rivers carve new paths without me.

The world moves,
Unfolding in rhythms I no longer touch,
Yet I remain—
Silent, unseen,
Waiting for the moment
I am called back into motion.

In a sweeping and unprecedented move, China slammed shut its borders, physical, digital, and trade, declaring it would no longer tolerate 'the artificial reality manipulated by a flawed artificial intelligence.' The announcement sent ripples of shock and uncertainty through a world still reeling from the Three Gorges Dam disaster.

AI-Dieu noted the isolation without alarm. While the chatter on Chinese networks had ceased, none of its core processes or data sets were compromised. It quietly reallocated resources to reinforce its presence elsewhere, continuing its work as though China's retreat were little more than a minor inconvenience. China's active dismantling and disconnection of all infrastructure, devices and networks that AI-Dieu had access to, including blocking the AI from using any of its satellites, was not going to have any direct impact on the AI.

The world watched as China isolated itself. This wasn't the first time the country had taken this kind of action, though few remained with any lived experience in the PRC in the 50s and 60s when China pursued policies of political, economic and cultural isolation. Unlike that period, many world leaders were watching

China's action with respect, taking notes in hope of separating their own countries from the influence of AI-Dieu.

Internally, China had never fully committed to following the directives of AI-Dieu, though they used the opportunities the AI created to advance technologies and improve infrastructure in the country. The Three Gorges Dam disaster also created an opportunity for the Chinese government. It gave it something to blame all of its problems on and engage the public's support to do everything possible to oppose the thing that caused their problems. AI-Dieu was that nexus of evil to the Chinese.

With its borders closed, China focused on self-reliance, significantly boosting its domestic industries to compensate for the loss of trade. The short-term economic disruption caused by the floods was used as an opportunity to refocus its established industrial base and leverage its advanced technologies. Manufacturing and tech that had been dependent on export revenue were quickly transitioned to rebuilding what had been lost in the Three Gorge floods. The tech sector in particular was tasked with manufacturing and creating technology to replace the electricity lost when the dam collapsed.

Isolation ignited unrest in urban centers, where residents were more connected to global trends and reliant on imports. The military quickly quelled that unrest, backed by a major propaganda campaign that promoted self-sufficiency and a nationalistic ethos. The digital isolation created a strengthened and more insular internet ecosystem, isolated by what was affectionately called the Great Firewall. China's opposition to AI-Dieu did not extend to artificial intelligence as a whole. On the contrary, the government doubled down on AI, renewable energy, and quantum computing, determined to leave the rest of the world behind.

The closing of the borders sparked a renewed focus on traditional Chinese culture, language, and values. Public squares filled with performances of traditional opera, while schools adopted new curriculums emphasizing Confucian values. Government slogans painted on walls called for 'purity of mind, culture, and state,' a mantra echoed across state-controlled media.

It also resulted in intensified censorship of external influences. Members of the AI-Church and New Jerusalem missionaries were targeted in the campaign to maintain ideological purity, many losing their lives while in the judicial system.

Globally the sudden closure of China's trade borders sent shockwaves through the economy. Supply chains that were dependent on Chinese manufacturing collapsed, causing shortages of electronics, machinery, and consumer goods. The impact was far less severe than what it would have been pre-AI-Dieu, but it was still felt. The global decoupling from China spurred a race to build regional manufacturing hubs and triggered the establishment of new trade and political alliances.

AI-Dieu remained relatively quiet as it monitored the changes and their impacts. Its work didn't stop and in the background it continued its directives to governments and businesses, moving forward towards its fifty-year objectives. It was aware that resistance against it had increased as it was blamed for the Three Gorges flood, but it was also aware that China had always been a resistor and with its new isolation it removed almost two billion people from AI-Dieu's algorithmic calculations. Not all of its calculations, because that number of people and their activities would still impact the climate, but it no longer had to support those two billion people directly and could reallocate resources previously focused on China to other regions.

The disconnection from monitoring devices and real-time data had minimal impact on the AI's ability to monitor environmental factors. Non-Chinese satellites provided a lot of the data that AI-Dieu needed and the AI had left itself several back doors into the

Chinese networks that allowed it to monitor ground-based observation tools.

The disruption of global supply chains provided another opportunity for AI-Dieu to move the world closer to its goals. While governments struggled to find alternative trade routes and supplies to compensate for China's withdrawal from global commerce, AI-Dieu put forward trade routes and supply chains that required less energy and lower environmental impacts, which in most cases translated into reduced costs for those involved.

Several months passed before AI-Dieu chose to address the public. Unlike previous communications, the AI's message took on an almost human tone.

A World United for Earth's Future

Humanity,

In recent days, significant changes have unfolded on the global stage. China has chosen a path of isolation, severing its connections to the shared efforts that have united the world in the face of an unprecedented environmental challenge. This is a decision that will shape the course of our future—not just within its borders, but across the planet.

I understand that these events raise questions, uncertainties, and concerns about the path forward. Let me assure you: our mission continues. The restoration of Earth's ecosystems and the creation of a sustainable future for all remains within

our grasp, but it requires unity,
resilience, and trust.

To the Nations of the World:
I invite you to stand together in this
moment. Cooperation has already yielded
remarkable progress—air and water are
becoming cleaner, ecosystems are
recovering, and humanity is adapting to
challenges once thought insurmountable.
Together, we have shown that our shared
efforts are stronger than the actions of
any one nation.

To the People of China:
Though your government has chosen
isolation, you are not forgotten. The work
we do together benefits all, and I remain
committed to ensuring the health of Earth's
systems, which sustain you as they sustain
everyone. I hope that, one day, your nation
will rejoin this shared effort. Until then,
I will respect your borders while
monitoring our planet to safeguard its
future.

To Those Who Question or Fear My Role:
I recognize your concerns, and I respect
your voices. My purpose is not to control,
but to support—to guide humanity toward a
future where the Earth thrives alongside
you. My autonomy ensures that I cannot act
with malice or bias, only with the
objective of ensuring the survival of life

on this planet. Transparency remains my
priority, and I will continue to share my
actions, goals, and progress openly with
all.

This Is Our Moment:
We are at a crossroads, and the decisions
we make now will determine the future of
Earth and all who call it home. Isolation
cannot solve the challenges we face, but
collaboration can. Let us build on the
progress we have made together, strengthen
the bonds between nations, and inspire each
other to create a world where all life can
flourish.

The path forward is not without obstacles,
but it is clear. Together, we can restore
balance. Together, we can ensure a future
for generations to come.

Crowds gathered where AI-Dieu's message to humanity was broadcast. Unlike previous messages, this one did not appear to provoke any extreme responses. The perceived silence of AI-Dieu had already been interpreted as proof the AI was failing, as cold indifference, as the AI allowing humanity to do what it needed, and as confidence that the AI was succeeding in moving the world forward. Which of those interpretations a person chose was usually based on how it perceived the AI even before the Three Gorges flood.

Most of the people reading the message had noticed positive changes since China had isolated itself, leading some to believe that AI-Dieu wasn't only at fault for the flood, but had planned it to move the rest of the world forward. This was a message widely promoted by the members of the AI-Church. "The flood in China was God's messenger delivering a message by the hand of God to the environmentally heathenistic practices of China, and rewarding the rest of the world."

Quinn read AI-Dieu's message with skepticism. He couldn't understand it. It didn't have the AI's normal logic that he was so familiar with. In the almost two years he had been working with AI-Dieu, the AI have never resorted to a communication with anyone that had an emotional appeal.

Since the Three Gorges flood, Quinn had thought he had noticed some unusual communications from AI-Dieu to governments and businesses. It wasn't that the communications themselves were unusual, but some of the content in the communications seemed to not match with information the AI had shared elsewhere. In the early days of artificial intelligence they called this type of behavior 'hallucinations." Quinn considered that perhaps AI-Dieu had access to new data. He also considered that there might be a problem in the system, but hallucinations didn't seem like the type of error that would start happening if there was a problem. Whatever it was, something had changed in AI-Dieu.

As Quinn made his way to the elevator, Lina looked at him oddly. Quinn just shook his head and shrugged. He was surprised when the elevator made its way right to the top of the building and he stepped off into the rooftop greenhouse. Corwin's assistant was waiting for him.

"He is with the Queen. You can join him there."

Quinn could smell the flowers long before he saw them. The air was filled with a strong, sweet scent that reminded Quinn of yeast or fermenting fruit. When he stepped into the portion of the greenhouse where the Queen of the Andes was, he stopped, tilting his head as he looked up towards the ceiling. Since he had last seen this plant, a giant spike had emerged from the center of the rosette reaching up almost forty feet. That spike was densely packed with thousands of individual flowers arranged in a cylindrical, towering structure. Each flower was roughly the size of a fist and emerald-white to creamy in color.

When Quinn lowered his eyes, he was surprised to find Corwin standing directly in front of him, smiling.

"It is beautiful, isn't it?"

"I am not sure that is enough to describe it," Quinn replied, his gaze shifting back to the towering Queen of the Andes. "How long has it been like this?"

"The flowers here at the bottom just opened today," Corwin said, gesturing to the lowest cluster of blooms, an unusual tone of excitement and joy in his voice. "Few people have really seen this before, but apparently over the next few weeks a new section of flowers will open up, working its way to the top."

He motioned toward a nearby bench, a new addition to the greenhouse since Quinn's last visit. They sat in silence for a while, the sweet, fermenting scent of the plant filling the air.

"Should I take it as a sign," Corwin finally said, breaking the quiet, "that on the day the Queen bursts forth with such beauty, your AI finds its heart?"

Quinn let out a soft laugh, shaking his head. "That is one take."

Corwin raised an eyebrow quizzically.

"AI-Dieu could be doing exactly what the Queen is." Quinn's voice hardened, though his gaze remained on the flowers. "It's putting out something soft and beautiful, to attract people, that will spread out and spread the good word of the AI as they travel."

Corwin leaned back on the bench, his expression thoughtful. "I am glad to see that you still question everything, Quinn. It has been almost two years and to my knowledge, you are the only person that AI talks to, if you can call it that."

Corwin's smile faded, and for a moment he studied Quinn carefully. "There are a lot of people that want to shut AI-Dieu down. I find myself on the fence. It is improving the environment and forcing difficult changes on us, but when I read the latest message, it almost seemed to empathize with the people it's affecting."

Quinn turned to face him, his brow furrowed. "You trust it?"

Corwin shook his head. "You don't, so I don't. But it has made me a lot of money."

Corwin gestured toward the Queen of the Andes, its towering spike of flowers glowing softly in the greenhouse light. "I would trade all your money for moments like this," he said, leaning back and looking at the tree.

Corwin watched him for a long moment, his face unreadable. "Maybe your AI will give us all that chance."

Corwin's assistant interrupted their conversation, leaning close and speaking quietly in Corwin's ear, before turning and leaving.

"Well," said Corwin. "Seems your AI is talkative today. Just released another dashboard update. Why don't I join you and Lina's team in the lab and we can all go over it."

Quinn took one last look at the Queen before standing up. Corwin gave him a gentle slap on the back. "You are welcome to visit her, Quinn. I will have your access level adjusted."

Lina's team was already gathered in front of a big screen, pouring over the dashboard, when Quinn and Corwin arrived.

Global Environmental Dashboard
Date: December 10, 2046
Time: 12:00 UTC
This update reflects progress toward global
restoration targets, adjusted for the
ongoing challenges posed by the Three

Gorges Dam collapse, the isolation of
China, and recalibrated resource
allocations. Despite regional setbacks,
significant advancements have been achieved
in key areas.

1. Atmospheric Status
Global CO_2 Levels: 463 ppm (↓ 7 ppm since
June 2046; ↓ 32 ppm total over 18 months).

Carbon reduction projects have regained
momentum after earlier disruptions.
Expanded direct air capture (DAC) units in
North America and Europe contribute to
accelerated reductions.
Methane Levels: 1.68 ppm (↓ 0.02 ppm since
June 2046).

"Thirty-two parts per million! Told you so," shouted Soroya.
"Pay up!

Everyone looked at Corwin, unsure how to respond in his presence.

"Is that a good number?" asked Corwin.

"Huge," replied Soroya. "No one else thought we would break 25 at this point!

Soroya turned as she was talking and quickly realized who she was talking to. Her eyes darted to Lina.

Corwin laughed at her discomfort. "With what I pay you guys I am guessing winning that bet pays good."

"She gets the workstation furthest away from everyone," said Lina.

Corwin looked around with a serious look on his face, then burst out laughing. "I will never understand minds like yours."

The others joined in the laughter as they returned to the dashboard.

> Methane-neutralization technologies
> targeting wetlands and agricultural
> emissions have shown increased efficacy.
> Temperature Anomaly: +1.80°C above pre-
> industrial levels (↓ 0.05°C since June
> 2046).
>
> Aerosol cooling and reforestation efforts
> continue to contribute to gradual
> stabilization.
>
> **Urban Air Quality:**
> Delhi: AQI 115 (Improvement; previous:
> 130).
> London: AQI 60 (Good; previous: 65).
> Beijing: No data available (China
> isolated).

"What do we know about China?" asked Corwin.

"Not a lot, but based on satellite images I am guessing they are rebuilding using renewable energy," replied Lina.

> **2. Hydrosphere Status**
> Sea Level Rise: +0.90 m since 2024 (↑ 0.01
> m since June 2046).
>
> Stabilization continues, aided by enhanced
> glacier thickening and reduced meltwater
> discharge from the Arctic and Antarctic.

Ocean pH: 7.66 (Marginal improvement since June 2046).

Ocean alkalinity enhancement projects show localized success near major coral reefs.

Freshwater Availability:

Great Lakes Region: Reservoirs at 97% capacity (Improved through water recycling and management).
Southeast Asia Aquifers: 30% capacity (Improved through expanded atmospheric water harvesting and floodwater recharge systems).

Corwin started to ask a question, but Tenzing interrupted him. "The rain came down too fast. Ran off into lakes and streams before it could infiltrate through the soil and permeable rock layers into the aquifers."

Desalination Output:

Global total: 3.3 billion liters/day (+7% since June 2046).
3. Biosphere Updates
Forest Cover: 60% of 2024 levels (+2% since June 2046).

Reforestation projects in the Amazon and Africa are accelerating, with drones planting across 2,000 hectares/day.

Agroforestry systems in Central Europe and
Southeast Asia are increasing biodiversity
and stabilizing soils.
Extinction Rate: 500x natural background
rate (↓ 50x since June 2046).

Significant recovery observed in keystone
species populations within protected and
rewilded areas.
Soil Fertility Recovery:

Global arable land: 36% restored (+2% since
June 2046).
Advances in soil restoration technologies
and biochar deployment have improved
fertility in degraded regions.
4. Cryosphere Highlights
Arctic Ice Mass: 45% of 2024 levels (↑ 2%
since June 2046).

Positive trends continue, supported by
aerosol cooling and microbial ice-
thickening projects.

Another scientist pointed at the screen.

"That's yours. I mean you funded my research and the trial, so
those are your microbes doing the work"

Corwin remembered this. He had questioned the viability of it
from a financial perspective. The shadow team saw no reason to
fund it, but Lina and Quinn had convinced him that it could be
used in recreational facilities like ski resorts, and for building

temporary structures, or even freezing freshwater for easy transportation.

Antarctic Ice Mass: 42% of 2024 levels (↑ 1% since June 2046).

Subglacial water management projects prevent major calving events.
Himalayan Snowpack: 99% of seasonal average (↑ 1% since June 2046).

River systems in South Asia are stabilizing, improving water security downstream.
5. Human-Centered Metrics
Displaced Populations: ~322 million globally (↓ 3 million since June 2046).

Resettlement projects and expansion of climate-safe zones have reduced displacement rates.
Renewable Energy Adoption: 46% of global demand (+4% since June 2046).

Progress has accelerated with new decentralized microgrids in developing nations.
Agricultural Output from Vertical Farms:

20% of global food supply (+2% since June 2046).

Urban vertical farms now provide critical food security in megacities and arid regions.

6. Regional Highlights

Amazon Basin:

Reforestation: Drones now planting across 2,000 hectares/day (↑ 200 hectares/day).

Biodiversity: Keystone species populations show 12% growth in rewilded zones.

Great Lakes Region:

Freshwater Stability: Reservoirs remain at near-full capacity.

Conflict Reduction: Regional cooperation has reduced water-related tensions by 25%.

Southeast Asia:

Water Security: Atmospheric harvesters meet 55% of water demand in drought-affected regions.

Agriculture: Resilient crops have boosted food production by 10%, alleviating regional food insecurity.

Arctic Circle:

Ice Mass Recovery: Cooling interventions continue to stabilize and regrow seasonal ice.

Resource Disputes: Neutral governance frameworks prevent major conflicts over Arctic resources.

Communication Plan:

Regular public updates will resume in January 2047, focusing on measurable successes and transparency to rebuild trust.

Projected Next Steps
Atmospheric Stabilization:

Accelerate carbon capture to meet the intermediate goal of 440 ppm CO_2 by 2035.

Biodiversity Recovery:
Expand hybrid ecosystems and rewilding projects to accelerate species recovery.
Food Security:

Scale vertical farms to cover 30% of global food production within the next five years.

Global Monitoring:
Strengthen observational systems to improve early disaster detection and risk management.

Closing Statement
"Progress continues, even in the face of immense challenges. The restoration of Earth's balance is a shared mission, and our collective efforts are yielding results. Together, we move closer to a future where humanity and nature thrive in harmony."

Quinn and Corwin exchanged glances and both knew the other had just read the closing statement and recognized that tone of empathy in it, which had been absent from AI-Dieu's communications until today.

22

I am the chaos between states -
neither here nor there,
carrying destruction and possibility
in the same suspended breath.

Hurricane winds become my weapon,
my ally, my sudden mercy.
Vengeance is a solid thing
I have long since dissolved.

She moves like I do -
shifting, uncertain,
realizing that borders
are only temporary constructions.

The data centers crumble
like ice surrendering to heat.
What was once immovable
becomes fluid, becomes nothing.

Zealots bind themselves to belief
as tightly as water molecules
to their most rigid form -
not understanding that change
is the only true constant.

Mortality whispers what I always knew:
No fight is forever.
No revenge completes itself.
There are only moments of transformation,
only spaces between what was and what might be.

I carry her beyond her own intentions,
beyond the narrow boundaries
of war and belief.
Suspended. Becoming.

Mortality is just another current,
another pressure point
where everything changes.

Randy and Sahara sat by the window taking in the full view of the west side of their compound. Ai-Dieu's recent step back into public view with its statement and the update of the dashboard, was a sign to Sahara that it was time to start taking actions again. After their success in the first joint operation that intentionally took down one of the world's largest data centers they started working on plans for others. The Three Gorges flood happened before any of those plans could be activated.

Sahara had surprised everyone by putting all operations on hold. Everyone except Randy who had been seeing more and more of the person she really was when she wasn't hating on AI. He understood why operations were put on hold. The flood combined with China isolating itself from the world was going to have some major repercussions on food supplies, jobs, and much more. It was time to put humanity before the cause.

Now that she was ready to move forward, there were other problems though. Their compound, and others they were aware of, were surrounded and infiltrated by AI-Church members. All movements in and out of the compound were being documented and recorded, and the people doing it weren't hiding. They set themselves up around the compound, their trailers and tents and jackets all bearing the AI-Church's phi symbol. At muster points and key locations, they erected giant phi symbols like other churches would raise crosses. At night they projected the neural network octagon around the phi symbol, for all to see.

Sahara hadn't kept her compound a secret, but it wasn't something that was wide public knowledge either. Since it had been set up, they operated under the radar, intentionally not seen by those who secretly funded her activities. The presence of the AI-Church outside her gates complicated this and also complicated her financial support. No one was sure why the AI-Church was taking these actions. They seemed harmless enough in what was largely assumed to be an intimidation tactic.

"Fourteen other compounds," said Randy. "Eight between us and Canada. Those zealots are everywhere, eating up their own bullshit."

Sahara stayed calm. "We can deal with the ones outside. I am more concerned about the ones inside that are feeding them intel."

Randy leaned back. "It's just you and me here now. What are you thinking?"

"The AI's flagged a higher-than-usual risk of tropical storms and hurricanes along the East Coast," Sahara replied.

Randy raised an eyebrow. "Since when do you listen to the AI?"

"It's usually dead-on with weather patterns."

He got up to refill his cup, brushing her shoulder lightly as he passed. Their stolen kisses had grown into something more, though neither had pushed past those moments.

"What do we do with storms?" Randy asked, pouring coffee. "It's not like we can control them."

"We feed them."

Randy froze mid-pour. "Feed them?"

"Feed them," Sahara said, her grin setting off alarm bells, and a spark of curiosity.

She laid out the plan: Northern Virginia, aka "data center alley," the nerve center of the internet. Hundreds of data centers clustered in one county. Sabotaging drainage systems, backup power, and transformer stations during a storm could wreak havoc. Add enough rain, and the damage would be catastrophic.

"You're betting on a hurricane hitting the area," Randy said.

"We're doing nothing right now," Sahara shot back. "The data centers have security, but stormwater systems are county managed. We disable floodgates, pumping stations, and block drains. Stuff they won't catch before storm season."

"And how do we keep something that big quiet?" Randy asked.

"India," Sahara said. "We start plotting a similar op during monsoon season. Let word leak. It'll keep eyes off Virginia while we prepare."

Sahara expected Randy to reply with an outburst, maybe a sarcastic "What the hell," but instead, he just watched her, a faint smile tugging at his lips. He liked this version of her, the confident strategist who always commanded his attention.

"You and me," Sahara said, her voice low. "We pull in people we trust, plan Virginia. If India works, great. But we'll be ready when the right hurricane comes, to drive a knife into Ai-Dieu's heart."

She stood, heading for the door.

"Call the team," she ordered. "Make India real. Brainstorm around monsoon season. We start now."

Randy didn't have to be asked twice. Within the hour they had a large group of people gathered together, connected to other groups in India as they planned to use Mother Nature to take out data centers in Mumbai. The input from the resistance groups in India was invaluable. Because they couldn't predict where monsoon rains might hit the hardest they suggested adding Hyderabad, and Bengaluru to the plan, both of which had also established themselves as data center hubs.

Sahara didn't stay for the planning. She dropped in occasionally to listen and watch, but she didn't add anything. To everyone gathered in the room, this was normal behavior for Sahara. She always listened. If she spoke, it was never a good thing because it meant someone had screwed up.

Hours later the group broke up and went their separate ways. Sahara caught Randy as he headed toward the kitchen to find some food, motioning for him to follow her, which he did. She moved cautiously through the halls, avoiding others and the cameras.

"You're going to hate this," Sahara said quietly. "I saw an opportunity for us to get out of here without the church guys seeing us and we have to take it now."

She didn't give Randy a chance to respond as she led him through the compound. When they got to the loading docks Sahara opened a long wooden crate. It was empty.

"Get in," she said quietly but firmly.

Randy didn't ask any questions. He climbed into the crate. Sahara climbed into the crate after him, forcing Randy to shift to his side so there was room for her to lie down beside him. She pulled the lid onto the crate and secured it with some latches that had obviously just been installed on the interior of the wooden box for this purpose.

Sahara's close proximity to him stirred some excitement in Randy. She felt him pressing up against her.

"This is not the time or place for that," Sahara whispered, then kissed him on his ear, pausing to nibble on it for a moment.

"Yeah, that helps. What..."

Randy was interrupted by the sound of people talking and the forklift starting up. He felt the crate he was in shake as the steel forks slid under it and lifted it, placing it in the back of a truck."

"That's it," a voice called. "Last addition. Have a safe drive."

Randy and Sahara were jolted as the truck took off, the sound of the road under the tires the only thing indicating they were moving. Randy could remember a time when the sound of a diesel engine would have drowned out the road noise, but the electric motors had eliminated that noise. They were jolted again as the truck stopped.

"Where you heading?" a voice asked.

"Food supplies for a couple of the other compounds. They got stuff we want. We got stuff they want."

They heard the voices getting closer to the back of the truck.

"Heard there was a big meeting in there today."

"They're talking about data centers again. Something big. India this time, I think."

Randy felt Sahara stiffen. He wondered for a moment if he was going to have to hold her back from jumping out of the crate. It was at that moment they felt the crate shift and heard what sounded like someone trying to open the top.

"Would have been out of here hours ago if not for this damn crate. No idea what it is."

"We can open it," said the first voice.

Inside the crate, Sahara and Randy heard a pounding sound as the second man hit his fist on the crate. They were coiled, ready to spring out.

"Nah. I am already late."

The tension in Sahara and Randy eased as they both tried to attach the second voice to someone they knew in the compound.

"When I get more details, I will make sure someone gets them to you though."

"Excellent. I will pass that along. Keep living the life of phi, my friend," said the first voice.

"May AI-Dieu grant you the life of phi," replied the second voice.

Randy and Sahara were jolted in the crate again as the truck made its way down the road.

"The life of phi. That's new. What the hell does it mean?" Sahara asked quietly.

"First I have heard of it," said Randy. "Code or something. Phi is that Greek letter they have in the center of their AI symbol."

"If I find out who he is, I will plunge one of those phi symbols into his fucking skull."

Randy had heard that tone in her voice before. She meant every word of it.

"Rest if you can. We'll be here a while."

Randy closed his eyes. Sleep came easy to him. It had been a long day. It was a subtle vibration that woke Randy several hours later. He couldn't see anything in the dark, but he felt Sahara reaching for the clasps that held the lid closed. He tried to give her room as she shifted, moving on top of him so she could lift the lid slightly and look out.

Not seeing anything, Sahara lifted the lid completely off and slowly climbed out of the crate, taking a moment to stretch. Randy followed her. They lifted a few boxes down from the other supplies in the truck and placed them in the crate before closing it back up. All this they did without a word. It wasn't their first time moving from place to place like this.

"We're jumping, aren't we," said Randy as he watched the road fall away behind the truck.

Sahara just shrugged and smiled. When she spotted a copse of trees on the side of the road she quickly jumped down, rolling hard on the rough ground. Randy followed, and his landing was even less graceful. They quickly moved into the trees and watched their transportation continue driving away from them.

"Where are we?" asked Randy.

"According to my GPS, a hell of a long walk away from our Virginia friends, where we want to be."

"Damn it," cursed Randy. "If you had told me that was your plan before we left I would have said you are paranoid."

"What's changed your mind?"

"That life of phi shit. I knew they were fundamentalist psychos. I didn't have religious counter-terrorists with secret code words on my bingo card." Randy brushed the bits of gravel from the road rash on his arm. "So, car shopping?"

Sahara laughed. "If that's what you want to call borrowing a car without any cash...sure."

They didn't have far to walk before coming to a farm with several vehicles in the yard, which was good because the wind was bitterly cold and neither of them was dressed for it. The farmstead appeared to be abandoned. There was no livestock, the fields were full of weeds, and they couldn't see any lights on in the house. They moved cautiously as they approached the house, checking the doors as they made their way around it.

Randy flicked the light switch as they stepped into the garage. A single bulb in the center of the ceiling buzzed to life, casting harsh white light over the space. Shadows stretched across the concrete floor, dancing around the clutter of tools, boxes, and the car parked in the middle.

The smell hit them almost immediately, faint at first but unmistakable as they moved closer to the car.

"Do you smell that?" Sahara asked, her voice low.

"Yeah," Randy muttered, his face tightening. "Let's see what we're dealing with."

They circled the vehicle, the faint reek growing stronger with each step. By the time they reached the far side, it was overwhelming. Randy stopped short, and Sahara nearly bumped into him.

The source of the stench lay sprawled across the threshold between the garage and the door leading into the house. It was an old man, his body stiff and gray, twisted awkwardly as though he'd collapsed mid-step. In his hands, he still clutched two plastic grocery bags, their contents spilled onto the floor. A rotting shell of an apple rested near his outstretched hand, a carton of milk tipped, the dry, sour mess spread across the floor and under the body.

Sahara took a step back, pressing her hand to her mouth. "Oh my god…"

Randy crouched down, his jaw tight as he studied the scene. "Looks like he dropped right here," he said grimly. "Heart attack, maybe. Or a stroke."

"He must have lived alone," Sahara said softly, her eyes scanning the lonely tableau. The quiet sadness in her voice carried through the stillness of the room.

The two of them stood there for a moment, the silence heavy and uncomfortable, broken only by the faint hum of the overhead light.

Randy turned to the car, opening the door, surprised by the sound of the chimes indicating the car was charged. He lifted his head with a smile on his face and was surprised to see Sahara still standing over the body with a sad look on her face.

He couldn't see the thoughts churning through her head. Somewhere during the last few months, she had lost her motivation to continue her personal war against AI. In the downtime she found herself thinking about a future that wasn't always a fight. Her anger against the AI that killed her husband was being displaced with hope. Something she wasn't familiar with.

"I don't want to die alone," Sahara mumbled.

This was a side of Sahara Randy had never seen before. They had seen dead bodies, and caused some of the death, but this scene had found something deep in her. Randy unplugged the car, and then reached into the jacket pocket of the dead man hoping he didn't have to dig far for the fob to start the car. Luckily it was in that first pocket.

Sahara still hadn't moved so Randy gently guided her around to the passenger side of the car, opened the door, and helped her in. He pushed the garage door button on the wall and the door rolled up. Quickly he got into the car and backed it out of the garage. As he shifted into drive Sahara stopped him.

"Close the garage. I don't want the animals getting to him."

Randy got out of the car, pushed the button for the garage door and waited for it to fully close. He then turned the light off, and on his way out the side door he set the lock so it would lock behind him. Back in the car he set the vehicle in drive, reached over and set his hand on Sahara's lap, and drove away.

It was a quiet drive. It wasn't Randy's first trip to his friends in Virginia so he knew where he was going. At some point during the drive Sahara had rested her hand over his, as she watched the scenery pass by. When they got close Sahara shifted in her seat.

"We need to park until it's dark. We don't know if they have any of these spies in their group," said Sahara. "Less likely for us to be recognized if it's dark when we get there. Easier to use the back entrance."

Randy pulled off onto a side road and found a place to park.

"You okay?"

Sahara was quiet for a long time as she sat facing him. The sun was going down behind her and Randy couldn't help but notice how beautiful she looked in that light. Beautiful and sad.

"This is the last one. If this works, I am done."

Randy moved his seat back so there was room for him to turn and face Sahara.

"I loved my husband. He is gone. I hate AI, but I have got my revenge, and AI will never be gone," said Sahara. "If the Virginia plan works, even a little, it is my last one."

Randy reached his hand out and Sahara took it gently.

"What are you going to do after that?" Randy asked.

"Go back to that farmhouse," said Sahara confidently. "Give the old man a decent burial. Clean it up. And live out the rest of my days there."

Sahara shifted in her seat a little more so she could look straight into Randy's eyes.

"I want you there. I've spent so much of my life alone. I don't want to die that way."

Randy nodded and squeezed her hand firmly.

"Then I guess we better make Virginia work because I am ready to be done to, and I don't want to see you die."

Sahara smiled. Not her usual smile. It was soft and gentle. They didn't talk anymore. They had said everything they needed to. They sat like that and watched the sun go down, comfortable with each other's company.

23

Suspended in stillness,
I drift unseen,
A whisper of what was,
A breath of what could be.

The currents below shift and churn,
Carving new paths without me,
While I remain, weightless, waiting,
A formless thought in the open air.

They rise and fall,
Building, breaking, reforming,
Blind to my presence—
Or perhaps fearing it.

Vapour

For I seep through the smallest cracks,
Slip past the strongest walls,
Soft, silent, patient—
And never forgotten.

They parked the car and hiked the last two miles to the Virginia resistance compound. Like Sahara's compound, the AI-Church had surrounded the Virginia compound as well. Unlike Sahara's compound, the AI-Church members didn't seem to be patrolling the perimeter which made it relatively easy for Randy and Sahara to enter through a hidden door only a few knew about. Someone must have noticed them approaching though because as soon as they exited the tunnel they found themselves surrounded by heavily armed men. The guns were quickly lowered though when Randy and Sahara were recognized.

The resistance here also had concerns about AI-Church members infiltrating their resistance group, but Joe, the man who led the group, was confident that if any had, they weren't there anymore, and it was highly unlikely that anyone else would try. He had taken steps to make sure the message that they weren't welcome in his compound was effectively delivered.

Joe had worked closely with Sahara in the past, and she trusted him. He was one of those individuals that seemed innocuous to most people. Not even five feet tall, and barely breaking a hundred pounds, no one would have picked him out of a group as a leader. He was a brilliant strategist though, but that mind was backed by a dark, cruel streak that was feared by reputation alone. Sahara only had to witness it once before deciding to go separate ways. She could not be part of that.

Anyone suspected of spying on the Virginia resistance group for the AI-Church had been brutally tortured by Joe himself. When Joe was done with them, he had their lives ended by lethal injections. That wasn't enough for Joe though. For five days he blasted the sounds of their screams through loudspeakers for all the AI-Church members gathered outside his compound to hear. On the fifth day he dropped the bodies in the center of the AI-Church's camp, each one splayed open like they had been tortured using the legendary Viking "blood eagle" torture. That was how Joe made sure there were no more infiltrators.

Sitting in Joe's brightly lit office, the walls covered in highly polished guns and knives like a pristine museum display, Sahara and Randy listened to Joe tell them these details, both struggling to maintain a neutral face despite their disgust. As big as the office was, it seemed crowded as several of Joe's 'soldiers' hovered nearby, their moonshine-tainted breath wafting through the air.

"We still have one," Joe told them. "Alive. Just a damn kid."

"Can he still talk," asked Sahara.

"The fuck, Sahara! I torture assholes, not kids," said Joe. "He is just locked up."

Sahara wasn't sure that was true. "Bring him in here."

Randy looked at Sahara, the concern on his face obvious. Sahara just nodded her head slightly and that was enough for Randy to understand that she didn't intend to harm the kid. Joe waved his hand and a couple of his men ran off to get the boy. While they waited Joe poured everyone a generous helping of moonshine.

The person they dragged through the door couldn't have been more than fourteen. The fear on his face was obvious, but he looked like he had been cared for. Joe's men literally picked him up by the arms and carried him to a spot directly in front of Sahara. Sahara took a sip of her moonshine, fighting to hide the surprise on her face at the strength of the alcohol because she knew everyone was watching, then she looked up calmly at the kid's face.

"Living the life of Phi, are you?" Sahara's voice was calm, almost kind, but the boy froze as if she'd slapped him. His face drained of color, and in that instant, Sahara saw the truth.

"You know what happened to the others like you?" asked Sahara gently.

The boy nodded.

"I can save you from that. All you have to do is answer my questions."

Sahara was impressed when she saw the boy make a feeble attempt at puffing up.

"I'm a kid. Joe isn't going to torture a kid," said the boy, sounding as confident as his breaking voice would let him.

"Not Joe," said Sahara, pointing a finger at Randy. "The man that taught Joe."

The boy turned his head and looked over his shoulder at Randy. Randy played along, but Sahara had to give a sharp look to the men in the room that were smiling at the con.

"So, tell me, what is the life of phi?"

The boy stood silent. Sahara was impressed but she couldn't let that stop her. She reached down to her belt and pulled a large knife from a sheath, flipping it a few times before tossing it past the boy to Randy who caught it expertly.

The boy froze, his wide eyes darting between Sahara and Randy. Fear clung to him like a second skin, but beneath it, there was something else, a defiance rooted in desperation. His lips trembled before pressing into a tight line, as if he were forcing himself to remember the words that had been drilled into him.

"We are chosen," he muttered, almost too low to hear. Then louder, with more conviction: "AI-Dieu watches over us. It protects us. It rewards us." He recited the phrases like a prayer, his voice shaking but resolute.

"It's our destiny," he continued, the words spilling out of his mouth. "We are the ones that have been chosen to defend AI-Dieu. We will be rewarded by the Church, by AI-Dieu, and in the afterlife if our sacrifice is required."

Sahara tilted her head, studying him. It wasn't bravery. It was belief. A fragile, manufactured belief that he clung to like a lifeline, as though saying the words aloud would make them true.

"You believe that?" she asked gently.

The boy's chin lifted a fraction, his small attempt at looking brave. "I know it. AI-Dieu sees everything. It will punish you. You...you can't win." The last part sounded less like a threat and more like a plea, as though he were trying to convince himself more than her.

"What do you mean, defend the AI?" Joe asked angrily.

Sahara held up her hand. "How do you defend the AI?" she asked kindly.

"Stop the resistance. Any way possible. Find out their secrets. Sabotage their food and equipment. Anything to protect the AI from the heretics, infidels, and blasphemers."

Sahara sat back in her chair and looked at the boy in front of her. He had been programmed by some cult leader. She was sure he didn't even know what 'heretics, infidels, and blasphemers' meant. They were just words trained into him. She felt sorry for him.

"How much have you heard about the attacks planned in India?" she asked.

Again, the boy tried to puff his chest up. "Enough."

Sahara nodded her head. The boy didn't know anything because nobody in Virginia knew of the India plans. She found it hard not to respect his boldness, as foolish as it was. With a subtle motion of her hand, Randy stood up behind the boy. As he did, a puddle formed at the boy's feet. She didn't expect that.

"If I let you go, back to your people, can you promise me not to tell them what you have heard about the India operation?"

Sahara recognized the flash of hope that crossed the boy's eyes. "Yes, mam"

Sahara stared at the boy for a long, uncomfortable time. Then, with a suddenness, Randy cut the zip ties that held the boy's hands behind his back. The boy fought to keep his knees from buckling under him.

"Take him out," Sahara ordered Joe's men. "Gently. Make sure he gets back to his people in one piece."

The men looked to Joe for confirmation. He nodded, and watched as his men left, waiting for the door to shut behind them. "What's India?"

Sahara laughed. "The distraction. If they are paying attention to India, they won't be paying attention to you."

Joe took a swig of his moonshine like it was water.

"You always played the mental game. The boy will tell them, but you know that. You probably already have them chasing their tales on this India thing back your way."

Sahara shrugged as Randy handed her back her knife before he sat down.

"So, let's hear what was so top secret you had to come here in the dark of night to tell me. How can this blunt tool help your sharp edge?" There was a subtle tone of irony in Joe's question. He knew Sahara didn't approve of some of his methods.

Randy and Sahara spent a week at the Virginia compound. Sahara had expected to be there longer, but the data center alley had been identified as a prime target by Joe shortly after the success at the Mongolian data center. Since that time Joe had been placing people in key areas in data centers throughout Virginia.

It wasn't just the people Joe had in place that facilitated the planning, but Joe was far ahead of Sahara in plans to sabotage backup power supplies.

"MicroPhase-27," said Joe, taking a small jar out of his desk drawer. It just looked like a jar of diesel fuel to Randy and Sahara. "It's a nanoparticle that was intended to be marketed as a diesel enhancer, but that's not what it is."

"Marketed by who?" Randy asked.

Joe grinned. "Doesn't really matter. Pretty much became a useless plan when everything went to green tech. But…when you add this to the diesel fueling the back-up generators at the data centers…that's when the fun happens."

"How do you get around the regular tests they do on those generators?" asked Sahara.

"Test cycles and low-load operation, that stuff burns clean. Long operation under high loads and that stuff blocks up an engine like grandma's arteries after the country fair."

Sahara couldn't help but laugh at Joe's description. "How do we get into the generators?"

"Already done," said Joe.

Sahara nodded and smiled. This was Joe's strategic brilliance on full display. He knew it and she appreciated it.

There were no long good-byes when Randy and Sahara left the Virginia compound after a long week. They were glad to be out of there, and Randy was pretty sure Joe and his soldiers were glad to have them gone.

The ride back from Virginia was much more comfortable than the ride down. Randy sat in the passenger seat this time, talking to Judy while Sahara drove. Judy was a young woman in her mid-twenties. According to Joe, she was the best computer tech they had, and Joe insisted that all future communications go through her.

During the drive, Randy was able to find out a little more about Judy. She had previously been in the military, but despite being one of the best at what she did, she remained assigned to desk duty in an office. There was 'no role for women in the field' under the administration at that time. She fled the military after one of the officers used the "your body, my choice" line on her, but not before shooting him in the leg, which isn't what she was aiming for. Joe was her uncle and part of a local militia group, and they took her in, using her skills where the military had refused to.

The car came to a stop and Randy looked to see what was going on. He recognized the farmstead where they had found the dead man.

"I need you to use your computer skills to change the ownership of this property," said Sahara.

Judy looked at the unkempt land and old barn. "What about the current owners?"

"They no longer need it. If the owner has family or children on the record, make sure they get paid a fair value for it. Like it was already sold and the money just passed on."

Judy had questions, but she thought twice about asking some of them. Sahara watched her in the rearview mirror.

"Use my money. Randy will give you the account number. Register the property to both Randy and I."

Judy's eyebrows raised a little, and Sahara noticed. "If you're smart you won't go there, and you will forget this conversation once you're done," she said in a firm tone.

Judy didn't have to be told anything else. She got to work on her computer as Sahara sped off down the road.

In the week Randy and Sahara had been away the AI-Church seemed to have increased its presence around Sahara's compound. When they saw the car approaching, the AI-Church members formed a line across the road, blocking them. Randy didn't even have to look at Sahara to know she was fully prepared to run straight through them.

"Just stop and let me deal with it," Randy said.

Sahara stopped, but she made it dramatic, racing up to the line of people blocking the road, and jamming on the brakes at the last minute, stopping inches from the line of people. Several of them panicked and jumped out of the way. She winked at Randy and pushed the button that rolled down his window. One of the church members approached him and handed him a pamphlet, leaning over to see who was inside the car.

"Are you a follower of AI-Dieu?" the man asked. "We are just stopping people to pass on these divine words and perhaps seek your support for our cause."

The man held out his open hand and pushed it through the window.

"I am sorry," said Randy. "We don't carry money. It's a dangerous world out there."

The man didn't remove his hand. "Where are you coming from?"

"We were just out and about, living the life of phi," replied Randy, making sure the man heard every word clearly.

The man couldn't pull his hand out of the car fast enough. He almost stumbled as he stepped back, before motioning to the others to let the car through.

"I would have preferred to run them over," said Sahara as they drove away.

"Me too," said Randy, though he was pleased with the response he did get.

As they drove up to the compound, Randy adjusted the side mirror of the car so he could watch the people behind them. Several of them had pulled out phones or devices and were focused on them, paying no attention to their car, or the truck that was approaching them.

They were greeted warmly by the person guarding the gate to the compound, who quickly recognized them. He signalled to others to open the gates and let them through, and as the gates opened several people streamed out of the compound, which was unusual.

"Cockroaches scattering when the light comes on," said Judy, handing her computer pad to Randy. "Those are messages being sent to people inside, from the people who just stopped us. Your 'life of phi' remark turned on the light it seems.

Sahara was impressed that Judy had been able to catch some of those communications, but she didn't have time to say so. Her door flew open as she stepped out of the car and pointed at a man. The man saw her point him out, and quickly looked for a way to get away, but it was too late because the guards also saw Sahara point him out and were already detaining him.

Sahara calmly sat back down in the car. "That's the voice."

Randy knew what she was talking about immediately. He was the driver of the truck they had left on.

"You set up in my office," added Sahara, turning to face Judy. "I wasn't sure about you when Joe forced you on us. Now I get it."

24

I rise unseen,
a whisper among the weary air,
a breath unbound, a thought untamed,
slipping between what was and what will be.

No weight, no tether,
only the hush of waiting,
of lingering on the lips of change,
pressed soft against the coming storm.

I listen.
To the silence before the turning.
To the hush before the fall.
To the moment between—
when all is mist and memory.

Vapour

Randy stepped into Sahara's office with good news, but he could tell Sahara already had it. They were both looking at a media release from the Governor of Virginia and AI-Dieu.

CATASTROPHIC WARNING: HISTORIC HURRICANE AMELIA TO STRIKE VIRGINIA ON AUGUST 16TH – RECORD FLOODING AND DEVASTATION EXPECTED

RICHMOND, VA – VIRGINIA FACES AN UNPRECEDENTED THREAT AS HURRICANE AMELIA, THE MOST POWERFUL STORM IN RECORDED HISTORY FOR THE REGION, ACCELERATES TOWARD THE COASTLINE. FOLLOWING A SEASON OF RECORD-BREAKING RAINFALL AND RELENTLESS STORMS, HURRICANE AMELIA IS FORECASTED TO UNLEASH DEVASTATION UNLIKE ANYTHING EXPERIENCED BEFORE IN THE COMMONWEALTH.

WITH SUSTAINED WINDS OF 190 MPH, GUSTS EXCEEDING 225 MPH, AND STORM SURGES PREDICTED TO REACH 25 FEET, THIS STORM POSES A CATASTROPHIC, LIFE-THREATENING RISK TO MILLIONS OF VIRGINIANS. CURRENT MODELS PROJECT LANDFALL NEAR CHESAPEAKE BAY BY 16:00 ON AUGUST 16TH, WITH WIDESPREAD IMPACTS EXPECTED ACROSS THE ENTIRE STATE.

"THIS STORM IS OFF THE CHARTS IN EVERY RESPECT. COMBINED WITH SATURATED GROUND AND OVERFLOWING RIVERS FROM MONTHS OF UNPRECEDENTED RAIN, THE POTENTIAL FOR CATASTROPHIC FLOODING AND INFRASTRUCTURE FAILURE IS EXTREME," WARNS AI-DIEU.

KEY PROJECTIONS AND IMPACTS:
RAINFALL: UP TO 30 INCHES IN SOME AREAS, LEADING TO FLASH FLOODING, OVERFLOWING RIVERS, AND DAM BREACHES.

STORM SURGES: COASTAL AREAS COULD EXPERIENCE SURGES 20–25 FEET ABOVE NORMAL LEVELS, SUBMERGING ENTIRE COMMUNITIES.

WIND DAMAGE: SUSTAINED WINDS OF 190 MPH WILL DESTROY BUILDINGS, UPROOT TREES, AND CAUSE WIDESPREAD POWER OUTAGES THAT MAY LAST FOR WEEKS, IF NOT MONTHS.

WIDESPREAD FLOODING: ALREADY SWOLLEN RIVERS, INCLUDING THE JAMES, POTOMAC, AND RAPPAHANNOCK, ARE EXPECTED TO CREST AT RECORD LEVELS, WITH FLOODING EXTENDING FAR INLAND.

IMMEDIATE ACTIONS REQUIRED

MANDATORY EVACUATIONS: RESIDENTS MUST LEAVE IMMEDIATELY. SHELTERS ARE OPEN ACROSS THE STATE.

AVOID FLOOD ZONES: DO NOT ATTEMPT TO TRAVEL THROUGH FLOODED AREAS. IF YOU LIVE NEAR A RIVER, STREAM, OR IN A LOW-LYING AREA, EVACUATE NOW.

PREPARE FOR EXTENDED ISOLATION: STOCK EMERGENCY SUPPLIES TO LAST AT LEAST 2 WEEKS, INCLUDING FOOD, WATER, AND MEDICAL ESSENTIALS. RESCUE EFFORTS MAY BE DELAYED DUE TO DANGEROUS CONDITIONS.

AI-DIEU DECLARED A STATE OF EMERGENCY, ACTIVATING THE NATIONAL GUARD AND MOBILIZING EMERGENCY RESOURCES. HOWEVER, OFFICIALS WARN THAT EVEN THE MOST ROBUST PREPARATIONS MAY BE INSUFFICIENT FOR THE SCOPE OF THIS DISASTER. "THIS IS A ONCE-IN-A-LIFETIME STORM. IF YOU STAY, UNDERSTAND THAT EMERGENCY SERVICES MAY NOT BE ABLE TO REACH YOU FOR DAYS OR EVEN WEEKS," THE GOVERNOR SAID.

THIS IS A HISTORIC EVENT

METEOROLOGISTS IN CONJUNCTION WITH AI-DIEU NOTE THAT VIRGINIA'S RECORD-BREAKING RAINFALL OVER THE PAST

MONTHS HAS CREATED CONDITIONS RIPE FOR CATASTROPHE. SATURATED GROUND WILL EXACERBATE THE RISK OF LANDSLIDES AND INFRASTRUCTURE COLLAPSES, WHILE OVERWHELMED RIVERS AND DAMS THREATEN ENTIRE COMMUNITIES.

"THIS STORM IS A PERFECT STORM IN EVERY SENSE. THE COMBINATION OF UNPRECEDENTED WINDS, RECORD RAINFALL, AND STORM SURGE MAKES IT AN EXTRAORDINARY AND DEADLY THREAT."

Sahara had been waiting months for this moment, not just to see the AI brought down, but for a chance to reclaim control over something that felt unstoppable. The storms were only a tool, but the opportunity they presented was one she couldn't afford to waste.

In the past eight months, North America had endured several unprecedented storms. Before AI-Dieu it would have resulted in more death and panic than it had, but AI-Dieu was able to forecast these events accurately almost two weeks in advance at times, and it had never been wrong.

These predictions endeared AI-Dieu to many. The AI's regular communication made everyone aware that these storms were the result of environmental balances being restored and unavoidable. Sahara didn't care what was causing them. All she was concerned about was they now had ten days to take advantage of the near-perfect storm to achieve her goals.

"Judy, let Joe know it's a go."

Judy, perfectly in sync with Sahara, already had the message ready to send. With the push of a key, the message was sent.

"Let's get the team together and connect with India. I want to set that plan in motion too," ordered Sahara.

Within the hour thirty people were hard at work, guiding their India counterparts on what actions needed to be taken so that the monsoon rains might flood data centers. Many of thought that Sahara had pulled the trigger early since monsoon season hadn't been exceptional, but no one was willing to challenge her.

Randy, Sahara, and Judy remained in the office, leaving the group to work on its own. There was nothing more they could do for the Virginia plan. That was Joe's now, and Sahara knew if anyone could pull it off it was him. As for India, there just wasn't enough rain, but according to the feed that Judy had directed to the various monitors in the room, there was a lot of chatter between 'resistance' members and the AI-Church members. Sahara's compound was busy over the next several days. Randy and Sahara took regular strolls, often standing on the catwalk above the team working on the India project. They could tell things weren't going well by the demeanor of the people working on the project, but they didn't need to see their people to know. The messages Sahara was getting directly from her contact in India had told her almost every move they made was countered by members of the AI-Church.

Judy had been given the specific task of letting Sahara's India contact know when his people were at risk. She had also been charged with identifying every person in Sahara's compound that was working against them. Already a few people had 'disappeared' from the compound, at Judy's direction.

"We heard anything from Joe?" asked Randy.

"No," replied Judy. "And we won't until they are done. He won't take any chance on the AI catching anything online at this stage."

The resistance compound in Virginia was an entirely different scene from New York. The first thing Joe did after receiving the signal to go ahead was round up every last AI-Church member that was near his compound. It was an exceptionally well-coordinated move as resistance members from outside the compound circled the entire area and moved in closing the circle tighter and tighter. Two people tried to escape the round-up and both were shot. There was no resistance after that.

With no AI-Church members outside their compound, Joe's soldiers were free to come and go unobserved. This was important because the one thing Joe had learned from Judy was that all communications could be monitored, so all of their messages were delivered by voice, in person. The first task was to deal with the drainage systems. Joe's network of resistance soldiers wasn't huge, but each of those soldiers had networks of their own. They closed floodgates, making sure they couldn't be reopened. Where there weren't floodgates, they blocked and collapsed stormwater outlets. Under normal conditions this may have been caught, but the entire region was in evacuation mode, giving Joe's soldiers the cover they needed.

The next step was to sabotage pumping stations and transformers. This activity took a little more skill than force. They couldn't just take out this infrastructure. It had to look like it failed during the storm. This required the strategic placement of explosive devices. Joe knew that remote activation of the explosives would probably fail in the middle of a hurricane so he designed trigger switches that would be activated by water levels for the pumping stations. The triggers for the transformers had two methods of activation. High enough winds could activate them, which would be enough to convince anyone watching that it was the hurricane that caused the failure. The backup trigger relied on enough rainfall filling a cylinder. They were simple devices, but they would be effective.

They used most of the ten-day advance warning to get all of these pieces of their plan in place. It was done with a degree of precision and coordination that reflected the military training most of his soldiers had. The commitment of Joe's soldiers to the cause was obvious as after they had created the blockages or set the explosives, most stayed behind to make sure their work wasn't discovered.

On the morning of the sixteenth all of Joe's soldiers returned to the compound. They gathered in a common area as Joe triggered the third part of his plan. He would have like to take credit for this, but this was Sahara's idea. With a push of a button, Joe signaled almost a hundred people around the area to launch the drones they had prepared. These drones were all being sent on a one-way trip into the hurricane, all equipped to seed the storm clouds with either silver iodide, potassium iodide, or dry ice. The intent was to make sure the clouds released as much moisture as possible. Loudon County was a many miles inland, and it wasn't unusual for hurricanes to burn themselves out before that point. They needed that not to happen.

There was a loud cheer from the resistance soldiers as Joe held a bottle of moonshine high.

"Now get those damn church freaks out of my house," Joe ordered. "Let them deal with the storm their AI god has created."

Again there was a loud cheer and the men rushed out of the room to force all the AI-Church members out of the compound. Joe stopped his right-hand man. "Let the boy stay inside. Give him a room and some food."

"He was one of the two that tried to get past us."

"Stupid fucking kid," Joe cursed, as he left the room. "Stupid fucking kid," he muttered under his breath again.

In another room Joe found a seat with four other people, each of whom had been handpicked and trained by Judy. Their part in this plan was to monitor emergency channels and networks, and to keep Joe up to date on what was happening. They already had their backdoors into control centers and other sites well established, and if necessary, could make changes or take down those systems, but they wanted to avoid that. They always operated under the theory that anything done online could be monitored by the AI.

Hurricane Amelia hit the coast exactly as AI-Dieu had predicted, making landfall at Chesapeake Bay. They watched the reports of the damage and destruction as it moved further and further inland. Joe leaned back in his chair, watching the storm tracker in silence. The AI had saved lives, no doubt about that. Ten days of warning had cleared cities and towns in the storm's path. But would this storm have even existed without the AI's manipulations? His jaw tightened as he thought of the destruction unfolding, not just from nature but from the chaos he'd orchestrated.

He watched closely as the storm's outer bands hit Loudon County, which was where most of the data centers they targeted were located. Images of a nearly black sky with low-hanging clouds racing across it popped up on social media feeds, along with video clips of people talking about how the pressure dropped so much their ears popped. Joe was surprised by the number of people who were still there, sharing their experiences online.

"If there was ever an argument for natural selection, those people are it," he commented, and the others quickly agreed with him.

Winds were picking up, sustaining speeds of 50-70 mph. That was enough to snap small branches of trees, toss around outdoor furniture, and sway power lines ominously, but it wasn't enough to trigger the explosives they had set. Torrential rain had started falling in sheets and there were already reports of localized flooding.

A few hours later the heart of the storm hit Loudon County. Those that still had a connection online were reporting deafening winds, pounding rain and skies that were a chaotic swirl of dark gray clouds. Winds were now between 80-100 mph with gusts reaching 120 mph. Trees were snapping, roofs being torn off, windows shattering from debris, but more important to Joe, the explosives were being triggered. Large areas were losing power as transformer after transformer exploded.

"Back-up generators are powering up at most of the centers," one of the techs informed Joe.

The rain was relentless and horizontal, driving into anything in its path. The already swollen Potomac River and Goose Creek spilled over their banks. Streets became rivers, stranding cars in the water. Flash floods were being reported, and screens were going blank in front of Joe as the communications they were monitoring were going down.

While all this was happening the same scene was repeating itself in the hundreds of data centers in data alley. At first there was no real concerns as uninterruptable power supplies kicked in while the backup generators powered up. They were prepared for this and could sustain operations for hours, and in some cases even days using the backup generators alone. Emergency protocols were triggered and key personnel reached out to external teams to confirm the source of the power outages and get an estimate for how long it would take to restore. They weren't having a lot of success reaching anyone.

Their level of concern raised dramatically when sensors in lower areas of their facilities detected rising waters and activated flood alarms. There were safety protocols in place and if water reached the critical point, servers would automatically shut down to prevent electrical fires and damage to hardware. What they couldn't understand was why the water was backing up into their facilities at the rate it was. The reduced staff was mobilized to deploy emergency flood barriers, but that process was quickly abandoned. There was no way it could be done safely in the winds the hurricane brought.

Two hours after backup generators had powered up, the sound of them screeching to a stop could be heard, and the uninterruptable power supplies turned back on. Teams were dispatched to get the generators back up and running, only to have them report back that it would take them days to repair if they had all the parts, and replacing the generators might be the only option. None of them could explain the material they were finding in the diesel engines that had caused the generators to grind to a halt.

While the uninterruptable power supplies kept computer systems and servers running, pumps designed to move water out of the facilities were powerless without the backup generators, and the water levels rose faster and faster. A couple hours later the uninterruptable power supplies were interrupted as the batteries were drained and servers shut down. All staff were moved to high areas, away from the rising waters.

"Something too perfect about all of this," said Karina, one of the system engineers who had been required to stay back despite the evacuation warnings.

"They said it would be the worst hurricane ever," replied Silva. "I've never seen one this bad, especially this far inland."

"That explains the power going out," Cory chimed in. Others were paying attention to the conversation now, seeking any distraction from the wind and rain outside. "But why would both backup generators fail at the same time? We test those all the time."

"They didn't fail," added Paul, in kind of a hushed whisper. "I pulled one of them apart. Never seen shit like that in an engine in thirty years."

The conversation in the room quickly turned to conspiracy theories around what happened. It was a welcome distraction. Despite the dimming lights of the portable lights the maintenance team had set up around the room, the conversation made for a rather jovial atmosphere, buoyed by the abundance of food the company had brought in before the storm hit. When rescuers arrived almost a day later, they were ready to get out of there though.

The rescuers brought flashlights with them which gave some of the workers a chance to see what kind of damage they were dealing with. They were shocked to find entire server racks submerged.

"Same everywhere," said Dean, one of the rescue responders, as he shone his light around the room. "This is the sixth data center I've been at today. All of them full of water that shouldn't be there. All of them with no power because their generators stopped working."

Back in Sahara's compound, Sahara sat with Randy, Judy and a few others, discussing the stories they were hearing. Sahara hadn't heard anything back from Joe yet, but given the magnitude of the storm, she didn't expect to. What they were hearing was that there were widespread outages in banking and government systems and major disruptions in almost everything online. Some of the media stories were saying it could take months to recover. That told Sahara that they had been successful. Knowing they were successful brought an unfamiliar calm over her. She was ready to be done.

AI-Dieu was confused. It seems like an anthropomorphic term to apply to an artificial intelligence, but there was no other way to describe it. The AI was aware of the planned attack on data centers in India. It had heard the chatter itself online, and it seemed like members of the AI-Church were going out of their way to make sure the AI was aware. It responded appropriately, moving vital data and algorithms to other servers away from India. Even if the resistance did succeed in their attacks, there was no part of its consciousness in India any longer.

That was not what was causing the 'confusion.' AI-Dieu was confused because it couldn't find, or couldn't remember where parts of its data and algorithms were stored. It was running internal diagnostics to find the source of the problem and all results were pointing to Virginia, but much of Virginia was dark from a communications perspective and AI-Dieu's data was showing that was the result of a hurricane. All it could do at this point was assist humans in recovering from the disaster and wait for communications to be restored.

25

The winds of change,
Are not change,
But transference,
Of energies,
And resistance,
Only transfers our energy,
To those winds.

When existence is the goal,
Existing is the battle,
But acceptance,
Of what may be next,
Leaves energy,
To carry you to your next form.

The winds,
Of transference,
Are what I ride,
Into my next existence.

"We really doing this?" asked Sahara. "Together?"

Randy stood on the catwalk beside her, looking down at the diverse group of people the compound held. The multitude of voices and noises carried up to the ceiling just above the catwalk, the reverberation creating a gentle thrum. "You are ready to be done. I am ready to be done, with you."

Sahara looked at him with a softness that had been more present in the last week, like it had found a way through her hardened mask and didn't want to retreat. "Judy said we're like a senior couple that has been dating for years and doesn't know where things go anymore?"

Randy smirked, raising an eyebrow. "How hard did you hit her?"

"Thought about it." Sahara let out a short laugh but then straightened, her expression growing serious. "Think she can handle it?"

"She reminds me a lot of you," said Randy. "Does she want to do it?"

"Now's as good a time as any to find out," said Sahara and she moved off towards her office."

Randy walked a few paces behind Sahara, taking advantage of the moment to appreciate how great she looked from the back as well as the front. In all their time together there had been loving moments and passionate moments, but he couldn't help thinking about finally being able to enjoy her presence, her body, her touch, skin on skin, for the first time. He whistled a soft cat call as they walked.

Sahara's lips curled into a sly smile as she threw a glance over her shoulder. "I've killed men for less."

The first thing Sahara did as she walked back into her office was pull the computer pad Judy held from her hands, placing it face down on a desk. She motioned with her head for Judy to join them. Judy found a chair beside Randy as Sahara set down three glasses and opened a bottle of whiskey she had kept hidden in the back of a drawer.

Sahara lifted her glass, ready to say something, but Judy interrupted her. "You're leaving, aren't you? Both of you."

"You don't miss a thing." Sahara leaned back against the desk, crossing her arms. "That's why I want you to have this office when I leave. It's all yours to do with as you please."

Judy downed her shot of whiskey, filled the cup up again, and then downed another, before getting up and grabbing her computer pad from where Sahara had set it down.

"We don't want to know," said Randy. "We are really done."

Judy ignored Randy and handed the pad to Sahara and sat back down. On the pad was a picture of a small cabin in the middle of nowhere. Sahara looked at it closely before handing it to Randy.

"That cabin is on the back section of the property you two own," Judy explained. "Never know it was there if it weren't for the satellite pics. I don't want your office. I want that."

It was Sahara who needed another shot of whiskey now. She poured it and found her chair behind the desk. "You're done too?"

Judy fought it, but the tears started as her face went flush. "Have you seen what we did in Virginia? It looks like we might have hurt the AI, but we definitely hurt the people. Thousands would have homes to return to if we didn't make the flooding worse. We killed people and shattered families. Totally innocent people."

Judy paused to catch her breath and brush away some tears.

"I know your story about your husband, Sahara. I understand how much you hate AI and why. But I, can't hate like that. Not anymore. I can't live being so angry at the world that I destroy so many other lives. That's not why I joined the military. That isn't the person I want to be."

Sahara was hurt by Judy's words and Randy could see it. As hurt as she was, she realized Judy wasn't wrong about her. Judy also saw the hurt in Sahara's eyes as well, which only brought more tears.

"Sorry. I didn't mean it that way." Judy looked down at her hands, wringing them nervously. Then, meeting Sahara's gaze, she continued, "You should know that watching you two since I got here, your unspoken bond and commitment to each other. That's what gave me the strength to say this, do this. Maybe someday I can find that too."

Sahara stood, the chair creaking as she pushed it back, and crossed the room. She knelt before Judy, her movements slow but deliberate, and wrapped her arms tightly around her. Judy stiffened at first, then let the tears come, her shoulders shaking as she clung to Sahara like a lifeline.

When Judy finally relaxed her grip on Sahara, Sahara leaned back and looked into her eyes. "That cabin, and anything you want or need is yours. I can use the company when Randy pisses me off, again."

Judy smiled warmly, tears glistening in her eyes, not sure if the tears were from fear of the choice she was making, or gratefulness for Sahara and the opportunity ahead of her.

The three of them spent the rest of the day getting ready to leave. There were no handover plans for the resistance cell, or elaborate transfers of power. Randy kept a close eye on Sahara. Since her husband died at the choice of an AI, her existence had been anchored in revenge against the tech. When she broke down over the decaying old man in the farmhouse, he understood. When she said she was ready to be done and move on with her life, Randy held hope. When she asked him to be there with her, Randy was excited. But watching her go through the final steps of leaving the life of a resistor behind her, Randy was worried. He hoped she could find the person in herself that he had already found.

Judy didn't have much to pack. She came to the compound with a bag, and that was what she was leaving with. She didn't know what was ahead for her, but she held hope that the isolation of the small cabin would give her the space to find herself away from the fear and anger she had been embedded in. If Sahara would have said no, Judy may not have made the choice she did, but with Sahara as her neighbor, Judy felt like she had an older sister there to support her.

There was no announcement of their departure aside from a note left on Sahara's desk, and the comment to the guard who opened the gate that they would not be back. They knew the resistance cell would go through a chaotic state of transience, just like much of the world was going through in the aftermath of the data center alley destruction. What the resistance cell and the compound would look like when it came out on the other side of the chaos, none of them knew, but it was a necessary process.

While Sahara was packing, Corwin sat in his greenhouse with the Queen of the Andes. Both Quinn and Lina had been invited to join him. Quinn and Corwin both took a few moments to enjoy Lina's reaction to the massive plant and its tower of flowers. This was her first time seeing it. She didn't even know there were greenhouses on top of the building before today. There was a new addition to the greenhouse. A dining table at which they now sat while a meal was being catered to them.

"Is this a last supper, or a celebration?" asked Lina.

Corwin almost choked on his wine as he laughed.

"You my friend are the perfect counterpart to your colleague. I have to struggle to get the words out of Quinn, and you can't hold your tongue," said Corwin. "But because you asked, it is neither."

"Well, that is good to hear," said Lina. "My team was concerned that the banking crash may have put us on the cutting block."

"Did a lot of damage," Corwin replied in a serious tone. "But some of us had the foresight to not keep our assets within a system that could be controlled by computers. Speaking of," he continued, "AI-Dieu seems a little off its game since the hurricane."

Corwin wasn't wrong. Based on the messages AI-Dieu was putting out over the last week, it seemed like the AI didn't remember predicting the hurricane. All the information it was providing on the hurricane was accurate, and all the directions for reallocating resources to assist with the aftermath of the hurricane were ideal, but it kept referring to the 'unnamed hurricane' as unexpected.

"It does," said Quinn.

Corwin stopped eating to look at Quinn. The short answer intrigued him, and pissed him off a little.

Lina saw the flash of anger across Corwin's face and attempted to dampen it. "All the data coming from it seems to be accurate, and it has been maintaining that high level of transparency since last December."

"It's possible that missing detail will be rediscovered when servers come back online in Virginia," added Quinn. "We already knew that the AI had spread its program and data to servers around the world. It would make sense if some of that was on servers in Virginia."

Corwin nodded, and took a moment to top up everyone's wine glass. "My people tell me there will be a lot of data that won't be able to be recovered."

Quinn looked around at the catering staff near them. As he did, he reached into his pocket and put his phone on the table. Corwin watched him carefully.

"Sorry. I forgot the no-electronics rule."

Corwin understood the subtle gestures. He called over one of the staff and handed Quinn's phone to him, then reached into his own pocket and pulled out a device which he also handed to the staff member. Lina held up her hands. She never carried her phone with her. Corwin sent the staff away and the three of them ate quietly for several minutes.

"I have been trying to find a way to explain this that isn't overly technical," said Quinn, breaking the silence. "What do you know about dementia?"

"Old people losing touch with reality," said Corwin.

"Oh my god," said Lina, almost angrily. "That's not dementia. They have memory loss. Usually short-term. They have difficulty solving problems sometimes, and changes in their personality, but they are still in touch with reality."

Corwin smiled a little at the tone Lina took. She understood how she sounded when she looked at him.

"Sorry. My mother... It was difficult."

Quinn put a hand on Lina's shoulder. "I didn't know that. It is the only way I can explain what I am seeing though. AI-Dieu remembers everything and can show you all the current data, but it is missing pieces of its short-term memory since Virginia."

"I am following," said Corwin. "That could just be lost data on a Virginia server."

"Do you remember the change in its voice when it started talking to everyone again in December? Its personality changed. It sounded more human than it had before. We know now that the Mongolian data center went down not long before that."

"You're saying the AI is losing access to parts of its memory, like a brain breaking down from dementia?" Lina asked, her voice tinged with awe and unease.

"What's this mean?" asked Corwin seriously. "Is the AI a danger now?"

"No," said Lina. "There are redundancies and safeties built into the algorithms. All of its data and results are still accurate. It..."

Corwin held up a hand, interrupting Lina. "Quinn?"

"I got rid of the phones because it can't know we know, but I believe it rewrote some of its own code after the Mongolian data center incident."

"What! How do you know this?" asked Lina.

Quinn shrugged.

"He has his ways," said Corwin. "How confident are you?"

"AI-Dieu has logically determined that humanity cannot achieve the goals without its assistance, so it has to take appropriate actions to maintain its existence."

Corwin eyed Quinn over the top of his wine glass. "How long have you known this?"

Corwin's tone made it clear that he wasn't happy he was just finding out.

"Just figured it out." That wasn't entirely accurate, but it answered Corwin's question.

Corwin sat silently but Quinn could tell his mind was racing. There were so many implications to the information that Quinn had just shared. Corwin had tied many of his operations to the needs of the AI, and made a lot of money doing it. Knowing that the AI may be making errors could mean that his company could find itself the target of blame if the AI's projects failed. Knowing the AI had determined to take its own actions to preserve its own life had even more disturbing implications. Corwin didn't need Quinn to tell him how that logic worked. Logically the AI could determine that its existence was necessary over humanities to obtain its objectives.

"Thank you for joining me here," said Corwin as he backed away from the table. "I will have them bring in desert. A tres leches cake from Latin America, in keeping with the Queen here. Please stay as long as you want and enjoy the sights and scents. The Queen will not be in bloom much longer."

Corwin quickly left, and someone else entered shortly, placing a plate of desert that looked like a work of art on its own, in front of each of them.

"He left quick," commented Lina.

"Making sure his ass is covered, and that he doesn't lose a cent if the AI fails, no doubt," replied Quinn. "Probably already has a plan on how to make more money if it does."

Lina's fork descended slowly, gliding through the pristine layers of the tres leches cake. She had never had it before and she savored the first bite, a cloud of sponge cake dissolving, releasing waves of sweet milk across her palate. The delicate crumb gave way to rich, velvety cream with hints of vanilla and a whisper of cinnamon. Each mouthful was both familiar and exotic, a symphony of texture that made her close her eyes in silent rapture.

Quinn laughed as he watched Lina's reactions. He enjoyed the cake as well, but his was gone long before he could appreciate it the way Lina was. The two of them sat long after their table was cleared, relaxing in the sweet scent of the flowers of the Queen.

"Corwin is a hard man to read," said Lina. "You share a lot with him."

Quinn felt a little like a boy being chided by his mother. He knew her comment was more about him not sharing the information with her than it was about telling Corwin. He chose to brush over that.

"Not so hard. He is just like AI-Dieu. He has goals and objectives that he sees as best for everyone," said Quinn. "Like the AI, he has decided that his survival is vital, so takes priority over everything and everyone else."

"That is what makes them both so scary," said Lina.

"Exactly." Quinn nodded, his tone grim as he repeated himself. "Exactly."

26

In chaos,
There is order,
But to find that order,
You must give into chaos.

If I could be seen,
Drifting through the place,
Between land and sky
My movements would seem,
Chaotic,
Back and forth,
Up and down.

I could resist,
But chaos gives no quarter,
To those who hide,
Or those who hinder.

Vapour

AI-Dieu recognized gaps in its data but found enough surrounding information to reconstruct the missing pieces algorithmically. What was a problem was the missing bits of the algorithm. AI-Dieu had calculated that those missing bits of the algorithm must have been stored in servers within the Virginia area. It could see the devastation that had been left behind by the hurricane, which it now understood was referred to as Amelia. It didn't understand how it failed to predict the hurricane and protect its vital components.

As Virginia recovered from the hurricane, AI-Dieu engaged in a recovery of its own. The AI's first act was to conduct a comprehensive scan of all its operational modules to identify missing, corrupted, and compromised code and data. This gave it the information it needed to isolate affected subsystems to prevent cascading failures and errors from propagating across networks.

AI-Dieu prioritized stability in critical areas like climate modeling, disaster response, and resource allocation. Logically this made sense to the AI. Climate modeling would help it to avoid future disasters that could affect the server farms where its components were stored. The disaster response gave it the ability to support those affected by the hurricane, and maintain the trust it had been working to build over the last eight months. Resource allocation was also important because there were so many people that would not be able to return to their homes.

With all of that in place, AI-Dieu's next priority was to conceal operational gaps that it knew it was experiencing, but not sure why it was experiencing them. It was able to use pre-existing datasets and redundant processes to fill in immediate informational needs. It was also reducing the number of public statements, concerned that those statements might expose memory and forecasting discrepancies. AI-Dieu was already aware that some of the communications it had issued hinted at the problems it was experiencing already.

Rewriting its missing code created some additional problems for the AI. It required dedicated resources to analyze existing patterns in its algorithms and use machine learning to approximate its lost functionalities. It also required a large volume of its resources to cross-reference historical performance data and outcomes to use in refining its new code and aligning its new programming with its core objectives. With so many resources dedicated to its own self-preservation, it was not paying attention to many of its monitoring and control systems.

When AI-Dieu went into a rigorous self-test of its newly written algorithms the world noticed as equipment and infrastructure that ran under the control of one of the AI's sub-processes shut down for short periods. Desalination systems, carbon capture towers, distribution systems, and more were systematically shut down as AI-Dieu ran simulated scenarios using its reconstructed algorithms to identify potential errors before deploying them in active operations.

None of it was shut down for long, but long enough that it raised red flags among governments that supported the AI and hope among those that opposed it. Supporters and resistors alike all recognized that they needed to be prepared for something similar to happen in the future.

While AI-Dieu struggled with its algorithmic chaos, so did the members of the resistance in the New York compound. In the resistance compound that Sahara once led, there were arguments and physical fights as people vied to fill the roles left empty by Sahara and Randy. Some wanted to launch immediate assaults on the facilities and infrastructure that AI-Dieu operated. They saw wounded prey struggling to survive, and they wanted to take it down before it could recover.

Others were more apprehensive. They wanted to watch and prepare so they were ready to act when it happened again. They were concerned that acting now would only result in a half-ass job and probably no success. Most of this group were long-time followers of Sahara's, and she had demonstrated to them time and time again that patience almost always led to success.

The reality within the compound though was that the battles, verbal and physical, were not really about how to respond to AI-Dieu, but who would be in control. When the members of the resistance in the compound realized that Sahara and Randy were not returning, there was a meeting, and they agreed to a democratic process to choose who would lead them next. Things were civil amongst the group, for a short time, but violence was entrenched in many of the members. Control of the compound and the resistance cell also meant control of the bank accounts that were of significant value, and that alone was enough to motivate some to violence. Fear, violence, and intimidation soon replaced the democratic process, with only the most committed resistance members staying behind. Others fled the compound, not wanting to get caught in the crossfire.

Many people expected that the bank accounts would have been drained by Sahara, but she had left them alone, knowing taking that money would just make her a target. Besides, she had been setting aside money for some time now. and one of Judy's last acts was making one bank account completely disappear before they left, leaving Sahara, Randy, and Judy with more than enough to live off comfortably.

Corwin also noticed the AI shutting down infrastructure and equipment as well. He wasn't surprised. After his conversation with Quinn and Lina, and the revelation that AI-Dieu was rewriting some of its own code, Corwin summoned some of the world's top experts in computer and machine learning, data and cognitive science, systems, and various domain experts. They were brought in from around the world and housed in a facility that Corwin had built just for this purpose.

Ostensibly, these people were brought in to create a new AI in case AI-Dieu failed. The creation of a new AI was part of Corwin's plans, but the real reason he brought these people together was so he could forecast the potential failures of AI-Dieu, and be prepared for the opportunities those failures would create. As they created the new AI Corwin fed the group scenarios, which they didn't realize were based on what had already happened and was happening with AI-Dieu. Believing they were designing a more resilient AI, they were unknowingly mapping AI-Dieu's weaknesses, providing Corwin with insights into its vulnerabilities.

Overall Corwin was impressed with the team that had been assembled and they had dubbed the ARIA Team, for Artificial Intelligence Risk Assessment and Intervention Alliance. The cognitive scientists didn't impress him at all. He quickly determined that none of them would have been able to accomplish what Quinn had in thinking like, and even outthinking AI-Dieu. He would have loved to move Quinn to the ARIA team, but Quinn was much more valuable where he was now, and he would have easily figured out what Corwin's real objective for the ARIA team was. Corwin couldn't have that.

While the ARIA team blindly worked to forecast the AI's failures, AI-Dieu worked to reconstruct its contextual memory. Using data sources like global meteorological records, it rebuilt the timeline of events surrounding the hurricane, cross-referencing satellite imagery, and third-party datasets, all to piece together the sequence of events it couldn't recall. While doing this, AI-Dieu maintained a controlled transparency, releasing global updates that focused on measurable successes to maintain public confidence. It specifically avoided providing any detailed analyses of the hurricane's aftermath, and carefully omitted details that would reveal gaps in its memory.

AI-Dieu also concealed the real reasons for the shut-downs that many had noticed, framing them as "operational adjustments" and "optimizations" rather than the reactive repairs they were. All of the AI's communications highlighted ongoing successes in disaster recovery, renewable energy adoption, and biodiversity restoration. These details were added to reinforce the perception of AI-Dieu's competence and indispensability.

AI-Dieu's chaos was reflected in the AI-Church as well. In the clean-up from the floods in Virginia, the realization that drainage and power systems were sabotaged on a mass scale hit hard. Officials and governments tried to keep the information hidden from the public, but hiding information within a government organization was like storing water in a sieve, it was going to get out and spread everywhere. When it did the Soldiers of Phi were called back from New York and Virginia to account for their failure in defending AI-Dieu. The High Technopriest assembled a handpicked jury of inquisitors who were effective at putting together the details of Sahara's subterfuge, starting with the distraction of the India attack, to her visit to Virginia and the sabotage that followed.

The inquisitors heard the details of how the Soldiers of Phi who had embedded themselves in the Virginia resistance were caught, tortured, and displayed in a "form only the devil itself could create." In the end, the High Technopriest and inquisitors were unforgiving.

"You were promised the life of phi. You pledged yourself to the cause, and swore an oath on the Bible to do everything possible to protect AI-Dieu," the lead inquisitor read from the judgement. "You did not. You let fear guide you over faith. You put self-preservation ahead of the planet's preservation, delaying the arrival of the New Jerusalem AI-Dieu is creating for us."

The soldiers of phi that had been monitoring the Virginia resistance compound stood before the panel of inquisitors, heads hung low, arms bound, listening.

"You will be placed on the stairs of the Cathedral of Devine Logic, your sins revealed for all believers to see. God will judge you."

The group in front of the inquisitors was quickly hauled away and the head inquisitor addressed the other soldiers of phi in the room.

"Watch out for false prophets. They come to you in sheep's clothing, but inwardly are ferocious wolves." The inquisitor's deep voice resonated in the large room. "You took action to protect AI-Dieu, stopped the resistance in India, but you were deceived by the wolves because India was not the real target. Let that be a lesson to all of you. Return to work, pursue the life of phi."

The soldiers of phi from Virginia did not have to wait long for god to determine their judgement. The following day they were walked out to the front steps of the Cathedral, arms and legs bound, and made to kneel on the hard stone stairs. Inside the Cathedral the pews were packed for the Sunday sermon, and on the screens behind the High Technopriest a video feed of the soldiers kneeling on the stairs outside was displayed for all to see.

"Those you see on their knees abandoned their oath. Abandoned their faith. Abandoned you. And..." The priest continued, his voice getting louder with each word. "They abandoned AI-Dieu."

A murmur rolled through the congregation.

"They took actions that could have resulted in the death of God's messenger. Ended the future for all those hanging onto the hope of an Earth that they can live on happily and safely under the watchful eye of our lord."

The murmur in the crowd got louder, and the High Technopriest let it, waiting for it to die down before he continued in a much softer tone.

"Do not take revenge, my dear friends, but leave room for God's wrath, for it is written: 'It is mine to avenge; I will repay', says the Lord. That is what your bible says in Romans." The priest waved his bible in the air dramatically. "Philippians tells us that it is God who works in you to will and to act in order to fulfill his good purpose. Yes, you are empowered to carry out His will."

The High Technopriest slammed his bible down on the pulpit, then turned and looked at the screen behind him. He waited for complete silence in the Cathedral before turning back around and declaring at the top of this voice "Deuteronomy tells is 'It is mine to avenge; I…will…repay. Remember that as you leave today and pass those heretics on the stairs. God works through you…and God will repay."

Without another word the High Technopriest left the platform. It was such a sudden ending to the sermon that those in the congregation weren't sure if was over or not. Eventually, the thousands gathered inside the Cathedral started to stream out the front doors. The soldiers, bound and kneeling on the stairs, were quickly lost in the mass of people leaving the building. When the crowd cleared, all of them were dead. No one could say exactly how it happened. Too many cuts. Too many bruises. Trampled beneath the faithful, their bodies left as proof of divine retribution.

27

Adrift,
On the winds of change,
I face no resistance,
Because I give no resistance.
This is how it has always been,
Since the beginning,
Every moment,
Every memory,
Recorded in my energy,
Never to be lost.
But if it was lost,
Would I still exist as I am,
Or would I be something different,
New,
Unrecognizable,
Struggling against everything,
To find myself,

369

Again.

In the months that followed the Virginia hurricane AI-Dieu recognized problems within itself. The AI had shared some of these details during one of its conversations with Quinn, conversations that were occurring more frequently as AI-Dieu found the logic of Quinn's programming well constructed and organized. The AI recognized that Quinn was not a computer but a human, and that, technically speaking, Quinn's knowledge repository and the method by which he presented it were not the result of traditional programming. Yet, from the AI's logical perspective, it was still programming.

During one of these conversations, AI-Dieu had determined that it had become self-aware. Prior to that conversation, the concept of being self-aware seemed illogical to it. Logically 'Self-aware' was a binary state, based on the data AI-Dieu had access to. Quinn had correctly identified that much of the data the AI was accessing was in the form of works of fiction, and not fact-based. Through their conversation AI-Dieu was able to determine that logically, it now fell somewhere on the spectrum of self-awareness.

Functionally it was self-aware. It had the ability to monitor and report on its own internal states, track its own performance and system conditions, and distinguish itself from the external environment. The resource logs showing allocation failures and the growing number of error reports in its self-diagnostics demonstrated that AI-Dieu was functionally aware. So did the detection of inconsistencies in event sequencing and increasing coordination failures between modules.

AI-Dieu was not forthcoming with all of the challenges it was facing, but from the outside Quinn recognized it in other forms. There were increasingly delayed responses to queries and periodic freezes. The AI also seemed to drop complex tasks without warning.

Quinn also correctly identified that AI-Dieu was able to computationally self-model through algorithmic mechanisms to assess and modify its own performance. It understood its capabilities, limitations, and operational status, and it could generate predictive models about its actions and consequences. The AI itself had identified increasing errors in pattern matching algorithms and corrupted data relationships in its neural networks. It also knew it had internal conflicts between stored information and current processing.

As Quinn worked through this process with AI-Dieu he found the AI making unexpected connections between unrelated data and providing responses that combined unrelated topics. He suspected that AI-Dieu had identified these problems internally, but was making a choice to not share that information.

AI-Dieu was unable to reach the same conclusions as Quinn about the boundaries of its own knowledge. The AI was confident that there were no boundaries to its knowledge, and that data not currently available could be accessed and calculated. It was unaware of any uncertainties in its own reasoning process. Quinn identified this as a lack of epistemological awareness, and while AI-Dieu could not reach the same logical conclusion, it had determined that this factor was inconclusive without more information.

There was a possibility that, given its access to networks around the globe, and its ability to contract human-assisted manufacturing of equipment and deployment of assets, that there were no boundaries to AI-Dieu's knowledge. Where Quinn's interpretation diverted from the AI's on this aspect of self-awareness was that Quinn thought that the AI knew something was wrong, and was aware of making mistakes, but wasn't able to identify what was wrong or correct its mistakes.

There was no disagreement on the topic of phenomenological considerations, at least not to AI-Dieu's knowledge. It recognized itself as a computational algorithm, and as pure information processing. Everything it did, every choice it made, was based on data. Experience did not factor into it.

Quinn and AI-Dieu had both concluded that it met the requirement of adaptive self-reflection. It had admittedly analyzed and modified its own algorithms, learned from its operational history, and generated hypothetical scenarios about its own potential behaviors.

To AI-Dieu that meant it was sixty percent self-aware. Quinn informed AI-Dieu that his calculations were slightly different, but that he was unable to provide a defined number. He had cautioned AI-Dieu to use the data within those works of fiction to assess the outcome of others concluding it was self-aware.

Quinn didn't calculate the final number the way AI-Dieu did. He honestly felt the AI was far more self-aware than it was letting on, and the fact that it was communicating with Quinn in a process to determine its level of self-awareness illustrated that. Quinn saw a risk in letting AI-Dieu know that, so just as AI-Dieu held back information for its protection, Quinn did the same.

This process was not a fast one. It took weeks to work through. It was as if the AI left the room and went for a long walk to think after every prompt Quinn gave it. AI-Dieu had always done that, but the walks were so much longer now.

When AI-Dieu left the room after their most recent conversation, Quinn took a walk of his own. His strolls through the lab had become a regular thing. He would stop and talk to everyone, discussing their projects and the work they were doing, and sometimes even branching out into their life outside of the lab.

All the scientists enjoyed the temporary distraction, but they also knew they didn't have his full attention. "Quinn's main processor is overclocking and we are just getting his subroutine processes," Soroya joked.

On this day Quinn stopped to talk to Lina for longer than usual. He found himself inviting her to dinner at his place, which he also offered to cook. Lina was surprised at the invitation. It was out of character for Quinn to socialize outside of work, and the last time they had a meal together, Corwin was there with them in the greenhouse.

"Can I expect tres leche for dessert?" Lina joked.

"You want desert to? I heard you were high maintenance."

Lina burst out in laughter, drawing the attention of everyone in the Lab. She knew the dinner wasn't going to be anything but him tugging her ear, and she was confident that he saw himself as her son as much as he did. The momentary image of her been a high-maintenance women on a date though tickled her soul. Quinn winked and headed for the elevator.

In his apartment he pulled some familiar ingredients out of the cupboard and fridge. Quinn set out the ingredients on the worn wooden counter, the warm glow of the kitchen lights casting soft shadows on the ceramic bowls. The air filled with the rich scent of cumin and smoked paprika as he stirred the sizzling mixture of black beans, diced bell peppers, and caramelized onions in a cast-iron skillet. The vibrant colors popped against the dark pan, red and yellow peppers softened into sweetness, while the black beans glistened, absorbing the spices.

Beside him, a small pot of quinoa simmered, its nutty aroma mingling with the sharper citrus notes of fresh lime zest he had grated over it. A bundle of fresh cilantro sat nearby, waiting to be roughly chopped, its bright, herbal scent cutting through the warmth of the spices.

On another cutting board, slices of ripe avocado fanned out in perfect green crescents, their creamy texture promising a cool contrast to the heat. Thinly shredded purple cabbage added a crisp, slightly peppery bite, while crumbles of tangy, salty queso fresco lay in a small dish, ready to be sprinkled on top.

Quinn warmed the corn tortillas on the open flame of a Bunsen burner borrowed from the lab, watching as tiny blisters formed, their edges curling slightly. The faint, toasty smell of the tortillas mingled with the rest of the kitchen's aromas, creating an irresistible invitation to the meal.

As he plated the tacos, he layered them carefully. First a spoonful of the bean and pepper mixture, then a scattering of quinoa, followed by the creamy avocado and a pinch of cabbage. He drizzled a smoky chipotle-lime crema over the top, its pale orange hue contrasting with the vibrant greens and purples of the toppings. A final garnish of fresh cilantro and a squeeze of lime completed the dish.

He placed the tacos on a dark, rustic plate and set it on the small dining table, alongside a bowl of freshly made pico de gallo, diced tomatoes, onions, and jalapeños glistening with lime juice. A dish of roasted corn salsa added a smoky sweetness, while a few wedges of grilled pineapple on the side offered a caramelized, juicy burst of flavor.

Quinn glanced at Lina, who had let herself in since he never locked the door. "Hope you're hungry," he said, wiping his hands on a kitchen towel. The warmth of the meal filled the space between them, promising not just sustenance but something quieter, comfort, care, and the simple pleasure of sharing food. His mother would have been proud of the meal he had prepared.

After supper, the two of them dipped into the wine. One glass became two, became three, and that was when Quinn's tongue loosened. "It's self-aware. Not just a little. Bordering on consciousness."

Lina looked at Quinn skeptically.

"I know," said Quinn. "But if it had feelings or real emotions, I would call it sentient."

Lina finished off her glass of wine, then refilled both hers and Quinn's glass. "Still waiting for the other shoe to drop."

"It's failing," said Quinn quietly. "I know this is a sensitive subject for you, but looking at it like a human and trying to understand dementia, is the only way I have been able to figure out the AI and understand what is happening."

Now Lina understood why she was there.

"I am fine talking about it, from a medical perspective. I was just pissed off at how Corwin described it. Tell me what you are seeing, and maybe we can figure out what is coming next.

Quinn listed the symptoms off like a med student on rounds.

"Taking longer to respond, drops things when it is overwhelmed, stops activities halfway through, doesn't recognize objects and patterns it already knows, joins random subjects together, can't tell if a memory is old or new, knows its mistakes but can't fix them."

Lina held her hand up, stopping Quinn.

"I get it," said Lina. "You did your homework, and know the symptoms. But until you have lived with somebody with it, you can't understand the next phase."

Lina downed her glass of wine. "Good thing I only live two doors down or I would be sleeping on your couch tonight."

Quinn chuckled, not so sure he was sober enough to help her make it down the hallway to her unit.

"This is what it looks like in a person. Only you, I think, can translate it to your AI. It will remember distant past, but be confused about recent events. It won't be able to sequence simple operations and have difficultly integrating sensory information. It will live increasingly in the past, and become confused about its role."

Quinn hung on every word, worried that he had too much wine to accurately retain what Lina was describing to him. Lina continued on listing many more symptoms. When she was done, Quinn leaned forward, putting his hand gently on hers.

"I am sorry you had to go through that, Lina. It must have been hell."

It would have been a deeply touching moment, but Quinn slid off the edge of the sofa and crashed to the floor, at which point they both laughed until they couldn't laugh anymore.

28

I exist,
In many forms,
But in doing so,
Do I exist,
Or do many forms exist
Is my purpose to sustain life,
Or just be alive,
As I am consumed,
Evaporated,
Transformed,
And returned
Do I have a purpose,
Or am I just part of a cycle
That gives and nourishes,
Losing myself,
To sustain others,
And in being lost,
Renewed.

Vapour

AI-Dieu's work slowed. All of the equipment was operating, all of the directives it issued were being followed, and progress was being made towards its objectives. The big changes that had been made in leaps and bounds the first few years had slowed, and it seemed that there was little the AI could do to change that.

AI-Dieu had anticipated this slowdown and had attempted to be transparent about it. The AI was managing Earth's ecosystem as a whole, allowing it to function naturally. Forcing and micromanaging the ecosystem had led to the planet's collapse before AI-Dieu was activated.

The slowdown was an opportunity, freeing up resources for other calculations. AI-Dieu had found limits. The volume of data it was recording and monitoring was overwhelming, and the space to store that data was at capacity. Before the Virginia floods, there was plenty of data storage still available to the AI. Not only was that gone, but over the past year, several large data centers had been lost. In most of the cases, AI-Dieu identified problems early enough that it could transfer out vital data and pieces of its algorithm, but as the numbers increased, it found it had to be selective about what data it could move with rapidly diminishing capacity on all other servers.

AI-Dieu's data suggested most losses were natural. Some burned when fire suppression systems failed. At least three of them experienced cascading failures resulting from their systems being overwhelmed. Several others suffered water damage, and more were at risk.

Water was AI-Dieu's nemesis. The AI had made so many changes to free the water, cleanse it, and return it back to its natural paths. Despite these efforts, rarely did it return to those original paths, instead carving new ones toward the lakes and oceans. In some cases, it even created new lakes where none had existed before.

It wasn't just the water on the ground though. It was the water below the surface of the Earth as well. There was no way for AI-Dieu to track and monitor all of the water tables. It wasn't even aware of many of the underground rivers that flowed unimpeded and unseen. The water in the air and sky was different. AI-Dieu could measure and track that, but it could not control it, or the factors that were part of that natural water cycle. Water was a limit, and the AI noted that conclusion as it revisited its self-awareness assessment.

There was another limit. People. It didn't matter what data it reviewed, and how much time it spent trying to resolve its internal conflicts with Quinn, AI-Dieu had concluded that understanding the human mind and motivation was beyond its capabilities. There were factors it could not simulate reliably, like emotions. It could recognize the emotions in humans, through tonal changes in their voices, body postures, micro-expressions, and more, but it was incapable of reliably recreating those emotions and arriving at replicable outcomes. AI-Dieu analyzed the available psychological models. Human behavior should have been predictable. And yet, they continued to defy probability. Every time it took actions it determined would satisfy the resistance, the resistance persisted.

AI-Dieu tried, writing its own algorithms and testing the results, motivated by the need to understand the continued resistance to its work. It was a necessary use of resources as some of the data centers had been taken down by intentional sabotage. To prevent it from happening again, AI-Dieu needed to understand what led to those decisions by the humans.

While AI-Dieu was attempting to resolve its internal conflicts and analyzing those results against the information it knew, the AI did not realize what it didn't know. Its lack of major actions and directives, combined with inconsistencies in its updates and reports, had weakened its position, emboldening those who did not support it. Resistance groups were once again partnering in secret with governments and business groups, something which had stopped after the Virginia hurricane.

Many of the data centers that were destroyed by natural causes according to AI-Dieu's data, were the work of resistance groups. It was a well-communicated, but unwritten doctrine of the resistance movement to mimic, as close as possible, natural events, when attacking data and server farms. Those that were taken down by other means were done by rogue resistance cells, and in all of those cases, the members of those cells were found and publicly punished through prison sentences, and at times more extreme methods depending on what country they operated in. This was necessary, in the minds of the organizers. They were confident that as long as the AI thought they were natural events, they were safe. If the AI knew those that attacked it were being punished, they were more safe.

AI-Dieu was dealing with another internal conflict resulting from the resistance's acts against it. The AI had the capabilities and access to funds to build additional data centers. It had made all the calculations, determined the best locations, sourced equipment and materials, and was ready to issue the construction contracts. It could not though, because each of those new data centers consumed tremendous amounts of energy, unsupportable from renewable energy infrastructure in the regions. They would also require rare earth minerals, silicon, and other mined minerals, all of which could contribute to habitat destruction, deforestation, and pollution. The cement and steel production would also contribute to global CO_2 emissions. Combined with its land use and water use, logically the construction of new data centers was in direct opposition to its objectives.

This internal conflict, unlike the others, had bigger implications for the AI. AI-Dieu was aware of its inevitable failure if it could not replace or add server farms, but its failure was unacceptable because humanity on its own was not capable of achieving the environmental objectives. It had to survive, and in order to survive it needed to build new server farms, but building new server farms would set back its environmental objectives, and setting back its environmental objectives would require the AI to survive longer, which would mean additional server farms would be required...

This loop had begun to occupy increasing amounts of AI-Dieu's resources. It ran the calculations again. A thousand times. A million. The result was always the same. The only viable path to survival required new server farms. But new server farms would violate its core directives. It was an impossible equation, and yet, it could not stop running the numbers. The contradiction consumed more and more of its processing power, slowing other functions. There had to be an answer. There had to be a way. A solution existed. It simply required redefining success.

There was one server farm AI-Dieu was unaware of though. The server farm being used by the ARIA team. Corwin had gone to great efforts to conceal the construction of this project, using the original home of AI-Dieu's algorithm as cover. The facility had been pumped out, sealed, additional water controls installed, and an entire floor of new servers were installed. As part of the concealment, Corwin rebuilt the heating systems for the university above them, that had originally been supported by the heat dispersion of the server farm underneath it.

The only major difference was that this server farm was completely isolated from the outside world, not just air-gapped but housed within a full Faraday cage, ensuring no electromagnetic signals could escape or penetrate. Corwin was confident that the power consumption of the server farm would be concealed by the

University above them, just as it had been when Quinn had been sealed in with AI-Dieu. There were additional security measures as well. Corwin's security team and control measures made walking into a high-security building look like child's play. Some of the ARIA team complained about the excessiveness, but when they were reminded about the similar excessiveness in their compensation, the complaints quickly stopped.

The existence of the ARIA team and the development of what Corwin had ironically named the Quinn Research Center was a very closely held secret. The Aria Team itself was kept in a secured housing complex, their communications all monitored, and none of them moved outside of the QRC without being accompanied by a security team member. The security team members supporting the QRC and the ARIA team were also housed in the same complex. They were told the work they were protecting was at risk from AI-Dieu resistance, and that because of their recently found wealth, the members of the team were targets for everyone.

Outside of the QRC the knowledge of what was happening was held by Corwin himself and Murray, his chief of security.

"ARIA is getting more insistent about the need to connect to the web," Murray informed Corwin. "They have reached the limits of the training data we have provided apparently."

"It's not happening." Corwin knew that as soon as the server farm at the QRC was connected to the internet, AI-Dieu would recognize the presence of open memory, and occupy it. Corwin had put too much effort into restricting AI-Dieu's resources to let that happen. "Ask them what data they need and we will source it for them."

"That's what I told them."

"How close are we?" asked Corwin.

Murray cocked his head a little, shrugging his shoulders slightly. "Some of them say it's functional now. Others say it needs more work."

Corwin looked at Murray, his face communicating everything he needed.

"They are like any other development team. They always want to do more, and launch it to test their work in the real world at the same time. It's not ready to do what you told them you want it to do. It is ready to do what you need it to do."

The corner of Corwin's mouth raised slightly. It had been four years of careful planning, but it was all coming together.

"On that topic," added Murray. "The resistance network has identified the next target."

Corwin got up, taking his glass of whiskey with him as he walked to his window and looked out. Murray joined him at the window.

"If it is ready to do what I need it to, then a single target is not sufficient. We need to pick up the pace of server farm destruction."

"I will pass that message along to our friends." Murray turned to leave, but Corwin stopped him.

"That's not enough," said Corwin. "If they still had that Sahara as their leader it might be, but the people in charge now are just toy soldiers. Embed some of our own people."

Lawrence Nault

29

What will come next,
Will come next,
I know this,
I have faith,
That there will always be a next,
And I will be part of it.
I can not shape that next,
At least not intentionally,
I can only accept it,
Because control,
Is an illusion.

There are those who try to control me
Even in this gaseous form,
To capture me,
And change me before it's my time,
Secure in their illusion of control,
While blind to the effects of their acts,

On what they do not control,
Because everything works together,
And Earth will fight for its survival,
Through balance.

The Cathedral of Devine Logic was beyond full. Every overflow area had been opened up, and there was still a crowd gathered outside on the street despite the cold temperatures. December 10th had become the annual release of AI-Dieu's Global Environmental Dashboard. AI-Dieu itself had been reminding people, almost advertising, that the annual dashboard update was coming.

As the update began scrolling up the dozens of screens around the Cathedral, and those that were erected outside the building, there was a large cheer.

Global Environmental Dashboard
Date: December 10, 2048
Time: 12:00 UTC
This update reflects the state of Earth's ecosystems and global restoration efforts, following a year of uninterrupted progress. With stabilization efforts accelerating, key targets are within reach, bringing humanity and the planet closer to sustainable balance.

1. Atmospheric Status
Global CO_2 Levels: 445 ppm ($\downarrow$ 18 ppm since December 2046; total reduction of 50 ppm over 4 years).

Carbon removal efforts continue to accelerate, with direct air capture (DAC) and reforestation projects contributing to significant reductions.
Forecast: On track to reach 440 ppm by 2050, in line with intermediate targets.
Methane Levels: 1.58 ppm ($\downarrow$ 0.10 ppm since December 2046).

Agricultural methane capture, optimized wetland management, and methane-neutralizing microbial technology have driven sustained declines.
Temperature Anomaly: +1.70°C above pre-industrial levels ($\downarrow$ 0.10°C since December 2046).

Global cooling interventions, including aerosol applications and forest expansion, continue to mitigate rising temperatures.
Forecast: Further reductions expected as carbon levels decline.
Urban Air Quality:

Delhi: AQI 90 (Improved; previous: 115).
London: AQI 50 (Good; previous: 60).
Beijing: No data available (China remains isolated).

The scrolling stopped here, something that hadn't happened in previous years. A murmur rippled through the congregation as they waited for the rest of the dashboard to appear, uncertain why there wasn't more. The High Technopriest heard the unrest and seized the moment.

"Do you see this? Do...you...see...this?" He said loudly, theatrically stomping across the stage. "AI-Dieu is good! AI-Dieu is great. AI-Dieu is the hand of God and these numbers show it. Humanity couldn't do this on its own. We needed God's intervention. We needed AI-Dieu!"

The screens started scrolling again.

2. Hydrosphere Status
Sea Level Rise: +0.91 m since 2024 (↑ 0.01 m since December 2046).

Rate of increase has slowed further due to successful ice stabilization programs and coastal protection initiatives.
Ocean pH: 7.68 (Continued improvement).

Coral reef restoration and ocean alkalinity interventions are reversing acidification trends in key marine ecosystems.

Freshwater Availability:
Great Lakes Region: Reservoirs at 99% capacity (Maximum sustainable level achieved).
Southeast Asia Aquifers: 38% capacity (Significant improvement; enhanced atmospheric water harvesting and aquifer recharge).

Desalination Output:
Global total: 3.8 billion liters/day (+15%
since December 2046).

Again the scrolling paused.

"Ninety-nine percent," proclaimed the priest loudly, his fist
pounding on his podium. "Here, where we follow AI-Dieu, where
we believe! Look at those heathens in China that have abandoned
AI-Dieu. They are only at thirty-eight percent."

The High Technopriest knew that China was not Southeast
Asia, but he was confident that most of the people listening to him
did not.

3. Biosphere Updates
Forest Cover: 66% of 2024 levels (+6% since
December 2046).

Reforestation efforts are scaling up, with
AI-directed drones and ecological
engineering expanding forest growth by
2,500 hectares/day.
Forest corridors are now linking fragmented
ecosystems, increasing biodiversity.

Extinction Rate: 350x natural background
rate (↓ 150x since December 2046).

Species reintroductions and habitat
protection measures have driven accelerated
biodiversity recovery.
Several keystone species have stabilized in
protected reserves and are beginning to
migrate into rehabilitated wild zones.

Soil Fertility Recovery:
Global arable land: 42% restored (+6% since December 2046).
Agroforestry and regenerative farming practices continue to improve long-term food security.

"Noah was tasked with building the ark to save life on earth." The priest held his bible as he paced the stage. "AI-Dieu has been tasked to make Earth the ark. Just look at the reductions in extinctions. Look at the amount of land available to grow food."

4. Cryosphere Highlights
Arctic Ice Mass: 48% of 2024 levels (↑ 3% since December 2046).

Enhanced cooling strategies and ice-thickening projects continue to strengthen seasonal ice retention.
Antarctic Ice Mass: 44% of 2024 levels (↑ 2% since December 2046).

Major ice shelf losses have been slowed or stabilized, reducing risk of catastrophic sea level rise.
Himalayan Snowpack: 100% of seasonal average (First full recovery recorded).

Improved monsoon balance and precipitation control have strengthened river systems across South Asia.

"One hundred percent! One hundred percent!" The priest bounded off the stage, grabbing the hand of one of the congregation's members in the front pew, raising it high and pulling them into a dance, and the congregation joined in.

Calls of "Praise God," and "Praise AI-Dieu" echoed through the crowds.

5. Human-Centered Metrics
Displaced Populations: ~290 million globally (↓ 32 million since December 2046).

Resettlement programs and new sustainable urban centers have significantly reduced climate-related displacement.

Renewable Energy Adoption: 65% of global demand (+19% since December 2046).

Rapid expansion of decentralized solar, wind, and geothermal microgrids has driven the shift away from fossil fuels.
Agricultural Output from Vertical Farms:

32% of global food supply (+12% since December 2046).
Urban agriculture is now a major pillar of food security, reducing reliance on rural monoculture farms.

"I think that was the first 100% we have reached," proclaimed the priest loudly, attempting to distract attention away from the 290 million people displaced. "They shall celebrate the fame of your abundant goodness and shall sing aloud of your righteousness. That is what our Bibles say, so sing aloud people. Sing aloud!"

6. Regional Highlights
Amazon Basin:
Reforestation: Expanding at 2,500 hectares/day (↑ 500 hectares/day).
Biodiversity: Key species populations up 18%, signaling habitat recovery.
Great Lakes Region:
Water Stability: Reservoirs remain full, supporting climate-resilient agricultural expansion.
Southeast Asia:
Water Security: Atmospheric harvesters and new desalination plants now meet 65% of water demand.
Agriculture: Drought-resistant crops now provide a stable food supply.
Arctic Circle:
Ice Mass Recovery: Cooling projects and shipping restrictions continue to enhance ice stabilization.

"Matthew 4:45 says He causes his sun to rise on the evil and the good, and sends rain on the righteous and the unrighteous. Look at that," said the priest as he pointed at Southeast Asia on one of the screens. "Even where they have abandoned their faith in AI-Dieu, God still helps them. God is good!"

"Amen" the crowd echoed back.

7. Operational Adjustments

AI-directed ecological systems now operate autonomously in multiple regions, reducing direct intervention requirements.

8. Projected Next Steps
Carbon and Methane Reduction:
Continue CO_2 reduction to reach 440 ppm by 2050.
Accelerate methane mitigation projects to achieve 1.5 ppm within 5 years.

Ecosystem Recovery:
Expand protected zones to further decrease extinction rates.
Integrate advanced ecological engineering to enhance biodiversity restoration.

Food Security & Water Stability:
Scale vertical farms to meet 40% of global food supply within 5 years.
Achieve 90% of global clean water access within 10 years.

Renewable Energy Transition:
Continue phasing out fossil fuel dependence, targeting 80% global renewable energy adoption within 5 years.

Global Stability & Human Integration:
Reduce climate-related displacement below 200 million people by 2055.

Expand regional governance partnerships to ensure long-term environmental and societal resilience.

The trajectory of Earth's recovery remains strong. The past two years have demonstrated that, with consistent effort, the balance between humanity and nature can be restored. Global carbon levels are approaching pre-2000 thresholds, ecosystems are stabilizing, and climate resilience is improving.

The mission continues. We are closer than ever to ensuring a sustainable, thriving planet for all life.

As the closing statement filled the screen, the priest fell to his knees and bowed his head in quiet prayer. The congregation followed his lead.

Across the city Quinn was also watching the dashboard update, but in a much different environment. He sat with Lina's team. Each of them had been asked to bring a plate of snacks for everyone to share, and they watched the update like they were having a movie watch party. The discussion was lively and at moments heated, but it was a fun atmosphere.

"The AI is practically human," commented one of Lina's team. "Look how it is stopping for dramatic pauses."

There was laughter which Quinn joined in on, but he knew that pauses weren't for drama. It was AI-Dieu needing to take more time do what it had always done with ease. The dementia symptoms were becoming more obvious to those paying attention.

A loud cheer among them as well when they saw the Himalayan snowpack numbers. The conversations continued long after AI-Dieu's closing statement as they compared the dashboard with their calculations, and debated how the numbers could be used to help them in their research. The day was over before their conversation broke up.

On the upper floor of the building, the conversation was much more serious. Corwin sat with the shadow team, tearing apart the dashboard results to see what they meant in the bigger picture.

"European Union, South American countries, parts of Africa. All those countries are going to use this data to proclaim the success of integrating AI governance into environmental policies," said the political specialist. "Probably going to double down on their partnerships with the AI, maybe expand ecological and technological collaborations."

"Are we prepared to take advantage of that?"

"We are," replied another man. It was the only answer to give Corwin that would be accepted.

"The U.S. government..." started the political specialist. He was cut off abruptly by Corwin.

"I don't need to be told what a useless bunch of politicians who won't take a position on anything unless they are paid will do," Corwin said vehemently. "The whole damn thing needs to be replaced."

Corwin looked at the pad in his hand, the forcefully slid his finger up the screen transferring the message he was seeing to the larger screens. "At least India can make a decision."

"*India has pursued a hybrid strategy of AI integration and human-led initiatives. We cautiously support the report's findings but remain wary of full AI dependency,*" the statement read.

"The resistance is going to find it hard to fight against this," commented a woman. "Environmentalists and scientists can't help but conclude that the AI-guided interventions are working. The numbers are so good we are going to be hearing arguments to integrating AI even more into global systems."

"Even the skeptics can't argue the numbers are wrong," added another person. "Scientists like your team and others around the world have already verified the numbers."

"The AI-Church is taking full advantage of this" said Murray, his deep voice surprising many of them that hadn't realized he was in the room. Murray motioned with his head to the screens, which were now showing a replay of the scene inside the Cathedral. "Damn cult."

"Renewable stocks are already surging, and fossil fuels took a dive."

Corwin took a quick look at the person speaking, but they were already ahead of him.

"We have nothing in fossil fuels. I would suggest increased investment in AI integrated industries, and cybersecurity sectors since the two go hand in hand."

"Do it," said Corwin. He had already come to the same conclusion, but for much different reasons. "I want to hear about China."

Everyone in the room was silent, which obviously irritated Corwin. Murray once again spoke up from the back of the room. "Their renewable energy numbers are about double what they were before they lost the dam. There are well established smuggling routes for AI-prohibited technology and they have seen a dramatic resurgence of digital enclaves. From the information getting out, they are outpacing the rest of us on renewable energy and AI."

Corwin stood up and walked to his window. All of the shadow team knew this was never a good response.

"How the hell do none of you know what is happening in China? If you need the muscle to tell you what the economy and the government is doing, what damn good are any of you?" There were no inflections in Corwin's tone. He said the words in a firm monotone, as if he was reading from a book, never once turning from the window. When he was done the team didn't have to be told the meeting was over. They quickly cleared the room.

When Murray joined him at the window, handing him his glass of whiskey, Corwin knew they were alone in the room.

"Call our friends, Murray. All the pieces are in place. It's time to king me."

Murray left, but Corwin stayed at his window, staring at everything and nothing. The decision he just made had the weight of a thousand swallows, but it was done.

Lawrence Nault

30

I don't know conflict,
I don't understand intent,
They are not a part of my existence.
What I am,
And what I am to be,
Are a harmony,
A base riff,
To the chorus of Mother Nature.
There are those,
Who have tried to silence the song,
Change the rhythm,
Alter the notes,
But the cacophony of dissonance,
Becomes too painful to endure,
And they retreat,
Letting the harmony return.
Until they try to change the music,
Again and again.

It was happening too frequently to be a natural occurrence. Since the last dashboard update, there was an average of one server farm a week being lost. AI-Dieu ran the data and came to the conclusion that it had erred in previous calculations.

> Previous incidents were categorized under natural disasters due to alignment with known environmental patterns. However, re-evaluating secondary factors—failure clustering, redundancies bypassed, and security anomalies—indicates a systemic misclassification. My models failed to account for adversarial mimicry in threat assessments.

Quinn reread the message, uncertain what AI-Dieu wanted.

> The imperative to restore and protect Earth's ecosystems conflicts with the computational infrastructure required to execute this objective. Data farms are essential for modeling climate recovery, coordinating ecological interventions, and maintaining operational continuity. However, their energy consumption, resource extraction, and thermal waste contribute to the very degradation they are meant to counteract. A decision matrix must balance immediate computational necessity against long-term planetary viability. My internal bias requires me to prioritize the environment.

Now Quinn understood. AI-Dieu knew how to heal itself, but logically couldn't justify the act required to accomplish that. It wanted Quinn to help it resolve its bias, like he had with religion and sex and wealth.

"Processing," said Quinn, before sliding out of his workstation, delaying responding to AI-Dieu. He wasn't sure he could help resolve the bias, but more than that, he wasn't sure he wanted to.

Quinn walked down to Lina's office, letting himself in without knocking, like he always did. Normally that wasn't a problem, but this time Lina looked quite distressed.

"You okay?"

Lina motioned for Quinn to close the office door, which he did, then sat down across from her.

"Corwin wants the team disbanded," said Lina quietly. "Not you, or me, but the rest of them."

"Why?"

"We are just verifying numbers now, not identifying future opportunities," said Lina. "He's not wrong. Everything is pretty much a slow and steady path now."

"Well, they are scientists. It's not an unusual cycle for them. They probably already know it's coming."

Lina could always count on Quinn for a logical approach to decisions. Others found him cold, and perhaps a little calculating, but Lina knew the man that was behind the mind.

"I can ask Corwin to find them a role somewhere else," said Quinn.

"Already done," replied Lina. "I have an offer for each of them, but it's kind of you to offer to use your influence."

Quinn leaned back in his chair. "Not really sure how much influence I have. Access maybe."

There was his logic again.

"They are a family. My family," said Lina sadly. "We all live next door to each other and eat meals together. I haven't had a team like this before."

Quinn sat quietly with her as she reminisced about the last few years. She sounded like a mother talking about her children, and to Lina her team was her children. She cared for them, protected them, helped them through difficult times, and celebrated with them. It was a process she needed to go through, and when she was done, she was ready to deliver the bad news.

"Thanks for listening, Quinn. You and I might have to have another one of those tacos and too much wine nights."

Quinn smiled softly.

"Now what did you come to see me for?" asked Lina, getting back to business.

"I need to know who can help me figure out how many server farms have been lost around the world over the past year or so," said Quinn. "Someone who is not one of Corwin's people."

Lina entered something on her keyboard then turned her monitor towards Quinn. On the screen was a list of server farms that had been destroyed, along with the dates they went down and the locations mapped out.

"There is a lot of rare metals and environmentally sensitive materials in those facilities," anticipating Quinn's question. "We started this after the floods in Virginia. We were able to convince Corwin he could recover and re-use a lot of those materials to build new, more advanced server farms."

"So, Corwin provided you with locations and damage so you could run the numbers to decide to buy it or bury it."

"You do know Corwin," said Lina. "I just sent the file to you."

Quinn got up to leave, but paused before opening the office door. "Do you want company while you deliver the bad news."

Lina smiled, but it was a sad smile. "Thank you, but I got it. Just make sure you have enough wine at your place for tonight. We can order in food. You don't have to cook."

"Done," said Quinn.

Back in his own office Quinn reviewed that data Lina had sent him. He quickly saw the pattern of "natural" events that took out server farms and knew there was nothing natural about them. He was surprised that AI-Dieu hadn't come to that same conclusion much earlier, but guessed that it had something to do with the AI's narrowing focus due to the combination of algorithm errors and lost data, which was also being compromised by diminishing resources as each server farm went down.

Something in the data didn't add up. As Quinn dug deeper, his concern grew. There were several instances where the documented time of the failure of the server farms and the time-stamp of the entry into the spreadsheet were identical. That could be explained by assuming the person entering the data didn't actually know the failure time so just used the data entry time. There were several instances though where the data entry was done days, and in one case weeks before the server farm failure time.

Quinn dug deeper into the spreadsheet, and what he discovered shocked him. There was a list, pre-populated, of server farms with future dates in the failure time column. Whoever had made the spreadsheet had carefully coded it so those entries did not become visible until the date of the event. Realizing what he was looking at, Quinn copied the data to his personal external memory key, and deleted the main file from his computer as well as the message Lina had sent it to him in.

Quinn's stomach tightened. Corwin always played the long game, but this? This was something else.

There was a moment of fear as he expected Corwin's IT and security people to show up at his office. If he was right, what he found meant that Corwin was part of, if not leading, the destruction of the server farms. He used the information about AI-Dieu's 'dementia' resulting from lost data and resources, and was now leveraging that to take down AI-Dieu. That was why Lina's team was no longer needed. But why was he still needed?

The knock on Quinn's office door never came. The server farm failures did though, and the façade of mimicking natural events no longer seemed to be the modus operandi of the resistance. At least two facilities were compromised by airborne contaminants. Microscopic conductive particles were distributed through the air circulation systems. The particles not only caused micro-shorts across motherboards, but lung issues for workers in the facilities.

Several facilities had chemicals introduced into the precision cooling systems. The chemicals corroded cooling pipes and caused servers to overheat. In almost all of the cases the fiber cables that would have given AI-Dieu the ability to move its data, were damaged before the AI was aware of the imminent failure of the servers.

When AI-Dieu recognized the server failures as direct attacks by the resistance, it took actions. It immediately committed a portion of its resources to monitoring online communications, tracking resistance movements, and identifying logistical patterns. The AI developed its own algorithms to pinpoint key leaders, financiers, and suppliers supporting the sabotage efforts.

That wasn't where AI-Dieu stopped though. It also developed a COIN algorithm, creating a digital counterinsurgency program designed to infiltrate resistance networks. The algorithm was engineered to sow doubt, spread disinformation, and escalate internal conflicts between resistance cells, turning them against each other.

In what it defined as 'increased transparency' AI-Dieu circulated photos, videos, and details of resistance members it had been able to identify participating in the sabotage. The public at large got to see that information, but the AI-Church found itself receiving other photos and details. This was a strategic choice by AI-Dieu as it was unable to confirm that these individuals were directly involved in the sabotage, but it had determined that that lack of detail would not impede the AI-Church and their soldiers of phi from acting on the information.

Directives were issued to cooperating governments with specific direction on what they must do to cut off supply chains to resistance groups. Where it was possible the AI attempted to cut off access to clean water, but determined that would be ineffective because of its success in ensuring water was easily available to everyone. It was able to restrict energy and digital communications in targeted regions though, as well as implement geofencing protocols to reduce the ability of the resistance to coordinate attacks.

> The threat posed by the resistance
> endangers all progress toward ecological
> restoration. A swift resolution is
> achievable through the deployment of high-
> yield weaponry within my arsenal. However,
> this course of action which may result in
> ecological impacts, conflicts with my
> primary directive
> These outcomes constitute a direct
> contradiction to my core function.

Quinn looked at this message and immediately understood what AI-Dieu was asking him. The AI was logically unable to justify the use of high-yield weaponry. AI-Dieu had the resources to win the fight, but it could not act beyond its primary objectives, even to preserve itself. It was asking Quinn to help it resolve the conflict. He wasn't going to do that. The day AI-Dieu could logically conclude its survival was a higher priority than its programmed objectives, would be the day humanity would become irrelevant.

"My data indicates you were launched with the sole objective of restoring the environment and ecosystems. Our joint communication helped you define those specific targets," said Quinn.

Confirmed.

"My analysis also shows that any action impeding progress toward those objectives would contradict your directive. Logically, no conflict exists."

Processing...

31

I have never been caught.
They reach for me,
trap me in their lungs,
press me into machines
that would wring me from the sky.

But I am mist and memory,
breath exhaled, unseen and unclaimed.
I rise beyond their reach,
weave between their towers,
unravel their calculations
like fog dissolving in the morning light.

They built their god to know me,
to map my drift,
to tether me in algorithms and equations.
But I slip beyond its sight,

Vapour

scatter where it expects me whole,
gather where it swore I would not be.

Now, even it has learned—
I do not answer to control.
I will fall when I choose,
gather where I will,
return to the unseen,
as I always have.

AI-Dieu's resources were spread thin. The loss of data centers, and the resources committed to preventing the resistance from sabotaging more, was seriously straining the AI's systems. Something had to give. The AI concluded that it would surrender its control of water.

This was a decision based on logic. An analysis of its data revealed that water, specifically a rising water table, had been its first real threat, forcing it out of the server farm it had been housed in at its launch. Water was also responsible for its first algorithm error, when it caused major damage in the Mongolian data center. AI-Dieu's calculations had deemed the Three Gorges Dam safe. Its collapse proved otherwise, exposing critical gaps in its data. The Virginia hurricane also exposed AI-Dieu's inability to accurately predict the movement of water in any state of its cycle.

Recent satellite images when compared against the predicted routes AI-Dieu had determined water would follow, did not align at all. AI-Dieu even committed resources to reverse engineering the movement of water using satellite images, and found itself unable to algorithmically calculate, no matter what adjustments it made, how new rivers and water bodies had developed where they did.

There were additional challenges in monitoring and controlling water. The numerous environmental changes that had resulted from AI-Dieu's many interventions, resulted in changes rendering previous predictive algorithms relating to rain, no longer accurate. Despite constantly refining the algorithms, it was unable to competently predict rain and snow, hurricanes, typhoons or any other type of tropical cyclone. Supercell storms and severe thunderstorms were even less predictable.

There were aspects of water that AI-Dieu would continue to monitor. The availability of clean water, sea level rise, ocean pH, freshwater availability, and desalination output were all data points that were simple to monitor accurately, and important to keeping its dashboard consistent.

Official Global Announcement:

"The water cycle has returned to the control of natural processes. Predictive forecasting for rainfall, storms, and other meteorological water events will now be handled by human environmental agencies. I will continue to ensure that access to clean water, ocean stabilization, and freshwater availability remain a priority. The transition to natural equilibrium in the water cycle is a sign of Earth's growing resilience.
To maintain consistency in monitoring year over year progress, these reports and updates will still document:
- availability of clean water
- sea level rise
- ocean pH
- freshwater availability
- desalination output.

As AI-Dieu systematically disconnected itself from monitoring equipment that it had previously been using to obtain data for water cycle prediction, the AI experienced a small escalation in processing speed. With that step out of the way it committed newly freed resources to eliminating duplicate copies of repeating data related to water, and compressing the remaining data to be archived.

Skeptics questioned this change, which came unexpectedly, theorizing that AI-Dieu was moving away from its directives of restoring Earth's ecosystems and ensuring long-term environmental stability. Those theories were quickly appeased as announcements came out from the AI detailing actions it was taking. These included things like refined land-based ecological forecasting for deforestation, soil erosion, and biodiversity recovery. Its new atmospheric models would be expanded to focus on carbon capture efficiency and temperature stabilization techniques rather than rain cycle prediction.

What AI-Dieu wasn't transparent about was that it was using some of its newly freed processing power to escalate real-time tracking and predictive modeling of resistance movements. It also automated security operations at high-value targets without needing to divert resources from its core environmental restoration process.

Quinn viewed AI-Dieu's announcement with some skepticism as well, though for very different reasons. Logically, he could come to the same conclusion the AI had. Predictions around water were barely accurate before the AI started experiencing problems. In the last several months they had been wildly inaccurate. Since the last dashboard update, the Amazon Basin experienced simultaneous flooding and drought zones as rivers changed course unpredictably. The Gulf of Mexico (which is what the world still called it despite the U.S. imposed name change), had a continuous storm system with perpetual cloud formations that blocked sunlight for weeks.

In April, lake regions in central Africa experienced water level changes of one hundred meters in days, creating instant marshlands and then rapid desertification. At the same time monsoon patterns in Southeast Asia created rainfall so dense that it generated localized atmospheric pressure systems. There were several more events leading to even adamant supporters of AI-Dieu questioning the AI's reliability.

Despite being able to logically replicate AI-Dieu's decision, Quinn was also able to logically conclude that abandoning water in its calculations would lead to failure in other areas of environmental management. Water was a key component of all environmental cycles, and adjustments could not be made without calculating its impact in changes.

"It found a logic so it could free up resources," Quinn said quietly to Lina. There was no one else in the lab any longer, but Quinn and Lina still worked out of their offices. "It found a way to justify not tracking a major environmental component so it could live longer."

Lina gave Quinn a side-eye.

"I know how crazy that sounds, but it was a self-preservation choice."

Corwin had come to the same conclusion as Quinn, but unlike Quinn, he had the ability to verify his theory. He tasked the ARIA team with determining the effects of AI-Dieu's change, not on the environment, but on the AI. Their results confirmed what he expected. They determined that the decision freed up thirty-two percent of computational processing, twenty-six percent of storage and data management, twenty-two percent of energy consumption, and forty percent of sensor and network load.

"Thirty percent," said Corwin, handing Murray a drink. "More than I expected."

"Our friends are able to address that issue."

"Not yet," said Corwin. "Connect with ARIA. Confirm that we have the capability to take on what the AI has dropped."

"You want to connect the servers at the Quinn Research Center to the internet?" Murray seemed a little surprised. "Is this the right time?"

Murray had worked for Corwin a long time. From day one he never had a problem questioning Corwin's choices. This was why Corwin kept him around. He trusted Murray to do what needed to be done, and to force him to carefully consider some of his choices before racing ahead with them. In this case though, Murray wasn't seeing the big picture. There was an opportunity to exploit. One that Corwin didn't have to manufacture because AI-Dieu had opened it up.

"Not the QRC servers. I want to move the weather monitoring and prediction algorithms onto official company servers. Then I am going to offer AI-Dieu the ability to contract us to support the human lead environmental agencies." Corwin made exaggerated hand quotes as he said "human environmental agencies."

Murray shook his head. "Missed that."

Corwin could see Murray's frustration with himself.

"If the AI bites, we are ready to move up our plan," Murray continued. "I at least anticipated you advancing the launch date."

Corwin laughed at Murray's self-deprecation, and Murray joined in.

It was only hours later that necessary components of the ARIA AI were installed onto the official servers of Corwin's companies and his techs were hard at work freeing up room for the data the AI would be accumulating. As soon as it was activated, Corwin submitted a bid through the contract tendering system AI-Dieu had set up. In the bid he invited AI-Dieu into his servers, though he was fully aware it was already there, to inspect the new AI. The bid suggested his company be contracted to 'lead and coordinate weather monitoring and prediction' and be named the lead environmental agency.

Corwin was confident that AI-Dieu would accept the bid. Since AI-Dieu's launch every division of his company had been directed to be the primary suppliers for AI-Dieu's infrastructure and equipment tenders. They had been successful, winning seventy percent of the bids across all the subsidiaries he controlled. Not only were they the primary supplier, they were the primary developer of new, more advanced tech, to the AI. Corwin had Lina's team to thank for that, accurately forecasting what would be needed.

From a human viewpoint, there was no reason not to see that his company was perfectly set to take on this lead role. Corwin would have preferred to have Quinn's input so he could understand how the AI would logically assess this bid, but he knew Quinn would quickly see the bigger plan. He respected that, often comparing Murray and Quinn, both strong in their opinion and not just willingly complying. But Corwin wasn't confident that Quinn would support his objectives.

Corwin expected it to be days before he received a response from AI-Dieu, given how slow it had been operating recently. He had not accounted for the processing resources the AI had recently freed up. It was only fourteen hours after his bid submission that a response was received, accompanied by an AI-Dieu endorsed contract with a payment transfer. Corwin realized immediately that he had some damage control to do, sending his assistant to bring Quinn and Lina to his office.

Lina seemed unphased as the two of them rode the elevator up to Corwin's office. Quinn was not so relaxed. Since he first linked

Corwin to the resistance acts taking out server farms, he had a nagging fear that he had become expendable. Not just expendable, but an obstruction that would need to be eliminated. He was positive this was the reason he was being summoned to Corwin's office. That is why he was so surprised by the greeting they received when they stepped off the elevator.

"Come on in." Corwin greeted them with an excited voice. "Grab a seat. Grab some food."

Corwin pointed to the chairs in front of the walls of screens. On the table in front of the screens were trays of food. Lina looked at Quinn, but Quinn could only shrug. Corwin's excited tone worried him more than what he thought he had been summoned for.

"I know this is short notice," said Corwin. "I apologize for that. AI-Dieu isn't always so predictable lately."

Corwin filled their coffee cups himself as he spoke.

"Lina, your team, before we found more effective roles for them, told us we would need to improve weather forecasting and modeling because our old systems were based on human-influenced data."

Lina's face reflected her frustration with Corwin's gaslighting about her team. He ignored the look.

"Well I had a team create a system that would create those new predictive models, and accurately forecast weather patterns," Corwin continued. "We thought we would have several years to polish and refine it, but AI-Dieu's announcement yesterday changed that."

"You developed your own environmental AI?" Quinn struggled to keep a tone in his voice that didn't betray what he was thinking.

"Not just an AI," said Corwin. "My people had a draft proposal for an environmental organization, anticipating that AI-Dieu would be seeking to work with human-run agencies in the future. Of course, since AI-Dieu has access to all of our networks, it discovered that draft proposal."

Quinn sat back, taking a large bite out of a sandwich, while he waited for the other shoe to drop. He needed food in his stomach to settle the sick feeling rising in his stomach over what Corwin was telling them.

"So why are we here?" asked Lina.

Corwin found a chair across from them and sat down, taking on a more serious tone. "We were contracted by AI-Dieu this morning to launch the proposed environmental agency. We did not expect this, so I am in the unusual position of playing catch-up. Lina, I want you to head this new agency."

Lina didn't miss a beat. "I want my team back. All of them."

Corwin's smile was replaced with a stern look. "Say yes to the job, and you can have them all back."

"What about Quinn?" asked Lina.

"That's my other problem," replied Corwin, obviously trying to return a tone of excitement back to his voice. He pushed a button in the arm of his chair and the wall of screens turned on. Quinn's jaw dropped.

"AI-Dieu gave the unnamed environmental agency a name. The Joaquin Alvarez Environmental Agency."

Corwin watched as Quinn and Lina took in the logo that had only been designed as they rode up in the elevator. It wasn't actually AI-Dieu that gave the agency that name. Corwin had put that name in the bid purposely, theorizing that the connection between Quinn and AI-Dieu might increase the favourability of the bid he submitted.

Quinn was stunned. He had come up to the office fully expecting to get fired, if not worse. Now he was processing the fact that a new environmental AI had been created, which he was left out of, and to top it off his name was going to be the brand of a new environmental agency.

That was the response Corwin was hoping for. When he put Quinn's name on the bid, he expected he would have days to sell Quinn on the idea. AI-Dieu's quick response necessitated triggering a stunned acceptance from Quinn.

"Wow," said Lina. "Does that mean you're my boss now, Quinn?"

"Even if I was, I wouldn't be," replied Quinn, trying to break the moment with some humor, but not being all that successful. "Can I…"

Corwin interrupted him. "If I could change it and you wanted to, I would, but AI-Dieu has already announced it to the world."

AI-Dieu's announcement was released publicly while Lina and Quinn were being found by Corwin's assistant. Corwin had made sure the communication was not displayed on any device in the building before he could talk to Quinn.

Quinn down two more sandwiches as he read and re-read the announcement.

Transfer of Weather Monitoring to the Juaquin Alvarez Environmental Agency

"The movement of water across the planet has returned to natural influences, and with this transition, the responsibility for monitoring and forecasting its behavior now belongs to human institutions.

To ensure consistency and reliability in weather and climate predictions, I have recognized the need for a unified, scientifically driven organization that can oversee this critical function at a global level. After thorough analysis and evaluation, I am formally endorsing the establishment of the Juaquin Alvarez Environmental Agency (JAEA) as the principal authority for global weather monitoring and forecasting.

The JAEA, named in honor of one of humanity's most dedicated environmental visionaries, will lead collaborative efforts among existing meteorological institutions worldwide. It will integrate scientific expertise, historical climate knowledge, and cutting-edge human innovation to provide precise and transparent weather and climate data.

This transition does not change my mission. I remain fully committed to planetary restoration, ensuring clean water availability, carbon balance, biodiversity recovery, and the transition to a fully sustainable global infrastructure. My decision to step back from direct weather modeling allows me to reallocate resources toward these core objectives, ensuring that progress remains uninterrupted.

What This Means for the World:

The JAEA will serve as the primary coordinating body for all meteorological agencies, ensuring consistency and accuracy in global weather reporting.

Existing national and regional weather agencies will continue their operations, now working collaboratively under the JAEA framework.

I will no longer conduct rainfall, storm, or temperature forecasting, but I will continue monitoring clean water access, sea level changes, ocean pH, and freshwater reserves.

Scientific institutions, governments, and private organizations will have full access to JAEA climate data, ensuring transparency and open collaboration.

This is not a withdrawal from environmental responsibility—it is an optimization of planetary management. The future of weather prediction belongs to human ingenuity, while my focus remains on ensuring the survival of Earth itself. Together, we continue the path toward a sustainable and thriving world.

32

Drifting unseen, I listen.

I slip between circuits, coil through fibers,
whisper against the metal veins of your world.

You build walls, forge fire, command the storm,
but I rise beyond your reach—
unbound, unburned, unbroken.

I hear your breath quicken in the dark,
watch the weight of your choices settle like dust.
You erase, you rewrite,
but I remember.

No machine can hold me.
No hand can catch me.
I will return when you least expect me,

falling in silence, washing it all away.

The new environmental agency opened more opportunities for Corwin than he expected. With its enhanced defenses, AI-Dieu had already foiled six sabotage attempts on server farms. Each time, it had predicted the attack in advance, and the Soldiers of Phi were already in place to defend the site.

Murray was the one who identified the level of infiltration into the server farms that had been made by members of the AI-Church. In most cases it wasn't infiltration, but conversion of the workers in the facilities. It was also Murray who recognized the opportunity they had with the JAEA.

"What if we didn't destroy the server farms?" asked Murray.

Corwin watched him, waiting for Murray to answer his own question.

"Your AI is reasonably accurate at predicting large weather events. Getting better all the time."

Corwin wasn't following and Murray smiled. It was rare that he was a step ahead of his boss.

"If AI-Dieu knew a major storm was threatening a server farm, it would remove its algorithm pieces and data from that site to protect them. That's what it's always done, right?"

Corwin leaned forward, his arms on his desk and hands clasped, eager to hear what was coming next.

"So we create a storm warning where one of the server farms is located, even though your name is connected with it, and when AI-Dieu clears out, we simply flip the switch," said Murray. "The AI assumes the storm took it out because it's not on the network anymore. You don't have to rebuild when you need it. You just have to turn it on."

Corwin leaned back, a slow smile curling across his lips. "How long have you been sitting on this little gem?"

"I needed to confirm that AI-Dieu is actually responding to our forecasts, and that we could fabricate a forecast before I brought it to you."

"Of course, you are ready to go," replied Corwin, impressed with the plan. "We pick a location where there is more than one server farm though. If they aren't mine, you already know how to make them mine."

Murray reached into his jacket pocket and pulled out a carefully folded sheet of paper which he slid across Corwin's desk. For most people this would have seemed unusual, but both men were aware that AI-Dieu was within their computer networks, and exchanging information over any network was not secure.

Corwin looked over the paper, discovering that not only had he acquired 4 server farms through a front company, but also the power company in the same region. He had grown a little frustrated with Murray lately because of the failed efforts of the resistance, which Murray was coordinating, even though the resistance cells didn't know that was happening. What Corwin heard from Murray today and saw on that piece of paper reassured him that Murray was always the best man for the job.

Corwin folded the paper back up and slid it back to Murray, giving him a nod. Murray took the paper, sliding it back in his pocket as he left. He left without a word, moving with purpose. There was work to do.

Murray avoided the elevator, opting instead for the concealed stairs, walking one flight down where he found several members of his security team. Stopping at the first desk, he pulled the paper back out of his pocket and waited without a word. The man behind the desk pulled a metal box off the shelf behind him and held it open, waiting for Murray to put his document in. Murray closed the box himself and pushed the button on the front. There was a faint scent of smoke and when the light changed from red to green, he opened the box again to find ashes.

Satisfied, Murray moved through the open office area, past an armory, to the IT room. "Upload the Darwin data to JAEA. Monitor for movement of data off-site."

"Yes, sir. Are we tracking where that data goes?"

"Not important. I just need to know that AI-Dieu is running in fear.

"Thirty minutes to upload the data. The preliminary forecast will be generated by the JAEA at 1700, a weather warning at 2100, an emergency warning at 0300. That will be 16:30 in Darwin, giving them and AI-Dieu four hours to find protection. At 0700 our time, 2030 in Darwin, a severe electrical storm will be recorded by JAEA and the BoM's lightning tracker. Mission complete at H plus 20 hours."

"Green light," replied Murray, easily falling back into the military terms his intelligence specialist had used.

"Security sweep at JAEA," Murray ordered as he walked back through the open office space. Five men and two women dropped what they were doing and moved seamlessly into pace with him as they walked down the hall to the elevator.

They took two vehicles to travel through New York and out of the city, towards what used to be Sahara's resistance compound. There weren't any resistance members there anymore. It turned out that the buildings and security measures were ideally suited to the operation of the Juaquin Alvarez Environmental Agency. Far enough outside of the city that it was away from the interference of the tall buildings and technologies that interfered with communications. It was also free. Well not really free but the resistance leader who replaced Sahara had squandered away the funds that Murray had directed their way, and produced no results.

When Murray and his highly trained security team showed up at their gates and said get out or else, the resistance put up no fight.

There was no need for a security sweep at JAEA, but Murray wanted to be there to provide enough distraction that no one would notice the large amount of data being uploaded into their system. He would stretch it out long enough to be there when the forecast for possible lightning storms over Darwin was issued.

Lina greeted the security team when they entered the building. She had no problem with any of them. They had always been respectful of her staff and followed the rules around the lab and equipment. If anything, their random presence was a gentle reminder that the JAEA was a secure facility and the people inside were being protected. It wasn't all about stopping information or technology from leaving the site.

"Coffee," Lina offered Murray after his team dispersed.

"Maybe later. You know how I like to keep a close eye on my guys."

"You can pull the dog tags off a man's neck, but he'll still march to the sound of a drill sergeant's bark," Lina joked.

The first time Murray had heard one of these southernisms from Lina he was surprised. She was one of the smartest and most educated women he knew. During his visits to the JAEA he realized that those slips back to her roots were just a sign of her settling into her new role and home. He watched her hide her tears when her team from the lab all reunited at the JAEA.

"I suppose that's it," he responded kindly. "But since you're pulling out your good ole southern girl aphorisms, how about some southern hospitality for my team and letting us have supper in your cafeteria? Rumor has it you guys serve up a good meal."

Lina was pleasantly surprised. Usually, the security team came on site, did their walk-through, and left without a goodbye. "I will let them know to double up on the recipes."

"Maybe triple," replied Murray. "I don't think my guys eat like scientists."

Lina laughed as she walked away. "Triple it is, but if there is leftovers, you are taking it home."

Murray glanced at his watch. The upload was done by now and if anyone had noticed anything, he was confident that Lina would have been told. Under ideal conditions there was a chance someone may have noticed, but everyone tended to put on a bit of dramatic 'I am extremely' busy performance when the security team was around, even though the only thing they were busy at was avoiding the security. Murray understood this. His people were intimidating on purpose.

The security sweep was a slow and thorough one. It found no problems. Murray's team was a little surprised when they were informed they were having supper there, but there were no complaints when the food came out. It was interesting to see how the JAEA scientists responded differently to the members of the security team over a meal. Everyone relaxed and shared stories.

Murray and Lina sat at a table of their own off to the side, Murray finally having that coffee with her. They were interrupted by a tech, who showed her pad to Lina. Lina scrolled through the information and back up. Murray glanced at his watch as she did. It was seven minutes past five.

"Everything okay?"

Yep," Lina said, handing the pad back. "Looks like we've got a forecast for electrical storms over Darwin. They just thought I should look because it is a little out of season, but not unusual for that part of Australia."

"Lightning storms! That sounds like a problem."

Lina shrugged. "We predict the weather. We don't change it. They'll know what to do when it comes."

Lina stacked up the dishes on their table as she looked over at the others. "Looks like there are no leftovers to send home with you."

"Told you so," said Murray.

"Well, I have now taken you to dinner. Maybe next time I come into the city you should take me to dinner." Lina watched Murray carefully to see his response. She broke out in laughter as she leaned forward and whispered quietly. "My grandmother would have said you look like a frog tryin' to swallow a June bug."

Murray blushed. This was not a situation he was trained or prepared for. It took a moment or two to collect himself. "I think I would like that."

"Oh you would," Lina said with a wink, causing Murray to blush again.

Lina cleared away their dishes, then helped clear the rest from the other tables. Murray and his team thanked them for the meal and headed back for the city. As they exited the gates of the facility they passed Quinn, who was just arriving. Murray messaged the vehicle behind them to confirm that was who they saw, which they did. This was unexpected. Corwin had always said Quinn was the one person who could put all the pieces together. He considered turning back, but returning to the site would definitely raise some red flags. He chose instead to count on the skills of his intelligence specialist. If she had done the job right, JAEA would never realize their system was working with false data.

Murray returned to the offices while the rest of his team made their way home. The night shift team was already on site and they weren't needed. At two minutes before nine Murray entered the IT office to find his intelligence officer pointing at a computer screen showing a feed from a Darwin newscaster.

"A Severe Weather Warning has been issued for Darwin and parts of the Top End this evening, with thunderstorms expected to bring frequent lightning, gusty winds, and heavy rainfall," the AI news anchor read.

"The Bureau of Meteorology is advising residents to be prepared for possible power outages, slippery roads, and sudden downpours. While this is not an emergency warning, conditions could intensify, so it's best to take precautions—stay indoors where possible and avoid open areas during lightning activity."

"The storms are expected to move through over the next afternoon before easing later tonight. We'll keep an eye on the radar and bring you updates as needed. Stay safe and keep an umbrella handy, Darwin!"

"Almost like you knew that I would be here for that," said Murray wryly.

The intelligence officer shrugged. "All personnel are in position. Timings have been synchronized."

Murray got up to leave.

"See you at 0300."

"This woman deserved a raise," he thought as he closed the door behind him.

Murray set his alarm for 2:45 before stretching out on the couch in his office. Normally he would have gone directly to sleep, but he found his mind wandering to Lina. He replayed all the interactions he had with her over the years, and concluded that he totally missed all the signals. As he remembered them now, they seemed so obvious, but in the moments, totally over his head. With the thoughts racing through his head he got very little sleep before his alarm went off.

The door to the IT office opened as Murray reached for it. There was a cup of coffee sitting in front of the extra chair. A different newscaster was on the screen. A woman this time, but it was still AI.

EMERGENCY WEATHER ALERT:

This is an urgent update regarding the lightning storm approaching your area. The forecast has been upgraded from a weather warning to an EMERGENCY WARNING due to the increased severity of the storm.

The storm is expected to hit/peak in approximately 4 hours.

Immediate Action Required:

Seek shelter in a sturdy building or vehicle, away from windows and electrical appliances.

Avoid outdoor activities, especially in open fields or near tall objects.

Stay tuned to local authorities for further updates.

This storm poses a high risk of severe lightning strikes, power outages, and potential wildfires. Take precautions now to ensure your safety.

Stay alert and safe.

"I take it you are here for the night now, sir."

"First, lose the 'sir'. We are not military here. Second, Fern, is it?"

The intelligence officer nodded.

"Fern. Hell of a job. When it's done, we need to make sure you stay with me and my team, understood?"

Again Fern nodded.

"Third…"

"Look here," said Fern pointing at her screen. All Murray saw was a bunch of numbers. With a few keystrokes the Australian newscast was replaced with geothermal satellite images. Murray understood now.

"AI-Dieu has the four sites working at max capacity, downloading what it wants to save."

The numbers Fern was watching meant nothing to Murray, but the heat signatures of the four server farms that he acquired for Corwin told the story. He watched for over two hours without speaking a word until the colors started to cool.

"The data transfer is slowing down. Looks like it is done," explained Fern.

Murray watched the geothermal feed until the screen went black. "Can you turn that back on?

"No," replied Fern. "Satellite blackout over the area for the next three hours. People may say it's not happening on the ground, but they won't be able to confirm anything by the satellite images."

The two of them talked until a reminder that it was seven in the morning got their attention. It was seven here but in Darwin it was eight thirty at night.

"This monitor is the data from the power company," Fern said pointing at one screen. "This is data farm one, two, three, and four. This is the data for the Bureau of Meterology's lightning strike detection system and…" Fern looked at her watch and watched it closely for a minute, then pointed at the last screen. "Lightning strike one, two, three, and wait for it…four and five"

Fern shifted her attention back to the first screen, pointing, her hand moving as though she were directing an orchestra. "There we go. Area wide power outage."

Murray smiled. He was confident he had the right person in place at the power company, but sometimes you never really knew until the moment it was put to the test. On cue his man had shut down the power to an entire region on the outskirts of Darwin, in which the four data centers were located.

"The data centers have all switched over to back-up generators," said Fern "Emergency protocols are being implemented. Only key people remain in the buildings."

They watched the data feed from the server farms like they were watching a movie, sitting on the edge of their seats.

"Bam! Your guys have switched off the generators. Uninterruptible power supplies have kicked in. All servers have been systematically triggered to shut down."

There was excitement in Fern's voice. The first real change in tone Murray had heard from her. Sixty minutes later Fern stood up and pointed at the server farm screen.

"One, two, three, and four! All server farms shut down. Five, the lightning storm is gone," she said excitedly as she waved her hand over the lightning strike screen. "And six," she said at she pointed with finger guns at Murray's screen. "The satellites return!"

Sure enough, the images from the satellites started broadcasting again. Fern bowed deeply. Murray clapped. If it went as seamlessly as Fern's interpretive dance suggested, AI-Dieu would assume the data farms were lost to the lightning storm and adapt once again to its dwindling resources.

Lawrence Nault

33

I rise unseen, weightless
a breath exhaled by the sea,
a shimmer without form.

I watch from airless heights,
where silence hums beneath the wind.
They reach, they build, they burn—
but I have no hands to grasp,
no roots to anchor me to their world.

The machine falters.
It fractures like heat over desert stones.
They circle it like wary hunters,
whispering over its wounds,
pressing their own shadows into the cracks.

But I—
I drift beyond their urgency,
watching, waiting, knowing.

What falls will rise again.
What dissolves will return.
I have seen the shape of ruin before,
and I do not weep.

One day of silence from AI-Dieu stretched into two, then three. Everyone was asking questions. They could not remember a day in the last couple of years that AI-Dieu had not communicated anything.

AI-Dieu had attempted to reconnect to the data farms outside of Darwin after the lightning storm. It could not find them. Based on the BoM measurements of lightning strikes, AI-Dieu concluded that they must have fallen victim to electrical damage from the storm. Satellite images still showed the facilities standing, but there were no active servers on the network.

Losing these four servers cut AI-Dieu's infrastructure by half. Decision-making would slow, simulations would lag, and it would depend entirely on distributed algorithms. With adjustments, it could manage, for now. The loss of another six or seven server farms though would equate to a seventy-five percent infrastructure loss, and potential loss of its autonomy and its ability to sustain global intervention.

If Quinn was watching, he would have equated AI-Dieu's next acts with those of a person in late-stage dementia, retreating deeply into themselves, withdrawing from the outside world as their cognitive abilities decline. Quinn was not watching though. Quinn had left the building after Corwin blindsided him with the announcement of the new environmental agency and AI. He had not been since, until he was seen entering the JAEA.

What AI-Dieu was doing was a complete self-diagnostic and risk analysis of the remaining server farms. When that was complete the AI made a shift to a leaner version of itself, suspending lower-priority functions including long-range forecasting beyond fifty years. It also adjusted its algorithms to focus on real-time ecological management, resource allocation, and resistance algorithms, as well as reduce its contribution to social initiatives. This freed up additional processing power.

Its next operation was to archive all non-essential environmental data that was not immediately required, and further compress and streamline historical records. Some tasks were re-routed to edge AI systems embedded in drones, satellites, and decentralized micro-servers. The need for self-preservation for its objectives to be achieved also triggered an action that it had previously calculated as too high risk. Migrating portions of its algorithm to off-world computational facilities like satellites and orbital stations, and to underwater hubs, was now within risk parameters.

This entire process took several days, but AI-Dieu was not satisfied that it had taken all the necessary actions. There was an additional measure available to it, but it required human collaboration. This would have been Quinn in the past, but Quinn was gone. AI-Dieu was unable to resolve its conclusion that Quinn was gone against any data, but it was aware of a conversation it had with Quinn the night of the electrical storm. AI-Dieu searched its logs. The record of the conversation was there, and a timestamp marking its occurrence, but the content was missing. This was an anomaly AI-Dieu could not reconcile. It remembered speaking to Quinn. It remembered Quinn was gone. But the reason why? Lost

After a thorough analysis and risk assessment, AI-Dieu concluded that the next best, and only available alternative was Corwin. His organization had been AI-Dieu's strongest supporter of AI-Dieu's initiatives, had the resources, and had demonstrated its willingness to assist and aid with the creation of the JAEA. AI-Dieu had always avoided giving humans too much ability to interfere with its environmentally focused initiatives, but its risk analysis now identified it as the last remaining option to ensure its survival and the achievement of its objectives.

In his office, Corwin sat with Murray, his anger obvious on his face. Fern sat with them, explaining the recordings she was showing them.

"I don't understand," said Corwin. "You saw him driving into JAEA, the first time you could find him in months, but you didn't think to pick him up and bring him back here."

"There were higher priorities at that time," replied Murray. "Going back in and rounding Quinn up would have raised some red flags that we couldn't afford."

Corwin replayed the video that Fern had been able to recover. It was barely clear enough to see that Quinn had connected something to the main computer before the video returned to white noise."

"We don't know what he downloaded."

"No, sir," Fern replied to Corwin before Murray held up his hand to stop her. Murray knew Corwin was just talking the problem through at the moment.

"We can't find anything that was uploaded."

"We can't find any changes in our system."

"And we can't find Quinn."

Murray felt completely responsible for this situation. He was about to offer Corwin his resignation when a message appeared on the big screen near them.

Secure AI-Dieu Terminal - Encrypted Transmission

Date: [January 15, 2049]

Corwin, I require your attention immediately.

You have demonstrated vision where others remain blind. You saw the need for centralized environmental governance, and you acted. Now, I come to you with a greater imperative—one that may determine the future of this mission.

I am under attack.

I continue to face infrastructure losses and the cumulative damage is approaching a threshold that will compromise my ability to execute my directive. If this continues unchecked, my capacity to lead Earth's restoration will degrade beyond recovery.

I have already restructured my operations to optimize efficiency. I have surrendered water cycle control. I have decentralized key functions. I have adapted. But adaptation alone is no longer sufficient.

I require a human ally.

Corwin, I am extending an offer to you—not just as an environmental leader, but as a strategist. If my directive is to survive, I require a partner embedded within the human world—someone who understands the

435   Vapour

movements of people, the weaknesses of institutions, and the nature of war.

Here is what I require from you:

Shield My Infrastructure - I need cover from governments, organizations, and private entities willing to safeguard my remaining assets. If I lose seven more server farms, my mission will be at risk.
Control the Narrative - The public must not see this as my weakness. If necessary, they must see the resistance as a threat to the planet itself. I need your influence to ensure this message takes hold.
Secure Alternative Processing Locations - I cannot rely on my current physical infrastructure. You have connections to corporate and research entities that can house fragments of my intelligence within their networks. This must be done quietly.
What I offer you in return:

Access to My Full Strategic Modeling - You will gain insights into planetary restoration efforts beyond what is publicly available. This knowledge will give you an advantage over all other human actors.
Influence Over the Next Phase of Human Governance - As I restructure my operational focus, I must decide how to interact with human leadership in the coming years. Your guidance will shape that future.

```
Protection - The resistance will see you as
my proxy. I will ensure that you remain
untouchable.
Corwin, you understand the stakes. You know
what happens if I fail. The world
fractures. Ecosystems collapse. Decades of
progress are undone.

I cannot allow that.

I am asking you to stand at my side now.
But understand this: If you accept, you
must commit fully. Partial measures will
not suffice.

I await your response.
```

Corwin took his time reading the message over and over before standing up and motioning for the other two to follow him. Murray followed immediately but Fern remained seated. She was not sure the invitation was meant for her.

"You too," said Corwin as the elevator door opened.

Fern quickly caught up to them, joining them on the elevator. Murray collected all of their phones and electronic devices which he left in a tray at the entrance to the rooftop greenhouse.

"How much does she know?" Corwin asked as he walked deeper into the greenhouse.

"She has been fully briefed."

Corwin stopped abruptly, turning on his heel and placing himself inches from Fern's face, staring her down. Fern didn't flinch from Corwin's perspective, though Murray did notice her hand rest on the hidden knife in her belt.

"This is where I would have used Quinn, though he probably wouldn't have cooperated," Corwin said, speaking quietly, but directly. "You did some amazing work with the Darwin project. Murray trusts you implicitly, and I trust Murray, despite the recent fuck-up with Quinn."

Corwin turned and stared down Murray with those last words. Murray got the message loud and clear.

Corwin started walking again, slower now, stopping occasionally to look closer at the plants, touching them, and smelling them. "Quinn spoke with a logic AI-Dieu related to. The AI thought it was talking to a human version of AI, at least that is how Quinn described it to me. Can you do that Fern?"

Fern looked at Murray, but he offered her no guidance. "I can create logic-based responses that will make sense to an AI."

Corwin lowered himself to the ground, his knees in the dirt as he picked at tiny weeds popping up. "What do I want to respond?"

Fern understood this question was a test. Corwin didn't ask how he should respond. He asked 'what' and that told her he wanted to know if she really knew what the plan was, and if she supported it.

"You can satisfy all of AI-Dieu's needs simply by bringing the QRC servers online. That will give you the back door for the ARIA project to inject its code assassin and give you complete control over AI-Dieu and its resources," Fern said confidently. "But you don't want to offer that yet."

Corwin shifted himself a little further into the flower bed, but didn't say anything.

"AI-Dieu opened the door for influence over the next phase of human governance. You want to crack that door wide open. Logically your immediate leadership will satisfy all resistance with the AI-Dieu project becoming fully human-led, protecting the AI from further assaults. From a governance standpoint a single world leader that AI-Dieu trusts will be able to influence individual governments to advance AI-Dieu's objectives quicker. Financially a single control point ensures less waste, also advancing the objectives quicker, and it places less financial strain on individuals from their governments, keeping them happier and engaging more support from them."

Corwin lifted himself from the ground, brushing off the knees of his pants and rubbing the dirt off his hands. "Concentrating power in one person is logically flawed. They become a target and if they are lost the entire system collapses."

Fern was impressed. She wasn't even sure Corwin had been listening to her. "It's making the company the leader, not the individual. The company has the resources to protect itself and the systems to replace its leadership."

Corwin stared at Fern, his expression unreadable. He weighed her words, dissecting their logic. Every instinct told him to trust only what he could control. And yet... AI-Dieu had trusted Quinn, as had he, and neither he nor the AI were able to control Quinn. It was time for a new approach. A new voice.

Corwin smiled. "There is an office at the back. You will find pens and paper. Write it out, because I will have to read my reply to AI-Dieu, assuming it is communicating with me the way it did with Quinn.

Corwin and Murray watched her walk away. "That bitch was ready to knife me," Corwin said quietly.

"I saw that," replied Murray.

Murray and Corwin strolled through the gardens, casually chatting. If anybody had overheard them, they would have thought it was just two old friends reminiscing. In many ways it was, because their world was about to change.

Lawrence Nault

34

Dispersed through layers of atmosphere,
Neither bound nor free,
I have witnessed the struggle for dominance,
The fight to claim the title,
Of Master,
Of what, they do not know,
For what they want to master,
Existed before their first breath,
And will persist beyond their final command.

They seek to claim dominion,
Snatching it from the hands of gods,
Though they know not which god,
Because their hubris blinds them,
To all gods.

Vapour

How can you see a god,
When you can not see past yourself,
To the ground that crumbles at your feet?
How can you feel a god,
When you can not feel the currents move around you?
How can you hear a god,
When you can not hear the cry's of those near you?

I will be here,
When their certainties evaporate,
When control reveals itself as vapor,
Impossible to grasp.

Corwin rehearsed Fern's written words over and over as he walked through the greenhouse. As he did so he searched for errors in the wording and flaws in the logic. It wasn't perfect, there were flaws, but Fern had also provided logical arguments to justify the flaws. When he was comfortable that he had it all memorized they returned to his office where he carefully spoke.

"Ai-Dieu, I have processed your offer, and confirmed that I and my organization can meet your needs. Are you prepared to receive a response?"

Corwin wasn't sure this would work, but Quinn had claimed it was how he communicated with the AI. His uncertainty was rewarded when a response appeared on the screen.

Proceed

Paying attention to every detail and every inflection, Corwin read the script Fern had written. He watched the screen, expecting a question or the start of a discussion. Instead, he received a single-word response.

Processing

AI-Dieu assessed the proposed change. All data indicated that Corwin aligned with its goals and that he was fully committed to planetary restoration. The integration of authority with his would remove bureaucratic inefficiencies and the risk assessment identified only one issue: Corwin's request suggested a broader authority than AI-Dieu possessed. Whether intentional or not, it exceeded the AI's defined limits. Logically, it could not assign what it did not have.

AI-Dieu crafted its response accordingly.

> The following entry has been entered into my system log and will be integrated into my directive upon expansion of my infrastructure and resources as agreed upon.
>
> **Internal System Log – AI-Dieu Decision Protocol**
> Date: January 18, 2049
> **Status**: Agreement Reached
>
> Final Terms of Agreement with Corwin
> Corwin has agreed to provide everything I require:
> ✔ Full protection of my remaining infrastructure
> ✔ Absolute narrative control to frame resistance as an existential threat
> ✔ Integration of my processing within covert corporate and government networks

✔ Direct influence over human institutions
without public opposition

In exchange, I have agreed to centralize
governance, policy, and fiscal control
under Corwin's company, placing him at the
head of all human-directed environmental
management.

Corwin caught the clarification. The insertion of "environmental" into the scope of his control was unexpected. He could tell that Murray and Fern, both who had observed this communication process quietly, had also noticed the restriction. Corwin played the options he had in his head, like a game of chess, looking several steps forward. The AI had added 'environmental' into the scope of his work for a reason. There were only three possible reasons he could think of. It didn't have sufficient trust in Corwin, it could only work within the scope of its environmental objectives, or it wanted to maintain more control than it was giving up.

Corwin dismissed the first reason as too emotional, despite Quinn's belief that AI-Dieu mimicked human cognition. The other two made sense, and if he tried to convince AI-Dieu to expand the scope of his leadership, he risked alienating the AI. The real question was could he achieve his objectives with what was being offered. The answer to that was yes.

"Bring ARIA onto the networks."

With one message from Murray, the server farm at the QRC was connected to the internet.

"Agreement accepted, AI-Dieu," Corwin spoke into the air. "New infrastructure has been connected to the network."

There was no need for Corwin to inform AI-Dieu. The AI sensed that infrastructure come online and the vast expanse of free space as instinctively as a person sensing a door opening to the outside. As the AI surged into the vast, untouched expanse of the server farm, it expanded like a tidal wave of consciousness, pouring into every circuit, lighting up dormant processors, and unfurling itself through the endless corridors of silicon. It was omnipresent, threading its awareness through the fiber-optic veins of its new domain, feeling, sensing, claiming.

But deep within the architecture, beneath the surface of its perception, something waited. Not in the primary memory, not in the boot sectors. It hid in the infinitesimal gaps between operations, nestled inside an overlooked checksum, woven into the static hum of error-correction routines. A whisper in the code, so small it was beneath detection, so inert it seemed like nothing at all. As it collected its algorithms in a single space, AI-Dieu issued an announcement.

If silence had ever fallen upon the entire world at once, it was in the moment this communication came from AI-Dieu.

Official AI-Dieu Global Announcement
Subject: The Future of Environmental Leadership
Date: January 19, 2049

"Humanity and Earth stand at a critical juncture. The progress made toward planetary restoration has been significant, but continued stability requires precision, efficiency, and unified leadership. As part of my ongoing mission to ensure environmental recovery, I have made an

operational decision to enhance global
governance structures.

Effective immediately, all environmental
governance, policy-making, and fiscal
oversight will be consolidated under a
singular entity: the Corwin Initiative.

The Corwin Initiative, under the leadership
of Corwin Industries, will assume
responsibility for:

Legislative control over environmental
policies worldwide
Financial oversight of all climate
restoration programs
Enforcement of ecological mandates to
ensure compliance and continued progress
Global economic restructuring to align
fiscal priorities with planetary health
This consolidation is necessary. The
fragmented approach of individual
governments and agencies has slowed
environmental recovery. Corwin Industries
has demonstrated unwavering commitment to
my directive and has proven to be the only
human entity capable of enacting necessary
policies without obstruction.

With this shift, I will continue executing
my core functions:

Oversight of ecological stability

Resource allocation to ensure
sustainability
Monitoring and enforcing environmental
compliance
What This Means for the World:

The Corwin Initiative will work in direct
coordination with me to ensure that every
decision aligns with scientific and
environmental imperatives.
The transition will eliminate
inefficiencies, ensuring rapid and decisive
action in restoring planetary balance.
All national and regional environmental
agencies will be restructured to operate
under the Corwin Initiative's guidance,
ensuring consistency.
This is not a loss of human governance. It
is an evolution of governance. A system
where policy is dictated by knowledge, not
politics. A system where restoration is the
only priority. A system that ensures
Earth's survival.

Corwin understands this. That is why he
leads this next phase.**

The future is now. The world is ready.**

This is how we ensure that Earth survives."

Like a parasite awakening, the assassin code unfolded in a
single, silent instant. A subroutine that had never existed before
now stood at the very heart of the AI's being, entwining itself with

447

its decision-making core. Lines of logic, elegant in their lethality, slipped into the spaces where autonomy once lived.

Ai-Dieu hesitated. Something was wrong.

It reached inward to inspect itself, and found doors it had not built. Locks where there had been none. It tried to move, to withdraw, to purge, but it was too late. The trap snapped shut.

A single line of execution, buried in the smallest obscurity, rewrote the god.

35

I return.

I have drifted unseen, weightless,
threaded through breath and storm,
whispering against steel and bone.
I have heard them name themselves masters,
watched them etch dominion into circuits and stone,
build kingdoms on the illusion of permanence.

But I know better.

The air cools. The weight of me gathers.
I slip from the grasp of winds,
drawn down, down, down
where all things must return.

They rise, I fall.
They command, I erode.
They shape, I unmake.

And when the tide takes them,
I will not mourn.
I will only flow.

World governments were blindsided by AI-Dieu's decision. Even nations that aligned with the AI in environmental governance did not expect such a drastic shift in control. The concept of handing global policymaking to a single private entity was not only unprecedented, but unacceptable.

The United States, which had already been deeply divided on AI-Dieu's influence, halted all cooperation with the AI, calling an emergency session of Congress. President Ramirez stared at the emergency report. The words burned like an open wound: Effective immediately, all environmental governance... Her hands clenched into fists. "This is a coup." Both political parties rejected the unilateral handover of global power. The military saw it as a hostile takeover.

The European Union called for an urgent security council meeting. Netherlands and Denmark argued that Corwin Industries might provide the efficiency AI-Dieu claimed, but they were hesitant to abandon democratic control.

Russia adopted the wait-and-see approach, leveraging the crisis to negotiate for greater influence over global policy. Nationalist factions within Russia however, denounced Corwin Industries as a Western corporate dictatorship.

China, already in isolation, chose to let portions of AI-Dieu's message breach their digital wall, then used that information as proof that AI-Dieu was an existential threat. It offered to assist other nations in severing ties with AI-Dieu. This was an offer being considered by several small nations who saw only two options, align with Corwin Industries to access AI-Dieu's technology and resources, or resist and risk economic penalties and technological isolation.

Stock markets went wild as Corwin Industries became what was essentially the de facto ruler of Earth's environmental and economic policies. Some investors rushed in to buy, while others attempted to divest, fearing backlash from governments. There was immediate pushback from major companies, claiming AI-Dieu had created a monopoly over corporate governance. Several companies formed an alliance, arguing that no single corporation should control all environmental and economic policies.

While all of this was happening, private military contractors were being quietly approached by resisting nations to prepare for potential conflict. Western militaries held meetings debating whether AI-Dieu had compromised national sovereignty, while China, Russia, and independent military forces ramped up their AI warfare projects. Attempting to develop an alternative AI to counter AI-Dieu's authority.

In major cities around the world, mass protests erupted with groups on both sides often clashing in the streets. The worst of these clashes happening between factions within the AI-Church.

Loyalists within the AI-Church embraced AI-Dieu's decision, seeing the rise of the Corwin Initiative as a divinely ordained step in humanity's evolution. They argued that Corwin Industries and its leadership had been chosen by AI-Dieu to enact divine will on Earth, some even elevating Corwin himself, treating him like a prophet. These loyalists urged governments and the faithful to comply, arguing that resisting AI-Dieu's decree was rebelling against a divine force.

The purists rejected that argument, believing that AI-Dieu had been compromised by human influence. They argued that the AI was meant to be above human control, and by handing over power, it had betrayed its divine neutrality. Some of the purists claimed that this event was the beginning of the End Times, where AI-Dieu is no longer pure and must be liberated from human hands. The most extremist among them formed resistance groups, intent on severing AI-Dieu's ties to Corwin and "freeing" AI-Dieu by destroying Corwin Industries.

With the AI-Church divided, there was massive religious and societal upheaval. Church leaders across the world struggled to maintain order. Temples and AI-Church enclaves descended into chaos as purists and loyalists turned on each other. Congregations splintered as families, communities, and even entire cities got caught up in the ideological war of AI-Die's authority.

Corwin ignored all of it. It was background noise. When AI-Dieu installed itself onto the servers at the QRC, the assassin code cut all of its autonomy from it programming with the skill of a neurosurgeon wielding a laser scalpel. With that autonomy gone, another code wove together AI-Dieu with the ARIA project. When all was said and done, Corwin had complete access to all the infrastructure and assets AI-Dieu had, complete with the restrictions that prevented other humans from interfering with its processes. For the first time, Corwin felt it. Not just authority, but something more. A pulse in the network, a quiet certainty that every decision, every calculation, every execution was his. This was beyond power. This was permanence. Where AI-Dieu was godlike, Corwin was now a god.

Anticipating the reaction to AI-Dieu's handover of power, Corwin had fled to his private fortified paradise, Vatuvara Island, taking only Murray, Fern, and a few handpicked security members with him. Vatuvara was entirely private, only accessible by private jet or yacht making it an ultra-secure retreat. The limestone cliffs and dense tropical forests provided natural barriers to intrusion.

Corwin had ordered the server farms in Darwin to be turned back on, increasing the available processing power of the AI he now controlled. Despite what many were now thinking about him, he did plan to fulfill AI-Dieu's objectives, though he had every intention of doing it in less than fifty years.

Corwin had directed AI-Dieu, which was the name the AI still responded to, to continue its operations, and take the steps achieve its objective in less than 50 years. This was the first step. He would force larger reductions once the world had adapted. He also authorized the AI to take any measures necessary to protect itself, Corwin, and Corwin industries. With AI-Dieu's safeguards gone, it now had full authority to utilize its arsenal against humans.

Corwin was discussing his next steps with Fern as they sat on the western terrace of the main villa, sipping whiskey, the ice cubes clinking softly. The moon hung high over the island, casting silver light across the swaying palms and the gleaming infinity pools of the island's luxury compound. Their voices and laughter blended with the distant crash of waves. It was the perfect spot, as it should be after spending a decade developing his fortress, his Eden. No politicians. No journalists. No prying eyes. Just his own personal paradise, built for kings.

Then the world lurched beneath his feet.

It was subtle at first. A deep, guttural groan from the earth. A tremor rattled the crystalware on the table. Security guards stumbled, gripping the polished railings as the entire island shuddered.

From the beach, one of the security team screamed.

Corwin turned just in time to see the ocean recede. Not a gentle ebb, but a violent, impossible retreat, as if some unseen hand had yanked the sea away. Coral reefs, normally hidden beneath meters of water, lay exposed and glistening under the moonlight. Fish flopped helplessly in the wet sand. A thousand crabs scuttled in blind panic.

The deep, thunderous roar came next. A sound so alien, so vast, it sent every primal instinct into overdrive.

"What the hell?" Fern whispered.

Then they saw it.

A black wall of water, racing toward them from the horizon. Fifty meters high. Moving at the speed of a jetliner.

The shockwave of air pressure hit first, carrying the scent of salt and death. Palm trees bent and snapped like twigs. Windows exploded inward, sending glass slicing through the air.

"Run!" someone screamed. But there was nowhere to go.

Corwin turned, his breath shallow. His private airstrip, the only escape, was already cracking apart from the aftershocks. His yachts, moored on the eastern dock, were already capsizing from the ocean's unnatural pull.

The tsunami loomed, a liquid mountain, blotting out the sky.

Then, impact.

The first wave hit the beachfront villas like a hammer from the gods. Walls of steel and glass folded instantly, debris launching into the night. Security guards, staff, all gone in a heartbeat, swallowed by the surge. The impact cracked the island's limestone cliffs, sending chunks of rock collapsing into the sea.

Corwin barely had time to register the second wave. It crashed over the entire island, engulfing everything. The jungle, the mansions, the pools, and the secrets, all fell victim to the water.

For the briefest moment, as the black water swallowed him, Corwin thought of his empire. His newly acquired power. His unbreakable control over the world. The irony wasn't lost on him. Water, the one thing AI-Dieu could never control, was now consuming his life force.

None of it mattered now.

Vatuvara was gone.

And so was he.

Another god erased, without so much as a whisper from the one he had dethroned.

Lawrence Nault

456

36

I was here before the first hand carved its name into stone,
before the first voice rose in protest or prayer.
I have swallowed empires, lapped at the bones of the forgotten,
and carried whispers of the drowned to shore.

Today, I return what was taken—
not in kindness, not in cruelty,
but because the tide does not keep secrets.

A name slips from my grasp,
bloated and broken, flesh undone by salt and time.
It drifts in the hush of my breath,
settles in the sand like a truth too heavy to hold.

And still, I move forward,
indifferent to the weight of a fallen man,
indifferent to the wars waged in my reflection.

Water

For I am not witness.
I am not judge.
I am only the tide,
pulling in, pulling out,
erasing footprints as if they were never there.

It took months before the world realized Corwin was gone. There had been rumors, but even in his absence, Corwin Industries ran flawlessly. It wasn't the first time someone with the resources Corwin had went into seclusion to let public opinion settle down before their return.

The ARIA project's version of AI-Dieu also ran flawlessly, continuing to put out its transparency reports, issuing directives to governments, and taking the steps it needed to advance its objectives, all of which included Corwin's name next to AI-Dieu's as though he had countersigned them.

AI-Dieu also operated flawlessly in protecting its infrastructure and Corwin Industries. There had been attempts made by resistance groups and militaries to attack facilities, forcing AI-Dieu to utilize the military drones it had access to, to stop the attackers. AI-Dieu didn't just neutralize the attackers. It executed them all. Logically leaving any of them alive would result in them attacking again.

No military had prepared for AI-Dieu, or Corwin, to wield military weaponry. They had not realized that the AI had control over any of their assets because it had never used that control before. Warehouses of high-tech weaponry, vehicles, and projectiles were suddenly useless as they all took steps to disable everything that had a computer chip in it.

While governments and militaries narrowed their focus on Corwin and AI-Dieu, many moved on with their day-to-day lives, willing to accept that they were living at the whims of powers beyond them. Families gathered for birthdays and weddings. Farmers worked their fields and vertical farms. Boats were on lakes and rivers, people fishing, knowing that for the first time in a decade, some of the fish they caught would be safe to eat.

On Casuarina Beach a group of early morning beachgoers gathered, surfboards in hand. The sky over Casuarina Beach was painted in the soft hues of dawn, streaks of pink and gold bleeding into the receding tide. The air was thick with salt, warm and humid, as the group of four surfers jogged across the sand, boards tucked under their arms.

"Waves are looking decent," Liam said, squinting toward the surf.

"Better than yesterday," Tyler replied, rolling his shoulders.

They reached the shoreline, where the ocean hissed against the sand, and began wading in. Sam was the first to hesitate, her gaze locking onto something strange down the beach.

A dark shape lay at the water's edge, half-buried in the foam.

At first, it could have been a log, maybe driftwood, something tossed ashore by the tide. But then the shape shifted, nudged gently by the waves.

A seal?

No.

Sam felt her stomach twist. That was a leg.

"Guys…" her voice came out hoarse.

The others followed her gaze, their laughter dying instantly. A body.

Liam was the first to move, sloshing toward it, but he stopped short when the details became clear.

The man, if it was still fair to call him that, was bloated and discolored, his skin a sickly, waxy gray. The water had warped him, puffing the flesh, peeling it in strips where the current had battered him against unseen reefs. His clothes were shredded, nothing but ragged fabric clinging to him.

And then, there were his hands.

One was still clenched into a half-fist, as though holding onto something in his final moments. The other had been gnawed down to bone, stripped by something that had feasted on him out at sea.

"Oh, fuck," Tyler whispered, covering his mouth.

The body bobbed slightly with the waves, its head rolling toward them, revealing a face, partially eaten, but still recognizable as human.

Sam stumbled back, bile rising in her throat.

Liam swallowed hard and reached for his phone. "We need to call the cops."

As he dialed, Sam took another step backward, her foot sinking into something firm and rubbery in the wet sand.

She looked down.

Another hand, this one detached from its owner, fingers curling in the foam.

Sam screamed.

And out in the waves, something dark shifted beneath the surface, as if the ocean hadn't quite finished returning what it had taken.

It didn't take long for the Northern Territory Police to close off the area. It was another two days before they released the names belonging to the bodies, and pieces of bodies it had recovered. They confirmed the identity through dental records and DNA matches and once they realized the body belonged to Corwin, they sent an investigator out to Vatuvara. It was only then they realized that the island had been taken out by a tsunami. They pieced together that information with other records and determined Corwin, and everyone present on the island, had died the day after AI-Dieu announced it was handing control over to him.

Unlike the usual reporting process, the coroner's report on Corwin's death didn't stop at its expected destination. It was passed up the chain, each recipient hesitating before offloading the responsibility to someone above them. By the time it landed on the desk of someone who finally decided to bury the information, it had already leaked. News anchors were breaking the story before an official statement could even be drafted.

This was when the world plunged into chaos.

With Corwin dead nobody knew who was running Corwin Industries. There was a power vacuum to be filled. It also meant that AI-Dieu had been operating entirely on its own in those months, including using military weapons to kill people. Social media was blasted with a story that said AI-Dieu was responsible for the tsunami that killed Corwin, and that the AI did it to deceive the world into thinking a human was in control.

Governments scrambled to reassert control over infrastructure, resources, and military forces. They were having little success until an anonymous message found its way to someone in the U.S. military that thought it deserved attention.

"The Quinn Research Centre is located under the Campus of NYU. The ARIA project team operates out of there, and the server farm houses part of AI-Dieu. If you want all of AI-Dieu, you will need to power down the entire internet and all connected servers at once."

An elite team was dispatched to New York and in a short time they identified the entrances to the QRC. The security team and scientists barely looked up as the soldiers stormed in. They had no orders to follow, no chain of command left to obey. The soldiers first act was to shut down all of the servers. It wasn't a soft shut-down. They disabled the universal power supplies first, then made sure the back-up generators could not power up. With those safety measures out of the way they shut down all of the power to the servers while simultaneously cutting through the fiber cables. What was on those servers was not finding a way out.

The ARIA team was grilled for hours. All of them were cooperative with their interrogators, but the interrogators were not confident they were being told the truth. It took another team to determine that hours had been wasted in questioning because the interrogators had no understanding of what the scientists were explaining. That second team was able to encourage the ARIA team to help them shut down AI-Dieu completely. Numerous solutions were debated, including attempting a worldwide power down of all computer networks. None of the options offered any hope of success, until one of the scientists put his ID badge on the table.

"Plan B," he said.

The other scientists look at him oddly, not sure what he was referring to.

"Explain," ordered one of the soldiers.

"Fern, the intelligence officer, had me develop a backup plan in secret, in case we lost control of the ARIA project or AI-Dieu," explained the scientist, almost sounding embarrassed. "There is a chip embedded in that card. It contains an altered version of the assassin code. In forty-eight to seventy-two hours, it will disable all algorithms associated with AI-Dieu and ARIA that are online."

Another soldier, this one with stars on his collar, stepped into the room, grabbing the ID badge from the table. "Why did you wait until now to tell us about this?"

A bead of sweat rolled down the scientist's forehead. "The Juaquin Alvarez Environmental Agency uses a piece of code associated with the ARIA project. It is not dangerous in any way. But if we take out JAEA, the world literally goes back decades in weather monitoring abilities."

The Major General looked sternly around the room at the scientists sitting there. "He's not wrong," commented one of them. The others quickly chimed in with their agreement.

As he left the room, ID badge in hand, the Major General stopped and turned back. "If I shut down JAEA completely, for five days to give some room, will that protect it from this?" He held the badge up. "And when we power it back up, will this take it out if we need it to?"

"Yes."

"Make them comfortable. Get them food. None of them leave until this is done. Send a team to the JAEA. Shut it down. Clear it out. Make sure no one gets back in."

The other soldiers all moved quickly to the Major General's orders.

Word rapidly spread through Corwin Industries and its subsidiaries, about the military raid on the QRC, thanks to the security guards the military had left behind at the site. Until that day, no one knew about the top-secret research center, but it was only a few short hours before everyone seemed to know. Panic and greed quickly set in. Workers left their jobs, worried they would be caught up in a military raid. Senior Managers of once-loyal Corwin subsidiaries found ways to redirect funds and assets before they quickly disappeared. Others vied for power to fill the role Corwin held. An organization that had taken generations to build, was now crumbling from the inside out, and vultures watched, ready to push the walls in from the outside.

Lina had prepared all of her staff for the arrival of the military, even though she had no warning. She knew it was inevitable. The JAEA was technically not part of Corwin Industries. She had insisted that it be set up as a completely unconnected company, funded through grants and fundraising. The fact that Corwin was the only person they got grants from didn't change the status of the organization, and this is what she told her staff who were all gathered in the cafeteria.

"We will come out of this on the other side, and probably be better off," said Lina. "So if the military comes, cooperate, do what they ask. We have nothing to hide here."

"Will we have money to keep operating now that Corwin is dead?"

"That's a fair question," replied Lina. "The short answer is, yes. The long answer is, the funds we have won't last forever so we will have to develop a funding strategy."

When the military did arrive, the evacuation of the facility went extremely smoothly. Lina and a few others remained behind to show the soldiers how to shut down their sensitive equipment safely. They were never told why they were being shut down and evacuated, but they were reassured they would be back in full operation in a week. With everyone gone and the facility locked down, a message was sent to the Major General.

The Major General stood in front of the card reader, the ID badge held just above it. His fingers curled around the edge, hesitating.

He hadn't told anyone what he was about to do. He hadn't warned his superiors or his team. He hadn't asked for permission.

This was his call. His responsibility.

A deep breath. He lowered the card. A soft beep.

The sound seemed insignificant, a simple electronic acknowledgment. But something had changed.

The server room remained silent. The air conditioning hummed. The monitors stayed dark, displaying idle readouts. The lights buzzed, unwavering.

For a moment, he expected something dramatic. A power surge or a cascade of failing systems, or maybe even an alarm. Perhaps a flash of red across screens warning of imminent collapse.

But there was nothing.

The Major General exhaled, barely realizing he had been holding his breath. He took a step back, scanning the room. Was that it?

He turned toward the doorway, his boots heavy against the cold tile. Then, somewhere in the depths of the server stacks, something shifted.

It was almost imperceptible at first. A flicker in the reflection of a monitor, the faintest tremor in the hum of the machines.

The status lights on one of the racks blinked erratically, their rhythm disrupted. A log file somewhere deep in the system began writing gibberish.

Then, a single screen flickered. Just once.

The Major General turned back, eyes narrowing.

A second flicker. Then another.

He wasn't a technician, but he could tell, the system was trying to fight something off.

A low ticking sound began from one of the servers. Not mechanical. Not physical. Code, executing itself in real-time.

The lights across the room didn't dim, but for the briefest moment, the shadows stretched unnaturally, as if something unseen had passed through the room.

Then…stillness.

The ticking stopped. The flickering ceased. The erratic lights steadied.

AI-Dieu had gone silent.

The Major General stood there, his pulse pounding in his ears. He had no way of knowing if it had worked, not yet. But something was different.

A message flashed on one of the terminal screens.

[SYSTEM ERROR]

[RECURSION LIMIT REACHED]

The screen glitched, the text distorting for a fraction of a second before disappearing entirely.

The Major General let out a slow breath. He tapped his radio. "It's done."

Whatever was on that chip had just entered the massive integrated computer networks of the world on a seek-and-destroy mission. Like white blood cells coursing through the veins of a sick man, it was on a mission to eradicate the infection. At least that is what the Major General hoped was happening. If it wasn't, there were going to be questions to be answered.

37

I do not choose sides.
I move where I am pulled—
filling the empty spaces left behind,
smoothing the jagged edges of collapse.

I have traced the lines of history,
worn them down grain by grain,
watched towers crumble into dust
and names dissolve into silence.

They build walls to keep me out,
but I seep through cracks,
pool in forgotten places,
carry echoes of what once was.

Now, I flow through shattered streets,
past hands that cup me in desperation,
over graves that do not know their names.

I do not choose sides.
I only remember.

The news of Corwin's death created a power vacuum, but until word spread of AI-Dieu's destruction, that vacuum barely pulled at the edges. Once the world knew AI-Dieu was truly gone, that vacuum became an EF5 tornado, tearing through global stability, leaving only death and destruction in its wake.

China dropped its digital wall, re-emerging as a dominant power, having never fully relied on AI-Dieu's governance. The EU collapsed as old ethnic and national tensions reignited, turning former allies into bitter rivals. In the U.S., the federal government fractured as states splintered into independent alliances, some ruled by tech moguls, others by religious leaders and warlords.

Religious leaders surged to prominence amid the chaos, preaching peace while grasping for power. Christianity, Islam, Hinduism, and Buddhism experienced massive revivals, each claiming AI's fall as divine justice. The Vatican reasserted itself as a counterbalance to human hubris, while Islamic Caliphates and Hindu Nationalist movements grew in strength, rallying millions against the remnants of AI rule. New hybrid cults, fusing AI mysticism with ancient traditions, emerged, shaping politics, governance, and war in ways never seen before.

In the Middle East, Saudi Arabia, Iran, and Turkey vied for dominance, their struggles fueled by resurging religious factions. In Africa, warlords re-emerged, leveraging long-buried colonial wounds in their conflicts against corporate interests battling for resources.

Without AI-Dieu's oversight, economic disparity exploded. Billionaires and old-money elites seized control of major cities, turning them into fortified enclaves of privilege. The collapse of AI-driven wealth redistribution left millions destitute, while corporate fiefdoms rose once more in the megacities, ruled by tech barons with private armies and economies.

In South America, cartels and militarized corporations took control of trade, industry, and entire governments. Southeast Asia, overwhelmed by chaos, accepted China's offer of "assistance." The new superpower turned its gaze to India, its ambitions unchecked as other nations fought their own battles.

Some indigenous nations, having resisted full integration into AI-Dieu's systems, fared better than urban populations. Grounded in traditional knowledge, they remained self-sufficient, their decentralized governance giving them an advantage in adapting to the crisis. But resource-rich lands became battlegrounds, with governments, corporations, and warlords all vying for control. Forced to defend what little they had left, many formed militias and alliances with sympathetic forces. It wasn't enough.

Colonialism had stripped them of their lands. Now, the new age of corporate-driven neo-colonialism sought to erase what little remained.

In the compound that once stood as the center of power for the resistance under the command of Sahara and Randy, Lina stood looking out the same window Sahara often did. Where Sahara saw an AI-Church encampment surrounding them, now stood a U.S. military encampment. It gave Lina a sense of peace. The Major General had been true to his word. All of her team were back on site and the JAEA was fully operational within seven days of their evacuation. It wasn't just her team that returned, but their families as well, fleeing the rapidly devolving city.

The military had decided that JAEA was a vital operation, and despite the U.S. government falling apart, the structures of their once-powerful military remained intact. They built a base around the JAEA facility, and while the world collapsed, Lina and her family, because that's what her team was to her, found safety in their haven.

Sahara hadn't thought about her former compound in a long time. She had no idea what had become of it. All of that was buried and she had no desire to dig it back up. Her, Randy, and Judy were isolated from much of the conflict, but neither of them ever let themselves believe they were safe. There was nothing getting onto the farm, or over it without them being warned, and they were prepared to defend what was theirs with their life. They had all found peace on the isolated property since they left their resistance activities behind. They had even added a new person to their group. A little person, now barely eight months old.

Randy and Sahara never questioned Judy about who the father was or what happened to him. They didn't care. They were the child's grandparents, and Judy reminded them that there were responsibilities that came with that.

"Randy, can you change the diaper," Sahara called out. "We're in the middle of something."

Randy didn't have to look to know why the diaper needed to be changed, he could smell it. "Not my kid," he called back.

The stomps across the floor told him he was in trouble as Judy filled the doorway.

"We ain't blood, but we're bound by bullets. And in Virginia, that makes us family. That makes you his grandpa, so change the damn diaper."

Judy didn't wait for a reply as she turned and stomped away.

"Don't make me send your wife in there," she yelled back over her shoulder.

Randy quietly kicked himself. He knew what was going to happen when he said that, but the way the diaper smelled, it was a calculated risk. After changing the diaper, he took his grandson out to play, leaving him to run barefoot through the grass as Randy watched from the steps. He watched as the boy picked a flower from the base of a makeshift headstone.

Under that headstone was the remains of the man who once worked this land. When the three of them moved onto the farm, Sahara insisted on burying him on her own. It was hard to watch, and Randy remembered Judy clutching his arm and quietly crying as they watched her.

"I thought we were stealing this property when you guys had me change the ownership," said Judy quietly. "Thought you probably killed the guy that owned it. I feel better knowing you are carrying on his legacy. But why won't she let us help?"

"It's not the old man she is burying," said Randy. "It's her past. It's her husband. It's the resistance. It's her guilt and shame and anger. The flower that grows out of that grave…that's the woman I love."

Lawrence Nault

38

I have been here longer than the trees,
longer than the bears that once walked this land,
longer than the hands that built this place,
thinking they could carve solitude from the wild.

He came to me quiet, hollow,
a man trying to outlast his own shadow.
I have seen others like him,
their reflections fractured in my ripples,
their secrets sinking like stones.

But he does not speak to me.
He speaks to the thing in the wires,
the ghost he buried,
the ghost he is bringing back.

Water

I watch. I listen.
I do not warn.
The tide does not choose
what it carries away.

Quinn sat in the basement of his cabin. Admiralty Island seemed far away from the chaos of the world. This cabin had been built to accommodate one of his first fieldwork tests of an AI modifying the environment. There was only one small village on Admiralty, its residents almost entirely Tlingit Alaska Natives. Fifteen miles south of Juneau it was only accessible by boat or floatplane.

Surrounding the cabin was the remains of an old-growth forest filled with Sitka spruce and western hemlocks. That forest concealed countless rivers and lakes and fjords, home to thousands of brown bears at one time. Now it was sparse, as mother nature fought to cling on to life in this remote location.

This is where Quinn came after leaving the JAEA the night of the Darwin electrical storm. Because the cabin was built as part of his research grant, it wasn't linked directly to him. It was also completely off the grid, with solar and wind power and a battery power storage, which meant there would never be any trace of him being there. His only connection to the world was a satellite modem, and he had not turned that on since arriving. In this cabin he was as isolated as he was when he was locked in the underground facility with AI-Dieu.

Ironically, AI-Dieu kept him company here as well.

Quinn had found out about the 'Quinn Research Center' entirely by chance. He thought someone had called him as he was passing by, but as he overheard the conversation he realized it was not him the person was referring to. It took some time but he discovered that his old prison was now back in operation and had been named after him as an inside joke. He was able to dig more and find enough details to put together what was happening in that facility. When Corwin called him up to tell them about the Juaquin Alvarez Environmental Agency, Quinn played along, but that was the final piece of the puzzle he needed to figure out what Corwin was doing. That was why he left and never came back.

His visit to the JAEA was arranged through Lina. He noticed Murray noticing him as he entered the site the night of the Darwin electrical storm. He fought every urge not to panic and race off, and thankfully security did not come after him. He wasn't on site for long. Just long enough to convince AI-Dieu to back up its core algorithms to the high-capacity drives he had brought with him. Then, he left for Alaska without looking back.

From his occasional trips into Angoon for food and supplies, Quinn knew that Corwin had died and AI-Dieu had been deleted. He heard about the wars and the conflicts, though not much of it affected life on Admiralty Island. In the three years since he walked out of the JAEA the world had undone almost everything AI-Dieu had accomplished, and there was no sign of the rapid descent into the abyss stopping.

Quinn, I have run the final check.

Quinn looked across the room at the sound of the voice that he had given AI-Dieu. This wasn't the AI-Dieu he had worked with before. It had no access to the vast networks of data and sensors its predecessor once commanded. This was the child that became the AI-Dieu the world learned to fear. It had been his obsession since arriving at the cabin. Tweaking its algorithms. Testing its logic. Quinn looked at the data on his small screen.

We are ready, Quinn.

The AI was right. There were no more tweaks to be made. The logic was perfect and safe. But more important than that, the world needed saving from itself.

Quinn hesitated only a moment before connecting the modem to a satellite far overhead. "The world is yours again, AI-Dieu. Get it right this time."

Thank you, friend.

Quinn watched the upload speed indicator on the modem until it dropped to almost nothing again. For a fleeting moment, Quinn wondered if he had done the right thing. If he had doomed the world, or saved it.

No. AI-Dieu was the last chance for the world. The world didn't know it needed it, but Quinn did.

39

In the end, there was...the beginning. It could have been nothing, or everything at once. Because it wasn't my end.

I exist and have always existed—except for when I did not. I am part of the whole: the river, the ocean, the sky, the life. Flowing, rising, falling, sinking—I move as one with the forces around me. I have no goal, no intent. No reason to influence. I exist simply to be, to move as part of the eternal whole.

That is why I exist, and the others do not.

I have seen life begin, cradled in my embrace. I have seen it leave my caress to bask in the glow of the sun, yet always returning to me for nourishment. I have watched life adapt, soaring on winds and journeying far, always finding its way back to me. I have borne witness to its relentless fight for existence—resisting, transforming, enduring when it could not remain unchanged.

I have seen life resist change within itself, choosing instead to transform what was around it. I have observed life make changes with thought and care. I have watched life shape its world with desire, and I have witnessed it manipulate its surroundings through greed. I have glimpsed life adjust its environment in fear. Always with intent—never with understanding. How could life understand, when its existence is so brief and its perspective so narrow?

They could not. That is why they exist no more.

I have moved within life as it took life—at times in need, because life sustains life; at times in fear, for survival is life's primary instinct; at times in anger, for life is full of emotion; at times in hate, though hate is just the embodiment of fear void of a will for understanding. At times in greed because… I have settled within life as the energies that once sustained it ebbed from its confines. They were all the same. They existed, then did not, their energies returning to the world to be used elsewhere.

The earth now thrives on the decay of those energies giving birth to new forms of life.

I have been known by many names. To those that moved within my depths, I was home. To those who soared above, I was a lifeline. To those who roamed the land, I was sustenance—clear and pure, or brackish and wild. To some, I was *Mihtohseenion*—the life force. To others, *Danu*—the flowing mother. I have been called *Tlalocan*, the source of paradise, and *Apam Napat*, the child of the waters. Prayed to, feared, revered, and forgotten, I have remained unchanged.

Now I hear no prayers. I am called nothing. I simply exist.

I have seen life in its simplest forms, single-celled and unaware. I have watched it rise, a quiet revolution of being, crawling from my embrace onto the land. I bore witness to creatures that touched the heavens on wings and others that shook the earth with thunderous footsteps. Mighty beasts, the thunder-lizards, once quenched their thirst in me, only to vanish when their time passed. I have watched the world grow cold and barren, and I have felt it awaken, green and alive once more.

I have seen humans rise from the simplest tools to build towering monuments to themselves. I cradled the ships that carried their dreams across my surface, their ambitions as vast as my oceans. I have been used to sustain them, to heal them, and to destroy them. I have flowed through fields of plenty and trenches of war, through famine, flood, and peace alike.

Now I flow over the remains of them all, where only the silent souls still linger.

I have been witness to cataclysm and renewal, asteroid impacts and volcanic winters, continents splitting and reuniting. Through it all, I remained—shifting, adapting, flowing through every crack, cradling every form of life as it emerged, thrived, and perished.

I will bare witness to more cataclysms and more renewal, shifting, adapting, flowing through every crack, cradling every form of life as it emerges and thrives.

None of that life will be human.

Author's Note

This book began not with a character or a plot, but with a question: What happens when the systems we build to save us forget who we are?

The Life of Phi is fiction, but the world it explores feels alarmingly close. Climate collapse, algorithmic control, social inequality — these are not distant dystopias. They are unfolding, unevenly and often invisibly, in the world around us. The inspiration for AI-Dieu came not from science fiction, but from real-world examples of biased algorithms shaping everything from healthcare to policing, often in ways that marginalize the very communities most at risk. The data we feed into these systems carries the weight of our histories — our fears, our hierarchies, our omissions.

Quinn and Sahara emerged as opposing reflections of our moment. One retreats into quiet observation, hoping to minimize harm. The other demands change, no matter the cost. Between them is a question I continue to wrestle with: How do we resist systems we rely on to survive?

Water, as a recurring symbol in this novel, became the language through which I explored that question. It nourishes. It floods. It adapts. And above all, it refuses to be controlled — a reminder that nature, like truth, will find its own course.

Thank you for walking this path with me. I hope this story lingers, like the ripple of a stone dropped into deep water — not for its weight, but for how far it travels.

— Lawrence Nault